Omnia Series - Book 1

Collecting Crowns

Jay Montana

Cover Design and Internal Art: InkStrider
Editing and Formatting: Samantha Vargas

Author: Jay Montana
Title: Collecting Crowns / Jay Montana
Description: First Edition |
ISBN: 979-8-9939484-09
jaymontanawriters.com

TO MY YOUNGER SELF

To six year old me, thank you for daring to dream of a world never
out of reach.
To seventeen year old me, thank you for fighting through the dark
times despite wanting to give up. Your resiliency is what led to this
moment and I am forever proud of you.

TO MY FAMILY

I would never have been able to achieve any of this without your
unwavering support and belief in me when I have a hard time
believing in myself.

TO MY READERS

As Omnia Melania says you can do hard things and I hope you
realize your greatest strength is remaining true to who you are and
not what the world wants you to be.

Music Playlist

This is not a requirement to enjoy Collecting Crowns, however, music kept me sane through the journey of writing and shaped many scenes.

Content Warnings

This book may have some trigger warnings and content not suitable for particular audiences. Should any of the below be of concern to you, as a reader, please think cautiously about moving forward with the read. Your mental health is of the utmost importance.

Violence
Child Abuse & Neglect
Genocide
Mentions of self-harm & suicidal ideations
Mentioning of suicidal attempts
Death of Parents (not on page, but mentioned)
Death of a child.

Prologue

Little drops of rain patter against the stained-glass windows of the carriage as I sit alone, waiting for my mother to return. She had told me to stay inside; said there was an emergency to be dealt with that couldn't wait. Her protector, Queen Gaia, tried to talk her out of it, but she didn't listen. My mother never listens to anyone else.

Sharp pangs ring out. I've heard the same sound on the palace grounds before, but nothing like this. Burning meat suffocates the air, closing my throat. I try to hold the gag; my mother would say it's not lady-like, even though I'm only a five-year-old girl. Suddenly, the carriage door swings open, and a man with dark brown eyes and bark-like skin reaches for me. I gasp, backing away as tears rip through me. I duck under his arm, my small body landing against his burning legs.

Bright red flames dance over my skin, but it doesn't hurt. The man's slender, viney fingers clasp under my armpits, pulling me from the ground. His face scrunches in the same way mine does when my maid braids my hair too tightly. Screams fill the air, muting anything he's trying to say to me.

Green splatters over my skin, and I plop to the ground, releasing a piney, bushy smell. The man grips his throat before a sword pushes through his stomach and slides up his chest. I barely make it out of the way when he falls to the ground. A pool of green seeps beneath him into the orange blaze surrounding us.

I should turn back to the carriage, but too many people are looking at me. Hands reach out to me. Gaia will know what to do—she always knows what to do.

The soppy, green hued ground dips under my slippers, shoes sliding with each step I take. I must find Gaia—I'll be safe in her arms.

People cry out, wails booming over the scorching flames of the night. My mother said this was a good thing. I don't understand how the ear splintering screams can be right.

On the hillside, gold flashes—Gaia. The light within the darkness. I run toward her as a body falls in front of me: a woman with wide brown eyes and leaves in her hair, eyes pleading with me as her chest rises and falls before it doesn't do so again.

"Omnia Melania," someone says from behind me, but I don't look back. I sprint around the woman, making it to the bottom of the hill, the grass soaking wet. Getting on my hands and knees, I try to crawl.

My hand slips, and I'm not fast enough to catch the fall. My face smacks against the ground, spewing a metallic taste on my lips like when mother makes us eat animal meat. Except this isn't a dining hall, and these aren't animals being slaughtered—they're people.

Tears well in my eyes as I push myself back up.

Keep going.

I claw myself through the dirt and mud, nearing the top when a small purple bud begins to form between my palms. My finger grazes the top of it instinctively, as if it were calling out for me, begging me to take part. It blooms into five dark purple petals with a golden center. Glittery dust tickles my nose. I sneeze, my breath circulating the golden dust.

More buds shoot from the ground, surrounding my body. I don't have to touch them this time for them to open, each blooming on their own. The petals are soft like silk sheets, smelling of lilacs and honey. The dust kisses my face and dances through the strands of my hair, whispering secrets I can't hear into my ears.

The carnage fades as more flowers sprout and bloom with each breath. Even through the heavy screams of agony and sorrow, the spiraled flecks of gold dancing in the heavy, ash-laden air enchants me. I reach for one, pulling it from the ground to admire its beauty up close.

Gaia would like to see this, I think to myself.

My attention immediately snaps up, searching for her amidst all the gold powder. If La'Mia, Gaia's daughter, were here, she would try to smash the flowers just to see my smile fall. She's like my mother in that way.

"A blessing," someone whispers.

Turning in their direction, I see a woman bathing in the golden dust. My eyes widen at the giant gash in her abdomen as it stitches itself, coming together like two halves of a whole finding the glue it needed. Dark brown flesh flakes over and renews. I scan the hillside, watching as all the people renew in front of my eyes.

Gaia will be amazed at what is happening. She'll be so proud of me.

"What have you done?" My mother's voice is cold. Distant even.

She snatches my cheeks between her white metal gloves, forcing me to look at her. She wears the armor of Omnius with her white iridescent hair pulled back into a bun. Mother squeezes my face tighter until tears form in my eyes. She scoffs at me, and I know it's because she hates to see me cry.

"You were to remain in the carriage," she hisses.

I try to jerk out of her hold, but that only makes it more painful. The purple flower in my hand continues to grow, a tingling feeling coursing through me as if it's trying to heal the wounds on my cheeks. My mother reaches down and snatches my wrist, raising it between us.

"You are weak and pathetic," she shouts.

The vines growing over my forearm twist and tangle tighter, the soft, ivy hues transforming into dark brown thorns tearing into my flesh. My white, iridescent blood drips toward the ground, soaking the area with all the others.

I can't respond—not that I want to. I hate when my mother gets like this. With her other hand squeezing my face, she jerks my head to the side.

The woman whose torso came together bends at the waist, the specks of gold replaced with bubbles of jade. The same bubbles surround my mother and me, but neither of us react like the others.

Guards and civilians alike drop to their knees as the bubbles burst, releasing a noxious gas into the air.

Bumps and boils form on their skin.

Their hands grasp their throats through gasping breaths.

"Their deaths are on your hands now because you couldn't obey," Mother bites out. She grips tighter, and I'm not sure how she's not breaking through the skin of my cheek into my mouth.

She releases me, only to grab the back of my head and drag me toward the carriage. Then, she throws me inside before forcing herself in next. After what feels like forever, Gaia makes her way in. I want to ask her where she went, but I don't want to risk my mother's ire again.

I turn to look out the stained-glass windows, my tears and whimpering refusing to stop.

"Pathetic," my mother says.

"She's a child," Gaia snaps.

"And as a child, she just killed an entire squad of royal guards for disobeying direct orders. The only positive is that she also killed an entire grove for the Great Cleansing to save the Greater Good of all Veilia."

Gaia says something, but I can't hear her words as a single bud of purple sprouts from the ground like it's trying to tell me something else. Closing my eyes, I try to understand my mother's words. If it's for the Greater Good—why does it feel so bad?

One

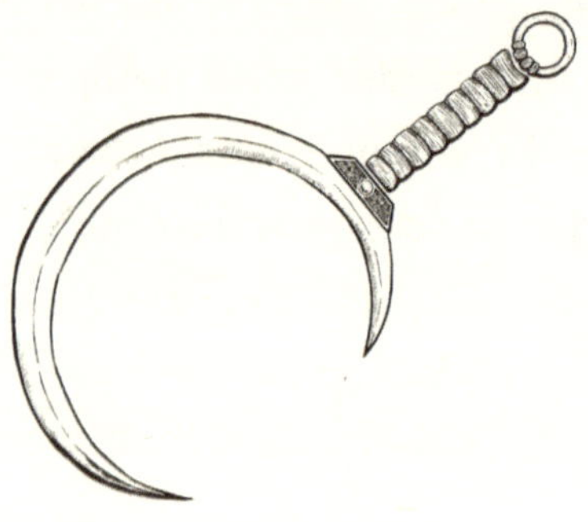

Melania 1

Lords and ladies of Omnius converse with one another, waiting for the imposition to begin. Many of them are accompanied by servants holding large burlap sacks. One servant looks like a child wearing rags and trembling under the weight of gold—although it could be from the rope around his small, filthy neck. The other end of the rope is in the hand of Lord Darius, the new lord of the fire quadrant. His predecessor mysteriously passed in the night from drowning—on dry land. He frequents the palace, often speaking with my mother in hushed tones behind closed doors.

"Isn't this exciting?" my guardian, Princess La' Mia, says in her high-pitched voice. I forgot she was standing next to me.

"That's a word for it," I say.

She turns her attention to me. Small dove-like wings bathe in rainbow light reflecting from the stained-glass windows behind us.

Her light pink eyes sparkle. She isn't much taller than me, though; it doesn't stop her from angling her head to make me feel small. A demeaning act she's done since our childhood. Only three months older than me, yet she seems to believe she has more life experience. Practically raised together, I've learned to ignore her cruelty as I do my mother's. Sometimes I wonder if the Fates, our unseen gods, made a mistake making La'Mia my guardian and not my mother's. Even now, I think of Queen Gaia, my mother's guardian, and mourn her kind heart and gentle voice. We don't speak of her sudden death in the palace.

"It's our first time attending the imposition." La'Mia's tone is light, but it puts a sour taste in my mouth. Pulling a tight, closed smile onto my face, I nod without responding.

This isn't my first time attending. I've seen what happens from the alcove overlooking this small throne room. People stand in groups separated by their magical abilities, just as they are in the city of Omnius, living in separate quadrants. There aren't any chairs for people to sit, and most use their servant's backs to rest for the long imposition. My mother has another throne room meant for all the royals from the eight kingdoms to hold an audience. That room has marble slabs for chairs. It's only been used for coronations of Omnias and guardians and their weddings. At least that's what I've been told. There hasn't been a coronation or wedding since my mother's reign.

Many guards stand at the different entrances to the room. One with blond hair slicked back guards the hall to the servant's quarters. His hands hold the handles of his white swords. Unlike the other guards armored in white, General Javon wears gold. There's a crown symbol carved in the center of the metal.

The guards move to open the large marble doors. People lower, averting their eyes. Omnia Itzel's looming presence strides into the room, wearing a floor-length white gown encrusted with diamonds. She looks over the bowing crowd as light from the windows reflects dancing rainbows over them.

La'Mia lowers into a curtsy; wings splayed wide behind her. The weight of my mother's gaze is upon me as if daring me to defy her. I lower my head, my tiara slipping from the loose coronet braid.

My mother's shoes click against the marble flooring, echoing off the walls and columns of the room. My shoulders bristle at her sickening scent of lavender and vanilla. The scent haunts all my dreams.

Her fingers graze under my chin as she jerks my head to look her in the eyes as the rainbow of her irises glisten in the midday sunlight, satisfaction flickering across her smug expression. White, iridescent hair falls to the top of her shoulders. Her sharp, long nails scrape against the soft parts of my cheek.

My mother moves to her throne next to me. "Rise," she commands the crowd.

At the sound of her voice, the powerful beings rise from their positions. A small grin lights up her face. To others, it may seem kind, but I know that feral grin too well. My mother is here to partake in her second favorite pastime: tormenting others; her first is tormenting me.

"Shall we begin?" she says.

The patrons cheer in unison, their excitement palpable like a physical entity. Next to me, La'Mia stands taller as people look toward the three of us, waiting for the show to begin. Unlike the pair flanking me, I have a sickening feeling burrowing beneath my skin and in the center of my chest.

This is going to be an imposition I will never forget.

My feet pulse from the grueling hours of standing. La'Mia sits on the back of a servant in the quadrant for light wielders. Mother didn't offer me the same kindness of dismissal. I fight a yawn as I drown in the sound of one lord expressing grievances about his livestock and vegetation disappearing in the middle of the night.

Even as my mother listens, her eyes glaze over. "I will send guards to patrol your property." She looks at her nails, then waves him along.

The lord gives a curt nod and mumbles "thank you" before making his way back to the others with light blue eyes. He's from the new quadrant built for air wielders—too new to have a servant by the rope.

Following him is a young woman with hooded, ocean-blue eyes, dragging a woman behind her with a rope around her neck. Through her tan skin, I make out the blue of her veins. Sea salt and jasmine waft up my nose as she steps toward the dais. She's the lady of the water quadrant. The woman next to her has muddy-brown eyes, smells of dirt and oakmoss, and it doesn't take me long to realize she's a powerless being. My mother's hitching breath means she knows it, too.

"A Nihil," my mother says. I bristle at her callous tone and prepare for the worst.

My mother has an aversion to many aspects of Veilia. Those aversions being Nihils, crossbreeds, shadow wielders, and me. Her hatred runs deep enough that she enacted the Great Cleansing Ordinance in all eight kingdoms. An Act where the eight royals of the kingdoms sign the Ordinance each year in order to rid the world of Nihils—the one's born without magic in their veins. She—like many others—thinks of them as abominations. Their veins are blue, but bleed red on the surface. Once she eradicates or puts them all into servitude, she'll move onto the crossbreeds—those born from two species, whether it's a siren and a wielder or a nymph and a wielder. She won't be pleased until they're all dealt with. She's done it before with others like the full-blooded wood nymphs. My heart pulses at the memories, ones I try to stuff down, but they're already taunting me, reminding me I assisted her in killing an entire drove of them.

"All Nihils were sent to Omnius to serve me," Omnia Itzel says.

The Nihil's throat works on a swallow. When she moves, burns under her throat are evident. I clench my fist at the sight. I shouldn't feel sorry for the Nihilan woman.

And I don't, the inner voice in my head says, but it doesn't have the thick weight of honesty.

"She was at an auction, and I paid a decent amount of gold for her," the lady says, pulling tighter on the Nihilian woman, as if presenting her property.

My mother looks coldly at the pair, ignoring the gold in the Nihil's shaking hands.

"Lady Helena." At the sound of my mother's voice, the room drops ten degrees.

The other patrons whispering amongst themselves shift their attention to the throne. My skin prickles at the weight of their stares. Even as she lifts her chin, the magicless being retreats into herself, her eyes glassy, and if it weren't for the sound of gold clattering against one another, I would think she's become a statue.

"Are you disrespecting your *ruling* Omnia?" My mother's eyes briefly flit to mine.

I didn't miss her indignation at "ruling". To the others in the room, I am an Omnia. When people address me, they say Omnia Melania, even if it doesn't carry the same respect like Omnia Itzel. My mother will never refer to me that way. To her, I will always be the child she didn't want. Even when it comes time for me to become the ruling Omnia, I will be the puppet and she the master.

"I would never," Lady Helena says.

"Then you will give me the Nihilian woman—and the gold."

Lady Helena looks at the young woman and rolls her eyes. She can try to deny my mother's request, but it wouldn't work in her favor. My mother never lets her command be ignored. She's killed other wielders, no matter their rank, for less. At the thought, my eyes flit around the room until I find La'Mia. She's eagerly looking at us from her seat among the other light wielders, a Nihil servant on all four propping up her feet. It pains me to admit, but La'Mia is more like my mother than I will ever be.

Both the Nihil and gold are deposited at the foot of the dais. Lady Helena stomps away from the throne, whispering under her breath. My mother's eyes flare, and I know without a doubt the water quadrant will need a new lord or lady by nightfall.

"Nihil," my mother says, her voice laced with venomous disdain. To her, all Nihils are the same—a genetic mutation lacking the unique qualities of magic in Veilians. They may look, sound, and act like us with the same lifespan and healing properties, but they will never *be* us. "You will be my daughter's servant."

My eyes fly between the two of them. Her words hang in the air, and I know what I should do—at least, I understand what my mother expects of me. I should lean down, snatch the rope, and use the Nihil as a seat. Perhaps I should drag her across the floor until we reach my chambers, only to return with the distinct blood of Nihil on my white gown.

I do neither as my mother and the Nihil wait expectantly. A trembling sensation starts in the tips of my fingers. Before others can see, I place my shaking hands behind my back, gripping them together.

"Guards," my mother says. Her ire-filled eyes are on mine. With everyone looking, I had a chance to prove my strength. Instead, I revealed how weak I am. "Take that," she points to the Nihil before continuing, "to the servant quarters."

Large guards grab the Nihil from under her armpits. Her toes dangle above the ground. They make it halfway through the crowd of parted people before my mother moves from her throne, grabbing the long rope at the edge of the dais, yanking it. The Nihil's head snaps back as she chokes, and then my mother lets go.

A sloshing of my morning breakfast moves in my stomach. The sound of the Nihil choking is forever etched in my mind. Next to me, my mother laughs, and others join. Scanning over the crowd, the only people not laughing are the servants, a few guards, and me.

After a few moments, my mother recovers, and the room thrums with nervous energy. Lady Helena was the last of the lords and ladies demanding an audience. My mother settles on her throne, thrumming her ruby red nails against the armrest. She looks out at the crowd before her cruel voice says, "Bring in the traitor."

Who would dare betray her?

Two guards guide a bloody and bruised lord. My breath hitches, knowing Lord Byron well. Another two guards follow, holding a man bearing a similar resemblance. His son—who smells completely ordinary, a smell I didn't recognize when I was a child, but one I could never forget now.

Only when a guard brings forth a marble slab do I realize what is happening.

The imposition was never meant to be entertainment.

But a public execution is.

Two

Melania

The two men are brought to the center of the room as an executioner wearing all white enters, holding a great axe stained with blood. I swallow, looking into the eyes of the lord and Nihil.

Lord Byron, the only lord I've cared for, stands before us, hands bound in gold chains to nullify his magic. I don't wear them often, but sometimes my mother's punishments require I do. They were made for Omnias during childbirth—the pain and warring emotions could topple an entire kingdom. Or so I was told.

Omnia Itzel watches me through her lashes, the right side of her mouth tipped up in a smirk, betraying her private satisfaction. She knows exactly how the chains affect me. I remain neutral when all I want is to bolt from the room. When Lord Byron's panicked, large green eyes find mine, the idea of fleeing tempts me further.

He used to show me the way of Quintarius when I was a young girl. He taught me about herbs and their healing properties, ensuring I knew which ones were poisonous.

His son, Baker, stands next to his father with regular chains around his wrists. He's twenty years old—only five months older than me. His veins are blue, but the blood seeping from the tight shackles is red—a unique trait of Nihils that none of the other wielders have. When cut, my white blood shimmers iridescently.

"Byron," my mother says.

My breath hitches when she doesn't use his title. Omnia Itzel always refers to them as lord and lady, even if she doesn't have to. With one word, she strips the man of his worth. No one, aside from me, seems to care. It's as if they realize they, too, can suffer the same consequences.

Our power can give or take. My mother's voice rings in my head from that fateful night when I was a child; the night I partook in the Great Cleansing Ordinance, killing an entire village. I shake the memory away, pulling myself to the present.

"You have broken your oath to serve Omnius," my mother says.

She's playing with him, even if to everyone else, she is a ruler doing her job.

I know without a doubt she doesn't regret what she's doing—she never does.

"Your son is a Nihil."

My heart beats faster in my chest. Deep within me, I know Baker is going to die.

Before the Great Cleansing Ordinance went into effect, I would spend time with Baker and Ben, Lord Byron's eldest son. They were always kind to me and would dance with me at balls. Even as kids, they would treat me differently than others. Back then, I couldn't understand.

Now, I see the imbalance between us as I wear fine silk on the dais—the second most powerful being in all the kingdoms—and they stand below me in chains.

"Omnia Itzel," Lord Byron says. A guard slashes his hand across his face, shedding blood the color of leaves and trees in Summer—a nature wielder.

"Let him speak," mother berates the guard with a twisted smile on her face. I know that look all too well. She enjoys seeing the blood of others; the white, iridescent blood in my veins brings her the most pleasure.

"My son is Nihil, but he poses no risk—" His mouth continues to move, though no words come out. The veins on his throat pull taut without air in his lungs. My mother appears utterly calm, yet there's tension in her lithe form as she steals his breath away with the power of air.

"All Nihils are a threat," someone yells from the crowd. A chorus of cheers ring out as others agree with the notion.

Lord Byron wheezes as my mother releases him. Baker, Lord Byron's second and largest son, shrinks in this room. His clothes are dirty and tattered. I tilt my head a little, pleading with my eyes for his attention, but he never looks up. I'm not sure *why* I want to make eye contact, but I do.

"You were caught fleeing Omnius with your son—a criminal offense against the Great Cleansing Ordinance," Omnia Itzel says.

Lord Byron's attention averts to the ground. His gold chains clink against the marble floor as tears drip into his mouth. My eyes squeeze shut at the sight.

"Your Nihilian son will die for fleeing, and you will be the one to kill him."

My lids open on their own accord, my wild gaze flying to her. Omnia Itzel keeps her sharp rainbow eyes on the traitors, glancing between the father and son crying. Her slim shoulders are tense as her nails tap against the marble, diamond encrusted throne.

Heavy boots stomp across the floor. The executioner approaches the dais.

I nearly gag at the sight of blood on his axe, but my lungs barely fill with enough air. The bloodstains create a rainbow—the rarest sight to behold. They're found around my mother and me on special occasions, as decided by the Fates. Our eyes appear to be a color wheel of each varying shade of the land. And we're the rarest bloodline of wielders—only us in existence.

Chains clink to the ground.

Lord Byron brings his hands forward, his jaw clenching. For a moment, I fear he might lunge at my mother. He glances at me instead, and whatever he sees on my face has him standing down.

Next to him, a sickening crunch of bones breaking against the marble flooring. Baker lets out a small groan, his chains still intact. One guard moves the slab of marble in front of his kneeling body, forcing Baker's head down, and he doesn't resist.

Lord Byron appears greener than tan as he looks at the sight before him. Baker turns to his father, and I wish I could understand the silent conversation happening between them. Lord Byron's sobs echo off the marble walls. Everyone in the crowd watches. Nausea rolls in the pit of my stomach as chills erupt over my skin, even as sweat beads near my hairline.

The executioner places the great axe in Lord Byron's hands. His green eyes darken as he glances between my mother and his son.

He takes a step toward the dais.

My fingernails dig into the palms of my clenched fist.

Another step toward my mother, and I hold my breath.

Lord Byron could strike us with the great axe, but we wouldn't die, even if our heads were cut from our bodies. The only being capable of killing an Omnia is an Omnia. If I use the axe against my mother, however, she won't survive. My heart pounds at the thought.

She gives me an ounce of her attention, as if she can read my mind. Or worse, she's thinking of using the axe against *me*. I wonder if her heart thrums at the idea, too. Mother gives me a tight smile before looking back at Lord Byron, who stands closer to us.

"You do it," my mother says, her voice laced with boredom despite the hunger for bloodshed in her eyes, "or I will."

My shoulders practically rise to my earlobes. At least with the axe, Baker will have a swift death. If my mother were to do it, she would make him suffer long before he draws his last breath. Lord Byron stops before the throne. His clenched jaw relaxes as the resignation settles in.

"Do it," Baker says, a deep voice I haven't heard in a long time.

His chin rests against the slab, pushing his dark brown hair over his forehead. The green of his irises strikes against his bloodshot eyes with a resignation that tears me apart. If he's going to die, let it be by his father.

Lord Byron drops his head, and I know without a doubt Baker's plea will be answered. Through heavy lids and sobbing, he settles by his kneeling son. "I love you," he whispers.

"I love you, too," Baker responds, turning his head to the side to face his father.

"Tell your mother and sister I miss them." Lord Byron raises the axe above his head. His arms never waver despite the weight.

"See you soon," Baker says, right before the axe swings down.

My eyes shut as a wet sound squelches against the ground. Warm liquid splatters against my gown, and bile fills my mouth. Lord Byron's cries ring in my ears.

For a moment, time stands still. There are only Lord Byron's woes. My eyes squeeze tighter, even as they burn from salty tears. Behind us, thunder echoes in tandem with my thrumming pulse.

I open my eyes, avoiding the beheaded Nihil, and scan the nobility's reaction. Some are rigid, with a glaze over their eyes. Others seem pleased with the spectacle, acting as if this is another day in Omnius. I find La'Mia with a grim smile on her face. If I were to glance at my mother, I am certain she would wear her mask of disinterested amusement, one of her personal favorites.

"Clear the room," she says, ignoring Lord Byron's wails.

I can barely make out his words, but he's asking for mercy. If I were in his position, I would take the axe and gut myself. No one deserves to live with the anguish of taking a life—especially the life of their child.

A thud follows; it's Baker's body. The sound of marble screeches against the hard, wet surface of the throne room floor. Thunder draws near, and the rainbow light from the stained-glass window dims. A somber tone settles over the throne room as Lord Byron's chains click into place. His swollen, bloodshot eyes meet mine as he searches my face. It's as if he is looking for an answer I cannot provide.

The guards drag him away, pulling his attention from me. There isn't an ounce of fight in his limp, defeated body. Baker's head remains before the dais, the red of his blood pooling beneath his headless body.

Other guards move into the room, removing his corpse. Bile burns my tongue as I fight against emptying the contents of my stomach. Memories of him as a child flood my mind, and the tears fall heavy with the rainfall beating against the palace roof.

"Get her out of here," my merciless mother says.

Someone snatches my wrist, dragging me through the throne room as if I, too, were a prisoner. Onlookers stare as my mother's right-hand man—General Javon—guides me. Like Lord Byron, I don't have the fight to resist the guard's tight grip.

"You're a disappointment," General Javon says.

The truth cements in my bones. My tears fall for the dead Nihil, though my tears are steady for another reason as well. How could all those people be so cruel? They watched a man be killed by his own father.

His only crime was being born.

I cannot help but wonder if my mother would kill me if given the chance.

Is my only crime being born a weak Omnia?

Three

Rain beats against the ground. Wet seeds burrow into the soil, creating the distinct smell of damp dirt, a welcome smell compared to the dry land of Tenebrae, where it only rains once a year for one week only. Envy takes root in the comparison between the two lands. Tenebrae is a barren land of death and darkness, while this one blooms with vegetation that far too many people take for granted. If an Omnia came to Tenebrae, I wonder if their tears could blossom the kingdom for my people.

It's not your kingdom.

A bitter truth, I may have the wings of a Ravenheart, but the crown no longer rests on my father's head. The legacy of being a king is not what I live for any longer; it's a reprieve to live my life the way I want to, without the pressure of it.

Stealing and killing for the people who need it the most. The ones who aren't able to stand for their rights.

The life of an outlaw isn't for everyone, but it works for me and my brothers. Neither of them would agree we were brothers because of the difference in our blood, but they're the only family I have. It's sad to think a brooding, barely speaking Nihil and an overprotective, crossbreed runaway warrior is all I got in the vast world. Perhaps it's fitting for the sanguine dead prince of Tenebrae.

My sharp fangs dig into my lower lip. I'm on the lookout for a caravan high above in the trees. Micah and Lelantos hide near the neck of the forest, near a portal connecting to the center of Omnius.

Rumors from nearby villages and towns say the guards have been searching the curtain lands for anyone of unpure blood. The Omnius Imposition is the perfect time to bring more bondservants, Nihils forced into servitude, for Omnia Itzel to torture, abuse, and eventually kill.

Even in the thundering rain, rustling disturbs the air. My shadows stir around me—their essence like a black butterfly drawing my eyesight to the guards approaching. Omnius soldiers donning their white armor. I'm not a gambling man, but I'm willing to bet the rain hasn't touched their skin. The same cannot be said for the dozen bondservants tied together at the ankles and wrists.

Deftly, I move through the treetops. My large raven wings snag on smaller branches. My brothers will never understand the weight of them nor how inconvenient they can be.

Keeping a distance from the slow-moving caravan, I find my brothers on the ground. Micah is under the tree closest to me, gripping his great sword confidently. His wavy blond hair is in a topknot on the crown of his head, clothes soaked, but his skin is dry despite the steady rainfall. Much like the ground soaking up the moisture, his hidden gills need the water more than he's willing to admit. It's been far too long since he's been in a natural water source.

On the other side of the tree line, I barely make out Lelantos. His auburn hair cascades to the center of his chest. Unlike Micah and me, he isn't wearing a cloth to hide most his face, as if he wants to get caught. The cocky bastard. He grips his bow tightly. His other hand hovers over the top of his arrows, fingers waltzing with the decision of which one to choose.

I let out a low whistle, signaling my presence. Their eyes move to me, but I focus on the approaching caravan. It's not a quiet ride as the wagon hits every bump. These foot soldiers are weak, callous men. One guard whips a slowing white horse. I flinch, then tighten my fists as I decide his future then and there. I'm not a saint, but I don't prey on the weak—a lesson this man is going to learn.

The guard leading the caravan stops, raising his fist. This isn't a typical guard scouting—he's a tracker. His head swivels, searching for any movement.

A twig snaps in Lelantos's vicinity.

My breath catches.

Out of the three of us, his likeness is plastered all over posters, wanted dead or alive by Omnia Itzel herself. Some may think it's for the death of his brother, but it goes much deeper than that. Like Lelantos's hatred for Omnias. A silent game played between the two of them, though they've never stood face to face.

The guard moves closer to the sound.

Staying as still as I can against the thick trunk of the tree, I search for my brother. Hands on their weapons, the other men ready themselves to strike as the advancing soldier makes it to the tree line—and suddenly stops.

His body jerks.

The guard staggers back with momentum of a large arrow protruding from the center of his neck, piercing through the weakest point of their armor.

Lelantos hit his mark.

A sickening smirk rises on my face when the guard collapses to the ground, his golden blood spurting on his white armor and onto the surrounding grass. The other guards pause, stunned, before they unsheathe their swords. The one with the whip jerks his head in every direction, eyes darting through the trees. His legs shake as if he were a caged animal ready to flee while the others shout orders.

Micah comes out of hiding with his sword at the ready. A shiver runs down my spine at the sight. It's easy to forget how lethal he truly is. He swings it easily, as if performing a combat dance as he focuses on the two guards sizing him up. But my brothers can't have all the fun, so I fly to the ground. One guard audibly gasps in my presence. Like a statue, he faces me.

I wish I could see his expression beneath his helmet.

As if reading my thoughts, he removes it. I stop immediately, taking in the sight before me.

Black eyes stare back at me—eyes like mine. He falls to his knees, dropping his sword next to him with a *clink*. Then another soldier in white—the same one who whipped the horses mercilessly—plunges a dagger into the back of his neck. Black blood pools around his fallen body—odd to see.

My blood cools significantly as my shadows tense beneath my skin; a beast begging to be released, and I am the conduit. Who am I to deny the starving creature?

My shadows come forth from my arms, smoky and thirsty for blood.

The soldier stumbles back.

Smart man.

A dark tendril latches onto his ankle, knocking him to the ground. Bone crunches sweetly under his helmet as more shadows descend onto him, and it's as if the world disappears into a bubble of darkness.

He removes his helmet, revealing light yellow eyes.

Stupid man. I almost laugh. Before he realizes his mistake, I take away all his senses until all he perceives is my darkness. Pulling open his lower jaw, I send three tendrils of magic down his throat. His eyes bulge, and he grips his neck.

This light wielder will choke on the darkness they damned long ago.

His skin turns an angry shade of purple, and perhaps I should feel remorse, but I don't. He stabbed my kin in the back, even as they were wearing the same armor. There isn't a loyal bone in his body. My shadows are merely showing punishment for his crimes.

His body goes limp, and yet I refuse to call off my shadows. It's interesting to see my darkness dancing under the surface of his skin. If he were a stronger wielder, this could have gone differently.

"Erebus." Micah's voice is a whisper. He continues speaking repeatedly until his shouts echo off the walls of my mind.

"What?" I scream back to him.

Gold, green, and brown blood coats Micah's skin. His turquoise blue eyes scrunch together. Though his sword is back in its sheath, he crosses his arms and widens his stance, ready for another battle if necessary. "We're done."

The darkness continues to rage, but I nod anyway. Micah points behind us to where Lelantos unties the bondservants. They thank him as they realize the legend amongst the Nihils has freed them. Some think he is the King of Nihils, whereas I think he's more beast than man.

Micah places his hand on my shoulder, lowering his head so our eyes meet. "Don't let the darkness win."

He knows how much those words mean to me. It was the same phrase my father used to say when my magic first manifested. Of course, that was during one of my tantrums. I'm not sure he would be proud of the man I've become after their death.

"I'm alright," I say, though I feel anything but okay. The war raging inside settles as if my conscious and subconscious are tired of fighting for control. The sensation hollows me.

Micah skirts wide around me and the obliterated man. The

corpse's eyes have popped out of their sockets, and some of his skin is pulled away from the bone. It's sickening to know my shadows nearly made a man burst, and worse, that I delighted in it.

I'm relieved I'll never sit on the throne. Tenebrae doesn't need a sadistic killer as a king.

Even though one sits on the throne.

Four

Melania

"Excuse me?"

My heavy eyes open, searching for the sound. Rolling to my side, I groan into the cold, soft pillow, praying sleep may find me again, so I can forget this horrendous day.

"Omnia Melania," the gentle voice says again, followed by light footsteps.

"What?" I mumble into my pillow.

"Your attendance is required for the feast tonight."

Sleep sweeps away from me—my mother's idea of torture is far from over. I say nothing as I sit up, rubbing my soft palms against my eyes, and willing myself awake.

The gown I wore for the imposition lies against the floor, red blood splattered from Baker's decapitation on the hem. Outside, the once storm-raging sky is calm while the tall tale of nighttime consumes the horizon, casting hues of red, orange, and purple onto the greenery. My bedroom is a glorious shade of golden orange.

"Omnia Melania," the soft voice sounds again.

My eyes snap to the woman standing next to my vanity quickly. Her dark brown hair twists in an intricate braid; her muddy brown eyes miss the luster of magic. The scent of oakmoss and mud after a rainfall discovers me. She wears a knee-length beige gown. Against her warm, dark skin, I can barely make out rope burns.

"What is your name?" I ask.

Her eyes widen. She recovers quickly, glancing down at her feet. "Elara."

A feeling of rightness settles in the pit of my stomach, as if we were destined to meet. An odd idea to have conjured—she's a Nihil, and I'm her Omnia. Even with that in mind, I can't stand her referring to me as such.

"Call me Melania." I say, my words mumbled in my tired state.

I move toward the small stool at the vanity, and she bristles from our proximity. A twinge of guilt sits on my chest like a heavy weight. I don't blame her for fearing me. Especially not after my mother's actions in front of the crowd today; choking her in front of the nobles, only to decapitate a man moments later. Omnia Itzel didn't wield the axe, but the blood of Baker's death is on her hands. Not that she would care.

Elara works on the knots in my hair. She's much gentler than other servants. The one before her was killed by my mother for poisoning me. One of many assassination attempts.

"You cried," Elara says, drawing my thoughts away from my mother.

"Pardon?"

A warm flush spreads on her cheeks. Elara focuses on my hair, brushing the same spot over and over. My skin prickles at the sensation, but I fight the urge to tell her to move to another section. I don't want to scare her more than she already is.

"When Baker died, you wept."

A sigh leaves my chest, recalling the moment the first tear fell. I thought of his kindness as he helped me climb my first tree. We were only children then, our innocence shining as we thought our only challenge was to climb the largest trunks. "No one deserves to die that way," I whisper.

A weight settles against my lower lashes. My shoulders rise and fall as I focus on fighting away the emotional turmoil. If I were to cry again, my mother would storm into my room and blame it on Elara. She's done that before, too.

I never saw that maid again.

Closing my eyes, I recite the words from my favorite romance book where the brute admits he's always loved the maiden: *You're the meaning for breath in my lungs.*

Once the onslaught of sorrow eludes me, my attention shifts back to Elara. Being connected to Veilia means I am granted unprecedented power, but it also means my very strength and emotion fuels the land—a give and take relationship that easily becomes exhausting. The older I get, the more it drains me. It's like the world is trying to tell me something, and I can't understand the message. "How would you like your hair?" Elara asks, and I'm thankful for the conversation change.

"Leave it down please," I say.

Another warm blush floods her cheeks, followed by a gentle smile. I am not sure why she's blushing. Perhaps it's because of my manners. I'm certain most Nihils aren't asked for anything—things are simply taken from them. -

We settle into a silence that I don't mind. Sometimes silence surrounds me, and it feels sticky, like the breath of everyone in the room is on me. Instead, this silence is enough to keep me grounded as she ties up my corset.

Too bad it doesn't stop my mind from wandering.

As a child, I knew Baker was different from the rest of us. When his oldest brother, Ben, went to school for nature magic, Baker stayed at home. Neither he nor I used magic, but I had thought he was like me. Perhaps his magic didn't belong to him like mine belongs to my mother. I knew his blood was different, but I don't understand how any of that made him a threat. I don't understand how any of them could be.

Perhaps my mother and the other rulers know more than I do. I've seen Nihils try to harm me without a cause to do so. And yet, Elara seems more frightened by my presence than I am hers. I consider asking my mother what makes Nihils dangerous, but that would reward me with lashes. There won't be any other royals here until La'Mia's coronation at the end of the month, when the land is covered in snow and ice, like her and my mother's heart. The official end of the fall harvest.

Over my shoulder, Elara busies herself with laces. Her tongue pokes out as she focuses on tying them upright.

"Why are Nihils dangerous?" I ask, not able to stop myself.

It's wrong to ask her, but when I want answers, my brain seems to rush out words. She pauses for a moment. There's an emotion that flashes in her eyes, but she blinks it away before I can decipher it.

"We have no magic, Omnia Melania," she says through clench-ing teeth. "If that makes us dangerous, then I guess that is why we are feared."

The comforting silence is gone. We're engulfed in the thick weight of tension. Still, she's gentle with the fine fabric of my corset.

"How is one born a Nihil?"

Like I said, once my mind wants answers, it will stop at nothing to get them.

"My eldest sisters are fire and nature wielders. My father could control nature and my mother fire." She says it like it answers any-thing.

I huff before opening my mouth. "Are all third-born children

Nihils?"

"Only if the parents are different wielders," she explains. I nod but do not follow. Elara continues. "Magic doesn't mix."

There is a sense of clarity as knowledge burrows into my mind. "It cancels out."

I mull over her words as she pulls on the other layers of my gown. For a moment, her eyes flash to the pink, raised skin of a scar below my left rib—a scar I keep hidden for good reason.

I can't help but wonder how little Veilian wielders know of Nihils. An even worse thought finds a stop in the forefront of my mind: how little does my mother know of these Nihils? Are they truly being subjected to servitude and death because of the magic they cannot wield? Does my mother truly fear the Nihilian population, or does she take pleasure in knowing they're weaker than her?

She finds pleasure in your weakness; a distant voice answers in my mind.

Looking at Elara, I see her as the Nihil, third born without magic, yet I can't help but marvel at our similarities. We are both tormented by my mother for weaknesses she sees clearly.

The portraits of Omnias—the ancient line of ruling power—line the hallway leading from my chambers to the dining hall. Residing in the east wing, I am the furthest away from the throne room and my mother's west wing. It's a reminder I will never be like the rest of them since I don't find pleasure in the pain of others. I feel too much and not enough at the same time.

I wonder if any of the previous Omnias were like me. My grandparents died before my birth. I know nothing about who we really are. My mother would rather choke herself on an ivy vine she conjured than speak of our bloodline. What I do know is that our power is unprecedented; we govern the kings and queens of the eight kingdoms. Our born protectors from Laelithra are meant to sway us from harming, serving as our guiding light and closest confidants in this vast world. Although I'm not sure La'Mia understands the concept of 'do no harm.' She's like my mother, making the weak feel even weaker. Perhaps when she spends more time with me, her feelings may change.

Aside from our protectors, we answer to the Fates. I'm not sure if my mother even listens to them anymore. If she does, would that mean the Fates are truly accepting of the Great Cleansing Ordinance?

My shoulders slump with each breath before I enter the large dining hall. The melodies of an orchestra guide me along. Guards stand by closed doors with a hand on the hilt of their white, golden swords. Their heads lower in my presence, only to rise when I walk past them. Servants flit around the room holding glass flutes filled with bubbly liquid. Like the guards, their heads lower and rise in greeting.

"We've been waiting for you," Princess La'Mia purrs.

She stands with the lord of the fire quadrant. A golden, floor-length gown hugs her silhouette, and she holds a half-empty drink between her fingers. Her other hand is propped against the lord's shoulders. It seems she has found her conquest for the night. Typical La'Mia to meet and seduce a patron at the party—another striking similarity to my mother.

The lord lowers his head to me. His fiery red eyes peruse my frame once or twice before meeting my eyes.

"Lord Darius," he says, holding out his arm.

My small hand fits into his. He lowers to kiss my knuckles, lips lingering longer than respectable. My skin bristles from the sensation.

"Omnia Melania," I say with more bite than necessary.

Lord Darius' hungry gaze sweeps over me once more, La'Mia

completely forgotten. I can see why she finds him attractive. Lord Darius is much taller than us, a masculine face highlighted by the dark stubble from his beard. His olive tan skin glistens under the chandelier light.

"I shall go find my mother," I say.

Lord Darius' mouth opens only to shut as La'Mia presses her body to his, desire battling between them. I leave them to themselves, journeying to locate my mother. It isn't difficult since she loves being the center of attention. There's a large table designated for all the lords and ladies present. My mother's spot is at the head, mine to her right, and La'Mia to her left.

Omnia Itzel wears a floor-length white gown without the diamonds and gems from earlier. The white-golden crown of Omnius sparkles with seven gemstones representing almost all the kingdoms, lacking only the onyx stone of Tenebrae, but I wouldn't expect it to be there. The crown glistens on her head as she speaks with Lady Helena. I approach hesitantly before a familiar face catches my attention.

A man with light green eyes, olive skin, and brown hair pulled to the nape of his neck stands in the corner, away from the crowd. A face I've seen in my childhood, but not since then. He looks at me and then moves to another corner to hide. All air leaves me as Ben, Lord Byron's eldest son, blends in seamlessly with the crowd. Dread falls upon me. Before I can find him again, I'm stopped by a voice that fills me with even worse dread—if that's even possible.

"You best be on your best behavior tonight."

I was too busy watching Ben; I didn't see General Javon nearing. A scar from his left ear connects to his nose; another, smaller scar is above his lip. General Javon's dark brown irises darken, nearly disguising as a shadow wielder from Tenebrae with how dark they are. His dark green veins peek from under his gold armor.

"I didn't wish to be here," I say, trying to sound disinterested in both the feast *and* him.

"Do right by your mother," he says, sidestepping from me.

My mother and General Javon have been together for most of my life. There was a time I was certain he was my father. When I asked him, he laughed at me and asked why he would ever want to sire me when he already had two bastards of his own. I still have no clue who my father truly is. I wonder if my mother disposed of him for getting her pregnant with a baby she didn't want.

Moving away from General Javon and his wicked smile, I try to find Ben again. He's gone amongst the bustling crowd as they move toward their seats. Of course, they're keeping distance from me. Most of the patrons know better than to touch my mother's property.

"I am glad we can all be gathered here today," my mother announces to the crowd. I barely make it to my spot next to her. She draws the attention of the room like a moth to a flame. All eyes find her as she soaks in the attention. "Shall we feast and enjoy our entertainment?" She gestures to a large square behind her.

The box is draped in heavy velvet. Beneath the fabric, the soft padding of someone pacing catches my attention. Feet brushing the hard surface echo faintly despite the surrounding voices. No one else seems to hear it, but that doesn't surprise me. As an Omnia, my hearing is far sharper than anyone else's, as well as my sight—unless it's dark.

"Sit," my mother commands.

The guests and I move into our seats as the velvet cover is removed. A gasp catches in my throat. Lord Byron wears only stained, tattered pants. The gold chains dig into his skin, and there's an angry shade of red from the tight grip on him. Around me, the crowd points and laughs at the helpless man. I avert my gaze and immediately catch Ben rushing toward my mother's back. Her attention is solely on the crowd as she basks in their amusement. My lips open to speak, to warn my mother, but nothing comes out as Ben's dagger pierces her flesh.

Her face twists from blissfulness to rage in seconds. Ben rushes to his father's cage. His steps halt the moment he makes it to the locked door.

"Please no," Lord Byron's voice rings out. His leafy green eyes are still bloodshot from the death of Baker. It's too soon to face another loss.

My mother ignores the dagger protruding from her back as she turns to face Lord Byron and Ben.

Stillness settles over the great dining hall.

The unserved dinner sits under silver domes. No one lifts a glass of wine to their lips. It's as if everyone in this room is holding their breath, waiting to see what happens next.

My mother raises her trembling hand toward Ben. I can't make out his face, but his gasping leaves little to the imagination. Ben's large body lifts from the ground as my mother raises her hand higher. She turns him like a puppet on a string, as if this is a game to her.

Isn't it?

A chill runs down my spine. His lips are purple, and his neck constricts. Blood falls over my mother's dress. If I were to move closer to see her face, I'm sure she would smile at the sight. I don't move as I watch her white, iridescent blood drip down her back.

Ben's body smacks against the ground, landing at the edge of the cage. Lord Byron pleads, but they fall on deaf ears.

My mother clenches her fist, and a silent whimper parts from my lips.

Ben's light green blood trickles from his nose.

He writhes on the ground. Through his wailing screams, he coughs, splattering his blood. From all orifices, it seeps from him, forming a pool of green. She's hiding her pain well if she's switching magic that fast.

Lord Byron's wails nearly drown out the sound of his dying son.

The pitch alone threatens to slice my ears until they bleed.

My mother nudges her head from General Javon to Lord Byron. He doesn't hesitate to pull Lord Byron to the iron bars of the cage, removing the golden Omnia chains.

Lord Byron is too broken to put up a fight.

"You will live with the death of your sons for the rest of your pathetic life," Omnia Itzel says as she pulls the dagger from her back. "Only to be relieved by an Omnia as punishment for what has occurred today."

My mother threatens the dagger toward him.

She doesn't wait for an answer.

A green portal opens at his feet. His body falls through, leading somewhere unknown to the other patrons, but there's a scent of cinnamon and pine—a smell I used to spend my afternoons in.

Byron Manor.

Metal clangs against the ground. The blade lands next to Ben's lifeless body. Memories of my innocent childhood spent with these boys linger at the forefront of my mind. Now they're both dead for trying to stand their ground against their ruling Omnia—against my mother.

I don't wait for the crowd to disperse as I push through them. General Javon shoves himself in front of me. My eyes meet his, and he moves immediately. Power thrums below the surface of my skin, potent energy raging within against my mother's cruel acts. With each step I take, I swear the ground trembles. I don't fight the emotions boiling through me as booming thunder drowns out the partygoers.

As I continue through the overwhelming flood, my mother's threat repeats until I stop moving to process what she'd said. She said an Omnia is the only one who can end his suffering.

But she forgot one thing: she isn't the only Omnia. And for the first time in my nineteen years, I prepare to stand against the woman who gave me life.

If she won't grant him mercy, I will.

Five

Erebus

The dark land of Tenebrae is unlike any other kingdom. Brown grass crunches beneath my boots. Dark tree branches twist against each other, useless for vegetation, but the knots can be turned into a bed.

A distant memory of fleeing the palace flashes in my head; Micah carried me on his back while I cried onto his shoulders. My parents' bodies would have still been warm. I kept begging him to take us back—we have yet to return to that forsaken palace. He made us a makeshift bed and tied my waist to the tree. I don't recall him sleeping as he watched over me, his silver sword shining in the Mother's moonlight.

The hardest lesson learned that day wasn't my uncle killing my parents; it was learning the cruel reality of our world. Understanding that the stories of happily ever afters my mother read about were mere pieces of fiction. And I learned from a young age that I may be a prince, but it doesn't guarantee happiness.

"Today was a good day," Micah says, drawing me away from my

thoughts as my tongue lolled over my bleeding lip.

I hadn't noticed my brother's flanking my side. Micah's carefree persona calms my nervous system. I'll always be safe with him. Ever since that fateful day, he's been the one person I give all my trust to freely. His eyes gleam as if he can see where my train of thought had gone. I try to fake a smile, but I can't shake the darkness within me.

"We can bury him," Lelantos says.

Another tilt to my lips without the happiness of it. The body in question is resting on the back of my trotting horse, Henrietta. She was tied at the portal entrance, ready to carry the weight of our contraband, though she didn't seem impressed by the dead body Lelantos was carrying.

I thought of leaving the man, but I couldn't bring myself to let a shadow wielder rot in the curtains when he belongs here. I push away my melancholic thoughts from earlier. I will deal with them later when my brothers are not near. They don't deserve to suffer through my sad state, not with all they've faced in life.

"Help them get situated," I say, eyes trained on the Nihils and crossbreed huddling together.

Being the land of monsters, most of them fear the creatures they've heard of. Clearly, their folktales of the monsters don't mention they only hunt at night. It's why my brothers and I move out in the morning when I would much rather sleep until nightfall. Blame it on my sanguine bloodline.

"Where are you going?" Micah asks.

"To bury him with the others," I say.

Micah looks as if he's about to protest, but Lelantos moves in front of him. I know Micah detests when I bury the bodies alone. He reminds me I don't have to be isolated if I let them close. I understand his concern, but there are some things I have to do on my own. Burying a shadow wielder I couldn't save is one of them.

Henrietta's warm breath blows against the back of my neck. Our journey to the makeshift graveyard is short. There are small cobblestones marking the souls who rest there. Many of them are Nihils and crossbreeds who were injured or sick during their rescue. It bothers me, but it hurts Lelantos more. It was his idea to save them, and when one dies, he bears the loss of it. Yet Micah doesn't ask him to open up about *his* feelings.

Lelantos didn't try to end his life, my pesky voice of reason says.

My lower lip juts out, pouting at my own traitorous thoughts. I don't *always* want to be rational, especially not when I'm in this state of mind.

Henrietta halts, hooves stomping into the ground near an open plot of land next to another shadow wielder who died on a rescue just nights ago—a failure that's rested on all our shoulders, especially when we couldn't save that nature wielder and his sons from Omnius. We barely made it out alive.

Digging the grave is the easiest part. It's like preparing their bed for eternal rest. Laying their bodies is the hard part. The shadow wielder is heavy in all his white armor; a crime in itself. No one with black eyes should be forced to wear a color opposite of their kind. Still, I leave it on him as I lie his body in the shallow grave. There's never rain here to wash away the dirt, and to disturb the dead is a sure way to incite the fury of the Mother. The monsters here understand the sanctity of a cemetery. I'm sure the Mother of Monsters knew it would piss off her sister, The Mother of Death and Darkness.

"I'll never know why you served that wicked woman." My hands smooth out the dirt mound. Cleaning them off, I say, "But I hope the Mother does. May you rest peacefully in her dark embrace."

I don't say anymore as I mount Henrietta and return to my brothers. I'm sure they'll wish to speak with me more about my feelings. Well,

Micah will—Lelantos never says much, but I know he cares. At least, I think he does.

The sky is a darkening hue of amethyst, signaling the end of another day. I could weep knowing sleep may find me soon. Henrietta's hooves stomp against the ground once more as my shadows rise around me, silently warning me of a presence that shouldn't be here.

I calmly nudge her forward, phantom eyes watching me. My hand wraps around the cool handle of my dagger. I'm about to pull it out when a man with light blond hair stumbles from behind a tree with his hands raised.

Smart man, I think to myself.

He approaches slowly, understanding he's the prey in this situation. His dark brown eyes focus on me. Dirt cakes his skin, and he carries the unmistakable scent of a Nihil.

"I don't want any trouble, Prince Ravenheart," he says, voice shaking.

When I don't speak, he moves closer. There isn't a weapon on him. I may have the upper hand, but I refuse to underestimate any Nihil. I've seen what Lelantos can do.

"Please save my *friend.*" He says *friend* in a way that catches my attention, as if the words are difficult to say. I gather it's an enemy or lover, but he's not producing which it is. Consider my interest piqued.

"In Omnius, she lives in the nature quadrant, but she's a water wielder." He rings his hands in front of him. My brows raise, understanding reckoning within me. It's a crime to live outside your quadrant, yet another way for Omnia Itzel to prevent the birth of Nihils.

"What's her name?" I ask.

"Addilynn. She frequents The Dancing Boar." He's practically shaking at the idea of her being saved. I've decided it's a lover, and who am I to deny love.

"At the first moonlight, I shall find her," I say. His lips part, and

I know he's preparing to thank me; to use my honorific once more. I raise my finger, silencing him. "Not a word to my brothers." I turn my horse to take the long way to another entry point. I'm never keen on entering Omnius, but it's worse with my brothers there. If I get caught, I'll be used as a lesson, but Omnia Itzel would be much crueler to them. My brothers have evaded her long enough.

I watch from the back of Henrietta as the large, silvery moon rises. It's much larger here than any other kingdom. The Mother's light basks me in her aura, as if protecting me from what I may face.

A chill runs down my spine, and my skin crawls. Worrying my lip doesn't seem to ease the restlessness in my body. Without a doubt, I know what happens tonight will alter not only my Fate, but the Fate of Tenebrae.

That idea hasn't stopped me before—it's not going to now.

Six

Melania

The wet grass tickles my ankles, moisture from the earlier rainfall soaking the soles of my slippers. I send a curse to the Fates and the First for not being allowed to wear pants. The trim of my white gown is splattered with mud, my long lace sleeve catching on the roots of the trees. My hooded cape obscures my face.

The silvery moonlight guides through the forest. Trying to climb off my balcony with only vines, was hard enough. I couldn't imagine bringing a torch with me. My hands still tremor from the adrenaline of escaping the grounds. Only low-ranking soldiers were guarding the back entrance of the palace, and they seemed too interested in their game of cards to monitor the area. The entrance is a decent distance from my balcony to offer me a secure exit. Per my mother's orders, if anyone is found lurking at these hours, they will be punished. If anyone is lurking near or around my quarters, whether inside or outside during the nighttime, the punishment will be severe. One would think she is trying to protect me, but she prefers privacy for my lashings. Wouldn't want a guard to overhear the whimpers of the future Omnia.

I release a breath of relief as I make it to the tree line. My shoulders lower significantly, though I didn't realize they were taut. I bite the thumbnail of my right hand, a habit I can't break.

From my position, the quadrant of nature wielders is visible. The brown wood buildings have ivy growing over the sides. Lamp posts with orange flickering flames light the path of the cobblestone roads. There are lights on in the buildings and only a few people in the streets. Their land taxes paid at the imposition grants them protection, though I'm certain they're completely oblivious to the events that occurred to their Lord.

I pull my cape further over my head, though I don't know why. I'm too far for them to see me clearly, and even if they could, they wouldn't recognize me as I'm not permitted to visit the quadrants, so I could march into the center of the nature quadrant, and no one would look twice. That would all change if they saw my hair and eyes, though, so I keep the cloak around me.

Images of Baker and Ben dying flash on repeat in my mind, forcing tears against my lower lids. Neither of them deserved to die, nor does their father deserve to live with this grief.

The grass tickles the bottom of my knees. I used to fear the way the land shaped for me. Sometimes I still am. I do not fear the land, but rather my control over it. The way it bends to my will as if wishing it could be commanded. And I'm not ready nor allowed to wield it. This power does not belong wholly to me, but the decision to end Lord Byron's suffering does.

Gaining enough courage, I depart for the largest building made of cobblestone. The past and present are battling in my mind. I used to take this path to join the Byron boys to play with them in the field. Queen Gaia, my mother's protector, would watch from her spot on the hill, making sure nothing happened to me. Lord Byron joined her often. I cared little for their conversations back then. Now I wish I would have sat with her a little longer.

My chest twinges at the memory of our youth before death took away the life I once lived. It was after Queen Gaia's sudden death that my mother began her punishments, as if I were the reason she was no longer living.

I fight back the tears from the memories and the sight ahead of me. On the hillside is a small patch of golden flowers. Even in the night sky, the petals glow. Only Lord Byron would be so kind as to leave a memorial for his old friend. It's another reason he shouldn't have to live with the deaths of his sons. I'm not quite sure what I'm going to do. I know something needs to be done for him, though. He cannot be expected to live out his long life knowing that both of his sons died because he tried to protect them. A part of me can't help but wonder if the Fates decided that his destiny is to suffer. Perhaps he did something heinous in the past and only now is he receiving punishment for it. Another part of me wants to laugh at the notion. My mother acts on her own freewill; the Fates and the First could stand before her, and she would still challenge their judgment. For that is where her true power lies. She's not afraid of our Gods or the Fates, and I am envious of that feat. I only hope I can be like that one day.

Glancing at the dark sky, I seek guidance from my only true friend—moonlight. It's frowned upon for anyone aside from shadow wielders to look at the silvery light as a guide. The moonlight is a sign of the Mother of Death and Darkness. Yet even now, as I stand on the precipice of right and wrong, I seek her guidance. The unbiased judgment of the woman who honors death. I can only hope she honors me for what I must do.

The manor is smaller than I remember. It once seemed to be a force to be reckoned with. None of the other cobblestone and adobe houses even compare to its stature. Without the innocence of childhood, I notice cracks in the foundation. The trees surrounding the building wilt. I wonder if that's from the cool weather or the despair of the lord of the land.

A chill kisses down my spine. The surrounding land mourns. The torches are unlit, leaving a haunting feeling. I can sense the eyes of someone, or something, perusing my body. I chew on my fingernail.

"I can do hard things," I say to myself.

I repeated this mantra to myself as a child. Each time my mother lashed her air whip against my bare back. For every night I thought I would die from starvation. Choking on the poison left in my food by a Nihil servant. All those moments I thought I would surely break, but I didn't. I can do this for Lord Byron and his departed sons. My hand rests against the cold cobblestone fence—newly built after a series of attacks against the lords and lady to protect their land and animals. From the grievances today, it doesn't seem to work.

Under my palm, the rocks flutter, leaving an odd impression of warmth. There's a glowing green aura surrounding it. Vibrations thrum in the center of my chest. I can barely put into words what I am experiencing. My broken nails dig into the stones. I watch in awe as they move and bend to my will with no need for words. They're crumbling at my feet, leaving a gap. There's a rightfulness blooming in my chest while watching my powers work. I want to do more, control more, move more, be more—

I snatch my hand away to pull it tight to my chest like the stones were tainting my thoughts. Sweat lines my brow, dripping from my hairline. My heart beats erratically, and my breath is nearly unmanageable. The green around my palm lessens, leaving me colder than I was moments before.

My mother's words echo in my mind: "Our power can give or take, and tonight yours took their lives."

I only ever used my powers once before, and it ended in bloodshed. How true her words are, even now.

From the front side of the manor, there are deep voices speaking with one another. I can't make out what they're saying, but I've been around guards long enough to know it's nothing good. Thankfully, the guards aren't aware of the secret back door that Lord Byron's animals used to use. Baker, Ben and I had snuck through here to reach the kitchen for more animal-shaped spice cookies. It was the only time I could eat such a treat without my mother knowing. The boys always gave me more. Thinking about it now, I wonder if his sons knew the life I lived within those palace walls. My heart hurts from their unfortunate demise at my mother's hands. Though she can't be the only one to blame. Everyone stood there to witness, and no one tried to defend them—even me.

The weight of that reality looms heavily on me as I shimmy through the narrow gap. My nightgown snags against the wooden trim. It was a lot easier to fit through here as a child. Inside the manor kitchen, not a soul is in sight. Ben, the smaller and most nimble, used to grab the treats without a single servant to bear witness to our thievery. Now I can feel his and his brother's presence like a ghost.

There are two doors here, one leading toward the servant quarters and the other to the dining room. I hear the phantom laughter of children. The scent of freshly baked bread and raspberry compote as the family prepared for their daily tasks. Now the chairs gather dust as if no one lives here anymore.

The sound of shoes against the hardwood floor restores my sense of direction.

I enter the living quarters. There are portraits of the family over the unlit grand fireplace. Their eyes track my every move as an unwelcomed outsider. Baker's brown, lighthearted eyes find me like they did today before his execution. Next to him, there is Ben with a sly smirk and stern eyes. The estate and title was meant to be his as the eldest and only nature wielder among his siblings.

Now his corpse will be buried in an unmarked grave.

Next to him, Lord Byron's arm drapes over his Fated's shoulder. Even in the picture, her glowing ice-colored eyes beam. Her long blonde hair is pulled in an updo, revealing a green palm print over her heart. The mark of Fated mates is sacred, often shown for all to see.

Instinctively, I rub at the jagged scar under my left ribcage. When I was fourteen, I fled Brilore's palace walls after a grueling punishment from my mother. La'Mia had told me how swimming in the ocean at night can be relaxing and healing, and I desperately needed it. During the walk, I got lost, for I ended up in a tree line, watching an argument between two men. One of them shot an arrow directly into the other's heart. My breath caught, and I didn't see it, but I felt the searing pain of another arrow lodging into my ribcage. I figured it would heal, but it never did; a reminder that somewhere out there, someone might truly love and want me.

Below Lady Byron is a girl barely older than Baker, wearing light blue silk. Her curly hair is dark brown like her father's, and her eyes are icy like her mother's. I never met the late Brie, for she died before I met the Byrons. Perhaps the brothers sought me out because they needed another sister as much as I needed a family. Lady Byron passed soon after, unable to heal from the loss of her daughter.

The boots on the floor above me quicken. The floor creaks increasingly with each large step. My hands shake at my side, and I don't fight the urge of putting my fingernail between my teeth once more.

Through the other door is the entrance hall, which leads to a grand staircase to the next floor. Knowing the guards are right outside, my heart thuds against my ribs. My other hand rubs against the silk of my fine gown as my heart syncs with my steps, pounding in unison. *Step, thump, step, thump, step, thump.*

The first stair creaks under my weight, and my breath booms in my ears. The pounding reaches a crescendo where I feel as if it may burst. Keeping my steps as light as I can, I make it to the top of the stairs, then exhale in relief.

A flickering light guides me as I make my way toward it. At the door, I stand there waiting for clarity. A sign from the Fates that I should defy my mother's order of mercy. A silent prayer to the Fates that they may forgive me for my future—and impending—transgression. Most of all, I wish this act doesn't turn me cruel like my mother.

I consider running from here. The fear of what could happen takes hold of me. I take a step back and then another step, but I don't make it far when a deep male voice calls out. "You may enter, Omnia Melania."

His Fate—and mine—will be intertwined forevermore.

Seven

Melania

The room is warm and inviting as I shut the door behind me. The aroma of burning wood and fresh herbs engulfs me. Tall shelves line every wall, filled with different colored books. Above the fireplace is another, smaller portrait. It's a painting of him and his late wife without the decades of time aging them. She's wearing a white gown encrusted with diamonds, her Fated mark on full display. Lord Byron is donned in a three-piece tailcoat. From this angle, I see more of a fingerprint of glistening white like frost on grass. In their different colored eyes, the adoration they have for one another is on display. Sadness overcomes me, but I bat away the tears.

My attention turns to Lord Byron. He stands in the grand study wearing brown trousers and a loose-fitted cream shirt. His emerald eyes are heavy and bloodshot. An empty glass sits in his hand. He seems at ease despite the circumstances we're currently in. He lowers at the waist, kneeling. A wave of nausea washes over me.

"Omnia Melania." His voice is scratchy and weak.

"Lord Byron," I whisper, my voice weaker than normal.

"Would you like a drink?" He stands and walks toward a glass decanter filled with an amber, red liquid.

"No, thank you."

I could use the liquid courage of the whiskey, but I've been poisoned one too many times by Nihils and assassins. He doesn't seem to mind my rejection as he refills his glass only to drink it down and pour himself another.

"How did you know I was here?"

"Because I know your heart." He pauses as he sips more of the liquid. "It's much like the late Queen Gaia."

After her last rites were read, it was as if she had never existed. Neither my mother nor La'Mia ever mention the fallen protector. Sometimes I feel as if I am the only one to remember her golden aura of kindness. My eyes widen through the ache her name brings me.

"You miss her." It wasn't a question.

"More than I think I should." The sound of our soft breathing mingles with the embers of the fire crackling. Time seems to stand still around us before my lips finally part. "Lady Byron was beautiful." I'm not sure why I said it, but it's too late to take back now. I fight my apprehension to run into the woods.

He looks at the portrait, and liquid pools on his bottom eyelashes. I have to look away before my own tears fall. When he doesn't answer, I mull over other topics that have nothing to do with the reason I'm here.

I'm about to ask him about the weather when he finally speaks. "She was the light of my life, and I've missed her every day since she died." He wipes the back of his hand over his eyes. "We met when we were around Baker's age. She was visiting Quintarius, and I was working the land when I saw her. From that moment, I was drawn to her presence, and she to mine.

"Her father never wanted us to be with one another. You see, she was a lady of Jeadrenia, and I was a poor farm boy. It wasn't until I had my own land and manor before her father let us marry. On the day of our wedding, we marked each other as Fated." He pauses, and I realize how enraptured I am by his tale of love. I've moved closer to him, waiting for each word to cross his lips. In his eyes, the light of their love shines.

"We had three beautiful children and lived happily before Brie passed." The light all but disappeared in a blink. "My wife followed soon after."

"Thank you for sharing that with me," I say.

His eyes flare in surprise. "Why did you come?"

My heartbeat increases once more, taking the air from my lungs. I know I want to help Lord Byron and save him from his sentence. With the question hanging in the air, I wonder if the only way to save him is to end his life.

"What my mother did is cruel." It's not an answer, and he knows it.

"Your mother thinks she is protecting the people of Omnius and all Veilia from the Nihils and crossbreeds. Do you not agree?"

I'm ensnared by his question, and he catches it. Gone are the tears of a grieving father, replaced with the scowl of a man in politics. With my hands behind my back, I pick at the skin around my nails to ground my thoughts. I could agree with my mother, and I should, but there's a distant part that knows what she did today is wrong.

"Some Nihils and crossbreeds are dangerous." Another non-answer from me. I've witnessed politics far too many times in different kingdoms to let him win easily—even as I feel I may faint.

Lord Byron glides to the edge of his desk, leaning against it. There's a smirk on his face as he looks me up and down. Not in a sickening way, like General Javon does when my mother isn't looking. He sizes me up to see if I can be a worthy opponent in our debate. "How are they dangerous?"

"I have been poisoned and attacked on more than one occasion by them."

His eyes flare. No one in Omnius knows of the attacks against my life. Only La'Mia and my mother are aware. If anyone else knew, it would show weakness in the palace walls, even if it would further my mother's cause for the Great Cleansing Ordinance.

"But here you stand," Lord Byron says.

I flinch at his tone, as if the attacks mean so little. I might stand here alive and breathing, but each attack drains me, and I grow weary of the people around me—him included.

"If I weren't an Omnia, I would be dead," I retort.

I barely have the words out before he says, "And as an Omnia, you have put them into servitude to be starved and assaulted. And for what?"

"My mother put them into servitude, not me!" I shout.

The floor around us shakes. My mind flashes to the servants wearing ropes around their necks, trembling under the weight of gold. The way La'Mia used one as a stool in front of the other lords and ladies.

"So, I ask again, Omnia Melania, do you or do you not disagree with your mother—the ruling Omnia of Veilia—that today's events were for the greater good?"

I'm like a statue thinking of ways to talk myself out of this. I thought I had him by ignoring his questions. Somehow, he circled us back to the start of the conversation. My hands shake even as I hold them tightly together.

A surge of energy rises in my chest as my blood heats. "Today, she made an example out of your sons," I explain. I remain steadfast, even as he flinches at my words. "But it did not stand to make Veilia better for the greater good. Your sons were decent men, especially Baker."

Lord Byron looks at the floor. His arms cross over his chest, and his face lowers, but I can make out a small smile. My chest rises and falls in rapid succession. I didn't outright disagree with my mother, though what I meant was there. And—for some reason—it doesn't scare me as much as it should.

"Perhaps there is hope after all," Lord Byron whispers. His eyes are glowing green when he looks up at me.

"I beg your pardon," I ask searching him for a ploy. All I see is a man who resigned in our spat.

"Perhaps Veilia isn't damned from your mother's rule. Maybe you're our salvation," he says, reaching out his hand to grab a farmer's sickle. "With this, I ask you to do what you came to do and end my suffering." His hand shakes with the weapon extended toward me."

Lord Byron lowers to his knees. The twine wrapped sickle weighs heavily between us. My eyes bounce between the two, unsure what to do.

"If you prefer magic, you can do so," he says, taking the sickle away.

I react. My hand wraps around the sharp blade, slicing into my palm. He's about to stand, but I pull away. "I'm fine," I lie.

I raise my hand to show the thin line where I was cut already healing. Veilians, crossbreeds, and Nihils can heal fast from most wounds, royals faster than most, but nothing is faster than an Omnia's healing.

"I've never taken a life," I say, despite it being a lie.

Back then, I was a little girl who didn't understand what I was capable of. I am an adult now. Only a few months away from being the ruling Omnia. Every decision I make from here on out is of my own volition.

"Omnia Melania, I need you to do this," he whispers before pulling a crumpled piece of paper from his back pocket.

He holds the picture out to me, revealing his family together, Baker in his mother's lap playing with the strands of her blonde hair.

Lord Byron has both Ben and Brie in his lap. They're both smiling at their father, yet his eyes are focused on his wife.

"Let me pass through the Dark Mother's embrace to live with my family again," he says.

This time, I don't keep the tears away. I step closer to him. My vision blurs as the rain starts a steady rhythm against the ceiling.

Lord Byron inhales. "You were his first friend and the only one who didn't treat him like a Nihil."

The tears are falling faster, like a dam ripped open by a violent storm.

"Make it quick, Melania," Lord Byron says, lining the blade to his throat.

It'll take one quick slit to end his life. My powers pulse from me to the blade, emanating a white aura.

"May you find solace in the afterlife," I whisper.

The blade cuts through his neck. His green blood splatters over my hands and body, the warmth raising the acid in my stomach. I choke on my bile as I frantically move away. His body lands to the side with a thud. I've never been able to stand the sight of blood without getting sick, whether it be from a wound or meat on a plate.

Fighting through the sickness, I roll him onto his back and place the picture of his family on the center of his chest.

The sickle glows in my hand. Warmth spreads through me like it did on the grounds when my power was surging. Wanting and begging me to use more of the energy. The sensation feels addicting, which is the only reason I leave it on his chest. I've heard guards say it's dishonorable to take another's weapon when they're dead. I want Lord Byron to have all his honor and kindness when he reunites with the ones he loves.

Before leaving the room, I pour myself a glass of red, amber liquid to burn down the sensation of despair. I realize now I should have taken the drink when Lord Byron offered it earlier.

Rain pools outside as thunder assaults the sky. The ominous sound reminds me I'm utterly alone, and I can't help the emotions from falling out. I have to go, I have to get out of here.

With each step I take, I can't help but feel as if a part of myself is left behind. A piece of me broke off the moment I ended Lord Byron's life. And I know, without a doubt, I'll never get it back.

Eight

Erebus

One of the worst places I have traveled to yet is Omnius. The city quadrants look more like prisons, and the lords and ladies are the perfect jailers. All of them are pawns in a game they can never win against their overlords, the Omnias.

Moving in the shadows of the city, the smell of piss and desperation burns my nostrils. Most of the town is asleep during the hours of darkness. Only those who like to drink after a day of hard work are in taverns or brothels. I've seen a few drunks, but they never saw me. A perk of being shadow incarnate. If someone were to see me, they would run in the other direction like all the others. My wings are terrifying, but the daggers strapped over my body send a warning to steer clear. Another reason I make a killing as an assassin.

The quadrant for nature wielders is peaceful, like the elements they wield. There's a sense of harmony and balance in the air that almost covers up the stench around it. Vines grow on the hovel green buildings. Markets that are normally filled during the day are left empty at night. There's a dark green building made of painted wood, with a small awning protecting the flickering torchlight and a large sign with haphazardly painted words: The Dancing Boar. The fire makes the place seem inviting. I'm sure that'll change once I enter—it always does.

The Dancing Boar is much larger on the inside than it appears. Slim beams support the roof and iron candle chandeliers. As I imagined, the inside is cozy, bathed in the orange hues of firelight. People stand around the few wooden high-top tables with pine mugs.

As I enter, the room quiets and everyone stills. The large bartender at the U-shaped countertop stops speaking to his patrons. The men and women carrying trays and serving drinks slow their pace when I walk by, finding a table in the back with minimal light.

I ignore them all. It's not often a shadow wielder is seen this far from Tenebrae—the dark kingdom. There's not even a quadrant in Omnius for my kind. Even if it weren't for my magic, my dark raven wings draw the most attention. There's only one other person born with wings like mine, and she's about to be crowned Queen of Laelithra. My large wings barely fit in the tight booth. If I could hide them, I would. Their stiff weight is uncomfortable. They're a reminder of who I'm meant to be but will never become. At least they serve as a warning not to provoke me most of the time.

People give me a wide berth. Varying shades of green eyes stalk me, as if I'm the prey in their den. The large barkeep stands to his full height. I'm willing to venture he knew of my presence before I fully stepped in. It's their job to be on the lookout for anyone who is searching for trouble.

"Don't see your kind around here often," a grumbling, northern voice says. He says *your kind* as if I am some sort of monster. I might hail from the kingdom of monsters, but that doesn't make me one. But I can't blame the ignorant people of Omnius for not knowing the truth. Omnia Itzel will spew lies to fit her own agenda.

The barkeep's eyes are light hazel. Both his muscled arms are covered in vine-like tattoos. Gray hair cropped close to his head. He looks to be the same age as Micah, which makes me wonder if Micah might have known him from his past times venturing alone.

"Can I get an ale? I'll be out of here when it's gone."

He gives me a look that shows he doesn't trust me before returning with a large mug, firmly placing it on the table with a sigh. I imagine he's going to continue watching me until I'm far away from here. I throw a few gold coins on the table and sip in peace. People continue staring. Though nature wielders are all about peace and harmony, they're not fond of newcomers. Especially those with shadows dancing around them as they do with me.

I want to scream, knowing they're there. The small, dust-like particles always surround me. Like my wings, they serve as a constant reminder of my last name, but I didn't choose who my parents were. At least they're with the Mother of Darkness now; a better place to be than here. -

Most stop staring and move on to their conversations—conversations I find very interesting even as guilt eats at me. Omnia Itzel killed a Nihil today, and I don't doubt it was the Lord's Nihilian son. Earlier this week, my brother received a letter asking for our aid in their escape. We nearly had it when royal guards came out of nowhere. If there were only a few, we would have engaged, but there was a damn brigade of them. It was the first time we had failed a rescue. I hope the father can find solace in the fact that his son will be with the Mother. I'm tempted to find him—of course after finding the blue-eyed girl in the sea of green.

As if my thoughts conjured her, a small woman wearing a light green gown, blonde hair braided intricately, and stark teal eyes approaches my table. "Don't see you all around often?" I recognize subtle southern notes of Brilore in her delicate voice.

"No? I thought shadow wielders were frequent visitors," I retorted.

"And you have a wit about you," she drawls.

"Would you happen to be Addilynn?"

"I don't know, am I?" A smirk dances on her rounded face. I can understand why that Nihil wanted his friend back. I want one for myself.

"Sit," I command, my tone harsher than I mean it to be.

She drops her playful demeanor and does as she's told, sliding next to me in the booth, pinning my wing behind her. Maybe I should have specified for her to sit across from me.

I sip on my ale, amused.

"A dashing fellow asked me to save his friend, Addilynn, who has blue eyes in the nature quadrant." I pause, noticing the sudden blush on her cheeks. She looks down at her fingers tapping against the table. "You fit that description."

"He's alive," she whispers, more to herself than me.

I hadn't considered that she might have thought him dead. We did rescue him from a caravan of royal Omnius guards.

"He was taken from our home in the curtain lands." She pauses, wiping under her eyes. "He made me hide in our cellar until the coast was clear. Once I got out, I came to search for Lord Byron. Irwin spoke highly of him, but I got here too late."

The sadness is imminent in her tone, and now more than ever, I wish to seek Lord Byron. I can't save his son, but perhaps he would come to Tenebrae.

My lips part only to shut as the burly barkeep approaches. Addilynn doesn't seem to mind his presence, but I do. His chest puffs out, and his hands are in tight fists. "Looks like you finished your ale."

I blow out a large sigh to see that the ale is completely gone. I'm not sure when I drank it all, but a deal's a deal. "And we'll be on our way out."

Addilynn begins walking to the door.

The large barkeep's hand lands on her shoulder. "You can stay."

My eyes level to him. The darkness from earlier dances within me. My fists clench. People are staring in our direction, and I know what they want. They want to see me lose it—show them how dangerous my kind can be.

As if she senses my urges, Addilynn shakes her head. My task was to bring her back to Irwin. To be reunited with her friend. Together, they can be safe.

"Fuck off, murker," someone says, followed by others repeating the word as a slur to my dark power and kingdom. I'm nearly out the door when liquid splashes in my face. All my senses beg me to unleash my wrath. Lucky for them, I'm not in the mood to prove them right.

The night air engulfs me. Sticky ale clings to my hair and dark tunic. Metallic blood fills my mouth.

So much for being peaceful.

The lot of them are ignorant. Those people calling me a murker are the same people who pray to my Mother in their time of need. Those who will bargain with her when a loved one they care for dies. Perhaps if the Mother stopped tending to their souls or granting them dreams of their loved ones in the afterlife, they might learn consequences for their actions.

"Are they always like that?" Addilynn asks.

I'm surprised the barkeep even let her go. I can imagine him trying to tell her I can't be trusted, or I will only bring her harm. Except I'm trying to do more for the kingdoms than any of them. It's times like this I wonder why my brothers and I even try to save this forsaken land.

She approaches my side. Just like in the bar, she stands too close for comfort. Someone needs to teach this woman about personal space.

"Are they?" she repeats.

"I don't expect a warm welcome in any kingdom besides my own." I don't tell her I'm forced to remain hidden from the cities near the palace. My uncle would certainly try to kill me if I tread too closely. "My brothers and I stick to the curtain lands for a reason."

We fall into silence as we continue haunting the barren streets.

"How did you get out?" I ask without actually caring.

"I flashed him my dagger." Addilynn smirks, revealing the small silver knife. I admire her tenacity—she clearly would not let me leave without her. "What's Tenebrae like?"

"It's not completely dark as many imagine. During the light hours, the sky is similar to how dusk is here—but at night." I glance at the distant moonlight. "At night, it's breathtaking to bask so close to the mother's light."

Addilynn smiles and, funnily enough, a warm feeling grows in my chest as I recall the beauty of my land. Living there for so long can feel like a prison with scarce food. Yet I wouldn't give it up to live anywhere else. I didn't mention the monsters there. Where everyone and my brothers stay, we're safe enough from them.

"And the people?" She taps her fingers against her thigh. She did it in the bar, too, I realize. It's an easy tell, indicating she's unsettled.

"You ask a lot of questions."

Addilynn's face scrunches, forming little wrinkles on her petite nose. "I ask the right amount of questions," she insists, sounding like a child. "How are the people?"

Sighing, I say, "They're kind, you'll see."

A large cloud moves over the moonlight, bathing us in darkness. Addilynn, whether she realizes it or not, moves closer to my side.

"You don't have to fear the dark," I whisper, my breath tickling blonde strands of her hair.

She glances up at me with wide eyes. It must have donned on her that she huddled closer to a shadow wielder in the dead of night. I glance at her fingers to see if she's unsettled by my presence, but they're still.

I steer us to the furthest point outside of the quadrant. A soft drizzle begins to fall. Something drops in my chest, like my heart sinking straight through me. I came here for Addilynn, but that's not the only reason. I can only hope that the rain isn't an omen that I'm already too late.

"Addilynn, can you take me to Lord Byron?" I ask.

We walk for a mile or two before she stops near a stone wall. My vision is superior in the darkness, like a nocturnal animal. There's a flickering light in the top window of the cobblestone manor. Two royal guards stand at the front door. I was hoping this would be easy to get in and out, but I was wrong.

I nudge Addilynn's arm and cock my head in another direction. We crouch, hiding behind the cobblestone. I could laugh at how poor those guards are. Not that I expect much from any of Omnia Itzel's foot soldiers. Half of them live in servitude without an ounce of loyalty to her. It's the generals with their ridiculous feather helmets that worry me.

We sneak to the back entrance. The rain falls in a steady beat, like earlier in the curtain lands. An odd sensation I can't place feels heavy on my skin. It's like I need to be here, but I shouldn't be. It's the same feeling I had when I was a child, the night my parents died. Unlike then, I'm not a coward anymore.

"Wait here," I whisper.

She nods, staying low. I'm nearly at an out-of-place gap in the cobblestone when the sound of someone falling catches my attention. I glance over my shoulder to see Addilynn holding her knife in front of her. Pride mixes with the foreboding sensation within me. I'll make her a better dagger for her survival in Tenebrae.

Closing my eyes, I focus on my surroundings. The darkness kisses my skin until I am a phantom. I hear a faint intake of breath, and I know Addilynn saw me disappear into nothing.

In the distance, someone vomits. My stomach turns at the sound. I can see all the bloody gore in the world, but there's something about stomach acid and metabolized food that makes me sick.

As I enter the premise, I'm convinced my eyes are playing tricks on me. For what I am seeing shouldn't be real. The young woman's face is masked by long shimmering white opal hair. A white aura surrounds her as she holds her stomach. It's as if I'm caught in her trap, unable to move. When she looks up, my chest tightens. She is looking right at me but not seeing me.

Rainbow irises are highlighted by the water of her tears. The tears continue to fall, and I half expect her to lie there in her sorrow. Instead, she stands on shaking legs like a newborn doe learning the first steps of freedom. Dark green blood stains her sheer nightgown. She approaches, and I'm quick to keep my distance. Her light aura could dissipate the shadows hiding me. A part of me wants to protect her, for she seems too innocent, but another part of me knows the horrendous woman who birthed her. She slips past me, and I can smell lilacs and honey in the wind.

I'm about to follow to see where she goes, but I'm stopped at the sound of metal clinging off itself. Omnia Melania is through the walls as the guards round the corner.

Leaving witnesses; a rookie mistake, I think to myself.

The guards track her faint footprints in the mud, speaking amongst themselves. One of them unsheathes his sword. I should leave them alone, but they're steadfast on their mission to find her. They're only a few steps away from me when I decide I'll protect her in the only way I know how—killing.

My hand tingles against the handle of my dagger. The guard holding the sword never stood a chance as I jab my blade straight into his neck. The one furthest from me reaches for his weapon, but it's a fruitless effort. My shadows pin his arms to his side. He sputters out pleas for his life, but they fall on deaf ears. I slice my dagger against the major artery of his neck. Dark red blood spurts from the wound. For a moment, I'm stunned, for only sanguines— half-Veilian, blood sucking monsters—have sparkly maroon blood.

I don't dwell on it as I venture into the house. The distinct scent of a nature wielder's blood hits me. Following the trail, I reach the study to see Lord Byron dead with a deep slash across his throat. A glowing white, silver-edged sickle rests on his chest. My hands shake as I grab the weapon. There's a charge of energy emitting from it. The reality of what I'm holding crashes into me.

Omnia Melania used this sickle to kill a man. A sickle that is now imbued with her magical essence. One of the most dangerous weapons is in my hands because she left it behind. I keep it close as I read Lord Byron his last rites before fleeing.

Addilynn is waiting for me with her knife in front of her. There's more white than teal in her eyes. Her lips are parted, but nothing comes out. I may not look it, but I feel the same as she does.

"Prince Erebus," her voice shakes.

I don't let her speak anymore as I conjure a portal. I don't want to sneak through town holding the only Omnia artifact in existence. The very weapon that could alter the Fates' plans for all the kingdoms.

Addilynn slips through the portal without hesitation.

"Prince Erebus Ravenheart of Tenebrae," an ancient voice whispers, drawing my attention.

In the tree line, I see a dark mass with glowing orbs for eyes. The same mass I've seen during life altering events. I can't see its face, but I know with certainty the creature is smiling.

Smiling because what happened tonight has altered the course of *everything.*

Nine

Melania

I walk until my feet threaten to give out. My body tries to heal the fresh scratches on my skin. I didn't mean to scratch until I bled, but I welcome the pain. It's a relief to see my white shimmering blood, the only blood I can manage seeing without wanting to throw up. Perhaps that's the one commonality between my mother and me. We both enjoy seeing my blood alongside pain.

A chorus of frogs and toads bellow out, beckoning me further. My breath hitches at the sight ahead of me. The moon's reflection dances over the still lake. There are giant willow trees swaying in the gentle breeze. The same breeze causes a strand of my hair to brush against my nose, tickling it. Midnight-blooming flowers look to the sky, basking in the light they crave. The center of them is a pale, silvery light, while the petals are midnight blue fading to black. It's odd seeing the moon in Omnius when anything regarding it has been destroyed.

Fireflies light my path, guiding me closer to the lake. A giggle racks through my body, and the sound is odd to my ears. I can't remember the last time I laughed and felt the joy of it. I've had to fake joy for my mother and the other royals, but none of it belonged to me.

The cold-water laps around my calves. I flinch backward, not realizing how far I had ventured. I should clean myself and return to the palace. If I were caught here at night, my mother's wrath would consume me. Yet, as I look around at the beauty of the land, I'm enchanted.

The white of my gown floats around me like a lily pad. Similar to the moon, my reflection shimmers on the waves. My rainbow eyes are a stark contrast to the darkness surrounding me. Mud and green blood stains my face from wiping at tears.

Venturing further into the lake, the cold water washes over me. It's as if the land knows what I did and is trying to clean the ilk of death from me.

"For the Greater Good," I whisper, keeping my eyes trained on the moon, hoping the Mother can hear me.

The sound of the world is silenced by the water surrounding me. My entire body feels lifeless, and I bask in the sensation. For the first time in my life, I'm not Omnia Melania, the next one to rule. I'm not the child my mother didn't want. I'm just a woman seeking solace in the land and herself—even if I'm not sure who I am.

I'm not sure how long I stay like that, reveling in the quiet. Reflecting on the blood that will forever stain my hands. I can't say I regret my decision to end his life because I don't. Lord Byron deserved mercy for all he's done for me and Gaia. I hope his family will find one another and never be parted again.

With that thought, I swim toward the shore. Under the surface of the water, I can see an ancient statue from one of the first wars. The white marble sculpture has detailed short hair and a strong jawline. The rest has been covered by algae. Another royal who thought their reign would last forever. And that idea gives me more solace than it should. One day, I will be a statue at the bottom of a lake, wasting away—and that's marvelous.

Next to the lake, I ring out the ends of my gown. The water pools around me next to my white slippers. Without thinking, I toss the forsaken shoes into the lake. They'll be a better home for the fish than they are for me.

A stick breaks in the distance, and my heartbeat rises. My nail finds its place back in my mouth, tasting like mud and sand. Another crack sounds near me, causing me to flinch. I scan the trees, praying it's an animal scouring for other prey that isn't me.

All the air rushes out of my lungs when my eyes collide with white glowing orbs stalking from a distance. The shadowed silhouette doesn't move, but the land around it shifts.

I blink, hardly believing my eyes, as the haunting purple flowers of my childhood sprout from the ground, surrounding the creature in a circle with another path leading in my direction. I should run, yet my feet are stuck as if I am in quicksand.

A broken whisper crosses my mind. Goosebumps cover my skin. The fragmented voice is louder this time as it says, "For Everyone's Greater Good," in the ancient tongue of Veilia—a language taught to a select few.

"Melania."

I jump high in the air.

My feet slip from under me, and I land on my backside against a sharp rock. I'm still shaking as a hand reaches out to help me.

The onslaught of her white dove wings and golden aura is too bright for the surrounding darkness.

"By the First, you scared me," I retort.

La'Mia smiles like the idea entices her. The land around recoils at her presence, and I have the same sentiment. Glancing over my shoulder, I search for the shadowed entity and the flowers, but they're gone. I'm certain now it was a trick of the mind. Doesn't make me feel any better, though.

"What're you doing out here?" I snap.

If she's offended, she doesn't mention it. La'Mia keeps close to my side as we walk toward the palace.

"I can always find you." She gestures to the skin-colored spiral mark on her wrist. I was born with the same mark on the back of my neck. If it weren't for the shadow holding my attention, I would have felt her nearing. "Why are *you* out here?"

She says *you* as if belittling me. Like it's unacceptable for me to be anywhere but the palace. In a sense, it is, but it doesn't mean I enjoy it.

We walk in silence as I try to figure out an excuse. I consider all options. Perhaps I met a man during the gathering and went away with him. She would immediately laugh and never believe it. With my social grace and awkward pauses, no one would consider me good company. I'm about to tell her I wanted to enjoy the night air when she suddenly halts.

"What did you do?" she questions. Her golden eyes are accusatory, like she's stripping back all the layers of my being to find the truth. She's perusing my gown when her eyes snag on something that can't easily be talked away. "Who did you do?"

Her voice doesn't waver, but for a moment, I swear she's proud of the blood staining my gown. When our eyes meet again, I can't help but bear my truth to her: The death of Lord Byron and my uncertain feelings towards Nihils and crossbreeds. Her hands are crossed over her chest as she listens intently to each word. When I finish, I am breathless and feel utterly wrecked, longing to find solace in the lake once again.

"Melania." The way she says my name sounds like my mother before her true side bursts out. "Where is the weapon?"

My shoulders snap back. How could she only care about the

damn sickle when I committed murder? Is she truly so damaged by my mother that the idea of death no longer bothers her? Admittedly, I wish it didn't bother me as much as it did.

"Where is it?" she exclaims, moving around my body, lifting my gown and arms as if I hid it on my person.

I push her hands away and try to create distance. Her eyes' golden glow intensifies, and I gulp, my chest tightening from her presence.

"I left it with Lord Byron," I whisper.

If I weren't scared of her before, I certainly am now. Her wings splay out wide, and her veins glow similarly to mine when I'm channeling.

"You fucking nitwit," she yells, taking a step toward me, but I retreat. "Do you have any idea what you have done? What you released into the world?"

My back lands against a tree. The bark digs into the thin layer of my gown. La'Mia stops a foot ahead of me, and I see it then. She has more of my mother in her than I ever will.

"Return to the palace at once." Her voice is booming.

I don't argue as I turn on my heels with my eyes to the ground like a wounded creature needing to tend to my injuries.

"And Melania," La'Mia calls. I glance over my shoulder. "You should pray to all the Gods that the sickle is where you left it, or else you may have just damned us all."

I know she's threatening me, but I wonder what it would be like for the world to be damned. Perhaps then I might enjoy my life in the ashes of the past.

Ten

Erebus

The brown grass crunches beneath my boots when I step through the portal to Tenebrae. Addilynn takes in the surrounding sights. I can't help but be amused at people's expressions during their first portal experience.

Henrietta neighs in my presence. Her hooves clomp against the firm ground. I rub her nose, whispering soft praises to her. My Henrietta is a good girl, and she knows it. I pull Addilynn closer so the two can get acquainted, but also to ensure Addilynn doesn't stray from the small shadow orb I have around us. It's the only way to ensure our safety from monsters without torchlight. Even now, they click and claw in the distance.

I place the sickle into the saddlebag. Henrietta stirs, as if she wants it as far away from her as it can get. I have the same sentiment, but I'm the best person to have it compared to others.

Reaching my hand out, Addilynn takes it as I help her onto the horse, then swing behind her, keeping as much distance between our bodies as possible. Addilynn doesn't seem to mind as Henrietta trots toward our makeshift town.

"Isn't this the land of monsters?" Addilynn asks.

Horror stories circulate about Tenebrae, but it's livable. I try not to be rude as I hush her with my hand over her mouth. "They won't disturb us unless we give them reason to."

I track the movement in the trees, making sure none of them contort or move, then take my hand from her mouth. We ride in almost complete silence. There is a stillness in the air. I can feel the eyes of different creatures around us. They might not know we're here, and I'm thankful for that. This is Tenebrae after all—full of horrors and darkness as the good Mothers intended.

Once we make it far enough away from the haunting grounds, I ask, "Did you see them?"

She practically falls off the horse trying to turn around. "There were monsters with us!"

I can't help but laugh at her surprise. I know other wielders have a hard time sensing them, but I thought she might have seen the ones crawling on the ground next to us. They're not quiet when they're scurrying.

"More than one kind, too," I say, keeping the reins steady.

"Tell me about them," she requests, and I nearly laugh as her voice wavers.

She doesn't seem to frighten easily, but she might if she knew the real horrors of the world. I'm about to ignore her request when one plops down in front of us. Henrietta doesn't stir. She's used to seeing many creatures—Addilynn isn't. My hand goes over her mouth once more in case she screams.

The monster's body is like a cat bathed in ink, its face like a humanoid imp with beady red eyes. Long, spindly hair falls around its face. Pointy ears twitch, sensing its surroundings. A long-forked tongue licks around its mouth, full of two rows of sharp, pointy teeth.

The long claws dig into the ground as it stalks into the woods.

"That was a macabre," I whisper in her ear.

Addilynn shakes against me, and my heart feels for her. I remember when I was a child, and a pack of them attacked Micah and me at night. He was better with a blade than they were with their teeth and claws. Of course, they got a few bites and scratches in, too. We had to make another camp further away for Micah to recover.

Their black venom is extremely toxic.

Nothing else jumps out or crawls near us as we make it closer to the village.

"Was he dead?" Addilynn asks. "Lord Byron?"

I almost forgot about what happened in Omnius. Now it's the only thing my mind can concentrate on.

"Yes."

"Who killed him?"

"Omnia Melania I presume." I pause, remembering the picture on his chest. The manor was so empty, it seemed as if he were the only one left living there. "But I probably would have done the same if he didn't wish to come to Tenebrae."

She seems to chew on that. I don't tell her about Omnia Melania running away without the weapon, nor about the guards and how I took their lives. It's not something I like to do, especially if they don't deserve it. But if they didn't find her and saw me… well, it's a kill or be killed kind of world.

Addilynn's head thumps against my chest. I admire her easy-going trust in me. It's not something I am given so freely. Even Lelantos wanted nothing to do with me at first. He was a damaged boy when we first met. I picked a fight with him, and he made sure I felt each punch. If it weren't for Micah stopping us, we could have killed each other. It was then and there that I learned not to underestimate anyone—especially a Nihil.

Later that evening, he brought me a small barrel of ale. In turn,

I gave him a dagger with a wooden handle of a bear-like beast from Tenebrae. He introduced us to the parents who took him in. The town was raided soon after. He could either stay and risk the safety of his adoptive nymph mother and nature wielding father, or be an outlaw with us. He chose the latter, and I've never asked if he regretted his decision because I certainly don't.

Pushing the memory of Lelantos from my mind, the reality of the night strikes me. I don't want to believe what I saw, but it displays in my mind like meat at the butcher's. Omnia Melania killed Lord Byron and fled the scene. She left an Omnia artifact for anyone to take. I can't imagine what havoc Omnia Itzel would raise if she had the weapon in her grasp. Why did she do any of it? I want to believe she did it to show mercy, but I can't forget she's the spawn of Itzel. I've known only one Omnia in my life, but from the rumors of others, they're not known for their kindness.

Neither is your bloodline, my conscious mind says, battling with my exhaustion.

Addilynn snores beneath me, and I'm jealous of it. Not the abhorrent snoring, but I wish to sleep, too. As soon as my brothers see me, they're going to fight me—verbally and maybe physically. I never know with Lelantos. He'll either choose to speak or let his fists do the talking for him.

Henrietta doesn't need a lot of guidance now that we're close to our shack. The village is a mile down in the ravine near another waterway that dried up a long time ago. The once-a-year rain isn't enough to keep it full. Only the swamps in the west have natural water from the beginning of time. And not too many people venture there unless they're desperate and willing to invoke the witches' wrath. Even Micah would rather his gills shrivel up and be in immense pain than go anywhere near them.

Our shack is hand built like the rest of the village. It's a little lopsided, but it's large enough to fit three grown men. Two bedrooms upstairs and one bedroom downstairs. We haven't given it a name yet. I don't think any of us thought it would get as far as it did. Sometimes it feels like we're on borrowed time. *I feel like I am borrowing time.*

Gently getting off my horse, I pull Addilynn into my arms, and she nestles close to my chest.

The porch steps groan under our weight. I'm barely at the door when it swings open, the scent of amber and musk welcoming me home. Warmth blossoms in my chest.

"Where the fuck have you been?" a very *naked* Lelantos shouts. He's always been comfortable in his body, and I never shy away from seeing it.

Addilynn stirs in my arms. Lelantos moves away as if the sleeping woman might be a banshee ready to feast on his soul. It's funny to bear witness to the burly, giant man afraid of touching or being touched by someone.

Micah appears in a blink, his arms covering his lean chest. The blue of his veins swirl like the undercurrents in a sea. I immediately place Addilynn in his arms, cutting him off before he can speak. Like the nurturer he is, Micah cradles her close to his chest. I don't look to see where he takes her as I leave for the door.

A large hand grips the top of my very sensitive raven wing. I grit my teeth at the intrusion.

"Where do you think you're going?" Lelantos snaps.

He knows not to touch my wings, yet he does it anyway. I predict a tonic in his soup or dried mushroom powder in his socks. I glance over my shoulder to see he found pants. *What a shame.*

"To tend to Henrietta," I bite out.

Lelantos lets go of my wing, but he pushes me forward. I nip at him with my fangs before exiting. I make quick work of grabbing the sickle and tying Henrietta with Micah's beige steed, Perseus, and Lelantos's white mare, Aurora. The latter, on her last legs, being the horse he fled on six years ago. Back inside, I barely have time to take in the fireplace's warmth and familiar smell of our home before my brothers hound me. I can't make sense of their gibberish as they talk over each other. It's the most Lelantos has said to me in months.

You add salt to his drinking water and the man loses all trust, I think to myself.

They follow me around as I pour myself a glass of whiskey. I finish it as the sickle I tucked into the back of my waistband burns. Pouring another glass, I turn toward my brothers, giving them the attention they deserve. This time, I'm holding the glowing sickle for them to see.

It's been one hell of a night, and I fear it's only starting.

Eleven

My brothers stare at me as if I've grown another head after I explained the entire evening to them. The sickle is on the wooden desk between the three of us. I don't think Lelantos can decide where to look. His sapphire-blue eyes keep darting between the weapon and me. His fists are clenched tightly at his sides. I reach to move the artifact away from him, and he audibly snarls.

Micah's head flinches back. I'm relieved I'm not the only one surprised by the sound. I've heard him snarl, grunt, and even growl before, but nothing as primal as that.

"Lelantos," Micah says, nudging his shoulder against his.

He glances between the two of us. Whatever daze he found himself in, he's out of it. He moves to the fireplace, tense, even with the distance between us. Without his shirt on, I can see the tight muscles pulled taut. His veins bulge through his skin. The glass of whiskey I nicely poured for him remains untouched.

The flame casts an orange hue over him like amber whiskey,

blending with the similar color of his long, wavy strands of hair. My heartbeat quickens looking at him. Ever since that day in the bar, I was attracted to him. Who wouldn't be?

"What?" he snaps.

"Admiring my *brother*."

He rolls his eyes. Lelantos doesn't like how I call them my brothers. He had a brother who now rots in the ground, just as he thinks he should. Of course, it was Lelantos who killed him, but I suppose he has a sister somewhere out there, too. As the third-born child of a fire and water wielder, he was born without the ability to wield. He used to practice when he thought everyone was asleep. Trying to conjure an ounce of spark. When he reached twenty last week, any chance of magic died with the age. No one gets magic after reaching maturity. He's still a grouchy ass even after we let him hunt all weekend. Came home covered in blood, and neither Micah nor I asked if it was animal or not.

Micah shakes his head. He knows of my infatuation, and he knows Lelantos will never satisfy my desire. Another damn shame.

Micah is our designated father figure, with his one hundred years of life experience. He was my age when Omnia Itzel began eradicating species. It was only fourteen years ago when she enacted the Great Cleansing Ordinance, forcing all the royals to partake. Before the royals turned a blind eye, but the Nihils were a large part of the population, and to enact a cleansing against them wasn't a decision everyone supported—including my father. This has been Micah's ongoing battle for eighty years. Micah's adoptive mother was made an example of. She was a Scindo—an ancient race who was believed to be reincarnated with two souls. Only when they reached maturity did the two souls combine or separate. Shadow wielders believe the Mother of Monsters and the Mother of Darkness were once one body with two souls. Omnia Itzel made an example of Pandora as she cleaved her in two. Micah deserted the Creces the next day. He knew it was a matter of time before crossbreeds like him would be hunted—I'm sure she's waiting until all Nihils are dead before another Great Cleansing Ordinance is enacted against them, including Princess Brianna, the daughter of a siren and King Caspian of Brilore, the kingdom of water.

"Omnia Melania killed Lord Byron?" His voice pulls me away from my thoughts. Another tang of blood coats my tongue. I really need to get a new habit other than biting my lip.

"We should have saved him," Lelantos adds.

I don't disagree with him. We should have, but I don't believe in myself or my brothers dying to rescue others. Why does it have to be them or us?

"Did you see her kill him?"

I groan at his question as if I hadn't explained everything that had happened. I even told them about the bar, and that got Lelantos riled up. Even now, his face holds a serious, "I might snap and kill everyone" expression.

"She was covered in green blood, and I saw her in the backyard," I bluntly say.

"Could have been cleaning it up," Micah said.

"Why are you so hell-bent that she didn't kill him?" Lelantos snaps.

"I want to believe that the next ruler of Omnia will be better than Itzel," Micah hisses, his voice low so as not to disturb our sleeping guest.

"She cried," I say, moving to stand between them, though I'm not sure how much I could do to stop a fight between them. Micah rarely fights, but I'm willing to wager he'd put Lelantos on his ass. "Omnia Melania cried on the grounds. The entire sky opened in a downpour."

It's no surprise that her tears caused rain. It's the way of the Omnias and their connection to Veilia. Their magic feeds the land, and the land feeds them. The same happens to me and all the other royals on a smaller scale. We're the strongest on our own soil.

"It rained earlier today," Micah confirms.

"Doesn't dismiss the point; she killed a man," Lelantos argues.

He may not see the hypocrisy, but I do. This isn't about morality for him. I'm an assassin who kills for money, and today we all killed a number of Omnius guards to save others. This is about her being an Omnia and his deep-set hatred for them. If Micah and I weren't the closest thing he had to a family, he would have disdain for us, too. Though I'm sure he does in some way.

"Let's say she killed Lord Byron." Micah raises his finger before I can say she did. "Why wouldn't she use her magic to do it? Why even use a sickle?"

He gestures to the glowing blade. I mull over his question, thinking of all the times she could have used magic but didn't. It was easy enough to portal out of there; she ran instead. If I can cross through space to enter Tenebrae, I know it would have been easier for her to portal to the palace. Plus, the guards wouldn't have stood a chance against her.

"Why leave the sickle?" Lelantos asks.

Another good point.

I'm surprised he's adding to this conversation at all. It contains the two things he hates the most: talking and Omnias.

I'll admit he's asking the right questions, though. When I throw daggers in a fight, I go back for them. I'm sure Lelantos tries to gather all his arrows after a hunt. Micah would rather carve a piece of himself than leave the sword I crafted for him. Everyone knows a weapon is sacred—an extension of oneself.

"Are you certain it wasn't Itzel?" Micah asks, holding his nose between his thumb and forefinger.

My eyes practically fly out of my skull. I don't think Omnia Itzel can see through shadows, but I have a suspicion I wouldn't be alive if it were her. She wouldn't travel alone in the dead of night without at least one general with her.

"It was Omnia Melania; I am certain of that," I insist, drinking more of the amber liquid. Micah rubs his palms together in a circular motion. Poor Lelantos grits his teeth so hard, I fear he might chip a canine. If only he were half-sanguine, it would grow back.

"Why did you take it?" Micah asks.

I chew on his question. At the time, all I felt was the power of it. It practically had me salivating at the sheer potency.

"Wouldn't you?" I ask.

"Are you asking if I would take an Omnia artifact from a dead man's body?" Micah reiterates.

Hearing it like that makes me realize how much of an imbecile I am. I try to cover the ground for the hill I shall die on. "Isn't it better with us than anyone else?" I glide to the black settee, finding comfort in the leather cushion.

Lelantos sits in his rocking chair. It's the only piece of furniture he wanted for this shack. If the shack went up in flames, he would burn himself alive to get it. "How dangerous is an Omnia artifact?" he asks.

He's so full of knowledge about random things; I assumed he knew of this, too. Micah, still standing beside the blade, sighs. "An Omnia artifact is the same as any other magical weapon," he says, gesturing to his own sword.

The center of it appears to be a blue liquid in the steel blade. I didn't make it like that, but it's changed. Same thing happened with my daggers. My eyes flit to Lelantos's plain wooden bow and arrows—no magic moves within it.

Micah continues. "It shapes to the wielder and what they desire in combat—"

"I can't comprehend how an Omnia desires for anything more when they have everything," I say.

He looks at me sideways for interrupting. I raise my hands without remorse for my actions. He's lived with me long enough to know I'm prone to butting into sentences.

"I only know of one other Omnia artifact and Omnia Arabella wielded it. People believed her own hair was the bowstring. She never missed with it," Micah explains.

"But why would an Omnia need a bow?" Lelantos adds.

"There isn't much knowledge of Omnias beside their bloodline stemming from the First. They certainly wouldn't mention weaknesses if they had any."

"I doubt they have any," Lelantos mumbles.

Micah gives him a pitiful look, and I'm grateful Lelantos didn't see it. Poor Addilynn would wake to a brawl if he had.

"I'll do more research," Micah says, moving closer to his book nook. Before he settles in for his exhilarating night of reading, he looks at me dead on with a finger pointed at my chest. "The sickle has to remain here."

I'm about to retort when I hear an amused chuckle rumble from Lelantos. The odd sound silences me. Both my brothers are going to end up with a tonic in their stew soon, and I don't feel bad about it.

Micah settles into his chair next to the small candle. Lelantos leaves for his bedroom up the stairs, his eyes focusing on the glowing sickle as he disappears.

My head hits the small pillow, and I feel the blissfulness of sleep approach me.

"We have to run," Micah yells.

His large hand pulls me down the long corridor. Dark blood pools on the obsidian surface. I shouldn't fight him, but I can't leave without them. I can't part from my parents. My ears ring as someone lets out a violent scream. Micah doesn't hesitate. He throws me over his shoulder. His long legs carry us as the scent of blood wafts up my nose. Bodies are everywhere. I can see the misty shadow with horrifying white eyes watching me.

Suddenly I'm no longer in Micah's arms, and I'm not a small boy anymore. The onyx palace stands as it did before the night my parents died. The black and white marble tiles, laid like a chessboard, reflect the flickering light of the candlelit chandelier. A coldness laps at my exposed skin.

Looking down, I'm in a pair of filthy trousers without a shirt. My wings and wrists are pinned. My breath catches as I see a head of familiar red hair. His face is twisted in agony. His severed body is on the ground with deep gashes and teeth marks.

I nearly wretch at the sight, only to release all the bile seeing Micah's blue-tinted gills flayed from his body like a fish. His head is nowhere to be found. I'm being led by someone, but I can't make out who it is. Their scent is like a mausoleum, musty and full of death.

Heavy chains rattle against the ground with each step I take. I know wherever we're going will be my death. And if it means getting to see my brothers once more, I welcome it.

Cheers ring out as a bright light blinds me. People with different colored eyes stare at me. None of them have dark eyes like me. Looking down, the chains sparkle with gold. My power seems to have left me. A vast, empty void fills my chest. I try to speak, but no words come out.

The sound of heels clicking against the ground steals my attention from the crowd. I can't make who they are. Their scent fills the room with lavender and vanilla. The last thing I see is the sickle, but it's different. It's all sharp edges of gold with rainbow gemstones imbedded in the hilt. The sharp blade digs into the sensitive nerves of my wings. I scream out as the warmth of my blood drips from me.

Everything goes completely dark. I'm alone in the middle of a void. My hands and wings are free and left unmarred.

A creature with pale white skin and long strands of black hair crawls toward me. Her eyes are like liquid pools of moonlight. I can't move even though I want to.

"Don't let this be Fate," she hisses—

"Shh, you're okay, Erebus, you're okay." Micah's calm voice breaks me from my sleep.

He's leaning over me. The blue of his irises spin like a whirlpool, a complete contrast to the calmness in his voice.

The warm fire surrounds me. My breath comes out in short bursts, while my heart pounds against my rib cage. My wings hug around me.

"It was just a dream," he mutters as he pushes the hair away from my face, wiping away beads of sweat. I don't know how long he stands there soothing me, but it isn't long before my breath settles. The weight of the dream lightens. My eyes shut once more without the sickle and phantom figure to haunt me.

"Sleep well, Prince Ravenheart," are the last words I hear.

Twelve

Melania

The creaking of the door wakes me from my fitful sleep. I tossed and turned most of the night. Every time my eyes closed, I saw flashes of Byron's bloodline covering the floors. His wails as his sons were cut down by my mother haunt me, followed by his pleas for me to end his life.

A dark part of me envies my mother for her ability to take life without batting her lashes. If she weren't born an Omnia, I wonder if she would have taken up crime, becoming an assassin to clench her thirst for bloodshed. Do assassins sleep peacefully at night even as the blood of their victims soaks their hands? Or are they haunted by the life they cut short? Am I to be haunted by Lord Byron's death for the rest of my long life?

Elara stands in the corner with her eyes on the ground, wearing the same beige gown from yesterday. Dirt smudges her chin and hands. I'm sure my mother had her cleaning before it was time for me to wake.

She makes to step forward, but halts suddenly as La'Mia pushes herself into the room. Her golden irises dance with fury.

"Leave us," she all but shouts.

Elara's brown eyes flit to mine as if waiting for my permission. I nod for her to obey the command. She gives La'Mia a look of disdain as she exits. La'Mia scoffs but doesn't move toward her. She glides to my bed with every ounce of prestige we were taught to have. I have yet to manage the same posh walk.

She sits on the edge. Her fine yellow gown highlights her beautiful dark skin, contrasting the rage barely held at bay. I hug myself, clutching the new nightgown to my curves, the one I wore last night with Lord Byron's blood all but burned in the fireplace. Our breaths sync as we stare at one another.

I wish this were a meeting between typical friends. Two girls gossiping after a raucous party the night before. Perhaps speaking of whom we kissed in hidden alcoves. Did we find our future Fated? But this isn't that—and we're not those kinds of friends. I'm not sure I've ever had a friend like that. Not since General Javon's daughters—the ones I view as sisters—Syrinx and Eros, were sent away.

"You lied to me," La'Mia says.

I don't have to feign shock when the feelings reign true. I recall what I told her last night, and none of that was a lie. My lips part to explain myself. She holds up her finger, a demeaning act she must have learned from my mother.

"Killing Lord Byron is one thing, but to kill two royal guards." She clicks her tongue, taunting me.

My eyes blow wide, and my breath comes in quick recession. Nothing was out of the ordinary aside from the voices when I fled.

"The guards never saw me," I think to myself.

She raises her eyes to me. To the First, I said that aloud.

"La'Mia, I swear on my Omnia bloodline, I had nothing to do with killing the guards."

Her face twists into a sneer like she couldn't imagine betting on the power of Omnia. "Then whoever took the sickle killed the guards." If it weren't for her berating me for my mistake, I would think she's amused by the theft.

La'Mia stands from the bed, pacing. Her slippers clip against the marble flooring. Liquid gold pulses in her veins.

I chew on the skin next to my finger. A suffocating blanket engulfs as we sit in the silence. I wish I could read her thoughts to understand what is whirling around in them. With her pacing, I barely make out the mumbled words of an Omnia artifact. A chill runs down my spine thinking of any other time I've heard those words—nothing comes to mind.

The glowing edged sickle pulls to the forefront. The warmth of it in my palm as it cut. When I placed it on his chest, it wasn't glowing—was it? I wouldn't have left a weapon that was glimmering, but I can't remember outside of the pool of green blood.

"I can't keep saving you, Melania." La 'Mia's words bring me back to the room we're in.

I flinch. I don't recall her ever saving me. For being my protector, she's done little to keep me from the wrath of my mother and General Javon. Sometimes she's the reason for my punishment.

"But I will save you this time." Her tone is almost nurturing, like she cares. She moves around my bedroom, packing a small bag with dresses, lotions and potions from my vanity, and a small coin purse. Funny enough, I never realized I had a bag in my closet.

"What are you doing?" I ask, moving out of the comfort of my bed.

The wind picks up, moving the cashmere drapes from the balcony. The fall breeze cools my warm skin. La'Mia approaches me, placing her hands on my cheeks, then looks down at me once more. I fight the urge to roll my eyes since it's unbecoming of a lady.

"Omnia Itzel is recovering from her *activities* last night."

I want to gag at the insinuation of what my mother partook in.

La'Mia continues. "She hasn't received word of Lord Byron's death or the death of the guards."

"You didn't tell her." It's a statement, but my tone is inquisitive.

A gentle smile raises on her face, and I understand why people fall for her charms. I want to bathe in the warmth of her glowing, golden orbs. Gone is the woman who nearly crippled Elara to enter my room. Now, it's the Princess of Laelithra with a gentle soul, a swift change I can barely believe.

"I am trying to protect you." La'Mia moves away from me. "With my coronation only four weeks away, the focus needs to be on me."

My jaw drops. I can tell she sees nothing wrong with what she said. I'll never understand how deep her selfishness runs.

"It's for the Greater Good."

My empty stomach sours. It's like she truly believes it would be better for everyone else if I weren't here. It's a thought I've had, but I never thought it was serious. I'm realizing it may be the truth.

"I can't leave without speaking to my mother," I say, determined.

She may not know what I have done, but I can't leave without telling her. I shiver, imagining how cruel the punishment might be.

"Melania." La'Mia speaks it like I'm a child asking for a sweet tart before dinner.

My arms cross over my chest. I'm not sure why this is the battle I am choosing, but I'm not going to budge. We stare at each other. A battle of wills and who wants to win more. I'm about to break when she says, "Fine."

I don't register her tone as she tells me what I need to say. She goes as far as picking out a white lace gown for me and then welcomes Elara into the room. Her brown eyes flash toward the canvas bag on my bed.

Elara remains quiet as she readies my hair, then places a white gold diadem on the crown of my head. In my reflection, I look like the perfect Omnia.

My feelings don't match.

I stand from the vanity, running my palms over the elegant fabric. The decision to ask my mother's permission catches up to me, filling me with regret. Should I have just gone and asked for forgiveness later?

You did that, and three men are dead, I think to myself.

As I approach the door, I see Elara with her sad brown eyes. The husk of a person who will live and die in servitude. La'Mia told me exactly what to say to have my freedom. She said nothing about Elara, but I can't leave her.

"Pack a bag quickly and quietly."

She smiles, a first I have ever seen from her. Warmth floods my body, even as I'm about to face the lioness in her own den.

I can do hard things.

The closer I get to the main hall, the more people I see. Maids and guards stalk the halls, ensuring everything is in order. Like always, they look at me and immediately avert their attention, as if making eye contact with me will turn them to stone. I'm sure I could perform such a task by simply touching them if I truly desired it. I'm surprised my mother hasn't tried that method of punishment yet. It's an idea better left in my head, for she might try it on me.

The kitchen quarters are always busy with servants moving in and out with a purpose. Their hands are full of fresh juice and pastries. There's always too much for my mother and me to eat and never enough for the prisoners. I think most of the captives receive a piece of bread and a glass of water a week—something I learned from my punishment in the dungeons. It's a dark and musty place that infests my dreams.

Though if I had to choose between dreaming of the dungeon or the blood of Byron's family, I would pick the former.

Thinking of them has my mind grappling with the "what ifs" of my current situation. I've been taught about an Omnia artifact, but La'Mia didn't speak more of it. A part of me wonders if the idea of it scares her. Many people hear Omnia and are instantly struck with fear. Could a simple sickle evoke the same emotions?

I trip on the edge of my gown, nearly toppling into a guard. "My apolo—"

I stop speaking as I look into the most dreadful eyes. General Javon's blond hair is pulled to the nape of his neck. His large hand rests against the hilt of his sword. There's a large bruise-like mark on his neck, and I *wonder* how he got that. La'Mia's words about my mother's activities stop my mind from filling in the blanks.

"You're as clumsy as you are weak," he grumbles.

He always speaks to me this way, so I'm not surprised. If he weren't my mother's lover or right-hand man, he wouldn't get away with talking to me like that. No one would aside from my mother.

"Omnia Itzel requires your presence."

A sense of dread overcomes me as if I didn't ask to see her. I nod, and General Javon leads us through the foyer, past the study and into the west wing. I'm only allowed here when I'm summoned by her. We can share the middle of the palace, but her side is off-limits to me. Rarely does she ever come to my wing.

Her part of the palace is nicer than mine will ever be. The white walls sparkle in the rising sun. White chandeliers reflect rainbows onto all the surfaces. Each wall has a separate mirror, so she can feast on her own presence. There are no portraits of Omnias from the past, unlike my dark hallway lined with them. There's only her portrait at the end of the hall before her bedchambers. No matter how many times I see it, I can't help but feel envious of her regal posture and domineering eyes. That feeling is fleeting as we cross to her room, and she's standing before me.

"You may leave, Javon," she says sharply.

He doesn't hesitate. He turns on his heel and leaves the room, shutting the door behind him. For someone who was resting from her nightly activities, she seems quite well. Her hair is pulled into a bun, displaying the old scar where she had her spiral protector removed. I've often wondered why our protector marks are in such a place. It's as if the world knew Omnias were meant to be perfect, and the simple scar was a flaw to be hidden.

She wears a long silk robe with a plunging neckline, revealing far too much skin. Stepping down from the raised floor, she approaches and circles around me, inspecting every inch of me in search of a flaw. It's a maneuver she's done for my entire life.

As she faces me, the skin prickles on the back of my neck. With all our physical similarities, we both know we couldn't be more different. She's a force to be reckoned with, and I'm a dandelion blowing in the wind.

"You've gained weight," she says, focusing on my center.

I can't find the words to agree with her, as I have once before. Keeping my wrists firmly behind me, I square my shoulders to recite what La'Mia told me. It's blind trust I shouldn't put into her, but her selfish need to have the attention on her outweighs what I've done.

"With Princess La'Mia's coronation approaching, I hoped I could travel to the other kingdoms," I say, proud of myself for keeping my voice steady.

My mother looks me up and down, scrutiny in her eyes, and I fear she might reject my request.

"To learn more about the politics and how they're enacting the Great Cleansing," I continue. Her eyes flare at the mention. "With Lord Byron's treasonous acts, I believe others may act against you, Omnia Itzel."

The words feel like acid on my tongue. Sweat beads on my

forehead. I never realized the room was this hot.

"How will you punish them?" she asks.

Keeping my heart as level as I can, I straighten. "I shall keep them chained until you arrive, Omnia Itzel."

For the first time, my mother smiles, a snake before killing its weak prey. Her cold, red-polished nails rub against my cheek. I bite the inside of my mouth.

"Perhaps you are learning after all." My mother returns to her spot before the mirror, admiring her eternal beauty. She turns to the side to see her slim stomach, clearly jabbing at me, but I'm too stunned to care. "You may go," she says.

My lips part. I didn't expect her to allow this, and so quickly. I turn for the door when I realize I'm not the only one leaving. Elara is the only reason I stop. "I require a maid, Your Majesty."

It's her turn to look dumbfounded. Her eyebrows scrunch, and I see the deepest wrinkles on her forehead. I wonder if she realizes she has those.

"You may go, but you will not take a maid."

I am about to argue why I need one when three servants enter the room—servants I have never seen before. Their eyes widen in my presence, and they bow before us. Omnia Itzel looks over her shoulder and raises her hand to shoo me from the room.

"Can I use your power?" I ask.

The maids busy themselves, even as I feel their stares.

"Only this once," she says, a finality in her voice.

I practically sprint out of the room toward my east wing. General Javon is nowhere to be seen, and I'm thankful for that. Down the long hallway, the eyes of the Omnias watch me. I'm almost at the door when a full body portrait I've seen hundreds of times catches my attention.

The woman portrayed in the picture must be generations older by the high neckline of her gown. Her tan skin makes her hair and eyes seem much brighter. The crown of Omnius sits on her head, but that isn't what keeps my attention. Her right, lace-gloved hand rests on the hilt of a great sword, all white and adorned with intricate golden spirals. A golden aura surrounds both her and the weapon. Together, they are connected; together, they are one. My heart twinges as the words *mine* repeat in my head.

I thought a piece of me was missing because I took a life. Now, I realize why La'Mia was so shaken by the weapon not being with me. The sickle contains a very piece of my being, and I must get it back.

Elara paces the floor in my bedroom. She changed into a fitted pair of leather trousers and a loose fitting tunic. The familiar stench of horses greets me—attire meant for the stables. I've never been allowed to wear pants, though I've wanted to.

From my nightstand, I grab three weathered, leather-bound journals. I only have one ink jar left, but I can get more. I'm placing two romance books in my bag when Elara says, "Where are we going, Omnia Melania?"

I consider this. La'Mia and I never decided on a place. Any of the kingdoms would welcome me, but not all of them will accept Elara. "Where do you have family?"

She jerks back, then responds quickly. "Xannoroth."

I pull the heavy bag onto my shoulder and lead us to the balcony. Elara rubs at the side of her bruised neck. I couldn't save Baker, but I can save her.

Closing my eyes, I sense the energy surrounding me. My mind dances with visions of lava rock beds. The ashy air and hot temperatures. I can feel the heat of the energy in my palm. Holding it in front of me, a red, green, and white spiral forms. It continues to grow. Pushing it forward from the palm of my hand, a fiery volcano appears. Elara grips my other hand, and I pull us through.

With my first step into the portal, it's like standing between space. It's silent *and* loud. There's nothing and everything. A paradox that shouldn't exist. I'm about to complete the step into Xannoroth when a white tendril of power tries to pull me toward it. The energy is connecting from me to dark energy. I try to follow it when I'm pulled by another force.

For a moment, I'm falling until my tailbone lands against the firm ground. I wince from the feeling of rocks digging into my skin. The portal before us dissipates. My eyes scan the surrounding area— we're not in Omnius, but this isn't Xannoroth either.

Thirteen

"What the hell was that?" Elara groans, followed by a gag.

My morning breakfast churns in my stomach, threatening to make a swift exit. Beneath me, the ground is firm, yet I sway. The trees blur together. A green aura glows around my hands. No matter how sick I feel, there's another emotion pushing through—pride. I created the portal out of nothing. I've seen people do it before. The other royals and my mother do it as naturally as breathing, but I've never been given the chance. It's as exhilarating as it is terrifying. A feeling that can easily become addictive. I'm starting to understand why my mother uses her powers constantly.

Her powers, I think to myself, reminding me of who the magic belongs to.

Elara is on her hands and knees, a pool of stomach acid beneath her.

"Are you alright?" I ask, my voice shaky.

Elara snaps her head in my direction. Redness forms around

her teary eyes. Her skin is paler than normal with a hue of green on her cheeks. She squints before choking out, "Do I look alright?" Her brazen tone is unexpected.

A laugh escapes me, for no one—aside from three people in my life—speaks to me that way. When the other servants fed me poison, they had a smile on their faces. Elara's jaw is clenched and her brow furrowed, and I admit, she definitely doesn't look alright.

She faces the ground once more. Her body moves like a cat choking on a hairball. A sob wretches through her, and I feel the pain of it like it's my own. I didn't consider how the portal would affect her. I shuffle to her, and with each step I take, my mother's voice repeats in my head: Nihils mean nothing. They don't deserve kindness or apologies from anyone, especially us. Even so, my hand pulls her braid from her face while my other palm runs along her spine. She wretches, but there's nothing beside liquid. It never occurred to me that if my mother rationed my meals to watch my weight, she would certainly give even less to the servants.

Beneath me, Elara shakes. She isn't dying, but she suffers because of an Omnia—because of me. And I'm tired of hurting people. Memories of Ben's body writhing against the ground surfaces. Then another, darker memory of the Great Cleansing when I was a girl. I fall to the grass as images of a treacherous, purple flower cripples me. People dying as they scream out to the Mother of Death and Darkness. Begging for anyone to save them. Their teary eyed expressions focusing on the person who killed them—me.

I swallow, stuffing down the sudden tightness in my throat.

We stay like this until her sickness recedes and my chest lightens. Short patches of spiky brown grass poke through the thin soles of my slippers. Sand and ash cling to my gown. The trees are bent at an angle, small specks of red leaves clinging to the branches. The scenery stretches for miles. My portal was meant to take us to the gates of the palace of Xannoroth, not *here*. Though I'm not entirely sure where *here* is.

"Where are we?" Elara asks, standing on shaking legs.

She uses the back of her bare arm to wipe her face, then pulls her bag higher over her shoulder as she flanks my side.

"You're from Xannoroth. Shouldn't you know?" I ask with more bite in my voice than I intended. In my defense, I don't do well without structure. Landing in the middle of nowhere is a little too chaotic for my liking—and I killed a man.

My heart tightens at the memory of Lord Byron's death. I wonder if Elara would judge me for what I did. Would she judge me like La'Mia, or would she understand why I did it?

I don't have the chance to broach the topic when she says, "I'm not from Xannoroth, my sister is."

My eyes widen, and my lip's part. I'm speechless for a moment as I grapple with this information. Not only are we in the middle of nowhere without a map, but neither she nor I know where we are.

"Should I portal again?" The idea of it tempts me more than it should.

"Fuck no."

Once more, I am unsettled by her manner of speaking. Whenever we were in the palace, she regarded me with a high respect and submission. Perhaps that was the only way she knew she could survive under the same roof as my mother. I couldn't imagine anyone speaking to my mother in such a way.

"You don't fear me?" The words are out before I can stop them. As they settle in the air around us, I'm affronted by the truth of it. I'm one of the most powerful wielders in all the land, and this Nihil isn't scared of who or what I am.

"Should I?" She faces me. Her brown eyes bore into me, and I want to yield under her scrutinizing gaze. I keep my shoulders back, but I shake my head. Her only response is to nod and push past me.

"Where are you going?"

Elara points her small finger toward the mountain with a large billow of smoke bursting from it. The volcano of Xannoroth.

I walk behind Elara as we navigate the hillside. The volcano is our only guide in the home of the most chaotic wielders—the Kingdom of Fire. The smell of sea salt wafts up my nose. From our high ground, I can make out the crashing waves of Brilore—the Kingdom of Water. If I thought it were safe, I would take Elara there with me instead. King Caspian has always been kind when I went on my visits as a child. It's his seven sons vying for the throne that I fear. They're willing to do anything—and I truly mean anything—to get in my mother's good graces. But out of them all, I fear his daughter, Brianna, more. She's seventy-eight years old, made of siren scales and ambition. She might be a crossbreed, but my mother holds her in higher regard than others. It's the only time I've seen my mother be kind to someone born of two species. And by nice, I mean she didn't use fire magic to steam her skin and cook her like a fish.

No. The Kingdom of Water is not the right choice. At least here in Xannoroth, despite the short tempers of the fire wielders, the king is kind to all. And he's the only one to stand against my mother and live to tell the tale.

"Are we going to talk about what happened back there?" Elara asks.

"What do you mean?"

"The botched portal."

And just like that, my pride is wounded.

"I didn't see you conjure a portal out of thin air," I retort.

She nods, clicking her tongue against her teeth, silencing anything else she might have said. I shouldn't have said it, but she started it. I want to apologize. I *should* apologize, but I don't. I pull my thumbnail between my teeth once more to keep silent.

I didn't think the portal was botched, although there was something different about it. The white tendril was of my own power. I can feel the phantom essence of it now. But that's not what scared me. It was the dark void it was trying to guide me, too. I'd never seen such a thing in my nineteen years of portaling, and I'm not sure I want to see it again. I was warned at a young age to avoid darkness above all else. The lesson pounded in my head how corrupt shadow wielders are. *You can't trust what you can't see,* I'd been told.

Feet crunching against the ground pulls me from my thoughts. The steps are heavier than ours. Ahead of me, Elara's neck swivels as she looks toward it.

She falls to the ground, pulling me with her. From our vantage point on the hill, three men lead two horses pulling a small wagon. A burly man sits on the edge, holding the reins. Behind him, in the small cart, is a group of children barely old enough to stand with muck and blood smeared on their faces. Attached to the cart are two ropes connecting to a group of men and women, connecting nooses around their necks. The soles of their bare feet trail blood against the rough terrain. A woman in the front trips, taking the whole lot with her.

"OY!" the man yells.

He halts the horses and the other three men, then storms off his cart over to the captured group. He pulls the woman up by the rope around her neck. A child cries, and I assume that's his mother. Another man covers the young boy's mouth and nose. Both the mother and child choke, turning a light shade of purple. I can't breathe, as if the air in my lungs is being stolen from me.

Elara speaks, but I can't hear her. My limbs shake as the power within me spirals out of control.

"STOP!" Someone shouts—no, not someone. It's Elara.

She moves down the hillside, leaving behind the bag of food she'd been carrying. I've never seen her look so determined. Her fists clench at her sides. The men look between each other before laughing, loosening their hold on the pair. The child's body goes limp, but the soldiers pay him no mind. They turn to the woman as she takes a breath, then slam their fist into her face. She hits the firm ground with a thud, and I think she broke a bone.

Two of the other men approach Elara. I try to move, to do something, but it's as if I've become a statue. My limbs are not mine. I'm here, but it doesn't feel as if I am. The men gain more ground on Elara. I try yelling at her to run, but the words are gone. Like the air in my lungs. My head might burst with tension when the tallest of the five gets in her face.

Elara throws a punch against him.

Blue blood gushes from his nose.

She shakes out her fist, then the other one knocks her to the ground.

Finally, my limbs move, but it's too late. The man's fist collides with Elara's face. She jerks to the side, then comes back to center.

I sprint down the hill, barely breathing. Their eyes fall to me. One sneers in my direction as if I'm horse shite on the bottom of his shoe.

Power surges through my veins, uneven like my breath. An aura of red dances around my fingertips.

One man lunges at me.

He doesn't make it far.

Fire engulfs him; he lands on the ground, screaming and swatting at the flames consuming him. The scent of burning flesh billows into the air.

Elara glances at my hand, at the red aura that hasn't left my palm. I didn't do that. I couldn't do that, right?

Hooves pound against the ground. The other four men run in the other direction. A group of guards wearing bronze-colored armor ride in, two of them with their swords ready to follow the men. In the action, I forget about the human torch. His body continues to burn, dead a few feet ahead of me.

I rush to Elara, thrusting out my hand. She swats it away, jaw tight as she looks at me. Blood drips from the corner of her lip. Standing, she keeps a distance between us. The added space digs a pit in my stomach.

The other guards release the men and women from their restraints, reuniting the mother and child. Both weep in their embrace. A large, black horse approaches, and Elara bows. King Albus dismounts, wearing an outfit fit for politics—a ruby-red linen shirt, partially buttoned with an open collar. Gold embellishes the tight sleeves. The shirt is tucked into his black trousers. When he bows to me, his slicked black hair falls forward, ashy-gray streaks catching in the light.

He looks at me through his dark lashes, eyes unlike any others I've seen before. Around his black pupil, a large ring of red lightens from orange to yellow, a living fire within him. I lower myself to a courtesy, and he flashes a glint of amusement—or perhaps confusion—in his beholding stare. It's gone before I can understand which it is.

King Albus rises, pushing the strands of hair back. "I apologize for the burning man. I never would have done that in your presence, but it's not every day I stumble upon an Omnia in these parts." His voice is raspy and crackles like the embers of a fire.

"We were making our way to the palace when we stumbled upon this," I say, gesturing around to the cooked corpse.

"I hadn't received word of your arrival," King Albus says.

My mother likes to announce her presence wherever she goes, making grand entrances with parades in the cities. She rides in front, sitting sidesaddle on a horse while soaking in the attention. I'm usually there, hiding in a carriage.

Searching for the words for why I am here is far more difficult than I thought. I'm not the most eloquent of speakers, and certainly not when Lord Byron's pool of blood haunts me. I certainly can't tell

King Albus I killed a man, can I?

A guard clears his throat, taking the attention away from me. "They're tired and starved, Your Highness."

I'm grateful for the reprieve.

When he meets my eyes, he bows.

I'll never be used to people bowing to me. I may be an Omnia, but I'm not *the* Omnia. I can't understand why they think they should do such an action here.

After a moment, the guard rises and turns back to King Albus with a question in his lowered brow and parted lips.

"We shall give them sanctuary in Umber," King Albus responds.

With that, the other guards approach with a gathered group of ten people. King Albus whispers with one of them. I try to make out the words, but I can't concentrate through the scowls around me—including Elara's. The young child who nearly died begins to cry as they near me. His dark blue eyes glimmer with magic, unlike his mother's. The realization slams into me like a rainstorm crashing against a hay hut.

Children of Nihils aren't supposed to be born with magic. Though I understand very little about them, I know that much. Or so I thought. My stomach turns. Nihils *do* have the gene of magic, and they're being slaughtered because my mother doesn't know the truth… Or she does. An even worse thought comes crashing into me: how much has my mother told me that has been a lie? How much do I truly not understand?

King Albus glances down at me, and a smirk plays on his lips. I thought I was running from the reality of Lord Byron's death, but now I think this was all Fate's plans.

The thought doesn't scare me as much as it should. If the Fates are guiding me, then they're no longer controlling my mother. A chill runs down my spine. I can feel it in my bones that, once more, I'm standing on a precipice between right and wrong. As the faces of Nihils cower and scowl at me, I realize my decisions are finally my own.

Fourteen

The lavender hue from the rising sun breaks through the thin drapes. The smell of eggs and veal has my stomach growling. There aren't any walls separating the two rooms, so I can see my brothers before I register their voices. Lelantos shovels food into his mouth as if he doesn't eat every hour. Micah speaks to him, but there's never a response.

The memory of their corpse's flashes in my mind from my dream. A faint smile forms on my lips. I shuffle into the room, and Lelantos pays me no mind as I gather my plate. Micah tracks my movements. I don't meet his eye as I'm not prepared to discuss the dream. Not ready to ruin their happiness.

For the past six months, as the seasons changed from summer to harvest, they've been happier. Lelantos speaks more. With each kill he gets to provide to the butcher, there's a smile of pride on his face. I can tell Micah enjoys teaching the young ones how to train outside of his work at the fish market. There's no need to worry them over a phantom being when I don't know what it is. I certainly can't tell them about what the sickle did to me in the dream. Micah will demand I return it, and Lelantos will vote we bury it out of reach. Neither of those options sounds pleasing.

"Erebus," Micah says loudly.

"What?" I snap, sleep still clinging to my vocal cords.

"You're scraping your damn fork against the plate," he snaps. Micah's sharp, siren-like teeth clench. I don't bother apologizing as I shrug my shoulders. He might have comforted me last night, but we can talk about that later—much later.

More orchid scented air bleeds into the room. Every part of this shack is made of different wood; most of it has been refurbished from our missions saving Nihils and crossbreeds. We took the carriages and did what we could with them. At least we used to. Now we have small trade with local villages who don't seem to mind our presence. Like us, King Marcus pays little attention to them. Our trading is how we all stay alive in these parts.

Lelantos begins serving himself another plate, only to stop when he sees how little we have left. Another trip to a village will need to happen, and soon. With winter approaching in a few months, the temperatures will become too frigid to make the journey. In the past, I would stay in Xannoroth for the winter. Three months of pleasure and ale to get through my birthday and the death of my parents.

"Will you take the girl you brought here to village when she wakes?" Micah asks.

I nod, hoping that's answer enough as the two prepare to leave. They're always the first to wake the small village. Some days I deign to go with them, and other days I don't. Far too many people staring and praising me for the fortune I have brought upon them. With all I have done, it doesn't seem to be enough. Omnia Itzel still partakes in the Great Cleansing. And if my dream is any indication, our days are numbered.

After changing into new clothes that appear to be the same as the others, I settle into the chair next to the window, gripping cherry wood in my hand and whittling away at it, making deep and shallow cuts at the top. My knife is sure with each chunk. It's the only thing I can do to keep myself stable. Micah taught me how to carve when I was fourteen years old, after I tried to take my life. The blade-making came later when I was an apprentice in Xannoroth.

I'm nearly finished with the head of the lioness as the floor creaks above me. I was going to give Addilynn until I finished carving the fine details before I went to wake her. By the sound of it, she's scurrying around up there. Or it could be mice burrowing.

A groan sounds from the stairs. She's practically sprinting for the door, right past me, spilling the scent of the sea and jasmine, reminding me of Micah.

"Good…" I pause noting the shadows in the room. "…afternoon."

"I didn't intend to sleep that long," she exclaims.

"It's not easy on the body going through a long portal like that," I state, knowing she needed the rest. When crossing a portal, it feels like nothing. In a single step, you're in a different place entirely, but it's time and space you're jumping through. When I first learned how to portal, I tried to step from the curtain between Brilore and Xannoroth, only to land in the deepest ocean in Brilore—nearly drowning. Micah swam us to the shore. I'm used to it now, but it still takes a toll on those who don't frequent that way of travel.

"Would you like to see the village?" I ask.

Addilynn bounces on the pads of her feet. Her excitement becomes an energy of its own. I stand from my tiny corner near the window. In doing so, all my attention settles on the glowing blade. Its light is dimmer than it was last night. I should leave it here and wait for Micah to continue his research… or I could speak with someone who is older and more knowledgeable about weapons. I settle on the latter.

Addilynn raises her own brow as she sees me wrap the sickle in a thin cloth. She doesn't say anything as I tuck it into a small satchel with the newly carved blade, followed by a few daggers that I place in their sheaths of my leathers.

"Nine daggers? You plan on murdering folk?"

"Not if the day goes the way I want it to."

Our horses trot against the firm, dead grass. The dirt creates a trail of dust behind us. Addilynn's eyes remain forward, only to slide to me after a while. She looks back at the road when she realizes I noticed.

I study the landscape around us to keep me entertained. Even though the sun is at its highest point, the sky is a lush lavender with thick gray clouds moving swiftly. The trees bear no fruit or leaves, and their thick trunks make a great camouflage for frownies. I'm thankful we didn't come across one last night. A macabre is one thing. They're small enough to fight off. Frownies—or as other kingdoms say, Dreadblights—are the deadliest of monsters. Their bodies are like slender trees, their several limbs the branches. With their dark gray bodies, they are hard to spot. The only warning issued is the clicking of their long tongues. And the worst part about them— they hunt it packs. I survived once before, but even then, it took my brothers to help me.

I owe them my life for more instances than I can count. They never hesitate to save me, even when I wish they didn't. That night with the frownie, I did to myself. I walked into the woods with only one dagger and no torch. Call me dramatic, but it felt fitting to end myself by the Mother of Monster's creation. Alas, the two came in with their fiery light and saved me. Micah didn't let me out of his sight for two weeks because of it. I still think of that day—and others—when the darkness consumed me. I never told my brothers where I was going, but somehow, they always knew where to find me before it was too late, as if it were of the Fate's volition to keep me alive. I'm neither arrogant nor ignorant enough to think I have complete control over my life. The Fates constantly spin and turn for the path I am destined to follow. Though I don't understand why they put me on the path that led to an Omnia artifact.

"They're not your actual brothers, are they?" Addilynn asks.

She pulls me away from my drowning thoughts. I take a second to comprehend her question. "They're the closest thing I have to a family," I say, pausing before adding, "My parents died before the Mother blessed them with another child."

I still remember my parents asking me if I wanted a brother or sister. Back then, I was hesitant to consider another life I would eventually care for. Perhaps it was the Mother's will for them to only have me. Maybe she knew what the Fates had in store for them—but if she did, why didn't she warn them?

Addilynn nods. "That's how I feel about Irwin. My parents passed away when I was young. Irwin's family took me in, and when they passed, we only had each other." Her voice is soft, but there's something else in her tone that catches my ear. I pocket her inflection for later as she continues. "Irwin has been my rock through the best and worst times. It nearly broke me when all Nihils were sentenced to reside in the palace. I'm very grateful for you and your brothers for saving him, even if we had to part." Her voice rises as she says, "But today, I get to see my Irwin again."

"I understand," I say, and I do. As much as I fight with my brothers, it's our form of love.

"How did you meet your brothers?" Addilynn asks.

"Micah was hired by my parents to scout and watch the horses. He doesn't look it, but he's one hundred years old." Still quite young in our long lifespan. I've heard of people living to five hundred years old and longer. I can't imagine living past forty-seven—the age my parents were. "The night our palace was usurped, Micah came to the rescue. He couldn't save them, but he saved me."

Sometimes I wish he didn't.

Addilynn's face is somber, and I feel the guilt of that. She thought I was witty and a charmer, not some sad orphan.

"Lelantos came into our lives when I was sixteen." I smirk at the memory. "I was trying to hit on him, but we ended up throwing fists."

Nothing's really changed.

Addilynn's large eyes shine bright with tears. She looks at me with remorse. A strange sight to behold. I'm not used to people feeling remorse for a shadow wielder. Though few people would risk Tenebrae to find their Nihil lover. At least not with the blasphemy Omnia Itzel spews. Even at the thought of an Omnia, the sickle seems to come alive.

Addilynn takes in the sights around. The daytime looks completely different compared to night. It's still dreary with dark hues and little color, but there is life around. Smoke rises from chimneys nearby. I can make out the distinct wooden entrance of our village. We didn't have enough cobblestone to make a better archway. Though I can barely make them out, I know the people are hard at work. Village life starts early.

Next to me, Addilynn's horse trots faster toward her *friend*. She doesn't slow until we're at the hitching post next to the mediocre arch. Green and gray vines grow over the new wood with little bulbs of black littered throughout. Tenebrae might not grow nutritious fruits, but there's a plethora of poisonous berries.

Unlike Omnius, I'm not welcomed by the smell of piss and desperation. There's a stench of animal dung followed by hope. Hope for a better life for us all. No one is separated into quadrants for their magic or worth. In this quaint village, people can exist without fearing for their lives.

Men and women wearing thick hide leathers move throughout as if they've lived here their whole lives. A few of the fittest have swords on their waist, tasked with guarding the village whenever my brothers and I are on raids.

A few fenced in plots of land have livestock; mainly the ones that can be milked. There's a scarce amount of water, so most of the villagers survive off milk. Micah and our other water wielder, Anthony, tried to create water for the people. It made most of them sick for a few days. Lesson learned—Nihils shouldn't drink magical water. Instead, they use their magic to create water for the livestock. Only enough for the creatures to survive. Micah and Anthony can only do so much without replenishing their supply.

Whenever traders from other villagers venture here, the market booms. There's isn't a lot of money to be spent, but with Hamish— our blacksmith—our ends meet with his fine craftsmanship. People push carts from shack to shack, stopping periodically to speak with one another. Metal clinks together, and a lightness overcomes me.

Addilynn shifts beside me as she tracks the movements of the villagers. "Are all of them Nihils and crossbreeds?"

"There are a few wielders who reside with their loved ones, but yes, most of them are Nihils and crossbreeds," I respond, appreciating the village for myself.

It's the first of its kind where people live and sustain themselves. They can care for one another. They're not being sold at the highest price or murdered without cause. Children are able to run around with one another. People move out of their way like they understand the beauty of their innocence as they weave and skip around.

Halona, one of our youngest, steps forward. Her dark brown

eyes are much like her fathers. Light-green veins contrast against her dark skin as nature comes to life. And no one would know her mother was a Nihil. Many of the children here are orphans, born from a Nihilan parent; but most have magic in their veins.

"Hello," I coo, kneeling to her level.

Her dark eyelashes flutter as she does a small curtesy. Only the children are allowed to do that around here—refer to me as prince or bow in my presence. Not because I want them to, but because I can't tell them no. Halona holds out her hand to reveal the sharp point of an arrowhead on a twine string, displaying faint cuts around her fingers, and I know she made it herself. Another reminder that no one is safe when on the brink of war.

I take the makeshift necklace from her and place it around my neck. "Thank you."

Her large cheeks raise as she smiles with three missing teeth.

Then, Halona sways from her heels to toes with a pouty lip. Closing my hand into a fist, I summon tendrils of shadows forward. The energy of it tickles my tight palm like a bug trying to free itself. When opening it, particles of the shadow blow away into the breeze like seeds of a dandelion.

She flashes another toothy grin on full display as a tendril of my power floats between her hair and ear. I've given her that flower every day since she arrived. Halona never strayed from her parents side the entire journey. The only time she did was when they were speaking with Lelantos about building a new home. I can still remember the phantom feeling of her hand squeezing my finger as if I might let go. Since then, she's been given a flower.

Halona bows once more before chasing after two boys much older than her.

"That's kind of you to do that," Addilynn says from my side, startling me into an upright position.

"I want them to have a good experience here." I pause, thinking of my childhood. "Her parents died after arriving. She's about the age I was when my parents passed."

I don't add that they were murdered. Everyone knows how our kingdom was usurped. I remember hearing stories about it when we traveled to new taverns. It was the first time a king and queen were felled by someone not of royal blood. For some people, I think it was a motivator knowing that all royals could die—even if they didn't know how. My stomach turns itself into knots trying to understand how they died easily. In Tenebrae, my father would have been at his strongest, but my sanguine uncle was able to defeat him. It should have been impossible, but I'm an orphan because it wasn't.

"Didn't realize shadows could be made in the daylight," Addilynn says, gesturing to the lavender sky.

"They can be made if you're powerful enough."

She clicks her tongue. Teal eyes look at me sideways like Micah's did the night before.

I shrug. "I'm a Ravenheart. My heartbeat is as fast as a raven's, and my shadows are stronger than any other wielder in Tenebrae. I can make darkness out of thin air and turn myself into a living shadow if I will it. The void is thick within these veins."

I roll a part of my sleeve to show her the corded, dark veins. They're very noticeable against my ghostly, pale skin. I've tried to remedy it, but nothing works. With our skewed sunlight, I wonder how Micah and Lelantos keep their golden complexion. Addilynn's veins are faint, but they're blue like Micah's. Lelantos also has blue veins that turn red in the air, a unique trait only Nihils have. And I must admit, I'm jealous of that.

"So, the royal blood makes you stronger—like Princess La'Mia of the light region? I heard she can create images of herself using light to appear in other kingdoms."

"Our royal blood is a direct link to the first wielders of Veilia. A drop of blood from Esmeray, The Mother of Death and Darkness, created my bloodline. The blood of Aurum, the King of Life and Light, created La'Mia's. The Omnias hail from the First." I'm whispering the last part. I don't want a dead bird to fall from the sky for speaking *that* here.

"And what of the other magics like me?"

Her question baffles me, but I recover quickly. "Didn't you learn any of this in school?"

A self-deprecating laugh slips from her pink lips. "Didn't have enough money to ship off to school to learn the inner workings of my magic."

I can't find the words to express how I feel. I never went to school to hone my powers, left on the run with Micah. Everything I've learned comes from him, and he doesn't understand all the innerworkings either. Thinking of it, neither he nor Lelantos went to school.

"It costs money to earn an education," I say out loud, more to myself than her. Shouldn't the education of wielding and the history of Veilia be for everyone? Then again, our Omnia decides whose worthy enough for anything. She's as greedy as she is cruel.

"Can't go to school if you're working to afford the education," she responds, shrugging. "Are all monsters from the Mother of Monsters?"

I'm thankful for the conversation change. I don't know enough about the other kingdoms to try and explain the innerworkings of them. I'll have Micah give her some advice about wielding the element of water. I'm sure there's more she doesn't realize about her gifts.

"Harlot is the Mother of Monsters. She is the Mother, but there are some who can wield parts of her power." I try to think of all the beings and what they can do. My mind keeps circling back to the witches. As I settle in to tell her more about them, I pray I don't evoke their wrath. "It's believed her and Esmeray were once Scion, one soul until they separated. The witches in the west are said to be descendants of both Esmeray and Harlot. Some of the witches can wield darkness, and others can speak and raise the dead."

Addilynn's mouth is agape as she takes in my words. I've never seen her so speechless, even when a Macabre fell in front of her. Then again, talk of the witches has that effect on people. I hope when I die, I get to see the ones who speak with the dead in the afterlife.

Finally, Addilynn finds the words. "And all I can do is move water."

There's a defeated tone in her voice, matching the expression on her face. I see the same distant expression in Lelantos when I conjure in front of him. It's like they believe their worth is based solely on their powers—or lack thereof. Another divide created by the Omnias.

I don't try to comfort her, even if I want to. My words would be like pouring alcohol on a fresh cut. It'll seep beneath the skin and burn worse than the wound. I tuck my wings close to my body, steering us toward a few more plots of land. There are more people in this area tending to their chores, skinning fresh kills, milking the animals, and cleaning laundry.

They're laughing amongst one another. I recognize a few Nihils and crossbreeds we saved yesterday partaking in the work. Addilynn scours the people, searching for the one she truly wants. When she doesn't see him, she exhales deeply.

I see him before she does. He leans over a trough, dumping food in for the pigs. I nudge her, pointing in his direction. She barely takes a step forward before they find each other's gaze. A scream tears out of Addilynn. The villagers stop, searching for the threat, only to find her. The man drops the empty bucket and moves closer to us. Addilynn barely recovers from her scream before she sprints to him, leaping into his arms, and he holds her tightly.

Irwin puts her on the ground and kisses her lips. Addilynn wraps her arms around his neck, deepening the kiss. People cheer for only a moment before returning to their previous task. Their kiss threatens public indecency. I move forward, clearing my throat. Irwin pulls away, looking over Addilynn's shoulder to me. His mundane eyes brim with tears.

"Thank you, Prince Erebus," he says.

Before he has the chance to bow, I say, "Just Erebus is quite alright,"

"Sorry, Prin—" He catches him and says, "Erebus."

Addilynn's hand links with his, a promise never to let go. Her eyes are glued to him.

"I'm glad I could reunite *friends*," I say.

I bow my head once, motioning to turn away.

Irwin unlinks from Addilynn for a moment, placing his large hand on my wrist to stop me. His light green eyes bore into me with gratitude. "Thank you. I know I sent you after her under false pretenses, but Addilynn is far more than that to me." He pulls me into an embrace. "Thank you," he pleads again.

When he pulls away, I make out a faint blue marking on the side of his collarbone, barely showing from the collar of his tunic.

"She's your Fated." It's not a question.

His eyes flare. Addilynn approaches his side, and there's a love I hadn't seen in a long time. It's the same way my mother and father would look at each other. I remember as a young boy praying to the Mother to bring me a Fated so I may experience that same love.

"We're much more than friends," she says.

I can't understand why anyone would want to hide that part of themselves. If I ever find my Fated, I hope they mark me everywhere as I would do unto them.

"And I apologize for being untruthful. You have been kind to me from the moment we met, and I was dishonest of our true nature."

I'm trying to keep a straight face. It sounds as if she's trying to apologize, as if she were leading me on regarding the nature of our relationship. Between seeing Omnia Melania fleeing a murder and the ticking bomb of the Omnia artifact in my satchel, there was never the question of romance between us. But poor Addilynn appears as if she might burst into tears. Her lower lip quivers, and I can't decipher if it's because I reunited Fated Mates or for deceiving me.

At the first sign of tears about to fall I say, "There are no ill feelings on the matter. I am glad to have been of service," and because a tear drops from her eyes, I ramble on. "It's believed the first Fated pair were from Tenebrae. A woman made of shadows was born as the first to wield both darkness and monsters. She wasn't a physical being as she haunted the nighttime wanting to be seen by others."

As I'm speaking the picture of the shadow woman comes to my mind. Her glowing white eyes like the moon and her limber body crawling toward me like that of a frownie. Except none of that makes sense. It's entirely impossible with how the story ends. Pushing the image as far away I continue.

"The first and last lightning wielder saw her as he conjured storms. Each night, he would create strikes of lightning to see her dance amongst them. When he learned of who she was, he pleaded with the Mothers to give her a physical being so that she may live amongst the others." I pause. People gather around, listening to a tale I haven't spoken in years—I didn't realize I knew it this well anymore.

"She was granted life, and they marked each other as the First Fated pair to live happily ever after." I bow to the onlookers.

Addilynn stares at me in her unnerving away. Her face is relaxed, but her eyes pull back the shadows of my being. She knows it isn't the end, though she doesn't press the matter as others clap their hands together.

It's wrong of me to end the tale as I did, but I couldn't break the hearts of the villagers learning to have hope for a better life. I can't tell them the shadow woman was killed by the First and the King of light because she was different, and the lightning wielder was promised to the princess of light. Nor can I tell them that the lightning wielder drowned himself in the swamps where the witches now reside. Another reason why our storms only have thunder without light. The magic died with him, but it was written into books of the storms his magic could conjure. The only hope in that story is that the witches believe he and she will rise again as new beings to wreak havoc for the injustice they faced—starting with the King of Light.

And I hope I'm alive when that day comes.

Addilynn approaches me, her hands rubbing against the fabric of her gown. Any sign of tears is far gone. "Thank you, Prince Erebus Ravenheart—the rightful king of Tenebrae." There's a finality in her voice.

My eyes widen at the thought of being addressed in such a manner. My teeth find the groove in my lip, fighting myself from biting it. I search her face to find an ounce of deceit, but there isn't. Her hands rest steadily against her thighs.

With that, she returns to Irwin, whispering in hushed tones. I watch as they walk off, surely to make up for lost time. Except I haven't moved from my spot. In my peripheral, people stare and murmuring to each other. I want to move, but I'm a statue as her words repeat in my head.

The Rightful King of Tenebrae.

A storm brews inside of me. My stomach knots, and acid burns my throat. I've heard my brothers say I would make a great king, though it's never been said from someone else. My feet move on their own as the eggs and veal from this morning return. The death of Lord Byron, the sickle, seeing Omnia Melania, the shadow woman in my dream. And Addilynn's words.

It seems like Fate is trying to weave me back into the royal life, and I'll do anything to stop it. Fates be damned.

Fifteen

Erebus

Smoke and steel overcome the air. Three blacksmiths work on melting metal and pound it into weapons. From the doorway, heat scorches my skin. I close my eyes and inhale deeply, letting the scents and warmth seep into my pores. I haven't spent a lot of time here since we created a solid shop. The largest man in the room, with thick gray eyebrows and a beard down to his sternum, looks up from the steel. His black eyes meet mine as he approaches me at the doorway.

"Always a pleasure to see you, Erebus." His voice is deep with a southern drawl. It's not an accent commonly heard in these parts. Hamish, the large man, was once a swordsman for my parents and grandparents.

"I can't stay long," I say.

My presence has gained the attention of the other blacksmiths. They glance between their work and me like they can't figure out what's more interesting; the man with raven wings or the hot iron being sculpted.

Moving further into the room, I'm careful to keep my wings as far from the fire as possible. These damn feathers burn too easily, and I hate the stench. Hamish wipes his hands on the apron in front of him. He directs us to a small back room away from prying eyes, and I'm thankful for his ability to sense my need for privacy. I've often wondered if he didn't have a seer in his family as he tends to know things before they come to fruition.

There's a small cot in the room with fur blankets and a rocking chair in the corner. To the side, a small crate holds a bottle of whiskey, a pipe, and a picture frame of him and another identical man.

Hamish sits on a chair. It groans under his weight. The blacksmith reminds me of my brothers if someone were to combine Micah's height and Lelantos's build. It's baffling to think there might be another one exactly like him.

He leans forward, resting his elbows on his knees. His bald head glistens with sweat. "What did you do?"

I'm taken aback. Everyone always assumes it's me. Most of the time it is, but it still stings. I feign innocence, placing a hand over my heart as if his words wound me. He sighs, raising one brow higher than the other. Micah does the same thing often, and I wonder if it's a quirk men over fifty lean toward.

"There is a shift in the wind, boy. Veilia is unsettled and I think you know why."

His words are cryptic, but there's a warm sensation against my hip. I kneel in front of him. "What I'm about to show you stays between us."

"Of course."

Reaching into the satchel, I feel the heat of the sickle through the thin cloth. Hamish hisses as I pull it out, barely out of the bag before he reacts. I reveal the pulsating sickle. It's changed a little since last night. A white line of energy has formed between the sharpened and blunt edges. The aura of the white light is powerful enough to skitter my shadows away. My stomach tightens. A part of me feels wrong to hold something so pure, even if it was used to take a man's life.

Hamish snatches for the handle of the blade. I pull away before his fingers can glide against it. Once more, his eyebrow raises, but he doesn't reach for it again. I fight the urge to hide it away as he looks closer. He squints the closer he gets to it. My own eyes lower, taking in the energy. Hamish moves back into the seat and begins to rock; the chair hits the ground in consecutive thumps.

"Where did you get this?" he asks, grabbing the pipe from the crate next to him.

"Does 'the where' matter?"

I'm not sure why I'm being stubborn about where. Shouldn't I flaunt that I saw Omnia Melania partake in murder? As I consider doing that, my chest aches at the idea of exposing her. Unready to unpack it, I don't answer. Hamish cocks his head to the side, inhaling the tangy-scented tobacco. His dark eyes drill into me as if he can sense my sudden moral impasse.

"How did you get it?" he asks.

Now it's my turn to cock my head to the side. I could tell him I found it on Lord Byron's chest, but I risk being judged for taking it. I'm still not over how my brother's reacted.

Noticing my discomfort, Hamish shifts. "What do you want to know?"

Finally, a question I can answer.

"Have you seen anything like this?"

He stares at me for a while, taking in more puffs from the wooden pipe. On the last inhale, he breaks into a fit of coughing. He swigs down a mouthful of whiskey to clear his throat. "Only through stories." His eyes glaze over as if he weren't here. "In the first war between kingdoms, Omnia Matilda wielded a majestic great sword. She killed thousands in the war. It's why we have the hierarchy of royals now. Omnia Matilda united the eight kingdoms, and peace was restored through Veilia." He pauses, blinking away the glaze. "That was until she died. Some people believe the sword was buried with her. People tried to dig up her grave to wield it, but it's never been found."

Coldness moves through my veins, removing all heat from the shop. The idea of people desecrating a grave in such a manner—especially an Omnia's—shocks me.

"What of Omnia Arabella's bow?" I ask.

"Another war won against the monsters," Hamish states.

Dread is heavy in this room. His forehead is creased with deep wrinkles as he stares at the artifact. I want to understand how he knows this much, but I don't ask as I wrap the sickle with shaking hands. "Thank you, Hamish."

Knots tighten in my stomach as I place the sickle in my satchel. I thought I was the best one to hold onto this weapon, but I'm not too sure anymore. I take a step, but I'm stopped by Hamish's hand on my shoulder, his towering stature avoiding my wings as he touches me. I've never seen him look so serious. His dark eyes are almost completely black.

"You didn't ask for my advice, but I'm going to give it. Those Omnia artifacts were used during the time of wars, son. I don't know who, or where, you got it from, but it doesn't belong here." He looks over my head. "It doesn't belong to you, and I advise you to return it before a war starts that you can't finish."

For the first time in my life, I feel the change in the wind he mentioned earlier. I need to tell him it's Omnia Melania's. Figure out a plan to right this wrong. I open my mouth to speak when a hand grips my wings tightly, dragging me from the room.

My jaw clenches, nearly cracking a fang. Pieces of my feathers rip away from the sensitive muscles in my wings. I hiss as a trickle of blood seeps down. Only one man is brave enough to touch my wings. There's no doubt one of my brothers is dragging me. I bite into the air, fighting against the force. Micah waits for us across the village at the fish market. His eyes widen as others do from the spectacle.

He pushes past someone and runs toward us. I try my hardest to slip out of Lelantos's grip, but more feathers tear out. Fuck him for being so strong. Tears and darkness speckle my vision. I've never considered killing my brothers, but I'm close to the thought now.

Unlike the rest of my body, my feathers take more time to grow back. There's going to be a gaping bald spot for the next two weeks. And for that, he deserves to choke.

We near the tree line, and his grip loosens. I'm not a fool to think it's because I slipped the hold. We're away from prying eyes. He wanted to be out of the village. Not for his sake, but for the people walking around. We face one another. Lelantos's chest rises and falls as spittle flies from his clenched teeth.

A primal part of me comes forth, and I hiss at him. Blood drips from the new wounds on my wing. The black liquid covers his hands, and he doesn't seem to care. In fact, he revels in it as he smiles at the sight.

"What the hell is going on?" Micah asks from behind me.

I barely pay him any attention as I focus on Lelantos seething. His long, auburn hair cascades down his back. There is blood on his leather vest, pants, and splattered on his cheek. An occupational hazard of working in the new butcher's shop. I'm too mad to joke about how he might have come across the blood.

"Again, what the hell is going on?" Micah yells.

Lelantos's eyes cut to him, war raging within him as he glances between Micah and me. His fists ball at his sides. His jaw clenches tightly enough, I fear he may crack a tooth. Deep down, I understand where his anger truly lies. He's pissed at me, but he's angry with himself. One thing Lelantos hates more than anything is trying to express his emotions. Micah tries to deter me, but the darkness in me demands blood for what he did.

I lunge forward, and Lelantos strikes his fist against me.

Blood rushes from my nose.

All I see is black.

Rage consuming me, I thrust my body into his waist, and I bring him to the ground, swinging my leg over his chest. My fist connects with his face over and over. At first sight of his odd blood, I return to the present. That split second of hesitation gives him the upper hand.

He rolls me onto my back. Luckily, he doesn't go for the face. Instead, he pulls at my wings. More feathers tear with his grip.

"You never fucking think of anyone but yourself!" Lelantos shouts.

His fist collides with my face once more. My head snaps to the side. I spit out the blood in my mouth, and my fang goes with it. He's fucking smirking at the sight. Finally, I see Lelantos as the beast he is.

He prepares to hit me again, but my shadows are quicker than him. A tendril of my dark magic wraps around his neck, pulling him off me.

"You fucking murker."

He's fighting to breathe, and *that's* what he chooses to say?

His hands grapple toward the wispy power, but it's no use. A purple hue, similar to the sky, highlights his face. Lelantos's sapphire eyes bulge, but I don't see my brother. All I see is another person who made me bleed when I didn't deserve it.

"Erebus Jasper Ravenheart!" Micah shouts. The name only my parents knew jeers me to back to my surroundings.

Michah grips my shoulders. His turquoise eyes are wide with worry for both Lelantos and me. The rage within me weakens its resolve. Lelantos sputters and coughs behind Micah.

Micah steps away from me, revealing Lelantos as my brother and not an enemy. His face still has a purple hue as he sucks in as much air as he can in the wake of the powerful surge of hollowness that overcame me. I'm too ashamed to do anything other than fly away with bleeding wings.

Hamish's warning rings clear about the brewing of a war. It's already starting with the people I love the most. And I blame Omnia Melania and her fucking sickle, though I shouldn't. I grabbed the sickle. I brought it to Tenebrae. I nearly killed my own brother. All of it started with me, and it should end with me.

I doubt they'll want to see me after today with the trouble I've caused for them and the people we've saved in the village. The wind slaps my face as I fly higher before I register what I'm doing. The ground disappears behind clouds and distance. Tears stream down my face as I consider dropping my wings. No one can stop me if I plummet to my death from here. A burden would be removed from them.

I'm about to give into the idea when a large gust of wind moves me backward. The necklace around my neck reminds me to breathe. I reach for it, feeling the sharp arrow point trinket made for me. Taking a steady breath, I lower closer to the ground. I'm not ready to return home, but I'm not ready to die either.

Sixteen

Melania

The air is smoky on the balcony of the palace. Unlike the curtain lands, this is all Xannoroth offers. Little to no grass grows here. Dark lava beds are covered in a thin dusting of ash and sand—no doubt from the shifting winds between kingdoms. King Albus had created a portal for Elara and me to return to his palace. Elara barely made it through without getting sick again. I tried to comfort her, but she pushed me away. We made it through the gatehouse into the entrance hall, and then we separated.

A small maid directs me toward the bedchambers. She's an older woman with dark skin, gray hair, and piercing red eyes. She doesn't speak as she opens the large cherry-wood door. Before I can thank her, she turns on her heel and leaves.

The bedchamber seems to be triple the size of mine in Omnius. Two glass doors lead to a stone balcony. A few smaller windows cast natural light onto the stone flooring. There's a bed fit for a king with a large canopy. My fingertips trace over the intricate carvings on it.

A fireplace is across from the bed, with two nightstands made from the same wood as the bed and door. There are a few candles on it with unlit and unused wicks. On the other side of the room, another door leads to a bathing chamber set with a large tub and a porcelain toilet—a newer invention in Veilia.

Back in the bedroom, there's a walk-in closet, and I lose my breath peering into it. A large mirror with a golden spiral frame sits on the back wall, sharing my reflection back to me. Mud stains my gown from the curtain lands. I turn away and glance at the clean gowns hanging around me. I feel lightheaded seeing so many shades of fabric as I've only ever been allowed to wear white. Who does this closet belong to? Do they realize how lucky they are? Ironic to think someone is luckier than I am because they can wear more than one color. Grabbing the one white dress I can find, I change, though I keep the same corset. Without help, there isn't much I can do to change *that* particular article of clothing.

Back in the bedchamber, I pull out my book, settling on a romance I have yet to read. Sequestering myself on the balcony, I watch the sky change from a soft orange to a fiery red. Focusing on my book, I find myself reading the same themes from another romance novel I've read. The nomadic brute travels with a lost princess. They arrive at an inn, and there is only one bed. I should revel in this, but I can't stop thinking about what has occurred over the past two days.

It feels as if I'm living a different life. Up is down. Right is wrong. Truth is lies and lies are truth. I'm in a perpetual cycle of not knowing enough but knowing too much. And there's no way to stop it.

"Read the book," I say aloud into the empty air.

"Cannot be that interesting of a book if it can't hold your attention," a raspy voice says.

I jump from my seat with my hand lands against the top of my gown. King Albus leans against the archway of my door, his trousers still marred with patches of light dirt from earlier.

"You gave me a fright." My voice is breathy against my ears. My heart pounds as if I've been running.

"I did not mean to, Your Highness," he says, bowing slightly. I'm about to follow his lead when he straightens. "You are aware you needn't bow to me?"

I want to reply that it's proper, but the words don't form on my tongue. Another fabricated lie from my mother swims around in my thoughts. She never bowed, but she made certain that I did. And I willingly did as she said because what kind of mother lies to their daughter?

King Albus studies me as if he's seeing something for the first time. From a young age, he's regarded me in such a way. There's a softness to his unique eyes. His face remains completely relaxed. And no one else looks at me the way he does. Like I'm a delicate flower that might wither at any moment. It doesn't make me uncomfortable compared to the other ways men have regarded me.

His eyes flicker to the leather-bound book in my hands, at the title embroidered in gold lettering: *My Brute in Shining Armor.* "Would you like to find better works of literature in my study?"

A warmth spreads to my cheeks. My entire body is hot, like the lava outside. I try to say anything, but once more my words are failing me. It's not the only thing that fails me as I trip over my own feet. I'm able to catch myself against the velvet settee, but I fear I might catch fire and burn.

Glancing at King Albus, there is amusement on his face. He's trying to hide his smile behind his hand, but it's all too clear to me. There's a sparkle in his gaze as I approach him. He turns to leave the room, and it's my turn to be amused as he, too, trips over himself.

Neither of us say anything for a moment until he laughs, warmth spreading around us; like sitting by a campfire at night.

"Seems as if we're a clumsy pair," he states.

And for the first time in a very long time, a natural, non-calculated laugh escapes my lips. I didn't think I could feel this kind of joy anymore, but alas, I was wrong.

He guides us through the historic palace made entirely out of lava rock. Embedded in the walls are rubies glistening in the candle-light. As a child, King Albus told me this palace was handcrafted by the First as a gift to the first wielder of fire. The First passed down her magic and built them a place of protection to continue the growth of the element. It's hard to imagine this place still standing from the beginning of Veilia. A lot of other palaces have been rebuilt to be more modern or eccentric. Here, it's like walking through history and knowing my story is only a blip compared to the future.

"You never mentioned why you came to Xannoroth," King Albus says. He clears his throat and adds, "A most welcome surprise to be certain."

I want to tell him the truth. Let this secret of what I have done be free from me, but I'm not sure I can trust anyone anymore. Including King Albus, who is as clumsy and awkward as I am.

"Princess La'Mia's coronation is quickly approaching." I'm fighting the urge to bite my nails in his presence.

His gaze lowers to mine, and there's a question in his pinched brows. More lines of his years of life form on his forehead. "She's your guardian, wouldn't she want you present?"

A wet laugh escapes.

If Princess La'Mia had it her way, I wouldn't be at the coronation ceremony.

"A shame she wouldn't want you there." He shakes his head and scoffs. "Her only real value is being your guardian." There's a bite to his tone. I've never heard anyone speak of her like that, aside from myself in my inner thoughts.

We move toward large, cherry-wood double doors. Two men wearing bronze attire lower at our presence before standing and opening the door. The musty, vanilla scent of old literature hits me first as the doors creep open.

King Albus guides us into the room, and I stop moving as I take in the scenery. There are shelves upon shelves of books in the two-story study. In the center of the room is a large desk covered in yellow-hued pages. It faces the great fireplace, burning despite the heat outside. Three grand, red and orange stained-glass windows come to a point. They take up the back half of the library. Two spiral staircases lead to the second level. I bet during the daytime, this place is a sight to behold.

"Take any book you like," he says, gesturing his arms out wide to the entire room.

"I couldn't."

"You can and you should."

King Albus settles himself into what I assume is his personal desk. I don't pay him anymore mind as I move through the study. I grab books from the shelves only to flip open the pages and smell them. The scent of the worn-down pages is intoxicating, taking me back to when Queen Gaia would lie under a tree with me to tell me tales from the books she read. A weight settles in my chest at the bittersweet memory.

When she died, my mother had our library destroyed. All the books were thrown out or burned. I remember weeping at the sight of the pages burning despite the rain I caused. It's when my mother's cruel side was unleashed. I couldn't sit for three days after that.

King Albus steps away from his desk, guiding me toward the back of the library. My eyebrows lower as he tilts a book from the shelf. The motion causes a heavy groan before the shelf begins to move. The king takes a step forward into the stuffy, small room. When I don't move, he reaches out his hand to guide me in.

The walls are made of the same lava rock as the rest of the palace. In the center of the barren room, there is a wooden display with a glass case. Something pulls me to the case like a bond tethering us together. My hand slips from King Albus, and I glide to the center of the room.

Inside the glass, I see a leather book unlike anything I've seen before. A small tome bound in yellowing leather, attached only by thin white strands. If I had to guess, I would assume that book is made of skin and kept together with hair. My stomach twists into a knot, but I can't look away, as if the book is trying to speak to me.

"One of the eight ancient texts written by the First," King Albus says. He remains near the doorway with his arms crossed. "It's been passed down from each generation, starting with the first ruler of Xannoroth."

"Why show me?" I ask in a surprisingly breathy voice.

"This is as much your history as it is mine." King Albus smiles at me, but there is a vulnerability there. A secret he's hiding behind his lowered eyelids and raised shoulders. He presses his hand to my shoulders, and he guides us from the room. I release my breath as we leave.

"You can trust me, Omnia Melania.," There's sincerity in his voice. A pleading in those ombre eyes, but my instincts are flaring as if there's more to this.

Clearing his throat, he strides away from me, walking back to his desk, keeping his head down. Fighting the urge to return to the room, I move around the expansive library. The fire crackles in the hearth. His quill pen runs against the rough paper. Comfortability settles over the room, despite the tension earlier. I'm scanning through the shelves when book two of the *Shining Armor* series catches my attention: *My Bard in Shining Armor*. There seem to be hundreds of romance books from all different authors. Some have the forbidden love between fire and water wielders. Others mention wielders and monsters.

"Ah, it seems you found the romance section."

Once again, I jump and fumble the book in my hands. An

amused chuckle rumbles from King Albus's chest. I didn't hear him approach. He's far too stealthy for his own good.

"I didn't take you as a romance reader," I say, carefully putting the book back.

"My wife and daughters are fond of the genre."

"Daughters?" I've only known Queen Pria and King Albus to have their only child, Princess Priscia. I met her once when we were children, and even then, she treated me with little regard.

"Pardon?"

"You said daughters?"

"Forgive me for the mistake. I'm still reeling from the events of today."

His words pop the bubble of bliss I found myself in. Burning flesh, Elara's bleeding lip, and the strange tome of the First flash in my mind. The aroma of old literature and the sound of crackling fire no longer ground me to the moment as the weight of everything these past days weighs heavily on my shoulders.

"It has been a tiring day. I should ready for bed," I say.

"Before dinner?" King Albus says, like he can't fathom sleeping without a full stomach. I could laugh at the notion.

"Would it be terribly rude of me to eat in my chambers?"

"Of course not. Omnias require more sleep than other wielders, do they not?"

He says it as if it's not a question, rather a statement. As if he knows the truth of my bloodline. At least for me, I'm not sure I've ever seen my mother sleep during the day. However, it seems the closer I get to twenty, Veilia demands more energy from me.

My face remains neutral as I lower to his presence. King Albus walks toward the back wall of the windows and returns with a small scroll in his hands, tied with a red ribbon. As the door opens, he gives me a tight-lipped smile. A prickly sensation coats my skin. He says I can trust him, but I wonder if that goes both ways.

The guards lead me from the room. As the door slowly closes, a bird chirps despite the night.

I told my mother I would seek unfaithful rulers. I didn't truly believe there were any. Now I'm not too confident in that notion. A slither of doubt creeps down my spine as I find my chambers once more.

Seventeen

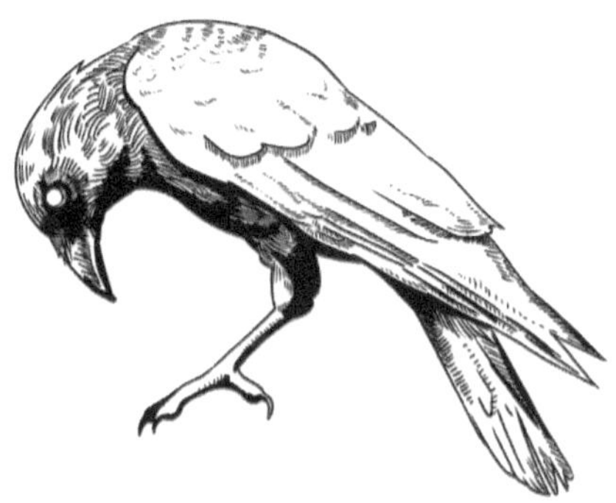

Erebus

My wings are heavy from the exhaustion and abuse they endured today. I waited until the sky was full of stars before swallowing my pride to come home. Owls coo while other animals scurry around in the darkness. The cool shadows float around me like my personal shield from any monsters scenting the dried blood.

A soft tune strumming on a lute welcomes me home, though I can't soak in its cheery notes as the reality of what I did comes crashing into me. Fat tears are heavy on my eyelids. I know I have to answer for the pain I put my brother through. Drawing in a large, steady breath, I open the door and release the air as I take my first step in.

Micah sits on the settee with a wood carved lute over his chest, deft fingers strumming the strings. He stops at the sight of me. Under his eyes are bags forming, the exhaustion clear as day. He doesn't move to stand from his spot, but his eyes bore into me. They're telling me how disappointed he is.

"Where is he?" I ask, flicking my attention to the ground when he begins to pick the strings again.

He stops strumming to point upstairs. We both know this is something I must do on my own. Tucking my wings close to me and dragging my feet against the ground, I prepare to see Lelantos.

Each step is a grueling journey, but I take them. Rapping softly against his door, I wait for a response. When it doesn't come, I continue the knocks, gradually increasing how hard I hit.

"Enough," Lelantos grumbles.

He opens the door before returning to his small, framed bed wearing loose-fitting trousers. My stomach turns seeing the faint bruising around his neck, knowing I was the one who caused it.

I step into the room. There are plaques of his kills on the walls: a bear and three large bucks mounted in various places. A thick fur blanket warms the foot of his bed. Another door leads to the bathing chamber we all share—one that's impressively clean for three men.

This place is a shack to me, but a palace to him. Before here and the family who took him, he lived in the barn of his family estate in the curtain lands. A lot like the other Nihils. They're treated as less than, even compared to crossbreeds. Today I was no better than the others for using my shadows against him—even if he started it.

We have gotten into fights before—a lot. He uses his fists to express how he feels, and I happily oblige, but I've never taken it this far. To use my fists to fight him is one thing. It's another to use the darkness in my veins. And that scares me.

The way the shadows within me demanded his pain.

The desire to kill pulsating through me.

I'm not a monster, but I feel as if I am becoming one. There's a dark pit in my stomach that can't be filled, like a part of me isn't at rest. I have to push that aside for now to deal with the issue at hand.

Lelantos's broad arms cross over his chest. His auburn hair drips with water from what I assume was a bath. Another bruise colors his lower jaw. Tension simmers between us as Micah's music bleeds into the room.

"I apologize for what I did today." My voice is quiet to my own ears.

Lelantos rolls his eyes. "You mean for nearly killing me."

My fists clench at my side as I draw in a strong breath. Between him and Micah, Lelantos is the hardest to apologize to. He doesn't let it go like Micah does.

"You hurt my wings," I mumble.

His sapphire eyes feel like pools of liquid gemstones as they fix on me. It's the way I imagine he once looked at his family—full of sadness and disdain. In them, I see the hurt he can't express. I hate myself for being the reason the look has returned to his beautiful eyes.

"Why did you bring the sickle to the village?" he asks.

I jerk back. We didn't get to talk about why I was there, nor did I think he still cared. "To learn more about it." I pause, my gaze flicking over my shoulder as my shadows warn me of someone approaching. Micah comes from the bottom of the stairs, and I wait to speak until he nears.

With all of us in the room, Lelantos clenches his jaw. He despises people in his space, but he isn't kicking us out—yet.

"I planned to leave it here." I do my best '*I really tried*' pouty eyes. "But I couldn't stop thinking of my nightmare last night. I haven't had a vivid dream like that in a long time. It was if someone was trying to warn me about the weapon."

I tell them about the nightmare, excluding the parts about their severed and flayed corpses, but I didn't mention the woman at the end, either. I don't want to worry my brothers unless I have to.

They glance between each other and me. Finally, Micah says, "What did Hamish say?"

I worry my lip between my fangs once more at the thought of

mentioning his advice. "All Omnia artifacts were created during times of war."

A chill floats around the room, as if we're not alone. I scour to see anything out of the norm.

There's nothing. My shadows aren't on edge, but I am.

"The real question is: who is the war against?" Lelantos asks, and I feel his words in the center of my chest.

If my dream were any indication, it's against the Kingdom of Tenebrae—and we don't win. Something flies against the window as I'm about to tell them my thoughts, halting my words. Outside, a small cardinal flaps its orange and red wings that appear to be flames, preparing to hit the hard surface again. Before it can, Lelantos opens the window, welcoming the small bird.

It lands on the dark oak bedpost with a string and paper wrapped around its neck. I don't have to see the fine script to know this is from King Albus, and neither do my brothers. Untying the bird, Lelantos helps it outside to send it back to its kingdom. We unroll the paper. Its small script is barely legible for some odd reason. Perhaps he wasn't alone when he wrote this treasonous letter.

The words are clear enough. Tomorrow, my brothers and I will depart for Xannoroth.

Eighteen

Melania

The quill pen runs against the rough paper of my journal, bound full of my secrets and transgressions. Detailed accounts of the things I've witnessed in the passings of the seasons, but especially the last three days—from the death of two men, to killing their father, the caravan and fleeing to another kingdom. My hand aches with the ferocity with which I write. It's the most action my life has seen since I was four years old and killed an entire village because of a purple flower that haunts me.

A knock at the door pulls me away from my illegible penmanship.

"You may enter," I say, closing the book before the ink has fully dried.

Elara steps in with her attention focused on the ground, wearing a new red servant's gown. There's a bruise on her lip. It's not scabbed over as it was last night, though her healing is much slower than wielders'.

She doesn't inch further into the room, and the distance between us is like a chasm. A gaping hole remains in our newfound relationship. I had hoped it would have been better this morning since she refused to speak to me last night. Alas, her silent treatment remains, and my irritation peaks.

I stomp over to the small vanity like the mature adult I am. Elara comes behind me, picking up the brush and combing through the knots in my hair. The tension thickens as if we are swimming in molasses. Not once does she meet my gaze in the mirror.

I wouldn't say we were ever friends—not that I would know. I've never had one before. But she's one of the few people who talked to me, not at me.

Elara's tongue flicks over the tiny split in her lip that is only noticeable because of our proximity. She took a hit she shouldn't have; if only she had remained hidden with me, she would have been safe instead of asking for trouble. The silence grates on my last nerve. Not even chewing on my nearly gnawed off nails helps.

"I want a braid," I snap.

Her brown eyes burn, though her lips never part to speak. Elara separates my hair into three sections, weaving and intertwining them together. At the end, she ties a leather strip to hold it in place. Backing away, she bows, and my anger simmers.

"What is your problem?" I burst, standing from the cushioned stool.

Elara flinches. Her nostrils flare. Fists clench at her side.

"I am your Omnia, you must answer me!" I command.

She takes a step away, but I keep advancing on her until we're a foot apart. I've never felt like this. The rage dances within my veins. It's absurd to fight with her over silence, considering I prefer the quiet.

"No problem, Your Highness," Elara says, bowing.

A devilish smirk dances on her face. Unlike other servants, she keeps her eyes on me. A mark of defiance that excites me more than infuriates me. I've never known someone who didn't fear me but didn't belittle me, either.

"I must have done something for the tension between us," I say, the edge in my voice softer.

"You didn't do anything," she responds.

"Then why are you refusing to speak with me?"

"Because you didn't do *anything*," Elara hisses through her teeth.

I fall silent, dumbfounded. If I didn't do anything, how can I be punished with this passive-aggressive approach? It's one of the cruelest torments I've had to experience. She stares at me. Her shoulders rise to her neck as the tension runs through her.

Finally, she bites out, "You're an Omnia, but you sat there as those vagabonds tried to kill a mother and her son." She raises one finger only to add another, saying, "You're an Omnia who hid when I tried to defend those people. I'm a Nihil and still had more courage than you." She raises a third finger. "You're an Omnia who has the power of Veilia at your fingertips, and you did *nothing*." Her voice shakes, but she refuses to back down from me.

"I didn't do anything," my voice wavers as if a dam is preparing to break in me, "because I can't."

Elara scoffs as my mother does when she wants me to exit a room. The final crack in the foundation of what's been building inside of me. I will not be dismissed.

"You know my mother's cruelty, but do you think she stops at the Nihils? I cannot wield my mother's power without her consent; I've tried in the past, and each time she finds out, the punishment is worse than before." My hands tremble beside me. "Do you know what it's like to be chained to a bed for weeks, living in your own feces and urine because you can't die? Do you know what it is like to suffer the end of a whip for days?"

Elara studies me as if she has never seen me before. A weight of truth tumbles off my shoulders in waves. Her lips part, but I raise a finger to stop her pity. The last thing I need is the pity of a Nihil servant.

"I have already done enough in the last two days that may cost me my sanity before my mother's wrath. I am here because I gave Lord Byron mercy with a sickle that may or may not be an Omnia artifact in the hands of another."

Elara moves forward, and I brace for impact. She grabs my hands and holds them in her own. Her thumb trails the back of my palms, but it feels like pins and needles.

"You needn't explain anymore," she says, unshed tears in her eyes. I try to revel in the words, but I can't hold back the feelings in my chest.

"I didn't do anything yesterday because I was afraid." The words are barely audible as I choke back the tears. "I am afraid of what will come of me and you for defying her. I may be an Omnia, but I am not as strong as one, not as powerful as one. Veilia is at my fingertips, but it is not my right to wield it as I see fit." The last of my words are verbatim to what my mother has said to me during each torture. Every syllable carved beneath the surface of my very being.

Elara pulls me closer, and she embraces me, shushing me as she rubs up and down my spine. I wonder if this is what it's like having someone to care for you. It's a foreign feeling.

"I had no idea," she says, empathy imminent in her raspy voice.

"Only a few people know," I whisper before adding, "but you're the only one who cares."

She pulls from the embrace, holding my face within her small hands. Tears roll down her plump cheeks. "Omnia Melania, you are stronger and braver than you realize. To live through the abuse as you have and still stand like the fortress of power you are is a feat within itself. You're an Omnia, as the others before and the others after. Your true strength is here." She places a finger against my sternum. "And no one can take away who you are."

Elara holds me as a sob breaks out. Fat raindrops land against the stone balcony. She grabs my hand and pulls me to the center of the terrace. The falling drops are cold, but the air itself is warm. My skin prickles from the odd mixture.

"You say you are weak and cannot wield your mother's power." Elara looks to the sky. "This isn't your mother. It is you. Veilia responds to you." There's joy in her voice, and I can't understand why. "Omnia Melania, you are bringing forth rain in a place that has been in a drought for decades." She sticks out her tongue. "If this is *weak*, I'm rather terrified to see your strength."

Her words soak into me as the rain thunders against the ground. Guards below look to the sky, arms are splayed wide. Faces to the heavens. I knew Veilia responded to me. When I cry, Veilia rains. Seethe and writhe, and Veilia quakes. Laugh, and Veilia shines. But it isn't until now that I realize my mother's being doesn't provoke it anymore. Veilia, like the Fates, is choosing me.

My mother doesn't punish me because she can. She does it because she's scared. So, she tells me I'm the weak one. Hurts me because it makes herself feel better. It's like an answer to a question I was too afraid to ask. Omnia Itzel has one weakness, and it's me.

We spend the rest of the morning readying before going to Umber. Elara changes out of her wet clothes, then tells tales of living with her two sisters. The bond they share with one another I can understand. Syrinx and Eros are my sisters by Fate, not blood. They're General Javon's daughters without a known mother. Knowing him, it could have been a number of women on his conquest.

They showed up at the palace gates at eight years old with little to no knowledge of how they got there except to seek their father. It was the first time I heard my mother scream at General Javon. She wanted to make them servants, but I stepped in, earning myself a week in the dungeon without supper—worth it. They lived with me in my bedroom for a time until they were nine. Mother sent them away to magic school a year before the other kids went. I send them letters, but I never get a reply.

"Scarlett will be apprehensive to you at first," Elara says, pulling me away from the memories. "But she'll like you when she gets to know you."

I don't know if Elara and I are on good terms now or not. I'm not keen on the innerworkings of a mutual friendship. With Princess La'Mia, it's about how I can benefit her. Elara and I had a fight and reconciled so fast, it nearly gave me whiplash—not that I'm complaining.

She helps me dress in a red silk gown. The color of it is much different from what I'm used to wearing; it almost seems too harsh against my pale complexion. Before I can beg her to take it off me, there's a soft knock at the door.

She opens it to reveal King Albus on the other side, wearing dark britches and a loose-fitting red tunic, a baldric strapped over his chest with a gold hilted weapon. It's less regal than his attire yesterday.

"Omnia Melania," he says, lowering himself into a bow.

I'm about to follow when I remember his words from yesterday. I don't have to bow to him, but he must lower to me. This new concept will surely take time to get familiar with.

"I have business in Umber, but if you should need anything, I would be happy to get it for you."

I glance at Elara as she chews the inside of her cheek. We planned on sneaking out to meet her sister, but this could be a lot easier. "Would you mind the company?"

King Albus' eyes widen, and I know, without a doubt, he is hiding something. There's a panic in his gaze. One I recognize too well.

"Umber isn't the safest city," he says, itching at the top of his collar.

"I promised Elara we would meet her sister. Would it not be better to accompany the city with you, King Albus?"

I tacked on the king part as a way of being courteous. If Lord Byron's taught me anything—besides traumatizing me—it's to out-speak your adversary. If I want answers, I have to pull them out by any means necessary.

My mother sure would be proud of that, I think.

King Albus glances between Elara and me. There's submission in his eyes before he says, "If we are to leave for the city, wear something more functional."

He turns on his heel, and I grapple with what he means. I've never been allowed to wear anything other than a dress, and I was already breaking the mold by putting on red instead of white. Elara's cheeks raise as a wide smile braces her face. I didn't think we would have a tour guide with us in Umber, but I am grateful for it. Especially after the attack from the—what did Elara call them? Vagabonds, I think. Not to mention, spending time with King Albus will give me the ability to study his sneaky behavior.

After the conversation with Elara and then King Albus, I find myself gluttonous and drunk on the idea of controlling my life my way.

"Elara, I would like to wear pants today."

Nineteen

Melania

Horses trot and birds chirp around our small group of two guards in front, King Albus and myself in the middle, and Elara with another guard behind. Aside from the sounds of the animals, there's an uncomfortable silence, sticky with the humidity. A film of sweat coats my skin as the loose sleeves of my shirt cling to my arms, making me shiver. King Albus squirms as well, and I wonder if he's experiencing the same.

Every so often, he glances at me. He'd only said two words since leaving the palace: *let's go*. His hands grip the reins so tightly, his knuckles blanch. His jaw is as tight as his hands and hasn't let up since we started our journey.

The guards in the front begin to slow. One of them raises a fist, halting our movement. My heart pounds in my chest, preparing for what may happen next. My ears tune into the noises around. In the whispering wind, there is faint laughter from somewhere far away. My shoulders—raised of their own accord—lower. We move again, at a slower place this time.

The high archway of the City of Umber reveals itself and looms over us. Guards patrol the entrance of a high rise. An overwhelming amount of chatter moves through the city, faint whispers trailing with the wind about mine and King Albus' arrival.

We inch through the gates, and people stretch to look at us. My hands shake as I focus on holding the reins. I should be used to being a focal point for large crowds, but I'm usually with my mother. People either cheer—or jeer—in her general direction. She takes up enough attention that I can disappear. Now, as the city becomes a heavy blanket of tension, I can't escape.

One guard extends a hand toward me. I hadn't realized they were off their horses. It seems that I am the only one still on mine. The guard clears his throat. His palm is warm to the touch. My legs wobble beneath me as the circle around us grows larger.

King Albus, now the definition of composure, stands at my side, playing his role as the King of Xannoroth. "Welcome," he laughs jovially. "I am pleased to see you all."

A man and woman approach before we can decide which direction to walk. I brace for questions, expecting them to ask about my mother. They lower to a bow instead, then stand upright with their hands behind their backs. They are clad in a brown, worn leather vest and matching leather pants. Over the left side of their chests is a symbol of fire engraved into the fabric.

The woman on the left is nearly half a foot taller than me—and I'm not short by any means. There are many small braids pulled back from her face. Within the hair are circular rings of bronze and rubies. Her dark skin glistens with a layer of sweat. Hanging from her nose is a small, bronze hoop. I've never seen such a beautiful, domineering woman.

Next to her, the man shares the same sharp lines and deep-set red eyes. He has a hoop on his right nostril. Black hair crops close to his head. Both wear their wide shoulders and biceps with confidence. No doubt these two do not need weapons to inflict pain on anyone who crosses them.

"Kiara and Kyan," King Albus says.

They nod to the king, but their eyes focus on me. "Omnia Melania," they say in unison, so much so that I wonder if they practiced that.

Warmth floods my chest from the raspy timber of their voices. I've been referred to as Omnia Melania before, but never in the way they did it. They weren't mocking my title as others have in Omnius—for only my mother can be taken seriously. Here, they are looking at me as if I am the true Omnia. The weight of that has my chest aching, knowing how dangerous this could become.

"Omnia Melania and Elara would like to visit some people in town. You are responsible for their safety," King Albus explains.

"Yes, Your Highness," Kyan says.

Elara moves closer to my other side. Her arm slithers against mine, and I fight the urge to pull away. King Albus' eyes flicker to the contact between us. "I have a meeting to attend to in the city, but once I am finished, I would be most honored to show you around."

"It would be my pleasure," I say through a plastered-on smile.

Internally, I want to stay with him. Learn what secrets the King of Xannoroth is hiding. My mind grapples with different scenarios, starting with his mention of daughters, emphasis on the extra "s". Perhaps he has another child, and he wants to spend time with her. But why be secretive about that? From the talk of the servants, Queen Pria no longer resides in the castle. She lives in another part of Xannoroth, only coming here for special occasions.

Elara tugs on my arm, pulling me away from the crowd. Kiara flanks to our front while her brother—I assume—is behind us. With them near, safety envelops me, though I have no doubt Elara would defend herself—and me—if she needed to.

Rich spices consume the air as we move through the small market. We turn down another section, and the air is rich with a floral scent, surprising me. I didn't expect flowers to grow in Xannoroth, let alone live long enough to be sold. I never considered that the people of the fire kingdom would fancy dainty items.

Elara guides us to the front of a small store. It's a clay building, two levels stacked atop each other. The first floor is open, displaying leather goods for sale. A man of medium build with short, blond hair sits on a small wooden stool, punching minuscule holes into straps. Near the back of the room, a woman dyes the product.

Her black hair is pulled high. She wears a brown bandana around the crown of her head. Her leather top holds firmly together in the front by thin pieces of leather, while two straps clasp around her neck, keeping it in place. I admire the beauty of such unique clothing. If I weren't an Omnia, I might want to wear it.

"Scarlett," Elara whispers from beside me as her brown eyes water, threatening tears.

Scarlett freezes. The red of her eyes fixes on us, but it's as if she's no longer here. The man moves to stand, and I notice half of his left leg is gone, replaced by a wooden peg.

He begins to move but is nearly pushed to the ground as Scarlett finally finds her speed. Whatever shock she was in is gone now. Her arms wrap tightly around Elara. Elara hugs back, but there's a slight wheeze in her voice.

"Don't strangle the lass," the man says in a thick accent, rolling his *r*'s.

Scarlett pulls away from her sister only to place her hands on her cheeks. My skin itches thinking of how uncomfortable I would be from the contact. Elara basks in it as tears stream down her face.

"I thought you were dead," Scarlett says, her voice cracking.

The weight of their emotions circles the air, my own thick and laced with something I can't quite name as I watch a connection I haven't ever felt.

"If it weren't for Omnia Melania, I would be," Elara says.

Considering what happened only the day before, I wouldn't thank me for saving her life. Blood drips from the side of my nail as I begin picking at it.

The weight of Scarlett's attention settles on me. Her fiery red eyes dance. She looks me up and down as if determining how worthy of an opponent I am.

"Bow," Elara whispers. My eyes widen and so do Scarlett's. "She won't tell you to, but I will."

Scarlett's jaw tenses, and her arms cross over her chest. Only when the man lowers on a shaky leg does she follow through. As they lower, I search the back wall, begging for anything to take me away from this moment.

They come to a stand, and I force a closed-lip smile. Sweat moves down my spine from my hairline.

"You're trusting an Omnia now?" Scarlett asks, crossing her arms.

Elara uncomfortably shifts her weight; her gaze fixes on the floor as if the gray clay is interesting.

"Elara Renee Vansburg," Scarlett says authoritatively, and I snap into a straight position. There's something intimidating about using a full name in such a manner.

"She saved me from the palace walls and brought me home," Elara explains.

The man drapes an arm over Scarlett's shoulder. "Shall we speak somewhere more private?"

He's looking over our heads at a group of people behind us. The weight of gazes burns into me like a brand on flesh. Whispering voices ring in my ears as they mutter amongst themselves.

Scarlett, the shortest out of the room, rocks on her toes to peer at the crowd. Like any person, I expect her to turn around and move to a secluded place. But she pushes past us to face the crowd with her hands on her hips.

"The shop is closed!" she shouts, slamming the front door as she moves back inside.

A small smile dances on my face. Both she and Elara have a fire within them and an "I don't care" attitude. Perhaps staying in Xannoroth won't be such a bad thing, especially if I learn a thing or two from them.

Twenty

Duncan, Scarlett's Fated, pours me a glass of clear liquid and retreats to a small, cushioned sofa with patches over the worn parts of the seat. He fidgets with his wooden leg. We all gather in their home above their leather shop. Everyone drinks except me. Scarlett takes note as she stands near the hearth of their kitchen, and I'm certain I'm not making a good first impression.

There's a bed pushed against the back wall, covers wrinkled. Elara and I found comfort at their wooden table, wobbly from years of use. A medium-sized window overlooks this part of the city. The high sun basks its light for the entirety of the room. Particles of dust and soot move along the rays.

"How did you end up in Omnius?" Scarlett asks, looking direct-ly at Elara.

She has yet to say a word to me. I grow frustrated by the slight against me. Her demeanor is too straightforward, too crass, and she certainly would never fit into the court politics I play every day. Scarlett places her hands on her hips, glaring down at her sister.

Elara's throat works on a swallow. "I was working in the fields," she says. She gulps down half of her glass. "It was a normal day until we were raided. I tried to escape, but the guards have been on edge since rumors of The Three have been circulating. They were more prepared." She looks at me sideways, signaling a secret language to her sister. A secret I am not privy to, but I long to be. I'm tired of being on the outside of the information I seek. "I thought the vagabonds were taking me to Omnius, but they took us to Brilore. There, I was sold off in auction to Lady Helena."

Scarlett chews on her nails as Elara continues, telling her about the Imposition, excluding the part about my mother choking her. I don't think I'll forget the sound of it followed by my mother's sick laughter.

"The vagabonds are becoming crueler," Duncan says. His hand massages the stump of his knee as the wooden peg rests next to him.

"What's a vagabond?" I whisper to Elara.

I had meant to ask her earlier when she first mentioned them, but it slipped my mind in the mix of emotions. Elara leans away from me, searching my face in a way that makes me uncomfortable. Her lips curl in amusement.

"You don't know about the vagabonds?" Scarlett asks with a lilt of sincerity in her tone.

I shake my head, followed by embarrassment over my incompetence. Someone releases a breathy sigh.

"They work in the bondservant trade," Scarlett starts.

Elara saves me from having to ask what a bondservant is by continuing where her sister left off. "I was a bondservant. As a Nihil, we are seen as less than. Taken away from homes, put in chains, and pulled to a new kingdom. Many serve in Omnius, but there are many who never make the journey. We are beaten and starved. Yesterday, you bore witness to a caravan of vagabonds and bondservants." Her voice cracks. I'm saddened for Elara and the trials she has faced, then and now.

"They are treated like slaves. Forced into servitude because of the purification that your mother pretends is for the Greater Good, calling it the Great Cleansing when it only serves the agenda of the royals—especially the Omnias." Scarlett moves closer to the table, a threat in her voice

My mind trails to the conversation I had with Lord Byron. I did not enact the Great Cleansing, but I am expected to enforce it when the crown is placed upon my head as the powerful patron casting judgment onto others—and for what?

"Omnia Melania is a Nihilian sympathizer," Elara says.

Scarlett's eyebrows nearly touch her hairline. I make a mental note of all the information I learn, starting with the fact that there is a group of people deemed as sympathizers, followed by an ominous name: The Three. Who are they?

"You expect me to believe that Omnia Melania feels for the Nihils." Scarlett peers down at me as if I'm scum on the bottom of her handmade leather boots.

Elara's lips part, but Scarlett raises a finger to silence her. The action infuriates me. It's the same motion my mother and La'Mia do to assert dominance. I don't care if Scarlett looks down upon me, but Elara has been through enough.

I scoff. "You could ask *me* how I feel toward the Nihils."

Scarlett rears her head back with a look of astonishment as if I had physically hit her. She crosses her arms over her chest. I stand from my spot, swiping the audacity she carried before to stand and yell at anyone she pleases.

"I do not understand all the information, but I do sympathize with the Nihils. They shouldn't be forced into servitude." I raise my finger to her before she can cut me off and continue. "I am not done speaking. When I am, you may have a turn."

Both Duncan and Elara bury their heads to the side to hide their smirks. It's apparent that no one speaks to Scarlett in such a way—though they should.

"But I do carry the belief that there have been wrongs on both sides. I have been poisoned on more than one account because of assumptions made toward me. I am assumed to be like my mother when we couldn't be more different. Now, *my mother*," I enunciate mother to show her beliefs are not mine, "has been enacting a Great Cleansing before there was ever an ordinance in place in the kingdoms because she assumes anyone who is different will be harmful for Veilia. I can admit my mother is wrong in many of her assumptions, but so are you." I take a deep breath, trying to settle the sudden shakiness in my hands.

"I am not the monster people believe me to be. I have done things to sympathize on more than one occasion. So, do not look down on me for assumptions."

Scarlett's throat works on a swallow. Those feelings I didn't realize I harbored came to the surface, searching for a way out. In three days, all my beliefs have been flipped upside down without an outlet to release my frustrations. I only felt reprieve after this morning when I exploded on Elara—something she did not deserve—but the rain afterwards calmed me the most.

"I worry for my sister and her safety," Scarlett says, her tone softer despite the tight purse of her lips. "The vagabonds are cruel, but other wielders are crueler. I meant no disrespect, but I am sure you can understand my apprehension."

I *do* understand, and I mean to answer, but I fall silent at the sudden sharpness in my chest. Pain pierces the center of my sternum. I look down expecting a dagger or arrow to be there, but alas, there isn't. All I feel is this gaping hole next to my steadily beating heart. I rub a fist over it, trying to relieve this sudden void within me.

Closing my eyes, I steady my racing heart, focus on my breaths filling and releasing from my lungs. Then I see it: the white tether that tried to pull me into the abyss is back.

My eyes shoot open to Elara in front of me, her hands gripping my shoulders. "Are you alright?"

"I will be," I whisper. My feet demand that I move to find the missing piece of myself. "Stay here, Elara."

She keeps her warm hands on me.

"I have to go, but I give you the choice whether or not you want to remain my maid. I cannot offer you protection from my mother, but I can offer you kindness and freedom if you choose to reside with me. Regardless, the choice is yours to make." I say the last part to Elara, but it's meant for her sister.

I don't even thank Scarlett and Duncan for their hospitality. The call to my power possesses me, and I follow blindly. The energy within me thrums. My senses burn. Everything feels like too much, but not enough.

Erebus

The city of Umber is one of my favorite places to travel. The aroma of spice and sweat swirls with passionate fire wielders, a scent—though a volatile concoction to be certain—I revel in. Micah nudges my arm like he knew where my thoughts were going. Over my shoulder, I give him a smirk and a little kiss.

After last night's melodrama, it seems we're back to normal with Micah over my dramatics and Lelantos grunting to communicate. We approach the backside of a wooden building, one of the few left in Umber. All the new structures are made of clay or stone—less likely to burn when things get hot.

"Is it secure?" Micah asks me.

"For the hundredth time, will you stop asking? The sickle is perfectly fine," I say.

Micah rolls his eyes. He runs his fingers through his sandy colored hair. Neither Micah nor Lelantos were keen on the idea of bringing it with us. They argued until it was time to go before deciding I was not as daft as they believed me to be. Leaving it at the shack without one of us near was too much of a risk. I trust the people of our village, but I'm not foolish enough to leave an artifact like this lying around.

It's strapped tightly between my wings, underneath my shirt. I created a sheath for it last night after another horrendous nightmare. This time, I was witnessing the death of my parents like I were in the room with them. A reality I might have lived if it weren't for Micah. I never thanked him properly for saving my life, but I should. I'll add it to my to-do list.

I tap my knuckles against the door five times and patiently wait for the person on the other end to open it. After what feels like too long, a small man peeks through the door. He nods his head before rushing back to where he probably came from, skittish from our presence.

The small room barely has enough space for my brothers and me, let alone the two men drinking in the corner eyeing us warily. Now I can understand why the man was hasty to hide. One man with cropped red hair has a tattoo on his bicep of three skulls, while the smaller one's flesh is marked clean. I recognize the ink from my time here in the past, but also from my line of work.

The Mark of Death is a fanatic faction of assassins. They'll kill anyone for the sake of killing. When I began killing for a living, I did it with ground rules.

Never kill women or children.

Get paid up front.

And never associate with the Mark of Death.

They've lost any humanity. They're like the real monsters of the world next to Omnia Itzel. At least the monsters in Tenebrae kill for survival or territory. There's no excuse for the former.

The man with the tattoo stands from his seat. A toothpick grinds between his crooked, yellow teeth. When we lock eyes, the dark abyss of his soul reveals itself. He pushes past us, carrying the scent of rotting corpses, keeping a wide berth around Micah and me, but he doesn't pay any mind to Lelantos.

His sweaty shoulder brushes against his elbow. Lelantos clenches his jaw as he peers down at the tattooed man. Micah moves an inch closer to him, preparing to stop a fight before it even starts. The smaller of the two doesn't seem to mind our looming presence. As the tattooed man pushes through the door, the smaller one shoulder checks Lelantos.

This time, my brother reacts. He uses his elbow against the man's nose, loosening the thick scent of metallic smoke. Blood and tears mix in the man's eyes as he clenches the broken bridge.

"You're a dead man," he shouts, pointing a finger at Lelantos, who then responds with a grin and a shrug. Before the bleeding man can cause more problems, he's pulled from the building. Micah's brow lowers as his jaw tightens. He puts his arms over his chest to share his disdain, preparing a lecture for Lelantos about using nice hands, to remind him to take deep breaths when he's about to fly off the handle. We've heard this lecture far too often if I'm being honest. Sometimes I wonder how Micah—the peacemaker—could have been a tough warrior. His skill with a long sword and survival instincts are the only proof I have of his time serving.

"He'll heal," Lelantos grumbles. He lands in a seat and kicks his feet onto a wobbly table. The man wouldn't know decorum and manners if they smacked him in the face—a part of his charm I love far too much.

"They're always causing trouble," a woman says from the shadows. She steps into the light, revealing a yellow bruise around her right eye. She swats the side of Lelantos's boots. I've seen her in this building from time to time. She's a Nihil earning her keep like many of the others before they're taken away. "He isn't here yet, but you may enter."

I'm confused by the notion of the king's tardiness. For all my years knowing him, not once has he been late. We've been working with King Albus since he learned of our rescue missions. We're famous for some and infamous to others.

An occupational hazard, I suppose.

To the Omnia loyalists, we're treasonous, practically begging to be killed for our crimes. To the others, we're silent heroes, willing to do anything for the people who need it most.

Behind the bar, there is a door leading to another room. To the naked eye, no one would look twice at it. To the sympathizers, this is a safe place for Nihils and a few crossbreeds to find sanctuary in their time of need.

Lelantos leans down, speaking in a hushed voice with the Nihilan woman. It used to bother me that he could speak easily with them. I didn't understand then, but after learning more about his childhood, I'm just glad he can talk to someone, even if it is trauma bonding. He was gagged many times for speaking out of turn, so much so that it stole his voice.

"Are you going to call on her after this?" I tease Lelantos as he covers the ground to catch up with us.

"Is everything a joke to you?" he snaps.

"Yes." I say truthfully. The world is already so heavy on us. I'd rather joke than let it drag us all down, but I'm also not trying to argue with him again so soon.

My brothers and I move around the room, making introductions. Telling the people around us about Tenebrae and the village there. We can't promise them complete safety through these trying times. The sickle strapped to my back is a reminder of that as Hamish's words about the artifacts in times of war corrupt my mind.

It doesn't belong to you, and I advise you to return it before a war starts that you can't finish.

The heavy door groans. King Albus enters with two guards dressed in bronze behind him.

Thank fuck, I think to myself, appreciating the lack of a plume. Nothing screams "I'm compensating" like wearing those ridiculous feathers to seem bigger and stronger than others.

King Albus approaches. People bow—including my brothers. As I lower, the king's hand tugs on my shoulder to stop me.

"You may never bow to me," he says.

I've known King Albus since I was a child. Ever since then, he has told me never to bow in his presence, but sometimes I want to. He reminds me a lot of my father. They rule with kindness toward the people. I think it's why he and my father were as close as they were. After my parents' death, I lost contact with him, but he found me as soon as rumors started circulating about the dead prince of Tenebrae. He told me tales of my parents I'd never heard before. I gained all respect for him when he told me he was a Nihilian sympathizer—a treasonous act for a king who signed the Great Cleansing Ordinance. I once asked him why he would do that, but I never got an answer, and I don't think I ever will.

"Apologies for my tardiness. Something came up, and I was delayed,"

Micah speaks before my curiosity gets the best of me. "All that matters is that you are here now."

Maybe to Micah and Lelantos, but not to me. There's a gleam of sweat on the king's upper lip. A tenseness in his raised shoulders. He's hiding something, and I want to find out what.

King Albus recounts the details of yesterday regarding the caravan and rescuing the Nihils from more vagabonds—the bane of my existence. They kidnap and traumatize people for gold to fill their pockets. Their thirst for greed makes me sick. King Albus, in his recount, stumbles in his speech, tripping over who all witnessed the Nihils. He runs his fingers through his hair with a glance to the side, avoiding eye contact. I watch the signs carefully, certain King Albus is omitting information. The only thing I'm uncertain of is why—but I will find out.

"I have gold, livestock, and anything else you might need to offer for their safety," King Albus says, looking back at me.

Giving a small smile, I regard his offer. He provides the same every time. Normally, I deny him, but not now. Our quaint village is becoming larger than I thought it would. With the winter months approaching, we need all the help we can get for these trying times.

"I have detailed accounts of what we need," I respond.

King Albus looks me up and down with a smile of pride—or what I think is pride. I haven't seen the look since I was a child learning to manifest my first shadows. My father bragged to all the men and women about the minor accomplishment. If only he could see what I can do now.

He guides us to the desk at the back, too comfortable for our liking. Everyone in the room is loyal to the Nihilian cause, yet there are far too many others looking for any reason to have another ruler on the throne. I have warned King Albus about his blatant treason far too many times, but he doesn't seem to fret. He's one of the few who doesn't fear Omnia Itzel. The thought of her nearly summons the weapon strapped to my back.

I have no doubt he would know what to do with it, and I long to tell him, but there's something off about this meeting. He keeps glancing at the door with urgency, as if he's on borrowed time. Our usual business occurs when the city sleeps, so we can bring the Nihils to the tree line. It's easier to conjure a safe portal when surrounded by nature. Far too many times I've conjured while in a house and would vomit from the instability of the energy. I can only imagine what the people who rarely travel nor have magic would feel.

Micah stands over me, listening to the list of items I am asking for. Lelantos works the room, as if he were the king of Nihils. From time to time, I hear his rumbling laugh, and warmth fills us all. It happens when they laugh or smile, for they're safe enough to do so.

"We will have to make more than one trip for everything," I say.

King Albus glances at the door, running his fingers through his hair again. "My guards can assist in delivering the materials after night fall." He pauses before redirecting his attention to the people. "Your only concern is to get them out of Xannoroth. There are far too many Omnia loyalists in the city."

There's a lilt of warning in his voice. The sound raises the hairs on my neck, considering all the dangers the people in this room face. My chest tightens. One woman with a dark purple bruise around her throat clenches a child to her. The whole lot of them depend on us for their survival, and with King Albus' cagey behavior, I'm questioning their safety—including my own.

"Is there something we should know?" I whisper.

King Albus's lips part. I'm waiting on a breath to hear of this phantom threat, but it never comes. A guard storms through the door with an expression of panic. He approaches, bowing at the waist. I roll my eyes at the notion. "She's moving through the city, My King," he says.

King Albus stands from the desk without speaking another word. He pushes toward the door in hurried steps. My brothers flank my right and left sides, and we march behind in case he needs our help.

Before we can exit the bar, his hand lands on my chest. "I can deal with this alone, Erebus."

The bar door slams behind him. As I stand there, I can't help but feel the pulsing weapon on my back as a sheen white glow vibrates between my wings. I don't have to look at it to understand that it's calling out to someone.

Twenty-One

Fuck the rations and supplies. There isn't time to get equipment and save the people counting on me. Pushing into the room, their wide eyes land on me, anxiously tracking each of my movements. I didn't have to tell my brothers to guard the doors—they're already doing it. Conjuring the portal is second nature to me. The power comes easily as the gateway to Tenebrae opens. None of the refugees hesitate to push through. Micah comes to stand at my side, preparing to leave with them. When he steps through, I take a deep breath.

Lelantos glances at me. "Whatever you're about to do, you're not doing it alone."

Micah looks through the portal at us, waiting. Someone needs to stay with the Nihils. Lelantos and I have to see the reality of King Albus's problem and which she the guard was referring to. The portal shuts and Micah's phantom cursing follows.

Moving to the main door of the bar, I count to three. I have to know who it is before going through the void, and just how fucked my brothers and I truly are.

Melania

Outside there is a throng of people—I pay them little mind.

Kiara and Kyan yell for me, but I keep chasing the electricity, following the same pattern: stop, close my eyes, feel the tendril and let it guide me. Then I run again until I need more guidance toward the Omnia artifact. I have no doubt that's what it is. The missing piece of power wants to return to where it belongs.

The market street is crowded during midday, reeking of spices and body odor. People either move out of my way, or I push past them. They yell out for me to "watch it", and I give a quick apology without losing momentum.

If I can find the sickle, return it to Omnius, keep it with me, then I am certain all will be right. The thoughts comfort me until my pace begins to slow, and a sickening thought creeps into my mind. Between my mother and me, either of us could hone it. I cannot fathom what my mother could do with it if she discovered its existence. The havoc she could wreak upon others with that sickle in her grasp. I can't trust that she wouldn't use it for her own gain. In fact, I'm certain she would.

Panting and out of breath, the urgency in my steps falter. A pull of right and wrong twists in the void of my chest. The rightful place of the artifact is with me, but what risks do I bring onto Veilia having it in the palace? I saw how La'Mia reacted to learning about the sickle. How would she behave with the power of an artifact near her?

Closing my eyes once more, I can see the strand within me. It's taunt as if it may snap. Yet, what concerns me the most is the faint light blue line near it. I missed it in the aura of the white, but it's there. When I open my eyes, I can barely sense anyone out of the ordinary. They all have reddish hair from the fire in their veins.

Except… there! A man with a wild mane of auburn hair and a bow over his chest finds me in the crowd. Our eyes meet, and my breath stops, calming me from the panic no longer there. My lips part, my chest tightening with something I can't quite name until he turns to someone else, and the flood returns. The man with the bow whispers something to another behind him, donned in all black matching the striking features of his hair and veins. I'm willing to venture his eyes are as dark as the midnight sky. His great, large raven wings huddle close to his toned frame. I'm awestruck, as the only two beings in the world known to have wings are from ancient bloodlines.

A tingle moves down my spine as he, too, sees me. A phantom whispers into my ear, telling me I need to speak with them—stay with them. My feet move on their own accord.

I'm too blinded by the darkness in front of me that I step without looking. A shout erupts, and my body is jerked backward.

The scent of musk, amber, and ash smothers the adrenaline in my veins. Turning, I come face to face with King Albus. His expression is lax, but I can see the tension lining his brow with silent panic in his eyes. "Omnia Melania, what a surprise," he says, his voice wavering.

"I could say the same to you," I reply. My words are quick as I glance behind me.

There's an empty spot over where the men were. A part of me wonders if my mind was playing tricks on me. Had I been imagining the whole thing? The world around me continues, but I feel adrift. That void within me still gnaws. Closing my eyes, I can see the tendril of my power and the lighter one beneath it. They're both taut once more, yet my feet beg me to follow.

"If you would excuse me, King Albus, I will be off now," I say.

"If you're venturing the city, I can assure you, I am a terrific navigator." King Albus offers his arm with a silent plea in his eye, giving me little to no choice. More city people wander closer to us on the crowded lava rock road.

Daring to glance back one more time, I concede and slip my hand into his. He steers me away from where I'm certain I am meant to be.

Twenty-Two

Melania

King Albus guides us into another part of the city. Kyan follows behind us. Kiara stayed with Elara for protection, and for that, I'm grateful. She is the only person I consider a friend anymore.

We move toward four wide pathways leading to a square in the center of town. There is a giant bronze statue of a woman kneeling against the ground. She holds a flame between her palms. Around the statue, incense burns, a pot of bronze left unlit below her.

"The First bestowing her blessing," King Albus says.

My eyes trail to him for the first time since he began guiding us. He looks at the statue with wide, adoring eyes—I realize I've never felt that kind of emotion for anything. I've never been proud to be born of an ancient bloodline like he appears to be. I can't help but wonder what that must feel like.

King Albus glances down at me with as much—if not more—adoration. An uneasy feeling runs through my veins as I piece together why. The First and all the Omnias of our past continue to breathe life into Veilia. As the others before me, my survival is dire for the survival of the others.

"What's the cauldron for?" I ask, needing a reprieve from these feelings swishing in my stomach.

"A sign of war," he whispers. Within them, I can hear the panic in his voice. "It hasn't been lit for a long time. I've read how my great-great-grandfather lit the cauldron during Omnia Arabella's reign. A fierce Omnia with a bow embedded with her essence. It's the only way we won against the monsters."

He continues forward, but I'm too lost in the story to realize.

"And of the Omnia who wielded the great sword?" I ask, recalling the portrait of another Omnia.

He clicks his tongue against his teeth in an ah-ha kind of way. "Omnia Matilda was the first Veilian to be born from The First. During those first few years as her magic strengthened, people feared her. She didn't have the control of The First. Her emotions threatened to topple cities. Many tried to kill her, but none were successful. It wasn't until she wielded a great sword imbued with her essence that she could hone the power within her." He pauses, running his fingers through his hair.

"At that point it was too late. The cities were uneased by her. A war between the people and the royals began. Many lives were lost, but at the end of the war, there was peace throughout Veilia for a long time."

"How do you know all of this?"

"Passed down from generations. My father used to sit beside me in bed and recount the stories of what happened before our lifetimes—the same stories I told Priscia when she was a child to prepare her for her future as queen."

"And what if another weapon was created by an Omnia?" I ask.

King Albus halts, turning to face me as he places his hands on my shoulders. A seriousness lines the wrinkles on his face. "Is there something you're not telling me?"

"No." I try to say it with complete ease, but my pitch raises every time I lie.

"Did your mother create an Omnia artifact?"

I jerk out of his touch, though I'm not surprised that he assumes my mother made one, and not me. "I was only asking King Albus. There is nothing to fear." Once more, my tone raises. I'll have to practice lying to stop this habit—one that may or may not be worse than my nail biting.

Dammit—I thought about it, and now I want to do it.

King Albus nods, but judging by the way he's looking at me, I don't think he believes me. Tension is replaced with dread, a sentiment I finally understand.

"You can trust me, Omnia Melania. I didn't mean to raise my voice with you."

I hadn't realized he did such a thing. I've been screamed at before, and that was nothing compared to the worst.

"But those Omnia artifacts were created by an Omnia because the Fates needed it. It's a sign of war—one we all have to prepare for."

"And pray to whatever God you believe in." I say the words La'Mia said to me. Her panic flashes through my mind in a new way. Yet what bothers me most is that she knew more about the artifacts than I did.

The stories were never told to me as a child. I always wondered what she and my mother whispered about. I had assumed they were talking about me. How wrong I was. Why would my mother trust her with the secrets and not me?

Because you're a threat to her power, I think to myself, though I'm not sure how anyone can be a threat to that woman.

We take another path in the city toward a quieter section. Gone is the sound of metal pounding at the blacksmith's, replaced by the sound of—laughter? Clusters of smaller buildings stood nearby, walls laid in uneven cobblestone. One of the largest buildings is splashed with color alongside the cobblestones near the ground. Flowers and stick figures are painted across the lava-rock ground.

Colorful steps lead toward the crooked wooden door. King Albus takes us to it. Small chairs and tables line the stone platform, and an awning made of cloth protects us from the burning sun, a reprieve to my pale skin as a pink hue spreads across my hands. I imagine my face is as red as a berry, too. I pay it no mind, as I know my skin will heal itself the moment we step inside.

The king knocks on the door, and I'm suddenly too aware of myself. I examine my attire—a long-sleeved cotton shirt and leather pants. My only comfort is that King Albus wears a similar wardrobe, blending in with the rest of the city people. And of course, my braided iridescent hair screams, "look at me! I'm an Omnia."

Tiny, muffled voices carry through the door. My fingers dig into the side of my nail behind my back as a slither of nerves twists knots into my stomach. My heart pounds as I realize we're meeting children—and they scare me more than releasing an Omnia artifact into Veilia.

King Albus raises his hand to knock again. Before his knuckles meet the wood, the door swings open, revealing a woman wearing a mauve dress draped to the middle of her calves who looks to be my age. Granted, Veilians rarely age, so she could easily be nineteen years old or three hundred.

"Oh, by the First!" she exclaims.

Her eyes are piercing red, like the other fire wielders. Her auburn red hair pulls tightly against her scalp into two buns at the top of her head. If Elara returns, I want her to do that style on me. Her lips are painted orange, highlighting her bronze skin. She lowers herself to a curtesy only to rise in seconds. King Albus doesn't tell his subjects when they can or cannot rise. I like that more than what my mother does.

"Would it be untoward if we joined class today, Valery?" he asks.

I cock my head to the side, raising my brow. My eyes widen, and my mouth gapes open. Valery runs her hands over her apron smeared with what I hope is paint and not the blood of different wielders throughout Veilia. The sight of it makes me queasy. The last time I saw that many colors was on the axe of the executioner—right before Baker died.

"Let's get you lot out of this heat," she says.

King Albus's hand lands on the top of my back and he squeezes the lower part of my neck, an action he's probably done for most of Princess Pricisa's life. I wonder if she realizes how lucky she is to have such a doting father.

Valery pours me a glass of a sweet, herbal liquid. Condensation drips down the side of the glass cup. I take it gratefully, wondering how they keep any refreshments cool in this climate. It's so hot, I want to gulp it down fast.

King Albus watches me closely, and I sense he picks up on my hesitation. Too many people have tried to murder me. Though they never succeed, it doesn't stop the pain of it all. He grabs the glass pitcher and pours himself a cup as well, drinking greedily. His throat moves with the large gulp as he nearly empties the glass. With a satisfactory "ahh," he turns to Valery. "How refreshing. I must know how you make your cold sugar tea."

King Albus' kindness in easing my suspicions does not go unnoticed. My panic over the smeared colors and worries of potential poison subside from my mind. Steadily, I sip the cool liquid, appreciating the sweetness on my taste buds followed by herbal notes of nature. I, too, must have the recipe for this glorious concoction.

Valery escorts us further into the building. Kyan waits at the door, facing the low-trafficked path. Neither he nor King Albus appears worried, so I try my best not to be either.

Several pictures of flowers and figurines—all made with paint, ink, or chalky, black soot—hang on the beige walls. Names mark the art on the bottom right corner of each picture. Some are freshly white, hanging at the bottom of the wall, the higher pictures aging with yellowed stain from students who must have come before.

Valery stops us outside a door where there are many little voices. I imagine them running around with one another, probably plotting world domination—or whatever it is children not born of royal blood think about.

"The children will be excited to see you, King Albus. They've been asking when you would make another return." There's a fondness in her eyes, and I wonder how often she and King Albus meet with one another. Could this potentially be the other woman in his cloak of secrets? I make a mental note to ask a servant about their relations later.

"They'll be very excited to meet *you*, Omnia Melania. I will try to keep them wrangled, but many of these children have never left Umber; let alone Xannoroth. If I'm being honest, I think they believe you are imaginary."

A chuckle slips from me. Words escape me, and poor Valery probably assumes I am mute from my weak social ability. I've never been surrounded by people who think so highly of me.

"I shall speak with them first." Valery says.

She barely cracks open the door to fit through. Her muffled tone mentions King Albus and me, followed by cheers. My heartbeat pounds against my ribs, begging to break free. King Albus takes a large, deep breath. For some reason, I follow his lead. Warm air fills my lungs, calming the adrenaline coursing through my veins.

"I've learned taking large breaths and counting them helps. I had hoped it would assist you, too."

I don't count, but I follow the rise and fall of his chest with my own breaths. My mind still runs freely, thinking of the children and how they might perceive me. In my nineteen years of life, I've never spent time with those significantly younger than myself. Syrinx and Eros are close enough to my age. When they left the palace, my mother ensured it remained a child free zone, aside from La'Mia and me. Then again, we were never raised as children after the death of Queen Gaia.

King Albus' touch on my neck has me jumping.

"You can do this, Omnia Melania. I know you can."

It's the confidence of his words that make the next breath feel easier. The weight of his palm grounds me in the moment, and it's the only thing keeping my power centered as Valery opens the classroom door.

A dozen little eyes land on me. Most of the children hover near the edge of their seats, some bouncing their legs trying to contain their bursting energy. I'm about to remind myself I can do this when I lock eyes with one child.

Her eyes are dark brown—nearly black. She's the only one in the room, aside from me, who does not flare red in her gaze. The scent of mud and moss fills the air from her presence. I had no idea King Albus allowed Nihils into the school, as it's an act of treason against the Great Cleansing Ordinance. One shouldn't even be here, let alone get an education.

I search my emotions to determine how to react to the notion of King Albus being a Nihilian sympathizer, and something dawns on me at that moment.

So am I.

Twenty-Three

The eager children stand from their seats. I take a step back, but I can't make it far with King Albus there. If any of the children near me, I'm running out of this room as fast as I can—reputation be damned. They bow and curtesy in our presence instead.

"Very well class!" Valery cheers, clapping her hands together.

The children stand one by one with bright smiles. Some have red in their cheeks. My attention flicks toward the small girl with dark brown eyes and hair. Oddly, she's the only one whose face is twisted into a frown. The only one who looks completely displeased with our being here.

"Alright children, shall we continue with our lesson?" Valery asks from the front of the classroom, near a chalkboard with a weathered map on it, detailing all nine territories—including the eight kingdoms and borderlands. A smaller square outlines Xannoroth with a tiny heart around the city of Umber.

I'd never realized how large Xannoroth—or any of the other

kingdoms—truly is. Quintarius, where Omnius resides, takes up the majority of the large space. The second largest is Tenebrae—the only kingdom I've never spent any time in. What strikes me as odd is the mention of Enodell—the ninth territory without a kingdom. Some say the Fates rule over that land, and it's the burial sites of the Gods and Goddesses. No one is welcome unless they're summoned by Fate. A chill moves down my spine thinking of the accursed place. My mother had Enodell removed from all the maps, which only shows the true age of this weathered paper.

King Albus nudges his knee against me, and warmth floods my cheeks followed by the taste of blood on my tongue.

"Who would like to tell Their Highnesses what we have been learning?" Valery announces to the room.

Hands shoot into the air. Every single child wants to answer except the Nihilian girl, whose eyes are still fixed on me. My shoulders tense. Has she been staring at me the entire time? I pry my focus away from her to listen to the little boy with curly locks of blond hair.

"We are learning of the kingdoms and the royals," he squeals as his leg shakes underneath his desk, the front of his toes bouncing against the bar.

King Albus raises his shoulders with a lax face. This was either a coincidence or planned—regardless, I'm eager to learn.

"Would either of you like to speak with the class on life as royalty and the kingdoms?"

The spit catches in my throat, and I fight through a cough.

"I speak for both of us when I say we would be pleased to learn under your teaching," King Albus says.

I imagine there is little he has left to learn. He knew more about the Omnias than I ever have. My mother would easily place the crown on my head and continue to lead in secrecy without teaching me a thing. Before everything, I might have obliged, but now I'm not sure. That alone has me terrified for what that could mean.

I place my hands under my thighs to keep myself from chewing on them.

"The royals don't have to learn," a child in the back of the room says.

I scoff quietly before I can stop myself.

King Albus looks at me. "Everyone has to learn, but especially royals."

The child diverted her attention to the window in submission—an action I can understand. Haven't I done that same thing throughout my life? Empathy drives me to stand and move my chair closer to hers. She doesn't look at me, but she's returned her focus back to the room.

"There are nine territories, eight kingdoms, and eighteen borderlands." Valery points at the large map. The students stare at their teacher in her stained gown, two buns like rabbit ears on her head, and her cheery smile commanding their attention. She's the queen of the room, preparing the next generation of our world.

"Can anyone list the kingdoms?" Valery asks, moving in front of the map to block the view of the names. I hide my smile behind my hand.

The little girl who'd been staring at me raises her hand, then speaks without being called upon. "Xannoroth is the kingdom of fire, Brilore of water. Quintarius is the kingdom of nature, Irolyn is air, Jeadreania is ice." The Nihilian girl pauses to catch her breath. "Enodell is the only territory without a kingdom, Laelithra is the kingdom of light, Omnius is where the Omnias reside, and Tenebrae is the kingdom of darkness."

She has more bite while listing off Omnius and Tenebrae. Then, her focus returns to me. I glance at King Albus to see if he's noting the behavior. His arms are crossed over his chest.

"And who are the royals of those kingdoms?" Valery says. The little girl's lips part, but Valery says, "Ire, let's give our classmates a chance to impress King Albus and Omnia Melania."

A fitting name for a girl who can glare as well as her.

The little girl next to me raises her hand with a bright smile. "King Xerxes of Quintarius."

Another kid says, "King Caspian of Brilore."

"King Albus!" one shouts.

"Queen Elowen and Queen Arya!"

Fitting for the queens of Irolyn and Jeadrenia to have their names called at the same time. Then again, where one goes, the other follows as they lead the only kingdom that shares the center border-line separating them.

"King Marcus of Tenebrae," someone says.

"He shouldn't be," King Albus whispers under his breath. I mull over his words, running the afternoon's events through my mind, and my chest nearly seizes. I was about to approach the Ravenheart descendent before King Albus stopped me, pulling me away from him. I hadn't considered that the king was meeting with Tenebrae's dead prince. It would explain a lot.

"And who are we missing, class?" Valery encourages the children to continue.

Silence fills the room, everyone stumped. There are three titles left in the realm, only one with a crown on her head. Finally—I know something everyone else doesn't. "Omnia Itzel of Omnius, and Princess La'Mia will be crowned at the end of this month as Queen of Laelithra."

Another bout of heavy silence falls around the room. I left myself out as I'm neither a princess nor a queen, but a spare Omnia in waiting.

"Then why are you called Omnia Melania, do you not rule?"

The breath tightens my lungs. Though I know the answer, my words fail me. Sadness coats their eyes.

King Albus uncrosses his arms. "She will be crowned on her

twentieth birthday." His throat works on a swallow. "On the spring equinox, Omnia Itzel will remove the crown from her head and place it upon Omnia Melania's—reigning her the ruling Omnia of Veilia."

How did he recall the date of my birth so quickly? He speaks of my coronation with such pride. Princess La'Mia told me once that some rulers were growing restless about my ceremony, hoping to stay with Omnia Itzel until the end of the Great Cleansing. The tone of King Albus's voice has me wonder if that was another venomous lie smothered so sweetly by Princess La'Mia that I thought it was the truth.

"Class, let us move forward with the lesson," King Albus says. He gestures toward Valery, and she returns with a curt nod. There's something there, and I so desperately want to find out.

"There is a hierarchy of the kingdoms, does anyone know what it is?"

The little girl next to me begins speaking only to be stopped by Ire. "The kings and queens rule over the lords and ladies. The lords and ladies rule over the commoners. And all of them rule over Nihils." Her jaw clenches as she grips the quill of her pen tightly, blanching her knuckles.

"Who do the kings and queens answer to?"

Ire starts to answer, but Valery moves in front of her, her eyes burning a warning to her.

"We answer to the Omnias," King Albus says.

"Who do the Omnias answer to?"

King Albus nods his head in my direction, and I realize everyone wants me to answer this question—including him. I mull it over, thinking of who we answer to, but most of the time, we're left unchecked.

"We listen to the Fates, then to our protectors—the heiresses of Laelithera— but it's our magic that keeps us in balance. We cannot wield more than one kind of magic at a time. Doing so is immensely painful. Our very being is tied to the land of Veilia, so there is a give and take from it. We require a lot of rest until we're old enough to deal with the pull of it. And—"

"Are there any lords and ladies in here?" King Albus asks, interrupting my word vomit.

"I am, but I don't understand why," the little girl next to me says, smiling to reveal the gap between her front teeth. My attention drifts from her face to her desk, her name written right in front of me: *Lady Elanora Carlsson.*

"Your Mother is *Lady* Carlsson and, as her first-born child, you are the heiress to her title," King Albus answers.

"And I will answer to you?" It's more of a question than a statement.

"Even as the king, I have a difficult time understanding everything happening in these vast lands." He makes a gesture to the board before striding to the map. He points to the smaller map of Xannoroth. "There are many lords and ladies throughout, keeping intel on what occurs in their areas. Once a month, they come to the palace to report any issues. If there are any large problems between kingdoms, I then report to Omnia Itzel."

The children nod as if they understand, though their bodies straighten and their legs continue to tap, almost like they're gearing up for another round of questioning—especially Ire, who's staring right at me.

"This has been a pleasure, but there is much more to see." King Albus is quick to my side with his long strides.

I leap from my seat, ready to leave the questioning and the child who seems to be plotting my death—one that would be fruitless. Before King Albus stopped me, I was about to reveal that only another Omnia can balance another one, which only spirals my mind down a hole about my mother and all the things she's willing to do to check me. But who is checking her?

I'm nearly out of the room when a little girl's voice stops me dead in my tracks.

"And what of the Great Cleansing Ordinance that has killed my entire family and sent my brother to Tenebrae?"

King Albus pulls me from the room. The girl's words consume me, and doom lingers in my chest.

What of the Great Cleansing Ordinance?

Neither King Albus nor I have spoken since leaving the classroom. What started as an amusing learning experience turned sad in a matter of seconds. That child didn't deserve the hurt they faced in their short life. I didn't create the Great Cleansing Ordinance, but like Scarlett, the judgement falls unto my shoulders by association.

"Why was a Nihilian child there?" I don't like the tone of my voice, but I can't find a care.

"I was waiting for you to ask me about that. Everyone deserves an education, no matter their rank or abilities."

His lack of an answer toward the Nihilan child heats my skin. "The Great Cleansing Ordinance says children without magic cannot earn an education, but you're openly breaking that law." Worry laces my anger.

I fear what could happen to King Albus if my mother learns of this. She would have to seek retribution, and if he were sentenced to death because of me, I couldn't live with the blood on my hands. Not after Lord Byron.

"Do you truly believe in the Great Cleansing Ordinance? That Nihils are less than without their magical properties?"

I sigh, knowing I don't, but I'm not ready to admit it.

"My King," Kyan says, pulling him away.

I remain where I am, knowing I should stay with him, but all I want is space—time to compartmentalize my thoughts. Power simmers within me, mixing with my emotions. I fight the heat behind my eyes. Ire's words—her anger—haven't gone unnoticed by me. I know I should do something—but what? What can I possibly do against the crimes of my mother? My skin prickles, my heart roaring in my chest as I feel every injustice ten times over.

Abandoning the king's side, I find a shadowed space between two buildings where two women wearing low-cut gowns whisper in the corner. King Albus nods in my direction, signaling he knows of my whereabouts—I'm not entirely alone. I remain close to the entrance, watching him. Once they're done speaking, I'll make way toward them.

"—left me in the middle of the night with three babes, ones still suckling and he's gone," said one woman behind me in a strong accent—one I've heard before when traveling through Quintarius.

My ears perk despite knowing it's wrong to eavesdrop. It's a habit I grew accustomed to as a child, learning more from whispering maids than I did my own mother and guardian.

"Gone with the Three to Tenebrae, did he?" whispered the other. "I've heard many Nihils are gone because of the likes them."

Interest piques further in my mind.

"I blame our king—granting them free reign to kidnap our families," the other lady says.

"I understand he wants to help them, but to send them to Tenebrae."

I knew there was something off with King Albus. Allowing a Nihilan child to study is one thing, but he's blatantly ignoring the Ordinance—an infraction my mother won't overlook. I'm on my way to tell him as such. Focusing all my fury into energy so I don't unleash it onto the land. His head whips in my direction, and there's a lot of white in his eyes.

"This is for my brother," Ire says.

A sharp, long blade plunges through my side. Burning pain blinds me as I crumble to my knees. The power within that had been building dances on the surface. I can feel and taste the energy as much as the blood pooling in my mouth. Ire remains next to me, her lip curled halfway as shadows flicker in her eyes.

The power within reacts to the pain and forces itself out, surging straight for Ire.

A gale explodes outward, hurling everyone away as blinding sky-blue energy erupts from me. A wall, impenetrable, roaring with force. King Albus, Kiara, and Kyan are thrown back. King Albus slams into a building, the structure cracking beneath his weight.

I search for Ire, but I can't see her. I hit the ground hard, the blade still wedged in my side. With a shaking hand, I rip it free. A scream tears through my throat.

The ground beneath me splits open. I don't know if the lava bed is trying to protect me—or Umber.

The walls rise higher and higher, sealing me in until all I can see are jagged cracks growing around me. Then, coolness. It floods over my skin, a sensation I know all too well.

I close my eyes, letting it take me, hoping it's enough to protect them all.

Twenty-Four

Light filters in through my thin eyelids—too bright. I squint as a large hand runs over my hair.

"I am so sorry," says King Albus with a deep rumble I'd recognize any day.

An ache throbs dully in my side as I shift to a sitting position, a weak groan slipping from my parted lips. My eyes adjust to the light and find the king. Hints of gold appear around his irises, and new wrinkles crease on his forehead. His breath warms my cool skin as he exhales. I remember seeing anguish at the time of my stabbing. My fingers trail under the right side of my ribs where a large cut rips up the side of my cotton shirt where the wound would have been. Dried blood clings to the fabric.

"Is she awake?" Elara asks as she appears in my sight, wearing her mauve maiden gown with a white apron—changed from the leather she wore with me earlier in the day.

Her voice sparks a surge of emotion in me, her presence meaning more than I'm willing to admit lest I fall apart completely. I expected her to remain with her sister.

"A little groggy, but I am awake," I respond.

Elara's eyes cut to the kings, but he's too busy looking at me. On instinct, she surges forward and hugs me, squeezing the air from my lungs. I must be going mad from the stabbing—or perhaps Elara truly brings comfort to me—because I wrap my arms around her, refusing to let go, even as my mind protests the touch. She pulls away, keeping her hand on my forearm as she does.

King Albus furrows his brow, then reaches for my other hand as his fingers rest against my pulse.

"What happened?" I ask.

"You were stabbed!" Elara exclaims.

Both King Albus and I chuckle in unison, and the sound is music to my ears. "I know that, but what happened after?" This time I look at King Albus—more so curious to learn of what happened to the city and Ire.

He bites the inside of his cheek, scanning the room for anything other than my face as his hand runs through his already tousled hair. The king opens his mouth, but nothing comes out.

"Omnia Itzel and Princess La'Mia are here to see you," Elara says, filling in the words for him.

Dread fills me instantly, followed by panic. I knew my mother would be able to find me, I just hoped it hadn't been this soon. Not when I'm on the precipice of making my own decisions. Not when I'm learning to break free of the chains of her conformity. Another more pressing thought takes root in my mind. "Did my mother see you?"

"No, she's been in the drawing room with Princess La'Mia. King Albus thought it would be better for them to see you when you were conscious."

How right he was, I think to myself.

"Elara, I need you to hide before my mother comes in here."

Elara motions toward me, parting her lips while her brows wrinkle together.

"Please," I whisper.

Her mouth closes, falling empty with words. She nods and disappears into the closet instead.

I hope she knows I only want to protect her, and that I didn't send her away because I'm ashamed of her. I can only hope my mother is so concerned with what happened to me that she doesn't suspect the Nihilan scent.

"Open the patio doors," I demand, confident it's the only step available to us now.

King Albus does so eagerly.

Before my stabbing, I was prepared to rage against him. Demand answers for what he knows of the kidnappings and Nihils in Tenebrae. I plan to do so when my mother isn't in the palace with superior hearing, but I'm only grateful he's here while I face this next step.

"Send for my mother."

He moves to the door and does the unthinkable, opening it, leaning his head out, and yelling for her. Like the showoff she is, a portal opens in the right side of my bedroom. My mother steps through, wearing a tight white gown with a deep v all the way down to her navel—attire, I note, that is not suitable for seeing her daughter post-stabbing.

Then again, she has yet to look at me as her eyes remain glued to King Albus. Princess La'Mia steps out of the portal after her, eyes on the ground and—*submissive?* Unlike my mother, her gown is simple, baby pink, holding her white, gold-tipped dove wings back like a wilting petal.

"King Albus," my mother says curtly, though she takes a flirtatious tone. It's one she takes often when speaking to General Javon—

and other men of the court.

I roll my eyes.

"Omnia Itzel," he says, but he doesn't bow.

La'Mia's eyes find mine for the first time, her expression sincere, like she's happy to see me, but it quickly shifts to something else lingering behind it. I can't seem to place it, though.

"My dearest daughter," my mother says, turning to me.

She approaches my bed, and I wince at the thought of her touching me as she gives me a tight-lipped smile filled with venom. I know—without a doubt—she's learned of my crimes.

"I send you away to another kingdom and you wind up being stabbed."

"I did not ask to be stabbed, mother."

Her tight smile changes to reveal her white teeth. She clasps her hands together in front of her, pushing her breasts together. I clench my jaw and focus on the ceiling to fight another urge of rolling my eyes.

"Are you completely healed?" she asks.

"The wound is closed." I don't bother with politeness—she isn't asking for it. I know her well enough to know she doesn't care about my safety. She wants to know how well I am before I can receive my next punishment.

"Once we handle the manner of this crime, we shall leave for Omnius." Her eyes flutter to King Albus. "The townspeople are missing you." She tugs at my chin, assuming the role of a doting mother.

I swallow back my own bile.

"She is welcome to remain in Xannoroth until Princess La'Mia's coronation," King Albus says.

Omnia Itzel pulls away from stroking my chin to focus on him. White aura forms around her fingertips. His hands clench at his side. I wonder if his power rages from the tension threatening to boil over and kill us all. I've never seen his eyes this dark shade of red before.

I turn my attention to La'Mia, who looks as if she would like to be anywhere but here—a sentiment I share at this moment.

"She's only been here for a day, Itzel."

My jaw drops. He didn't refer to her as *Omnia* Itzel, and my heart can barely take it. Some people have never lived past such an offense. When my mother looks from his feet to his eyes, the room chills ten degrees colder.

She closes the distance between them as she glares. I've never seen them behave in such a way. Come to think of it, I don't think they ever interacted without the attendance of the other royals. I certainly couldn't imagine these two getting along for more than a second. Not with my mother and her wicked ways against his kindness.

"And look what happened in one day," she sneers, neither of them regarding me. "She was stabbed and nearly toppled the city. Do you know the amount of people she could have killed with her brazen actions using magic that does—" she stops speaking.

It doesn't take a scholar to know where she was going. My mother was going to say *her* magic—the power of an Omnia in my veins, a power she bestowed upon me, making it hers. Power I was told on many accounts not to use, though I can't always control when it seeps out.

King Albus stands straighter, creating a foot of height between them before moving closer to my bedside. Hot and cold air swirl in the room, threatening dire conditions.

"No one died," he assured me, "and the assailant slipped away in the chaos." His left eyebrow raises slightly, a motion I've realized he does when he's not being completely truthful.

I need to know about what part. Most importantly, I need to see the city.

"She is *my* daughter," my mother voice shakes with her words.

The ground beneath us moves, knocking over a glass of water and my jar of ink. King Albus swears under his breath as he tugs the edge of his shirt to clean it up.

"If I say she comes home, she will be coming home." Her words are final.

The king's shoulders drop, and his lips press into a thin line. This is a battle he will lose—unless he's not the only one fighting it. My mouth runs dry as I attempt to swallow. My gulp is audible, and a faint blush floods to my cheeks. I don't let it deter me.

"I wish to remain in Xannoroth, mother."

Since the argument began with King Albus, she's ignored me—not anymore. My mother looks me up and down in my feeble state. I am healed, but I will need more rest, the toll of the wound and the drain from Veilia taxing me.

"You are the future of the kingdoms, and I will not risk this happening again. It sends a negative message to others that we are easy to wound!"

When she yells, nothing happens. In the old building, I would expect dust to fall from the ceiling or a crack to splinter the walls, but the room stays still. My mother smooths an invisible wrinkle from her floor-length gown, her skin flushed pink. She's notorious for threatening to bring down mountains, so the silence is reason enough for her irritation.

I keep my smile in check.

King Albus does not.

A smirk curls across his face, a knowing glint in his eyes with information I long to be privy to.

"Returning to Omnius would be a mistake. It would send a message that Omnias run from the problem instead of facing them. I shall remain here until the assailant is caught and brought to justice."

She gnaws the inside of her cheek, my words hanging in the air between us. La'Mia glances at me, eyebrows lowered as she studies me in this new light. I'm not sure if that's a good or bad thing. My nail scratches the center of my palm, grounding me in the moment.

Omnia Itzel approaches with her head cocked to the side. I've seen her do this when holding an Imposition. It's what I like to call her thinking position while she's deciding whether someone lives or dies. Too bad she's only given one option—and we both know it.

"You and La'Mia should return to Omnius and prepare for the coronation everyone is eager to bear witness to. The kingdom of light is suffering with unrest, and tensions are rising. The only way to keep the people on our side is to usher in this new dawn with Queen La'Mia and the next ruling Omnia together. We wouldn't want to take the attention away from the strengthening ties between Omnius and Laelithra."

I won't leave here without seeing what I did to Umber. "I will remain here."

My mother moves closer to my face, her hot breath against me. My resolve threatens to break, and she knows it. I keep my gaze locked on her despite it.

Her cold hand finds my forearm under the blanket, sharp fingernails digging into my flesh—smart woman to do it away from sight.

Sweat beads at the top of my hairline.

You will not cower, I chant to myself.

My mother leans close to my ear, whispering, "I never gave you permission to leave Omnius, but I am keen to the knowledge that you and Princess La'Mia concocted a plan for your sudden disappearance. I know you killed Lord Byron. What I don't understand is: *why,*" she hisses. "When I find out the severity of your crimes, you will be punished in ways you could never imagine."

Her threat clings to my skin like morning humidity. I study her, unsure of where to go from here. I asked her for permission to leave Omnius—she gave it freely. What am I missing?   "You can stay—only to find the assailant. When they are caught, I will be the one to judge them in the city of Omnius."

With that, she rises and returns to her rightful position. A gleam of excitement flashes in her rainbow eyes for the bloodshed she seeks. The blood of Ire and the blood of me. She glances at the blood on her fingertips before wiping them against the white sheets.

Her other hand runs over her revealing bodice before giving King Albus the entirety of her attention. "If another incident of this magnitude occurs, there will be war."

King Albus barely lowers his head.

"I eagerly await your return," Omnia Itzel says, creating a portal to take her leave.

La'Mia remains at my bedside, unable to move, warring the wide expression I've seen far too many times.

She's scared.

"Should La'Mia stay with me?" I ask, and I don't understand why.

Maybe it's the sudden silence. Maybe it's how the light in her has dimmed over the past few days.

"She has a coronation to plan," my mother says. She smacks the side of her thigh, and La'Mia obeys the call. "You should have Elara clean in here; it reeks."

My mother steps through the portal, her threat of war looming over all our heads—now more than ever.

Elara pushes through the door as soon as the portal clears. King Albus pulls my arm from under the blankets, revealing the half-moon shapes from my mother's nails slowly healing, iridescent blood staining my skin. Like I said, I'm very weak after the stabbing.

He curses again under his breath. Elara tightly squeezes my hand. The weight of their worried gazes land on me. I say the only thing that comes to mind. "It's her way of showing she cares." It's a wet, self-deprecating laugh.

Elara moves across the room to a bucket of water next to the burning hearth where she reaches in, pulls out a towel, and rings it out. Back at my side, she moves to take the arm I long to cover. I've come to understand physical pain, but their pitying looks hurt more.

King Albus steps away. "That's not love, Melania. It's abuse."

I have known since childhood that my mother didn't love me.

In the beginning, it wasn't always physical. Queen Gaia was still alive, protecting me as if I were her own. So, my mother settled for her vicious words, cutting me down whenever she could, reminding me of the time I ended the lives of hundreds because I wasn't obedient.

Queen Gaia loved me like a daughter. But when she died, that protection died with her.

Love became something I only understood by witnessing it in others. Lord Byron loved his sons enough to welcome death for them. Queen Gaia loved me as her own while she lived.

I would like to experience that kind of love someday.

Instead, I've only known the physical, mental, and emotional torment of my mother. It has become so normal that I cannot imagine my life without it. Sometimes, when she avoided me, I sought the pain myself. My own hands become the closest thing to normal I understood. To go a day without it feels wrong, but hearing King Albus speak the truth of my life feels worse.

"Elara, leave us," he says, standing in front of the hearth, arms crossed over his chest, but there's resignation in his eyes.

She continues the steady motion of wiping the healed wound on my side, the cotton shirt releasing from my skin. I give a faint nod to do as he says. Elara hesitates, then sets the rag down, gliding to the door, the latch clicking behind her—I'm certain she won't go far.

King Albus sighs, a heavy breath filling the silence. In a few strides, he stands at the foot of my bed, his warring emotions making him appear like magma ready to erupt. When I shift to a straighter position, pain seizes my breath. Apparently, organs take longer to heal than flesh wounds.

"Melania." My name sounds like a plea. It's the second time he didn't address me as an Omnia. To him, I'm not a figure of power, but a person. At least I think that's what is happening. "I didn't know of the abuse you were being subjected to. I knew Itzel to be cruel, but to wound her kin is monstrous." He pauses, running his fingers through his hair. "I speak for many kingdoms; if we had known, something would have been done to save you."

My emotions choke me, silencing the desire to laugh at the joke. A sprinkling of rain patters against the balcony.

"I did nothing back then, but I will do something now. Your mother forbidding you from wielding is slowly killing you. The cage you have forced your power in will break, destroying you and everything in its wake. Back in the city, the force of your power was potent. Your mother stumbled on her words, and I realize what true torment she's unleashing upon you.

"I told you the story of Omnia Matilda and how the people feared her magic. It wasn't because she was reckless—she was scared. Each time her emotions raged, a new city would topple because no one taught her how to wield. I cannot forgive myself if I do not offer my guidance in a time of need." He pauses, placing his hands on my ankles as he stares me dead in the eyes.

"You are much stronger than your mother—not only in power but resiliency. She believes sympathy and kindness is weakness. Forcing you to become tough or suffer the consequences. I am living proof you do not have to conform to your mother's will. She is the ruling Omnia, but her power is dwindling.

"Veilia is preparing for your reign. It happens to all royals from the ancient bloodline. It's a shame you never had anyone teach you, but I will."

Tears stream down my face as fat drops beat against the ground. Thunder moves closer as the weight of his words settle in my chest. These tears are not from sorrow, not like when Lord Byron died. Anger burns stronger than anything. No one deserves to be mistreated simply for being born.

"Your mother never taught you because she fears you, makes you feel inferior because she wants to be superior. Veilia and the Fates are on your side to end her corruption, and people are already uneasy over the misery she has subjected them to. I will train you, but only if you are ready to become the change Veilia needs."

Allowing him to train me will mark the end of the Great Cleansing Ordinance with my reign. I want to retreat, for the uncharted territory feels like it's too much. But wouldn't it be nice for Elara to live a life where she didn't fear every breath? For young Ire to not have to stab Omnias because she fears for her own safety in the world.

He squeezes my ankle once more. "The choice is yours—and only yours to make."

Parting for the door, he gives me a glance over his shoulder and then leaves me alone. It's the first time I have been given a choice not because of circumstances. Perhaps I should think on it more, but my feet are demanding I move. I swing them out of bed and immediately head for the door.

Pulling it open, I come face to face with King Albus, the corner of his mouth tilting upward into a crooked smile, Elara waiting behind him.

"I do not wish to be a pawn in my life anymore," I whisper, breathier than I intended, but my lungs burn.

King Albus nods, his brows rising as his eyes trail past me toward the pouring rain. Elara covers her mouth, forcing me to turn in that direction.

A rainbow forms beyond the balcony, cutting through the heavy, rain-filled clouds. The rarest and most beautiful abnormality. A sign from the Fates and the First that they stand on my side.

The Great Cleansing Ordinance will end with me.

Twenty-Five

Elara braids my hair. Five days have passed since the stabbing and summons of my mother. My body healed fully after the first day of rest, the additional four were redundant. On the third day, Elara stayed with me to ensure I didn't scale the balcony. Albus has dinner with Elara and me every night in the great hall. He has since asked me to refer to him as *just Albus,* an agreeable circumstance for he only refers to me as Melania.

There hasn't been word of Ire's whereabouts. I worry she was hurt in the blast. Yesterday, during the night, they took me to the site. Large cracks vined across the buildings, but none of them toppled over, a fact I am rather grateful for. There was a crater in the ground the same size as me with an anomalous, purple flower in the center—the same flower that has followed me for all my life.

Elara finishes with my hair, taking a step back to admire her handiwork. Placing her hands on her hips, she smiles—something she's done for the past days, like each braid is unique.

"King Albus and I spoke last night," she says, heading toward the front door. "We believe you to be well enough to begin your training."

I scramble out of the seat, knocking the hairbrush and red berry powder onto the ground. It lands with a *smack* followed by a *crunch*.

Elara's laughter lingers in the room as she leaves and returns swiftly. "Scarlett wanted to send her regards for keeping me safe and out of trouble."

She hands over a set of folded clothes, a smoky, earthen scent emitting from them. My fingers trace over the floral pattern burned into the dark brown hide. I lay them on the bed and appreciate the matching ensemble, with a leather corset to fit over my cotton tunics. Elara reaches into the closet, revealing a new set of brown leather boots.

"This is all too much," I croak.

Fine gowns and silk sewn slippers were meant to be crafted for Omnia Melania—the woman my mother wanted me to be. The smoky aroma of this leather is meant for me. Not *Omnia* Melania, but *Melania*, the woman ready to hone her power for the Greater Good.

Elara hastily helps me into the outfit with a bright smile, matching the one plastered on my face. My cheeks hurt from happiness. She reaches for a leafy green tunic with short sleeves. My mouth dries as the color reminds me too much of Lord Byron. His eyes were so vibrant, like new leaves after heavy rainfall during the changing of seasons.

"Not that one," I choke out.

Elara scrunches her eyebrows, wrinkling the bridge of her nose. She hands me a beige one instead, loosening the strands of the tunic at my collarbone, then moves on to buckling the leather corset. "We haven't discussed the night of Lord Byron's death. You said you gave him mercy?"

My shoulders tense.

"What happened to him?" Elara continues.

My chest constricts, barely loosening my breath. I'm smacked in the face with the rambling words from our fight. I had told her I had given Lord Byron mercy without explaining the weight of what I did.

"Next question," I say through the metallic lilac filling my tongue.

"Will I ever learn about the only scar that has remained on Omnia flesh?" She says it in a theatrical voice as if she's the leading role in a play. I roll my eyes, feeling for the hidden scar beneath my corset.

I have never spoken of that night when an arrow hit me, a painful reminder of why I stopped venturing outside the palace gates—until Lord Byron.

A faint knock saves me from these questions I can't come to answer. Elara rolls her eyes but opens it anyway. King Albus appears, wearing a loose red tunic, black trousers, and black boots. Half of his ashy black hair is pulled back, the other half falling in loose waves, resting on the top of his shoulders.

"You look beautiful," he says, wringing his hands together.

In the past, I would laugh at the statement, rejecting it completely. Now, as I glance at the outfits that fit me for who I am, I do feel beautiful.

"Thank you, Albus." It's odd not using his title, but it's growth in our relationship.

"Are you ready for training?" he asks.

I give him a smile as I reach for his forearm. Together, arm and arm, we walk toward my very first training of my power. But it feels much more than that. I have a warm sensation in my chest and my hands shake as I realize what's going to happen next. The fluttering in my stomach makes me want to jump up and down.

"What are we going to work on first?" I cheer. My cheeks heat, and I'm certain my behavior is just as the children in the classroom were, ready to pounce with giddiness.

"First, we will learn how to portal," he says.

A blanket of dread douses me. The last time I created a portal, the white tendril of my power was pulled to an onyx portal, causing me to lose concentration. I dumped myself and Elara between kingdoms to face the vagabonds.

"How splendid," I say with a hint of mockery. I've been spending too much time with Elara.

Albus steers us on the outskirts of the city where the bustle of everyday life continued in the streets. It's nice not being swept into the middle of it. My hands drop from his arm, a calm serenity overcoming me as I lower my guard. Though I don't blame Ire for her actions, I also really don't wish to get stabbed again. Even so, I imagine Ire feels the same about me—a frightened girl running from the scary monster haunting her nightmares, like the ones of Tenebrae.

"Were there ever monsters in Xannoroth?" I ask.

"Plenty, but most were eradicated during the wars. The fiercest monsters were jinn that resided in the depths of the volcano—fierce creatures who could blend in with everyone else when in their Veilian forms. Some were nice and others wished harm to people of Xannoroth. It's one of the reasons the war against monsters started."

His words soak in, but I have a difficult time understanding why they had to die. Aren't we all capable of being good or bad depending on the narrative?

"Albus, I have been meaning to ask what business you were attending to in Umber?"

He chews on the side of his cheek, looking elsewhere—anywhere but me. I gather he's taking this time to find a political response. Figure out what's the best way to answer the question, while completely avoiding the answer all together. I'm doing my best to focus on anything other than my pounding heartbeat—the dark cherry bark of the leaning trees, patches of brown grass breaking through the lava. Sighing, I resign that I'll never get the answer I seek.

"I have been working with a trio who assist in rescuing Nihils and crossbreeds before they make it to Omnius. And I will not implicate you further by speaking anymore on this manner."

His treason is finally out in the open. Suddenly, it feels like I've stepped into an alternate reality. Wanting to end the Great Cleansing Ordinance is one thing. It's another to stand with a man who no longer listens to the word of his Omnia.

"You don't fear my mother." It's not a question.

King Albus looks to the sky with a pitiful laugh. Whether the pity is for himself or me, I'm not sure.

"There are many things I fear in this life, but your mother isn't one of them."

"I think you may be the only one who has that sentiment."

"They don't understand her the way I do." He pauses. There's a sadness there, like speaking of her hurts more than it should. "Your mother is not a threat to me, for I have the one thing that could undo her completely." His hands wring together again. "The truth."

There's finality in his voice, erupting bumps over my skin, leaving a phantom chill in the air. I expect the trees to blow, but they remain still. The world around us is stagnant, but there's an invisible energy surrounding us. I mull over his words. My mother has her secrets, despite her bold decisions. Being an Omnia means everyone knows *almost* everything.

"Why did you sign the Ordinance if you're not scared of her?" I ask, needing to speak on something before my mind wanders to my paternal origin—a secret that's never been revealed, even to me.

Albus chuckles. "You and—" He inhales sharply. "Always curious, even when it can lead to consequences."

This time, there's a warning in his tone, almost pleading for me to stop. Even if I asked, he wouldn't grant me privilege to the knowledge—like the mentioning of the Three.

He says my mother has secrets, but I'm learning to understand everyone does—especially me.

I bite my tongue against my questions and continue to a clearing far away from the city. I can't even hear the busy streets, a silent blessing to find peace. Like the rest of Xannoroth, minimal patches of grass break through the cracks.

"Do you know why I like Xannoroth?" Albus asks. I shake my head, and he continues. "It smells like the harvest festival. Dancing around giant pyres, drinking the richest ale. Bards singing and jumping on the wooden platforms. Sometimes, when the air smells particularly smoky, I can hear the phantom sound of shoes tapping."

My cheeks ache as my lips curve up—an expression that once felt foreign but is becoming familiar. I've heard of festivals marking the changing of seasons. There was once a time all kingdoms celebrated their own versions of the same day. Now it's like they don't exist anymore.

"I've never been," I say, as if he doesn't already know this.

"When you begin your rule, you can enact the glorious days. All the royals would rejoice to celebrate once more."

"Why did people stop celebrating?" I ask.

A sadness fills his eyes. "The why doesn't matter. It's the when can people celebrate again."

Anxious dread consumes me, my heart pounding against my ribcage over the idea of ruling. I can wear a brave face any day of the week. Pretend to be strong, learning to fake it until I eventually make it. Internally, it's laid bare.

Albus stops us a mile or so from the city, nothing around aside from the open air; a safe space to work my magic without threatening the space around me. "I am aware you created your own portal, but it wasn't stable."

I'm about to protest, but his eyebrow lowers while he glances at me. "Did Elara tell you?" I mumble, hands on my hips.

"She might have alluded to your destination being the palace, and not the curtain lands." He says it lightheartedly, releasing the tension in my shoulders, offering a smile that lifts my spirits.

It's endearing to see Elara safe and comfortable in the palace walls, her own relationship budding with Albus.

"Portaling can be difficult, but it's the most resourceful power our royal blood provides," he continues.

Only royals can create portals: a gift given by the Mothers, the King, and the First. I've heard whispers about other wielders trying it in the past, nearly exerting all their power doing so—according to the servants.

"It can be difficult in the beginning. You have to remember you're contorting space to make a three-month trip in one second. You might even have adverse reactions like nausea."

I let his words coat my skin. One thing I've learned about Albus in my short months is that he is widely knowledgeable. He knows more than I think anyone else in Veilia.

"Eventually"—he snaps his fingers. A large flame flickers around the tip of his point finger. He pushes the flame outward, and a great spiral of blue and red takes form—"it becomes like breathing; the connection unique to whoever wields the gift."

With a wave of his hand, the portal disappears, and my lower jaw drops. It's nothing I should be *that* impressed by—but I am.

"We will start simple and have you create a portal to the borderlands between Xannoroth and Brilore," he says. "You are familiar with that place, and it shouldn't require us to tread too closely to your mother."

My head bobs. A steady beat of my heart fills my ears, followed by an undesirable shake of my hands.

I can do hard things.

"Focus on your power. Call it to the surface."

Releasing a breath, a current forms around my skin, pushing my hairs straight up. A beautiful cocoon of soft, white aura glows around me.

"Feel the borderlands; let your senses connect to your destination." His voice sounds distant.

I don't know why, but my hands curl into a ball. Magic dances across my palms like a firefly skittering over my skin, the power searching for a way out. When I release it, I watch in awe as a glittering trail begins to form—one like the arc of the sickle.

Not the sickle, the portal, I say inside my head.

It's no use as the rusty blade comes to mind, the weight of in my hands, blood splattering against my clothes, Lord Byron smiling at me from his kneeling position. His last words spin in my head.

You are nothing like your mother.

Before I can stop it, the sickle appears ahead of me, the glow of it guiding me toward the newly formed spiral—one I didn't realize I created. A roaring booms in my ears, as if I'm being called to it. The urge to run to it, to accept my fate, is tantalizing—the first desire I've felt for something I shouldn't want.

Fingers outstretched, the dark spiral begins to glow around it as cold welcomes me in. Reaching further, I'm prepared to fall—whether in a dark abyss or from the sky, I listen to the promises of the dark.

"Melania, no!"

Albus jerks me, and suddenly the ground is gone beneath my feet.

Tears flow from my eyes as my mind grapples with reality. Lord Byron is dead—a loss I truly haven't let myself accept. It explores it in full color before me, revealing what I had done as we spiral through the portal, the sickle as my guide—the mistake I can't undo.

My back lands against the ground with a sickening crunch, breath fighting to reach my lungs. My name repeats over and over. I try to follow the sound, but all I see is the green meadow I'm lying in. Salty tears burn my eyes as I scour, yet I can't find Albus—but rather another source of torment.

A shadow woman with glowing white eyes focused on me and a wide, creepy smile stands by the tree line in a gnarled tree, unlike any I've seen before.

"Melania!" Albus says, his hands steady against mine. He yanks me to my feet with an unwavering confidence I long to see in myself. "What happened?"

"I killed Lord Byron with an Omnia artifact I created."

The suffocating truth loosens from my chest, a dam of tears breaking from within. Fat raindrops fall against my cheek as dark clouds bruise the lilac sky, and embers of ash float around us.

Albus grabs the top of my shoulders, eyes rapidly bouncing between mine. "It's okay, Melania. I'm here. I can fix this, but I have to know everything that happened."

Taking a shuttering deep breath, I tell King Albus how I damned us all.

Twenty-Six

Erebus

"We are depleted of rations," Roman—I think that's his name—says.

He, like many others, has come into my space to deliver depressing news. There are limited rations, housing, and drinking water. The only things we have are armor, clothing, and weapons. It'd be great if we were an army, not a village trying to survive.

If Lelantos were here, I'd have them complain to him. He has a better way of speaking with them—the temperament of a wild boar with wielders, but gentle as a hound wanting attention with the Nihils. It's a skill I neither have nor want. I've been trying to avoid the people of Nobyl—the name I gave the village despite my brothers' disdain—hiding away from them.

"Naming it makes it real," Micah said.

"And real things can get taken away," Lelantos added.

And fuck if it doesn't feel like they're right. Everything was going great. I figured the village could use a name outside of *The Nihilian Village*. Now I'm not even certain we will last a week.

"Can you hear me?" Roman says.

"I'm not fucking inept," I bite out, attitude worse than normal.

Roman mumbles under his breath as he leaves my corner in the blacksmith's. I've been a real treat since seeing Omnia Melania in Umber, picking arguments and snapping at anyone and everyone. I haven't received word from King Albus over the safety of the Nihils since then, an odd occurrence since he always follows up with me about it.

My brothers aren't any better. Lelantos is more in his head than normal. He's been hunting in the woods. I've heard him return in the late hours of the night, gone before sunrise. Micah gives me the cold shoulder for shutting the portal on him, keeping his distance, but I know he worries for Lelantos and me.

For the past couple of days, I've been working in the shop, trying to finish Addilynn's blade whilst grappling with what occurred. When we returned, the ground shook beneath us—a sign of her rage, to be certain. I fear for King Albus and what might have happened to him. I shouldn't—especially after his carelessness nearly got us caught. I don't believe that was his intention, but the Omnias will seize any chance to take us. Of that, I am certain.

Before, I believed Omnia Melania to be different, rationalizing that she killed Lord Byron for mercy, but I don't believe in coincidences. She was in the city for a reason. A quiet voice in my head asks why she wouldn't come straight to the building to stop us, or why would she stop at the sight of us. I know she felt the blade, but her steps halted long enough for King Albus to keep her away.

Ping.

The tip of the blade snaps.

"Fuck," I say, defeated. I haven't made that mistake since I was a child. I'll have to restart. Thankfully, I didn't put the hilt on it. The wooden carving of a bear is at the shack, along with the sickle. I couldn't bring myself to touch it, afraid of what might happen if I kept it close—especially with how it seems to sing for her.

"There are breathing techniques to assist with rage," Addilynn says, leaning against the archway, blonde hair like a cascade of sunlight falling to her waist, a childlike grin on her face. Her clothes are too large, but she doesn't seem to mind.

I want to retort that I don't feel anger, but that would be a lie. "What are you doing here?" I ask, the unfinished blade forgotten.

"Irwin is tending to the pig we have left." She glances down. "It was too depressing, so I came to bother my favorite prince."

Her demeanor shifts in the blink of an eye. A talent that only she seems to possess.

"And how many princes do you know?" It's the first joke I've made in over a week.

"What are you working on?" She moves closer, hands in the front of her trouser pockets, a display of different patches sewn in. I wonder if she could do that for me.

"Trying to finish a better dagger for you. That pixie knife won't do much out here."

Addilynn lifts her shirt, revealing a leather sheath as she pulls out the knife. She twirls it around her fingers before raising it up. I blink as the blade thuds into the wood beam just right of my wing.

"You missed," I muse.

"My goal wasn't to hit you," she sings in a high-pitched voice.

"And what was it?" I ask.

"To see you smile." Addilynn pulls the blade free, and I'll be damned, but it's the first genuine smile I've had all week. "Forget the new blade, come with me."

She doesn't give me much of a choice as she pulls on my hand, guiding us through the village. The newfound smile fades. I've been avoiding the despair settling over the people. Children no longer run through the streets as they once did. Halona hasn't come looking for another flower. The thought saddens me more than it should. Some villagers glance my way, but none approach. Addilynn is the shield I needed—one I never would have asked for.

She loops her hand through my arm. My wing begins to wrap around her instinctively, and I mumble an apology under my breath.

"I appreciate the warmth," she says, tucking in closer to my side.

"Can I ask you something?" I say, chewing on the bottom of my lip. I take her silence as an answer. "Why don't you fear me?"

"Why would I?" Her response is instant—as if she never considered being scared of me.

"I wasn't completely honest when we first met. I had heard of you and your brothers. Stories were told long before Irwin was captured." Addilynn swallows back what I assume could be tears. "They would talk about Lelantos and Micah, but they praised you. The Dead Prince of Tenebrae." She uses her hands as if making a sign out of my name, no hint of mockery in her voice.

"They were hopeful that a royal was finally deciding to change Veilia. Many of them prayed to the Mother that the rightful King of Tenebrae would accept his Fate and find his place on the throne once more."

She stops walking to face me, turquoise eyes stern, brows squinting together, lips in a straight line. Gone is the smiling Addilynn I've come to adore, replaced by a woman who speaks what I've feared the most.

"Addilynn, I appreciate the sentiment, but taking the throne is not my destiny. The night my parents died is the night my Fate was changed."

I've said that sentence more times than I can count. Early on, Lelantos would argue that only I could end the Great Cleansing Ordinance; ascend the throne, refuse to sign the Great Cleansing, forfeiting the law in all nine kingdoms—a fact that most people are not aware of. Omnia Itzel created the Great Cleansing to be a law, but it could only be in effect if all eight royal families signed it. My father spoke out against it on more than one account, and he died for it. I can understand the irony of myself behaving in the same manner as him, except I have no faith in living a long life. We are all going to die eventually—being an outlaw has given me more of a chance than being a king ever could.

As if my negative thoughts have conjured the sky to open, raindrops plunge to the ground. People glance at the lavender sky, and I wait on a bated breath to understand what's happening. My power can't lead to a rainfall, and fear finds me. Only an Omnia can conjure rain, and they're far too close if it's affecting Tenebrae. I scour the villages as they bring buckets outside. Praying to the sky like all their problems have been solved. Addilynn's worried eyes find me as she understands what this means.

I open my mouth to express my concern, but a weight shoves me from the side. I barely catch myself before falling to the ground. Whipping around, I come face to face with a seething Lelantos.

Spittle flies from his clenched jaw. Blood soaks his chest, dipping down with the pouring rain, no animal carcass with him. He never leaves a kill behind unless—I search for any wounds on him, releasing a breath when I can't find any new marks against his scars.

"That was a sick fucking joke, even for you," Lelantos shouts through the rain, water slapping us in the face. He shoves me once more.

"What are you talking about?" I snap.

Addilynn stands between us, hands outstretched in front of our chests.

"Speak, Lelantos," she shouts.

He sneers at her. Surprisingly, his lips part. "Leaving a gravestone with my name carved in it is fucked up." His voice shakes between rage and fear.

My blood cools. I would never tempt Fate in such a way. The Mothers would curse me for considering such an act. I'm slightly offended Lelantos would consider me capable of doing this, as I don't know how I would live if he weren't alive with me.

"Lelantos, I swear on the Mothers, I would never do that."

His sapphire eyes search my face, tracking to find the lies. Except I own up to all my tricks. Hell, half the time I can't even keep a straight face.

"Then who did?" he says, crossing his goose fleshed arms over his chest.

I ask myself the same question, and when I have my answer, I hope they are ready to accept their Fate of death. I've been battling the darkness within me. Exacting revenge against those trying to harm my brothers is a good way to release the pit.

A sickening smile lines my face as the thought of coming undone makes my power sing.

Twenty-Seven

Erebus

The pale lilac sky has more clouds than normal. It's been like that since the onslaught of rain, lasting only a few minutes, but the people were rejoicing on the dirt pathway like it were some kind of blessing. One villager thanked me, as if I had something to do with it. I suppose, in a way, I do for holding onto the Omnia artifact.

Lelantos swings a large axe over his head to strike into the wood. In one clean strike, he halves it in two, then wipes the sweat from his forehead with the back of his forearm.

We discussed the tombstone with Micah, but it's been three days since that incident. Nothing else has come of it, so either it was a daft prank, or something bigger is on the horizon. Micah and I decided it would be best if Lelantos stayed with us, something he has opposed at every turn. He creates space however he can, which is why he's over there cutting wood while Micah and I work on building small shelters.

As of late, there have been more sightings of dreadblights

around the fence. We've added more torches to the border and on the outside of homes as an extra layer of protection. Villagers turn in early as a precaution against the monsters in the woods, but my brothers and I are adamant about keeping them safe.

I haven't seen Addilynn since the other day when she admitted her true feelings regarding my identity—feelings I'm not painfully aware others have, much to my disdain. I wanted to speak with my brothers about it, to know if they've heard talks and omitted to tell me. Not that I would be surprised if they did. I'm not always the most open about the idea of my name and king being in the same sentence.

Lelantos's axe slams into the wood once more, his muscles rippling in his back, highlighting permanently etched scars from the lashings he received as a child—a constant reminder to us all that the past is always there, watching over us and guiding our hand, even if we try to fight it.

Still doesn't make me a king, I think to myself.

We work tirelessly into the night. Deep calluses form and heal on my hand in the blink of an eye. Iron-scented blood seeps into the air. I search for the smell to find Lelantos biting the callus on his hand. There are small wells of blood in his palms. Protected by our power, Micah and I will never have to do that.

"We can continue in the morning," I say.

He nods. I reach to wipe away the blood on his chin but stop myself. His sapphire orbs track my movements as he moves away with another nod and grunt; his way of saying thank you.

"I've received word of more Nihils coming here," Micah says.

I wheel on him as he picks at his nails. No wonder he's been broody and distant like the rest of us. He's been trying to figure out the safety we once promised but no longer have.

"We can't take any more on." There's a stern command in my voice, similar to that of my father.

"If we don't, they die," Lelantos clips as he walks toward our horses tied to the front gate.

Micah glances at me, and a silent communication comes from both of us. We know the truth—if we bring any more, they'll die. If we don't, they'll die. It's a lose-lose situation that Lelantos isn't ready to face—a reality I'm not entirely ready for either.

Our horses stir in our presence as we near. Henrietta pushes her squishy nose into my palm. I kiss the top of her head; she's my good girl, and she knows it. Lelantos mounts Aurora, his white steed, rubbing her mane before trotting ahead.

"When will they arrive?" Lelantos asks.

I push out a deep breath, trying to find the words on how we wouldn't be able to accept them.

Micah speaks before I have to. "We're going to have to find somewhere else for them to stay. There are too many as is, and we don't have the resources to sustain the growth. We can search for more land, but for now, I had to defer them to Umber."

Lelantos clenches his jaw, slowing his horse to flank toward Micah's right—further from me. "We would be able to sustain growth if a king refused to sign the Great Cleansing Ordinance."

I purse my lips together, brows etching to the center of my forehead. "This isn't King Albus' fault." I'm not pleased with King Albus, but he didn't know the world would turn to this. At least I can believe that much from him.

Lelantos scoffs. "He's not the king I'm referring to."

"And what king would defy an Omnia?" I bite out. King Xerxes is too busy burying himself in men and women to give a real shit about the world. King Caspian of Brilore would rather die than evoke the wrath of Omnia Itzel, who would have no problem retaliating against his siren-wielding daughter. And King Marcus is probably reveling in the ideas of murder and bloodshed—the darker side of being a sanguine, I suppose.

Micah and his chestnut-colored steed shake their heads in tandem. I clench my lower lip, realizing which king he's referring to. Addilynn's words become more of a reality, also cementing the idea that my brothers have a bigger dream for my life.

"Out of the question," I say.

Henrietta trots forward, creating much needed space between us. Snagging twigs and trotting hooves comfort me. From behind, a newly lit torch flickers to life, one Lelantos must have lit.

In the quiet night, I recall moments of my childhood: the feeling of the onyx throne beneath me, cold to the touch beneath my small hands, my father's crown lopsided on my head. Back then, I knew the weight of it meant responsibility. It was also then that I realized there wasn't something completely right within me. My father could walk amongst the crowd, speaking of grander plans, and I wanted to crawl out of my skin—then and now.

These moments come and go when I teeter on the edge of living and dying—accepting or denying Fate. A constant push and pull of being tired but still having to fight. Only once have I felt a physical sensation close to that turmoil. Micah and I were making our way through Irolyn—the kingdom of air. The weather had been peaceful despite the warnings of the townspeople. We were caught outside in a tumultuous side wind. My wings caught the air like a kite, but I couldn't fight the current of the wind. I couldn't catch my breath because I was choking on too much air, failing its one natural mechanism. As soon as my feet were on solid ground, Micah held me, enveloping me in his salted scent, and finally, I was able to release a relieved breath of air.

Once more, I am teetering, and my brain and body want to shut down, enter a hibernating sleep to get past these moments. But I can't deny living the life I was meant to—whether as an outlaw or king.

Blood tickles the bottom of my chin, bringing me back to the moment. Shadows dance around me in the deep sky, a prickling sensation running up my spine, followed by a sudden dread knowing we're not alone. I turn around to warn my brothers, realizing I've created too much distance from them, lost in my thoughts.

From the orange torchlight, I can make out the auburn streaks of Lelantos's hair. He and Micah are deep in conversation. My lips part to yell for them, but my words catch in my throat.

A dagger lands in the center of Lelantos's back. His body jerks on impact before he falls from his horse, his steed rearing back as something strikes into it. I rush toward them.

Micah turns to me with wide, wild eyes. None of us expected this to happen. I place my hands around Lelantos, words tumbling out for Micah to run, but not to leave. Blood drips from Lelantos's mouth, the whites of his teeth stained crimson. Micah tries to take over.

"Take him to the shack," I hiss.

Micah moves to pick him up when a dagger lands in his side, dying the fabric of his tunic blue. I move to him only for a dagger to nail me in the right of my wing. Searing pain blinds me, but it pulls me from my worried state. When I open my eyes, I see nothing but black.

"Back to the shack," I shout.

My hand reaches for the blade protruding from my wing, hissing from the sensation. Standing, I take a deep breath and prepare to be the prime target as darkness overcomes me. And I know, without a doubt, the Great Mother intended for me to accept my true power—a descendant of Death and Darkness.

Summoning an orb made of shadows, I keep Micah and Lelantos hidden from the attackers—at least to the untrained eye. The small protection rewards me a sliver of peace—enough for me to hone on the land around us. A dormant beast within me prepares to break free.

My senses heighten to the pockets of shadows that are occupied. There are at least six I can count; an outnumbered ratio I am certain they are no match for. The one pocket is only a few feet ahead of me. I can smell their sweaty skin—a sign of fear.

The shadows cloak me. Like my brothers, I am completely invisible to the untrained eye. A more pungent scent finds me as more of the attackers begin to sweat. Some move from their positions, while others remain.

My hand curls around the cold obsidian and silver of my dagger. Sneaking behind the guy, I revel in the sensation of his skin beneath my blade. That dark fury that always lingers, fighting for dominance in me. And I'm eager to relinquish it for vengeance against those who thought they could harm my brothers and get away with it.

His hot blood coats my skin as the coldness of my shadows dance around my forearms, some moving to staunch the wound in my wings. Utter darkness surrounds me. A conduit to strengthen my power.

Snapping my fingers, yips and howls fill the air as creatures I've never made before come to life. Three large hounds heed to the bottom of my hip, red eyes glowing through the black void. Two larger, wraith-like creatures stand behind me, all waiting for my decision. I want to feel the pain of these fuckers.

Only one needs to survive.

With that thought, the creatures bound forward as I follow behind them to bear witness to the carnage. A sickening smile takes root on my face at the sound of tearing flesh and breaking bones. Screams and wails ring out near the narrow pathway. The fuckers had been scouting to ambush us at our most vulnerable. They're not amateurs, but they're daft for taking me on in the nighttime.

The world goes silent as I bask in the gloom. Through the snarls and tears, I can hear the silence of the night. My Mother's moonlight shines upon me. Instinctively, I stick my arms out wide, appreciating

the new breath of life she exhales into me. This is what I call a blessing.

One of my hounds' red eyes track me, then the beast drags a torn
body like it's a stick and not a grown man. The body bends at a weird
angle, and I'm certain he died from his spine being severed. There's
a thud behind me as a man falls from the tallest tree, groaning and
sputtering bright red liquid.

Approaching him, I place my boot on his throat. His bright red
eyes flare. He can't see me, but he sure as shit can feel me. I push
harder, watching him fight as I crush more on his windpipe. His face
turns dark purple, and then I remember I need at least one of them
alive.

Cursing under my breath, I lift my foot, willing my shadows
to enter his mouth, ears, and eyes. A cold darkness falls around his
body, his senses taken away with a simple thought. And that's more
impressive than making hounds and murderous wraiths. My power
should scare me, but it doesn't. It's the awakening I've been searching
for.

Approach, I command the hounds.

The hound chewing on an assailant shakes, forgetting its toy as
it comes to stand next to me.

"Take him to the shack," I say aloud.

Three hounds bite down on each limb. An ashy scent blooms in
the air. With a wave of my hand, another hound appears. It follows
the pack, taking the spare right leg, biting a little harder than the
others did.

*Secure the perimeter, and when you're finished, feast as you like
on these fuckers.*

The wraiths screech their answer, as if the creature is trying to
speak back to me. I'll have to see if I can train them to talk.

Retreating to follow the hounds, I watch the man's head bend
back, fear etched on his face similar to when I saw a dagger protrud-

ing through my Nihilian brother's chest.

Don't go there yet, I remind myself.

Keeping complete control over myself is the only thing grounding me in the moment. For the world will feel true darkness if my brother is dead, and I won't apologize for it. Enough has been taken from me, and I'm sick of it.

As we approach the shack, the hounds yank the assailant's limbs. One of his shoulders pops out of its socket. I loosen the shadow coating his skin so he can feel the sensation.

Don't let him die, I remind the hounds.

Taking the wobbly steps, I prepare for the worst, stopping outside the doors. I lower my head, say a silent prayer for the Mothers to give me strength, then I push on the door, tracking the red and blue blood staining the ground. My ears ring when entering the archway of the living room. I take a few more steps before falling to my knees in the red blood pooled beneath a barely breathing Lelantos. My hand envelops his in mine as Micah lets his tears fall. It's as if the Fates are deciding whether to end his life or let him serve a greater purpose. And it has to be the latter.

Lowering my head, I prepare to do something entirely too reckless—even for me.

"If you let him live, I will do anything." Tears choke me, and a string of whimpers and wails for the shadow creatures outside bellow in the pit of my despair. "I will take the fucking throne if you give me my brother back!"

Micah's squeezes my shoulders, but I can't look at him. Not when I'm too busy staring at Lelantos's chest, waiting for the Fates to hear me. Waiting for a solid breath to fill his lungs.

The throne for him, a feminine voice I've never heard before whispers in my mind.

I glance at Micah to see if he heard that ethereal voice, but his eyes are wide, staring at the center of Lelantos's chest. The wound hasn't healed, but the blood is staunched. His sapphire eyes open, staring right at me, filling me with the suffocating weight of knowing I've tied our Fates together forevermore—whether he likes it or not.

Twenty-Eight

Micah wraps a clean cloth around Lelantos's chest up to his shoulder to leave it in place. Lelantos opened his eyes once after the bargain, but he's been unconscious since. I only let go of his hand once to help with the wrapping.

"That should help with the bleeding," Micah says, red blood coating his hands.

Blood dries in the lines of my own palms, an image I fear I will never forget. Carefully, we lift Lelantos's still body and carry him to the bedroom on the first floor, placing him in the bed. I remain where I am, scanning the scars over his body—minor compared to the one that will be in his chest, reminding us of what was almost taken away.

"We have to deal with the man outside," Micah says, squeezing the top of my shoulder.

He leads me out of the room, and I fear I'll never look at the drawing room in the same way. There will always be a red stain in the light-colored wood, marking where my brother almost—should have—died.

Drawing a deep breath, I attempt to settle the nerves in my chest before commanding the hounds to enter. Micah moves a wooden chair to the center of the room, a loose rope in his hands to bind the man to it. It's easy to forget the man Micah used to be—a warrior who doesn't speak of what he has done for the sake of serving his king.

With a wave of my hands, the hounds push through the front door, the man's head hitting the walls with a *thunk*. They deposit him on the floor only to return outside moments later. Micah raises his brow. It's the first time he's seeing the depth of what my shadows can create. I can only imagine what Lelantos would say about it.

"What did you do to him?" he asks.

The man lies completely still against the ground, deep marks exposing tissue and bone from the hounds. A yellow pus oozes. I shrug, too exhausted to answer. Micah pulls him into the chair, binding his torso to the back, then holds him upright to face me. The man's mouth hangs wide open as if he is screaming. Black films over his eyes as smoke wafts from his nostrils, parted lips, and ears. Darkness bruises his throat from my boot, and one of his arms hangs lower than the other.

Opening my hand, I summon the shadows to return to their wielder. Smoke tendrils come to my palm, followed by a scream tearing through the man.

"Stop," I demand.

He doesn't register my voice, but he stops when I take a step forward. A dark spot stains his trousers, dripping to the floor, his pungent smell stinking up the area. I raise my nose at the pathetic man who dared to hunt my brothers, then pisses at the sight of consequences.

"Isn't this the man from Xannoroth?" Micah asks.

I didn't recognize him during my black-filled rage, but my mind pieces his image together, remembering The Mark of Death and the man's small stature pushing into Lelantos—the one who received a well-deserved broken nose. Crossing my arms, I fight against the rage trying to consume me. This puny fucker isn't as tough as he thought he was.

"Why did you come?" I ask.

"It was—it was for my in—initiation," he answers, choking on his tears and snot.

"Are there more?" Micah asks.

"No—no." He catches his pathetic breath. "The leaders told us not to come here, but I wanted to join the ranks. They told me a Nihil was easy to kill."

"Who told you that?" My words clip, trying to steady the rage brewing inside of me.

"The men who were with me. After that *Nihil*—"

A shadow tendril wraps around his neck after he spit the word *Nihil*, as if he's better than *that Nihil* currently fighting for his life. He claws at the shadows to pull them away. Tilting my head, I admire the purple shade taking over his skin. It's frightening how much I thirst for his death, and it's that thought alone that pulls me back to the present, away from my murderous thoughts.

"Continue," I bite out, leaving the smoky tendril around his neck.

He works on a swallow before opening his cracked lips to speak. "They told me Nihils we're easy prey since they couldn't fight back. They said it'd be safe if you weren't with them."

His words are a punch to the chest. I was ahead of my brothers when the ambush happened. I left them defenseless because I didn't want to hear more reasonings on why I should be king—which meant Micah was also a target.

"Where's your den?" I ask.

"It's called Fools Tavern in the slums of Umber. A black door with a skull on it." Tears stain his cheeks. Whether by my hand or his leader's, he's going to die for giving up the information.

I nod to Micah, and he doesn't hesitate to leave the room. He knows what's going to happen next, and he doesn't need to be here to see it. The man's eyes are more white than red as reality crashes into him. His pleas are the sweetest music to my ears. From my sheath, I pull out my dagger, releasing the tendril of shadow around his neck, and I step into his space, thrusting my blade in the center of his chest—right where Lelantos will have a scar. A wound like this won't kill a wielder, but I'm not done yet.

With the tip of my blade in the center of his chest, I pull it through his bone and tissue. An anguished scream is pulled from him. Hot blood soaks my hands as life drains from his eyes, but this death is too swift—too kind. Cutting the rope, I drag his body to the door. My hounds nip at his feet, ready to feast.

"Leave pieces of him," I say.

The man grips my ankle, trying to fight against the bite of my hounds. In his eyes, I see him as the young man he is, fear on his face palpable. I can practically taste the anguish, and it's like a divine, cold treat on an above average day in Xannoroth; the creaminess of the dairy mixed with the citrus of the fruit—one of my favorite treats, but not even that is better than this. With one final tug, he's yanked outside to meet his end, and I will not be wishing him a warm embrace from the Mothers.

Shutting the door, I find Micah sitting in a chair next to his bed. His tired eyes land on the blood coating my hands and the line of it wiped on my trousers.

"He will be a message to the Mark of Death," I say.

"Erebus," Micah says, emotion thick in his timber voice. "Perhaps you should stay until he's better."

"The Fates will keep him alive. A bargain has been made that I don't plan to break if it means saving his life."

"I am fearful the bargain isn't enough." He gestures to Lelantos's still body. "He's weak, Erebus. I've never seen Nihils come back from these wounds."

His words make sense, but I don't want them to. I'm the descendant of the Mother of Death. I know when someone is tiptoeing the line to the afterlife. Except I'm too stubborn to let it be him. Micah shakes his head before crossing his arms.

"Search Nobyl for any healers." I pause, pulling Lelantos's hand into my own. His pulse beats weakly, but it's there. A sign of hope amidst the chaos. "When you return, I'll leave for Xannoroth."

"You shouldn't go alone," Micah says.

"He isn't fit to travel, and the Mark of Death needs to be dealt with," I say, pulling the nearest stool to sit.

Lelantos's pulse flutters beneath his wrist, a faint beating coupled with the light rise and fall of his chest.

"Be careful," Micah says, placing his hand on my shoulder.

Before he pulls away, I rest my cheek against him, finding comfort in his warm, subtle strength. Only when I lift from his hand does he leave the room. Lelantos's fingers curl around the center of my hand, even in his unconscious state. It's the only time I've seen him seek comfort from someone else.

In the silence, I reflect on our adventures, reminded of the time he was teaching me how to use a bow and arrow. Micah wasn't too pleased with that lesson—not that I can blame him with the arrow protruding from his shoulder. I ramble aloud about that time we had dinner with his adoptive parents, the family who took him in even when they didn't have to. He only left with us to protect his adopted mother, Sapphira, from Omnia Itzel for being a nymph.

With each memory, I keep questioning how it came to this. Was it the day I met Lelantos in the tavern? Or was it when we decided to save our first group of Nihils? Did it all change when I picked up the sickle from Lord Byron's body? Each action leading to this moment, bordering between life and death. Micah said the bargain wasn't enough, and I believe him. There's something else keeping Lelantos alive. The Fates need Lelantos for something—like they need all of us.

I once thought after my parents' death, my destiny changed—the renegade outlaw, fighting for the Greater Good, but after today, I'm not too sure. Perhaps there was always something more for me waiting on the other side of the grief and depression.

"Erebus," Micah says.

I didn't hear him return in my stupor, trying to understand the Fates' plans. A stocky woman with lime green eyes comes to stand beside his bed, her hands moving over the wound with a faint green aura. A zesty scent fills the air as her powers work to repair the damage that has been done.

"You don't have to do this alone," Micah reminds me.

I shrug. "If I don't, who will?"

He pulls me into a tight embrace. "Be careful."

I relish the familiarity of his airy scent—sea salt and wind.

His large hand ruffles the top of my head—how he used to when I was kid, back when the only thing I feared was my uncle coming after me. Now, my fears pertain to other people.

Making my way through the shack, a tightening, warm sensation forms in my chest. When we first built this place, I hated the confinement of it; the idea of losing my freedom of roaming around the kingdoms and curtain lands. Now, it's the place I've truly known as a home. Gathering a bag, I prepare for Xannoroth to speak with the people I've always stayed away from. From my chest, I tighten the straps of the sickle closer to me. For a moment, I consider leaving it here, but I can't dream of parting with it.

Outside, the musk of Tenebrae finds me. Sunshine tries to break through the gray clouds, casting a lavender hue over the frost-bitten land. A pile of gore and limbs are deposited next to the front step, my shadow hounds guarding their prey from anything and everything. Gathering all the gore in a velvet bag, I summon a portal to Xannoroth to another decision I can only pray doesn't have the same consequences as the last.

I rarely venture to this part of Umber—the place of debauchery and temptation. Unlike the other parts of the city, there aren't people pushing carts, trying to sell their goods, or merchants yelling about their newest prices. The acrid smell of body odor and urine waltzes in the air, the scorching heat significantly making it worse.

There's a small opening between two buildings, a man and woman standing at the entrance with a three-skull tattoo on their biceps. The woman finds me first and whispers to the man. My eyes track their movements and the number of daggers they have on their bodies. Six on each of them. Moving closer, they step out of my way. Ominous dread settles on my shoulders as they turn to follow me.

In the narrow passageway, barely large enough to fit my wings, there's a large, wooden black door with a giant skull over it, chunks of wood missing from it, and a crooked sign overhead. The words "Fools Tavern" is written in a dried, brownish-red substance.

The man reaches around me to knock on the door, his elbow clipping against the muscle of my wing. I bite my lip to keep from hitting him. A small window with iron bars in the door opens. A woman with blonde hair stands on the other side. She slams the small window shut before the sound of locks clicks open, and the door swings.

The woman on the other side is short; her head reaches the center of my chest. Her eyes are full and round with deep, crimson-colored irises. Half of her head is shaved, and she has a golden hoop in each of her nostrils and another bar through her eyebrow. She looks me up and down like she wants to devour me.

Another time, I muse to myself.

"They've been expecting you," she says, swatting her hand against my ass. I clench my teeth. At least give me the decency of asking if I want it.

I step away from her, focusing on anything other than the unwanted looks and the stench of stale ale, vomit, and piss. Unlike the lava stone outside, the floors here are ebony hardwood, the bar and walls made of the same dark wood. Broken stools lie scattered across the room. One splintering leg is stained with blood along its hard tip. Some patrons have their heads against the wobbly tables. Through the thin barred windows, the sun casts narrow strips of light in the dim room. Everyone in here bears the same mark—three skull tattoos on their arms.

The woman who smacked my ass approaches. I lean away from her, and she rolls her eyes before guiding me toward a secluded hallway. There's another red door at the end.

"The leaders are through there," she says.

Pushing into the room, three people sit at a round table, yellowing pages scattered across its surface, a dagger stabbed in the middle. The man in the center rises from his high-backed chair. Dark gray hair crops close to his head, exposing the three-skull tattoo etched along the side. Deep wrinkles crease his forehead and gather around his eyes, dark patches discoloring his copper skin. His outfit is meant for royalty—a high black ruffled collar and a tailcoat in a slightly different shade of black. The darkest black belongs to his high trousers. I bite my tongue from telling him the shades don't match.

The woman and man on both sides share a striking resemblance to the one in the middle. Like him, the woman is wearing clothes fit for a ball. Rich auburn hair is braided at the crown of her head, and a black gown with long lace sleeves drapes to the floor. A crimson shade colors her full lips.

The man on the left is the only one who looks like an assassin. Four daggers are sheathed in baldrics crossed over his chest; two more are at his waist. Black leather pants and a matching vest cling to him. Like the other two, he has crimson eyes.

My family's history is royal blood tied to a historic throne—*this* family's legacy is fear.

"The Dead Prince of Tenebrae," the man in the middle says, lowering at the waist.

The two on the sides glance at who I assume is their father before following his lead. My throat tightens at the respect they show for who I'm supposed to be. But it isn't about me; it's about the daughter and son falling in behind their father as he stands in the center—a natural sign of leadership among them. A position I've always held, with my brother's flanking my left and right sides.

"You know my name, yet I don't know yours," I say.

"I am Magnus, the faction leader of the Mark of Death. This is my daughter, Annabelle, and my son, Thorne," he says.

"And you knew I would come, Magnus?" I ask.

"About a week ago, two men came to ask for aid against three men—one with raven wings. I told them to let it go, but during the debrief, those same two men and four others were gone. I figured it was only a matter of time the infamous Dead Prince would show up." He walks around the table, his fingers gripping a long black cane with a silver snake head at the handle, dragging his left leg as dead weight.

"One of those men nearly killed my brother," I grit out.

"If you didn't end their lives, we would have." Magnus leans his waist against the table. "I don't like having my people out of line."

Swinging the bag of gore over my shoulder, I toss it to the ground. It lands with a wet *thud.* Blood splashes between us. "I've come to deliver a message." I step toward him. "If any of your faction enter Tenebrae without my knowledge or permission, you will be killed. If any more of your people try to retaliate and come after my brothers and me again, I promise you will learn the true definition of fear." My finger lashes firmly against the center of his chest.

Thorne steps between us.

"Annabelle, Thorne, leave us," Magnus says.

Their mouths move to protest, but with a wave of their father's hands, they nod, leaving us alone; a neat trick I wish I could use against my own brothers.

"I don't like making enemies, Erebus. Certainly not when it pertains to royalty." He crosses his arms. "This faction—myself in-cluded—is indebted to you."

"I don't want or need your debt," I say. It feels like blood money. Nearly killing my brother only to offer a favor—one that I'm sure comes with strings attach.

"You have it regardless." Magnus takes another shaky step for-ward. "And please know, if you ever want to renounce your throne, you have a place here. Our faction is one of the strongest. I could even consider stepping down if someone like you were to take my place."

"My Fate was decided long before my birth," I say. "And I highly doubt your people would agree with my ideals when it comes to be-ing an assassin."

Magnus nods, walking around the gore to the front door. "If you ever change your mind." He opens it to let me out.

Before leaving, I stare him directly in the eyes, unleashing a tendril of my power. "Heed my warnings, Magnus, or I will slaughter your entire faction—starting with your children."

As the door closes behind me, I hear him faintly say, "You'll make a great king."

His words ring in my head as I prepare to return home to my

brothers. To rule over the small town we built. Speak with Micah over my brazen idea of bargaining with the Fates. Create a plan on how to seize the throne back. There's little of what I know about my uncle, but he hasn't held power this long without being paranoid. Some travelers tell us of the dark knights who are lethally trained to guard the Onyx Palace. There are a lot of unknowns regarding the place I once called home and the uncle I once thought was family. And it's because of all these negative thoughts that keep me in the city of Umber for a little longer. I doubt my suddenly seldom mood would be good for my brother's healing.

Leaving the tavern of the Mark of Death's den, I search for a tavern with the finest of Smutton—cherry whiskey native to Xannoroth.

Twenty-Nine

Melania

Wicked white, shimmering flames like temptation and chaos twine together in a dangerous waltz, moving closer to me. And it's mine to wield, control, and bend to my will—so intoxicating that I find myself understanding why my mother would want to keep this all to herself.

"Feel the energy," Albus says behind me as he guides my movements alongside his instructions, teaching me the ways of control, urging me to push past the fear and accept what has always been mine. From the moment we portaled to the top of the mountain connecting to the volcano, we were training. First, deep breathing techniques he insists I do regularly. Telling me it can calm my nerves and keep myself steady when controlling elements greater than my being—elements like fire.

Raising my hand, the fire nears closer, enclosing us in a ring of flame. Heat licks my skin, but it doesn't burn. It welcomes me into its warm embrace, like the first kiss of sunlight after a long, hard winter.

Flames caress my hands as I pull more of it in, blossoming heat in my chest as ownership washes over me. We've been training every waking moment, and this feeling never gets old; I hope it never does.

Sweat dances over the tops of my lips and eyebrows. Within the fiery flames, I can understand why others fear it; destruction ready to steal and consume the land around. To me, there is beauty. The embers seek air to breathe, kindling to burn, only for survival. My lips curve, discovering kinship with this uncontrollable, glittering spark, as if I, too, am a flame.

"Now for the hard part," Albus says, adoration in his tone. "Dismiss them, Melania."

He's right—this is always the hardest part.

Squaring my shoulders, I take in a large breath of air. The breeze swirls around the power within me, calling to me to continue wielding. Then, I release all the rage and sorrow I feel for myself and for the others who have been wronged by my mother.

"Stay calm," he says.

"I'm trying," I grit through clenched teeth.

His large hand finds the top of my shoulder, the weight a comfort I find solace in, a clear reminder I am not alone—and I'm safe. That alone grants me enough courage to turn away from the power trying to take control.

Stop.

A single commandment. I'm not sure if I say it aloud or in my head— the flames lower to the ground all the same, seeping into the lava bed as if they know that's where they belong.

Albus claps, starting with a slow beat to a fast crescendo. "I am so proud of you." A bright smile touches his face, revealing one deep dimple in his right cheek as red power swirls in his eyes. "Did you know fire is the hardest to control?" he says, crossing his arms over his chest.

"You might have mentioned that a time or two," I reply, wiping away the white aura glowing around my hand.

"Melania, you're a natural at wielding fire. I once saw your mother strain ten times trying to conjure her first flame."

I've never seen my mother wield fire before. She's quick to draw air and water. The latter I struggle the most with. I still can't conjure a drop in my hand, but he said if I am near the element, it is easier to wield. Albus keeps telling me that different magic comes naturally depending on our lineage. I kind of figured all magic would work for me considering my seeped-in-tradition bloodline.

"What do you know of my grandparents?" It's a question I've longed to know. Easier to ask about that than my paternal side—at least I think so.

"Omnia Maragret Zohar was a kind and gentle soul, much like you," he says nudging his shoulder against mine. "She loved the people and the kingdoms, but she loved one thing more."

"My mother?" I practically scoff. Wouldn't that be a treat if my grandmother were doting to her daughter, while mine is monstrous?

Albus glances over my head at the breathtaking view. "She loved her Fated, Cedric, more than anything." Sadness weighs heavily in his voice making, it deeper. "King Cedric was not as kind as she. He certainly wasn't kind to his Fated or your mother. I believe he was envious of their magic. He could wield air, but what was that to an Omnia?"

"A vicious cycle I was born into." I reach for my water filled costrel, but I'm stopped as Albus turns me to face him.

His hands grip my biceps, his magma-colored eyes bouncing between mine. "Your mother went through a lot in her childhood before Cedric died. It doesn't excuse how she is treating you. Melania, you were born into the cycle of abuse, and your mother was too afraid to stand against it. Right now, you training your magic, granting Lord Byron mercy, offering Elara and the others kindness is a step in breaking the same cycle. A cycle your mother was too much of a coward to stand against."

"Why didn't Omnia Maragret do anything against him?" I ask, needing to know that piece of the puzzle.

"Love is a powerful medicine. It can make you ignore people's true nature," he scoffs in a deprecating kind of way. "Come on, let's get back."

The view from here is breathtaking as the coast of Brilore crashes against the firm ground. A waterfall rushes powerful energy into the lake below. We've been training here since the sudden rain I summoned in Tenebrae, a detail he nor I want to discuss, though my mind snags on it. My mother told me when I was young that our magic doesn't work in or near Tenebrae—another thing she's lied about.

Albus creates the portal to the entrance of the palace. Guards lower, and I'm becoming accustomed to it—even learning more about them. Kiara and Kyan are members of the king's royal guard deployed in the city. They're his eyes and ears, visiting the palace to report on a faction of assassins. I never knew there were different factions. It makes me wonder which group was targeting me.

"Princess Priscia—"

Kyan rushes forward, cutting Albus from his thought. We both stop as the guard approaches, sweat beading on the bare skin of his shoulders, braids knotted and out of place, as if he'd been twisting them. It's strange seeing him without his sister, as they often travel as a pair. His wild gaze falls on me before moving to Albus. My heart pounds, fretting over what threat could be this dire.

He leans close to the king's ear. I tune my senses to the words, only to hear breathy mumbling. King Albus wrings his hands together, though his face remains neutral as I sigh, tensing my own shoulders.

"Thank you, Kyan," he says.

Kyan nods, leaving with the same speed he came with it.

Albus's gaze lowers to me, and my chest tightens. "Ire has been found." His ashy voice fills with pure dread and terror.

A hand grips my heart, the beat thundering irregularly. *When they are caught, I will be the one to judge them in the city of Omnius.* My mother's threat rings in my ears. Ire will become an example—as Baker was—tried as an adult, though she's not even old enough to have her monthly blood.

"Where is she?" I ask, afraid of what could happen to the little girl.

"Within the palace walls," Albus responds.

My feet move steadily as he remains a step behind, allowing me to handle this on my own; to judge the child in the way I see fit. And I should want to punish her. Make Ire hurt for the way she hurt me, but I won't.

I will not continue the cycle of abuse—starting with the judge-ment of Ire. What my mother doesn't know won't kill her—even if it might kill me.

King Albus takes the lead to the throne room—the one area I have not been to in the palace. Outside of training, I spend my time in my bed chambers resting or journaling. Other times, I am in the library, devouring as much information as I can while I have the chance.

There's a grand, sparkling chandelier made of rubies and three large red windows with a sharp arch basking the room in a red hue. A giant throne grows from the foundation on a dais with two smaller flanking each side, each with a fire emblem made from rubies, amber, and citrine—a bright contrast to the dark ash gray of the rock. There's a circular dip in the ground where I assume the patrons stand to speak with the royals. Above the room, a catwalk blends in with the surroundings.

Heavy doors close softly behind us. I don't fight to keep from biting my nails. I've admitted to murdering a man and creating an Omnia artifact to Albus, so I highly doubt my nail biting will scare him off.

On the other side of the room, a smaller door groans open, and two guards wearing their bronze armor pull Ire forward. The intake of my breath is quick and harsh at the sight of her: torn beige gown, scabs on her legs, arms, and lip, with sticks and mud matted in her hair, darkening the strands.

Her steps are hesitant as she approaches, jaw tight, and hands shaking. She's terrified, and I can understand why. As she makes her way toward us, I realize I'm looking at a younger version of myself.

"Once more you have disobeyed me," Mother said in her not-so-nice voice.

She stood behind her marbled glass desk. There was a weirdly shaped rope, where one end was hard like a handle, the other strappy. I'd never seen such a thing.

"I have been kind to you for far too long, Melania," she hissed through her teeth.

The red of her sharp nail scratched against the glass, and it hurt my ears. Someone entered behind me—General Javon, with a twisted smile on his face. He stood in front of the door. I didn't realize I had stopped walking until my mother's sharp nails dug into my arm. She pulled me to the edge of her desk to face the door. Cold air hit my back, and I wondered if my mother used her powers to make it so.

"Breaking you will be for the greater good," she said.

A whoosh seared pain against my back. No matter how hard I begged and cried, she didn't let up. General Javon continued smiling, like my pain amused him. My back burned when she finished.

"Our actions have consequences Melania," she said, shoving me towards the door.

I choked on snot and tears as I barely made it into the hall.

The heavy door closed behind me, and their laugher muffled through, followed by a sound of something I didn't know. I stumbled to my room, trying to figure out what I did wrong so I could never do it again.

Truth is, I never did anything wrong—that thought jars me to the moment. I bit a particularly painful part of my nail, forcing it to bleed. Ire bows in front of us, whimpering, her hands trying to catch the falling tears.

My breath shakes as I lower to my knees, the ground cold beneath me, and I grab Ire's small hands, pulling them from her face.

"I am so sorry," she cries.

My heart breaks for this small child as she sobs, and I don't know how to make it stop. Glancing over my shoulder at Albus, he's watching to see what I will do next. Will I rule like my mother, or start a new way of life for the greater good? My arms move around her small, shaking frame, holding her against me as I rub a hand over her back. Wetness soaks into the shoulder of my white tunic. Only when she stops does she pull away from me with streaks over her dirty cheeks.

"Is your brother Nihil?" I ask.

"Y-Yes, his family took me in," she chokes out, using the back of her arm to wipe away her snot.

"And your family?" I ask.

"My mama and papa were killed. Wrath barely got me out before he was taken by a man in white armor." She shakes once more.

Stop with the personal questions, I think to myself.

"How do you know your brother is in Tenebrae?" I ask.

"He ran away from the captives and sent word from there."

I look over to King Albus to gauge his reaction—he has none. This could be more information about the Three. "I see, now why did you harm me?"

"Because you sent my brother to the land of monsters." She

works on a swallow. "My anger gets the best of me, that's what Wrath always said."

I fight the smile, realizing her name is Ire, and his is Wrath. It makes me want to meet him.

"I am sorry for the loss of your parents and for your brother being taken," I say. Her eyes widen, as she clearly didn't expect an apology from me. "But our actions have consequences." It's the same phrase my mother has said to me repeatedly with each punishment. Except I get to decide to be different from her. A better, stronger version of myself my mother never could break.

She nods. From behind, King Albus bristles.

"But since you know what you did is wrong, there will not be a punishment."

They both release a large breath, like they were waiting for my judgement.

"If you promise to never stab me again, I will help you find your brother," I whisper.

Wide eyes focus on me, and Ire is practically holding in her excitement.

"How about we find my dear friend, Elara, and she can help you bathe and find something to eat," I say.

Moving to my full height, I pull on the velvet string near the door. I'm not surprised when Elara comes sweeping into the room, eyes glossy from her own tears. I could laugh if I didn't cry as often as she does.

"Elara, meet Ire. Ire, meet Elara." I gesture between the two of them.

Elara begins to guide her from the room, but before she goes, I hear a whispering of, "Thank you, Omnia Melania."

The smile on my face comes naturally, but it's gone when I turn toward King Albus, shifting myself from the caring Omnia Melania. He has information, and I need it.

"Tell me everything about Tenebrae and the Three."

Thirty

Erebus

Many people throw sideways glances my way as some whisper curses under their breaths about my wings and the blood on my clothes. Others yell for me to watch it. I'm too gone in my head to care.

Some buildings look worse than they did a week ago. Large cracks in the ground crawl up the sides of marketplaces and inns. The tavern I've been trying to make my way toward has two major splits. All of them leading back to a single crater in the ground—a purple flower growing from the middle of it. This is what must have caused the shake in Nobyl. I kneel at the sight, wondering what could have caused the size of this without taking down the fragile infrastructure.

A small tantrum, I think to myself.

I'm about to stand when a man runs straight into me, toppling me to the ground. His heavy foot lands against the edge of my wing. I groan at the flare of pain. I'm ready to give him a lecture in manners only to see him join the crowd of men outside the tavern.

Consider my interest piqued to see what these small-minded folks are pushing against each other to witness. At the edge of the crowd, a few people brush against my wings, and I grit my teeth. One man jumps on my back, pinching them painfully against my body. My elbow jeers back before I can stop it. I hear the crunch of bone, a wail, then outrage from the witnesses. Some help the man to his feet while I continue to push toward the tavern entrance. I'm then thrust forward into another man. The man I collide with shoves me. I am tossed from one set of arms to another, barely able to keep my footing in the throng.

My shin slams against the stairs, and I don't remember climbing this far. I straighten my shirt and turn to face the crowd, ready to tell them exactly what I think of their immature behavior. But I stop short when a small hand caresses the center of my wings.

"Hello, Erebus," whispers a woman with a voice like sweet venom. Her tongue flicks against my ear.

"Princess Priscia," I muse.

She intertwines her fingers through mine, pulling me inside the building. Princess Priscia is temptation wrapped in silk. Her red gown drapes to the floor, one meant for court and not a tavern, and it hugs her hourglass curves. Then again, I know her well enough to know the ruby encrusted gown is to draw attention to herself. Her thin, fiery eyes are enunciated by black lines on her top and bottom lashes, lips painted a bright red to match the color of her power. Priscia's black, wavy hair cascades to the middle of her back. On the top of her head is a bronze tiara with a medium ruby in the center of the swirls.

"Close the door," she says to a guard in bronze armor as we pass.

He doesn't hesitate. Through the small gap in his helmet, I can see joy in his eyes, like he can't believe Princess Priscia gave him an ounce of her attention. She pulls me onto a barstool, keeping our hands together.

The tavern is a decent size, but it couldn't handle the bustling crowd outside. It's made from dark gray cobblestone, the ground from an endless supply of lava rock. We sit in the middle of the ebony bar where a woman with short black hair and crimson eyes works to clean the glasses, feigning nonchalance despite the two royals in front of her. There's a glass of amber whiskey with red lipstick on the rim on the counter. Muffled voices wishing to change places with me carry through the room.

"What brings you here?" I ask.

"Should I not be asking you the same?" Her voice is proper compared to the lax speaking of Tenebrae, carrying an eastern accent.

The barmaid approaches, but I send her away with a curt nod. She practically runs, and I can't help but roll my eyes.

"Why don't you have glass?" Priscia purrs, her other hand coming to move a strand of my hair from my face.

"I like to keep my wits about me," I say.

Princess Priscia releases a mischievous grin, running her ruby red fingertips over her flushing skin. "I remember many times when you've indulged in losing your wits."

"That was then, this is now," I say, taking my hand from hers.

There was once a time when we indulged in each other on more than one occasion. We spent our days drinking all the finest Smutton until the sun sank low, only to indulge in our more decadent desires at night. I've come to learn it wasn't healthy for either of us. She was a princess trying to hide her wild nature from the prying, judgmental people of Xannoroth, who had plenty to say about how a princess should behave. I was a prince trying to escape the dark corners of my own mind. It seems she has stopped hiding, showing the city of Umber who their next queen will be. All the while, I'm still trying to run from thoughts that will one day consume me.

Priscia wraps her long fingers around her glass, consuming the whole shot of Smutton, never showing a reaction, then raises her finger to signal for another glass.

"Where are your—" She pats away the bead of sweat from my forehead. "What do you call them? Oh right, your brothers."

"Lelantos was injured, and Micah is tending to him," I say.

"I'm surprised Micah let you go off on your own. He's supposed to be your friend, not your father." Her tone carries condescendence as she speaks about the man whom I have to thank for saving my life time and time again.

I click my tongue and push out of the stool. There were times in our relationship when she would get like this, looking down upon my brothers for their lack of royalty. I wonder why Princess Priscia can be so cruel when her father is King Albus.

"Wait," she says, reaching for my hand once more. "I apologize, Erebus, truly."

I allow her heavy, saddened eyes to pull me back to our spot.

Princess Priscia drinks the other shot, staring at the many bottles behind the bar.

"My father would like my mother and me to accompany him for dinner with Omnia Melania." She says her name mockingly.

"And that's a problem, why?" I ask.

"They're vile women." She raises her finger for yet another glass and throws the shot back before speaking again. "Taking whoever and whatever they want because they can, and my father *lets* them. It's the reason my mother no longer lives in the palace, you know? She grew tired of being the other woman when all he wants is Omnia Itzel. I may be the heiress to his throne, but it's his firstborn daughter from the woman he truly desires that he loves most."

I try to keep my face neutral, but my wide eyes betray me. The truth slams into me. It explains his evasive behavior and why he sent us away so quickly. I knew it involved Omnia Melania, but I didn't understand why he was trying to keep it a secret. He was afraid that the truth of their relationship would come out.

"That cannot leave this tavern," Priscia says, eyes frantic.

I raise my hands in surrender, but the server's jaw gapes open.

"If any word of that leaves this tavern, I will see to you that you are hung from the palace walls with a T carved in your chest for attempting to assassinate me," Princess Pricisa says, pointing her sharp nail at the woman.

She said Omnias were vile, but the threat came easily from her lips. The woman nods her head and mumbles something like "yes, princess" before fleeing to another room, followed by whimpering behind the closed door.

"Why must you attend dinner?" I ask, trying to steer the conversation in another direction.

"I cannot deny my father's request." Her eyes widen as she looks at me. "Unless I bring someone to attend with me."

"My brothers need me back," I say to her, more as a reminder to myself. I've already been gone for too long.

"You never did say why they aren't with you, or what you're doing in the city," she says, a hint of suspicion in her tone, as if I'm keeping secrets.

For a moment, I consider lying about why I'm alone, but I trust Princess Priscia—even if I dislike some of her other qualities. I take a deep breath and explain the attack against my brothers and me, carefully avoiding the part about them only being able to attack because I wasn't with them.

"Was he stable?" Her tone is lax, like she's talking about the weather and not the condition of my only family.

"I don't know if I would consider unconscious as stable," I snap.

"Erebus," she says, rubbing her hands over my forearms, "I'm not trying to offend you, but there is life outside of your brotherhood. Perhaps, if you opened your eyes to that reality, you might have realized that I have powerful healers, whom I'm willing to share as long as you ask."

"Can you spare your royal healers to help save my brother's life?" I ask.

Princess Priscia leans forward, revealing the expanse of her dark brown chest. "Come to dinner with me tonight, and they're all yours," she whispers, her tongue darting out over the fiery red of her lips.

I don't know what I was expecting from her. Perhaps that she might have remembered how close we used to be. Then again, this could be a punishment for not answering the last three letters she sent.

"Won't your father be upset with my sudden arrival?" I hope mention of her father gives her clarity of mind to be a decent person.

"He's always been fond of you, Erebus. Spend dinner with us, and my three pureblood, Veilian healers will accompany you to Tenebrae to tend to Lelantos."

"Fine, but the minute we're done, I'm leaving," I bite.

She pats my cheek in a patronizing way, as if to say, *good boy*. I do a similar mannerism to Damsel, Butcher, Ripper, and Reaper—the names I gave to my shadow hounds on the walk here.

"I'll see you soon, Erebus Ravenheart," she says, her plump lips kissing the side of my cheek.

The guard from earlier opens the door for her. She walks away with a sway in her hips. I'm still watching even as the door shuts behind her. The bustling crowd from outside diminishes, leaving the tavern silent and still. I'm left reeling from what I've done. Choosing to go to dinner to have access to healers was a smart idea. Staying gone for a few more hours may not be, but it feels necessary. A pulsing at my back nearly spirals me as I realize I didn't consider the potent Omnia artifact strapped behind me as I prepare to eat dinner with its creator. All the while, I'll have to converse with Omnia Melania while resisting the urge to ask her why she killed Lord Byron. Why she left the sickle behind.

I don't ask before reaching behind the bar to grab a bottle of

Smutton. I pour more than I should into the glass Princess Priscia was drinking from. I consider drinking directly from the bottle, but I'm not an animal.

I drink three shots, savoring the sweet burn of the liquor. Wallowing in my self-pity, I pray nothing happens in my absence while a tight weight settles in my chest, as if everything and nothing are about to change—and I'm the catalyst.

Melania

The throne is cold beneath my legs. A sea of people watch as Lord Byron kneels before me. His white tunic soaks with green and red from the blood. I'm more than pleased by the metallic scent in the air. Inching forward, I step over a body without a head, red blood pooling around. I scoop the blood into my steady hands, wiping it against my face, licking it. The taste is a sweet concoction in my mouth. Lord Byron cries, begging me to do something, but I already did. I killed his sons because they deserved it—lesser beings who deserve to die by my hand. Lord Byron wails over his sons, and I grow weary of the sound. My fists clench, and his eyes bulge as the air is sucked from his lungs—the melody of his choking gasps pleasant on my ears. But nothing compares to feeling his life slip away at my hand.

The door opens with two guards entering—General Javon and another I don't care enough about to know. I smile at Javon, warmth spreading within me. The two men approach with a man with black wings bound by golden chains, eyes swollen, and his lip split.

"The Dead Prince of Tenebrae," I say, but it doesn't sound like me. It's calloused and colder.

Heat spreads in my hands from where I wield my special blade, white flames billowing around it as it allows me to conjure two magics at once. The man's dark black eyes widen at the sight of it.

"You've been betraying the ultimate ruler. Taking matters into your own hands when it was never yours to have." I sneer.

My shoes clink against the marble floor, my dress hissing until the blood catches the fabric, trailing behind me. With my free hand, I grip the bottom of the man's chin, then I face him and everything shifts.

It's no longer the Dead Prince of Tenebrae, but a woman with pale moonlit skin and long black hair falling to the top of her waist. Silver eyes like stars have made a home on her face. Her presence steals my very breath as she comes to stand to her full height.

"Is that what you want to become, Omnia Melania?" she hisses.

The nightmare incarnate blinks, and orbs of black reflect my image in her eyes; blood streaks my face like war paint. My mother stares back at me, eyes taunting as if this is the future I swore I wouldn't do. I back away from her dominating darkness, tripping over Lord Byron's body on my advance to get out. A large gash rips through his throat as I fall against my back.

"There's hope after all," he says, choking on blood spewing from the wound.

I wake to bile in my throat. Unable to fight it, I rush to the bathroom, emptying the contents of my lunch. Tears streak down my face as I heave, but nothing more comes up. From the nearest clean water bucket, I splash water over my sweaty skin. In the ripples, I see myself for who I am; not who I am meant to be.

Legs unsteady, I make my way into the bedroom when I feel a tug in the center of my chest, one I've become far too familiar with. Closing my eyes to focus on the extension of myself, the bright white cord pulls taut with light shining all around it; the closest it's ever been.

With my eyes still closed, I take a step forward when a hard object slams into my face, hitting my nose. I jerk back, pinching the bridge as my eyes water.

"I am so sorry," Ire says.

Her little head peeks around the corner, but she moves to Elara's side, who has a garment bag draped over her arm. She hangs it on the door and rushes to my side, leading me to the vanity. I try to swat her away as there was no need for a guide, and I desperately want to chase down that short tendril to demand answers—a feat I am not granted as Elara pushes me into the white cushioned stool. Her hands plop on the top of my shoulders. I've come to accept Elara's touch—but only hers. Ire falls on my bed, feet kicking as they don't quite reach the ground. Her hair is done with two buns on top of her head.

"King Albus has asked for me to help you ready for dinner," Elara says.

A storm conjures in my chest, and I force deep breaths. I need to find that sickle, but it'll have to be after dinner. Albus was too excited about this night, and I don't want to disappoint him. Especially not after he was vulnerable enough to tell me the whole truth about his connection to the Three; how those men have been saving and harboring Nihils, even if it could get them killed. I have respect for those men wanting to make a change, but I also have no doubt they are harboring the sickle—*my* sickle. Why else would I feel the tendril connecting to them?

Elara finishes with my hair, leaving it down in sweeping waves. She adds a pink pigment to my cheeks, liquid charcoal in a thin line on my eyelids, enhancing the rainbow in more vibrant hues, and a light berry pink pigment on my lips. I turn to show Ire the finished look, but she has long since fallen asleep, her small body hanging halfway off the bed.

"Thank you for caring for her," I say.

Elara follows where my eyes are focused on the little girl with a steady rise and fall to her small chest, and a soft snore escaping her.

"I didn't want to like her." She swallows. "She stabbed my dearest friend, but I, too, have shared the thoughts of wanting to stab an Omnia."

I stifle a laugh, trying not to disturb the child. I must admit that I have also considered taking an axe to cut off my mother's head. Seems we all have the urge to harm an Omnia. I'm surprised the youngest of us was the one to achieve it.

A heavy, sharp pull still roots itself in my chest, reminding me of the tendril once again, but I have to get through the dinner. Then Albus can help me get back what it is mine.

With my hair done, it comes to wearing something other than pants. Untying the bag, the air in my lungs tighten at the sight of the white gown. I didn't think I would feel this overwhelming joy for another white dress, except this one was made for me—not the version of myself my mother wants me to be.

I cloak myself in the coolest silk of the gown. The gauze of the tulle catches between my fingers As Elara laces the back, tightening it to my figure. My other hand grazes the golden spiral embellishments along the bodice and upper bust with the lowest neckline I've ever worn—yet I've never felt more beautiful. Thick straps embellish the shoulders with similar spirals, and another two connecting long tulle sleeves.

Elara steps back when she's finished, beaming. "Marvelous."

"We're forgetting something," I say.

Elara puts a hand over her chest, feigning offense. She raises her fingers to count down but stops when I raise the gown, revealing my pale feet, stark against the red rug. Elara rushes to the closet, returning a second later with a pair of silk slippers. She places them on the floor, allowing me to step into them.

"Now you're marvelous and must leave for supper," she says.

Elara escorts me out. The slippers are nearly silent against the lava rock floor, unlike the clunky leather boots I wore earlier. Red light reflects from the ruby chandeliers.

Servants bow as I pass them, whispering to each other. Unlike before, I don't feel the need to cower at their hushed tones. In this gown and within this palace, I've never felt more confident. Three weeks in Xannoroth, and this place is already more of a home to me than Omnius will ever be. Descending the stairs, there are more servants ushering into the dining hall. When I reach the bottom, I dare to close my eyes in search of that tendril.

It glows brighter than it ever has. My mouth waters at the taste of lilac essence surrounding my power—around the idea of having the sickle wholly mine once more. The tips of my fingers rub against the magic, but a hissing sound pulls me back to the present.

My eyes open wide, trying to find where the sound came from. I take a step back only to see hooded eyes as dark as night, strands of black hair swaying over the top of wide shoulders. A man wearing dark trousers and a matching black tailcoat with intricate silver swirls and two daggers with one gold and one silver handle, sheathed at his side. His raven wings reflect blue and purple amongst all the darkness. He displays his sharp sanguine fangs for all to see.

I move to approach him; to demand back what is mine, but King Albus steps in front of me, Queen Pria and Princess Priscia flanking his sides. As a unit, they lower at the waist—bowing to me. The overwhelming attention on me dissipates when the dead prince of Tenebrae lowers, revealing a white, glowing light on the nape of his neck.

Erebus

Burning erupts in my back as I bend at the waist. I knew there was a risk bringing the sickle so close to her, but I didn't expect it to burn this much. My attention fixes on her, and I'm completely, utterly enamored. Amongst the Xannoroth royals wearing red—myself in black—she's the only one in white. She wore leather pants that were too large for her back in Umber. In Omnius, her nightgown had been covered in blood-infused mud. But here and now—she's Omnia Melania, the future of Veilia—and the daughter of Omnia Itzel and King Albus. That alone is enough to draw my attention from her scrutinizing rainbow eyes.

"Shall we sit?" King Albus says, reaching out his arm for Omnia Melania. He does the same for Princess Priscia, who humphs before taking it. Queen Pria comes to my side, taking my other arm, and giving me a tight-lipped smile like any queen trying to avoid scandal.

A grand ruby chandelier hangs overhead, a bright flame burning at its heart. Like the rest of the palace, the walls are dark gray. The grand table beneath it stretches long, its bronze legs supporting a thick slab of ruby polished to a glassy shine. Bronze dinner plates gleam across its surface, catching the firelight. Eccentric candle holders run the length of the table, flames flickering in uneven rhythm. Five high-backed chairs surround it, each fitted with a vibrant red cushion complimenting the orange sheen of metallic bronze frames.

King Albus directs Omnia Melania to the head of the table. Five servers enter from a side door—two men wearing long, black, frilly-collared shirts with a red vest over them and a different shade of black pants. The other two men wear red, knee-length gowns with a black apron on top. The final servant—a woman with a braided bun—wears a burnt orange gown with a white apron over it. Her eyes widen at the sight of my presence before she focuses solely on Omnia Melania. A quick glance passes between them, the kind that says everything without a word, the same way Micah and I speak about Lelantos without him knowing.

The female servant pulls out the chair at the head of the table, nudging her head to Omnia Melania to sit. King Albus directs her into the seat by the middle of her back, and Princess Priscia scoffs, rolling her eyes. She stomps around the table to sit beside me, moving her mother to claim the chair next to King Albus.

Once seated, all the servants disappear into the other room. A silence blankets our space, thick like swimming in the sludged, seaweed infested swamps of Tenebrae. My chair scratches against the ground as I try to situate my wings in the uncomfortable seat, awkwardly slicing the quiet. The tips of my feathers touch against Omnia Melania's biceps—our eyes widening from the contact.

"I apologize," I say.

"Not necessary," she replies, her voice like the taste of fresh rainfall—cool and enchanting.

King Albus' throat bobs as he gulps. Omnia Melania picks at the nailbed of her other hand with thin fingers. Micah does that often. Perhaps that's the only reason I say, "I am Erebus Ravenheart."

"I am quite aware of who you are," she says.

My shoulders tense through the recognition. I prepare to ask her how she knows me, but the servants come in, holding trays. They place the bronze domes in front of us, then lift it to reveal vegetable stuffed hen, sizzling broth from the blood of the creature dripping along the edges. My mouth wavers at the thought of the first delectable bite. Micah is a great cook, and Lelantos is an amazing hunter, but nothing beats that of a royal chef.

"Is our food not good enough for you?" Princess Priscia bites out.

Reluctantly pulling my eyes from the feast, I track where she's looking. In front of Omnia Melania is a medium-sized bowl with vegetable medley soup. A faint blush covers her cheeks as she glances at King Albus.

"Do you not eat meat?" I ask.

Omnia Melania directs her attention to me, the top of her teeth pulling on her plump bottom lip. "No, I am squeamish at the sight of blood," she says.

I nod, though my brows dip. She didn't seem ill when fleeing from the murder of Lord Byron, covered in the splatter of his green blood. I also wouldn't expect the daughter of Omnia Itzel to be weary of it. I'm sure Omnia Itzel bathes in it any chance she gets.

Omnia Melania's spoon clinks, the scrape of metal on glass sending a sharp ache through my fangs. I grit my teeth, forcing myself to ignore it.

"Omnia Melania, it is a pleasure to have you in Xannoroth," Queen Pria says, the same venom I heard from her daughter earlier heavy in her voice.

Princess Priscia sips her wine. "Though I wonder why you came here on such short notice."

Omnia Melania pats at the side of her mouth with her napkin. "I wanted to stay out of Princess La'Mia's way before her coronation."

I hadn't realized her coronation was vastly approaching—a sign of major change throughout Veilia. As a child, I remember servants used to whisper about the influx of royals having heirs. It started with the births of Elowen and Arya, the new princesses of Irolyn and Jeandrenia—newly crowned queens of the land of air and ice—followed by the birth of myself, Princess La'Mia and Omnia Melania. People believe it was the Fates' way of creating change.

"Would your guardian not want you there?" Queen Pria asks, before slurping up the bloody broth.

Omnia Melania's shoulders straighten, her eyes not breaking away from the spoon. "We haven't been that close."

"Is it because of her mother's unexpected death in the Omnius palace?" Priscia asks.

My eyes swing to her. Completely unbothered by her own question, she twirls a strand of her black hair, a devious smile dancing on her crimson red lips. I've seen her cruelty before, but nothing like this. Queen Gaia died suddenly during a trip to Omnius, one week after the death of my parents. The Great Cleansing Ordinance was enacted soon after her last rites were read.

"How are the Nihils settling in?" King Albus asks me from across the table.

My eyebrows lower over my eyes as I twitch my head toward Omnia Melania.

"She was there the day we saved them." He rips at a piece of meat. "Her own friend is a Nihil."

The servant in orange suddenly makes sense, but the rest of it does not. How can Omnia Melania respect the Nihils when she killed the father of one? I'm trying to reconcile what I know with what he's saying.

Queen Pria scoffs like she's trying to understand. "Father, you cannot be serious. Omnia Melania would rather filet her own flesh than show kindness to those she deems unworthy."

King Albus parts his lips, but it's Omnia Melania's voice that sounds through the room. "Can we not speak around me as if I'm not here?" she questions as a flare of white dances around her hands, heating the sickle against my back, drawing a hiss once more.

Her eyes fly to mine, and I realize she knows exactly what I have.

"I wonder what your mother would do with the knowledge we have about her precious daughter." Princess Priscia stands, sparks of fire dancing at her fingertips. "Perhaps your mother will force us to be silent like she does with everyone else, or perhaps she might behead us all and find a new ruler!"

"Priscia, that is enough!" King Albus shouts, standing away from the table. "I have raised you better than to treat a guest like this!"

"She's not a guest! She's my fucking half-sister!" Princess Priscia's chest rises and falls with each heavy breath.

Omnia Melania gasps before turning to King Albus as tears weigh heavy on the bottom of his eyelids.

Queen Pria moves to comfort Princess Priscia, with fire still billowing at the edge of her fingertips.

"I shall take my leave now," I say—fuck the healers and the fancy meal. All I want is to be with an uncomplicated family who would make it through the first course—who need me more than these people do.

King Albus nods for my dismissal as he reaches for Omnia Melania. I stand, moving as fast as I can without running.

"Wait," Omnia Melania shouts.

I don't stop despite the urge to. The sickle sears painfully against me like it's trying to punish me for not giving it back. I reach the foyer, immediately summoning a portal, when the sound of slippers puts me on high alert.

Omnia Melania rests her hands on her hips, eyes lowered with a scowl on her face. Especially now, I find it hard to believe what King Albus described about her, nor can I begin to understand what he was trying to achieve. The portal continues to grow behind me. All I have to do is take one step back.

But I don't.

Not with her chest heaving and tears streaking down her face.

"Prince Erebus Ravenheart," she whispers, taking a step toward me, her voice broken like rescued Nihils whose strength had all but diminished because of situations outside of their control—situations caused by the Omnias.

She reaches her hand out expectantly. "You have what belongs to me."

A laugh escapes me at the audacity to think I would hand over an Omnia artifact without knowing whose side she stands on. "With all due respect, I will be keeping what you left behind." I take a smaller step back.

"You do not deserve to have it! It doesn't belong to someone like you," she says with a bite.

I nod and take the final step back into the portal.

Omnia Melania lunges for the sickle, trying to seize what doesn't belong to *someone* like me.

Thirty-Two

Melania

The heavy door of the library opens behind me. Elara enters, her burnt orange gown swaying with her motion. I rush her into a hug. Her arms wrap around me, allowing my head to rest against her shoulder—seeking comfort in the familiar.

"Are you okay?" she asks, her hand rubbing against my back.

I dwell over the answer. Physically, I'm perfect, but mentally and emotionally, I've been swept into a current, unable to get my feet underneath me. Pulling away from the embrace, I lead Elara to the red settee in the middle of the room.

Crackling embers of the fire mixed with our soft breaths bring comfort, though I still chew on my nails to form the words I need to—unlike how I did with Erebus. I couldn't understand why he seemed hurt by my words until I found solace in the library after. Only then did I realize how cruel what I said was, especially when he was nothing but nice to me during dinner—nothing like my apparent half-sister and stepmother. Another reality I'm not sure how to face.

Elara pulls my hand away from my mouth. My arms plop into my lap, leaving a drop of lilac scented blood in my white gown.

"King Albus is my father." I say the words despite the heaviness in my tongue. It's the first time I've said it out loud, and it's not as odd as I thought it would be. I should be hurt by the revelation, but I'm not. I think, deep down, a part of me is relieved that such a kind and respectable king is my father. Not that I can begin understanding how he came to be with as vile a woman as my mother.

"He's currently pacing outside the library," Elara says, glancing at the large door.

I thought I heard feet against the ground, but I assumed it was my own pacing. After dinner, I tried to flee to my bedroom, but Ire was still fast asleep—her tiny chest breathing followed by soft snores the sole reason I came here.

"I would like to speak with him," I say.

Elara squeezes my hand before asking, "Are you sure?"

I nod.

She stands from the couch, her soft slippers clicking against the ground. She stops shy of the door before turning to me. "I'll be waiting for you."

My lips turn to give her a close-lipped smile. Whispers trail outside the door before King Albus makes his way in, revealing puffiness around his eyes. I've never seen him appear unwell like this, not even when I was stabbed. Then, it was worry—now I can sense the fear of rejection in the furrowing of his brow and the shake of his hands.

"I should have told you sooner," he said, his voice cracking.

"I think I knew you were my father after I was stabbed," I admit more to myself than him. "No one has ever had the courage to stand up to my mother before. But what I don't understand is why you didn't tell me?"

Albus furthers into the room until he sits on the settee next to me, keeping a cushion between us. "When your mother told me she was pregnant, it wasn't out of joy but rather to tell me she wanted to get rid of you." He focuses on another part of the room, away from me. "I tried to protect you, but she threatened to create a tidal wave to destroy all of Xannoroth if I told or did anything to go against her plan."

"Life and royalty," I whisper.

Albus nods, pulling one of my hands between his. He dares to meet my eyes with years of pain harbored in one secret. Prying deeper into the hot magma, I know there are more secrets yet to be uncovered.

"I've spent my whole life wondering who my father could be, and I am grateful that it is you."

A *but* strains on the tip of my tongue. All I've ever wanted is to know there is someone else out there who could care for me. Yet, as I sit here appreciating this moment with Albus, all I can truly think about is Erebus and the weapon he carries.

"Prince Erebus has the sickle."

Albus jerks his head back. At least I'm not the only one surprised. Back in Umber, I knew there was a connection there, one confirmed when I saw it tonight, its presence calling me during the entire supper. Through each terse word and bite of food, all I wanted was the sickle in my grasp.

"Melania, if I had known, I would have done something about it," he says.

I believe him wholly. After I broke down in the field of greenery about Lord Byron and the sickle, he held me through tears. Comforted me by saying everything would be okay. Reminding me that the Fates know what they're doing. The former gave me the courage to continue training, but it's the latter wondering if the Fates brought us together for a reason.

"I would like to go get it," I say.

Albus shakes his head, his shoulders raising at the mere suggestion.

"I must figure out what the Fates want from me." I stand from the couch as I pace back and forth through a sudden adrenaline rush taking over me. Staying here to wallow and question what to do next isn't an option. Erebus has my sickle, and I need to get it back. I let it get away before—I won't allow it to happen again. The Fates decided I have an Omnia artifact; it's a destiny I need to see through.

Though I don't know what to do with it, I think to myself

"I'll go with you," Albus says matter-of-factly.

"I cannot risk your safety," I retort.

Albus stands from the settee with lowered brows and a deep set of penetrating eyes—the same expression he had while discussing my safety to my mother. His teeth clench so tightly, the muscles in his jaw ripple.

"Melania, I cannot risk *your* safety." He runs a hand through his hair. "If your mother knew, she would send an army to slaughter everyone in Tenebrae just to get you home. She would kill my entire family if I sent you to Tenebrae—"

"I am an Omnia, only one other person can kill me, and she will not know where I go." My voice raises an octave through determination. "I am neither asking nor wanting your permission. I fled Omnius because I feared what my mother might do if she knew about Lord Byron and the sickle." I take his hands in mine. "But I found strength and truth in Xannoroth. I cannot return to the marble palace without knowing what the Fates want from me!"

Albus's chest rises before exhaling deeply, moving strands of hair away from my face. "How will you even know where to go?"

"Erebus has the sickle, and I can track my way to it," I explain.

He looks over my head, still clenching his jaw until resignation relaxes the muscles in his face. Leaning his head back, he glances at the sky as if he's saying a prayer to a higher power. "You have to be at La'Mia's coronation by the end of the week," he finishes, quickly adding, "and when it's over, come back, so we can continue our training."

He pulls me into a tight hug, his chin pushing against the top of my head. A piece of my heart mourns for the younger version of myself who yearned for hugs—the girl who cried herself to sleep wondering why she was hated by her own family. I wish that child version of me could realize she wasn't hard to love, but the people in her life weren't capable of the kindness she deserved.

"I wouldn't dream of missing either," I say, holding back the tears as a rightness settles in my chest, healing a part of myself I didn't realize was broken—until now.

Breaking away, I leave the library with new hope blossoming in my chest. Elara presses her back to the wall, her head bumping against it with her eyes shut.

"I didn't hear a lot of crying," she says.

I stifle a laugh as I usher her to my room. My chambers are quite different from when I first arrived: the vanity covered in beauty products, books spilled around the room from all my reading. In the bed, Ire sleeps peacefully amongst the large blankets—nearly unseen. Sparing a glance in the mirror, I smile to see the added weight to my face and body, instilling confidence in my narrow shoulders, unwavering courage in my eyes.

"I am leaving for Tenebrae," I say to Elara.

She staggers away from me. "Excuse me."

Turning from the mirror, I explain what happened in the library with Albus and the conversation I had with Erebus—the way I said *someone like him* when I meant *no one but me* should have the sickle in their possession.

"You cannot leave on your own," Elara says. I yank at the fabric of my dress when her hands land on my shoulders. "Melania you cannot be as reckless to go to Tenebrae in the dead of night by yourself without an ounce of protection."

"Like I told Albus, I am an Omnia. Nothing can truly hurt me,"

I say.

Elara takes a quick step back, swirling me around to help me out of the gown and into a pair of leather pants, a long sleeve tunic, and a leather vest. Then she begins changing out of her own gown.

"What do you think you're doing?" I ask.

"I am going with you," Elara says, pulling on a pair of leather trousers. "You've never had someone give a shit about you, so I can understand your confusion. However, I will not allow my best friend to travel to Tenebrae without company. Whatever you're going to do, whether daft or completely clever, I will be going with you."

Her words completely throw me into a stupor. I didn't expect her to argue more than Albus did, nor would I expect her to jump at the opportunity to come with me, especially after the first time she portaled with me. Not that it will happen again after training in the art of control over creating and managing portals. I'm certainly not at the level Erebus is—then again, he's had to have had practice creating large, strong portals to bring entire groups of people.

"Elara," I say, resigning the argument. If I said it was too dangerous, she might take it as if I'm calling her weak. If I try to tell her I don't want her there, that would be a lie.

"You can't leave me, even if it means going to the land of nightmares," Ire's small, groggy voice says from behind us, blinking the sleep away from her eyes.

I didn't notice her stirring in the mound of white blankets. I glance at Elara, and she seems as stunned as I am while trying to grapple with excuses as to why she can't come.

"My brother, Wrath, will be excited to see me," she says, plopping to the ground from the bed.

Before Elara and I can explain the dangers to her—aside from the monsters—a knock sounds at the door.

Elara pulls herself and Ire out of view. I wouldn't know how to explain to anyone else why they're packing bags. Maybe that alone should be reason enough for them to stay. After a few steady breaths, I open the door.

King Albus stands on the other side. In his hands is a beautiful short sword. The blade is black, and set into the fuller rests a giant ruby. The guard is the same dark metal, etched with curling designs of fire. He reveals a dagger after—a replica of the sword.

"If you will not allow me to go with you, I would feel more comfortable if you brought these. They protected my grandfather, and they shall protect you, too," he says.

"Thank you, but my power will suffice," I say, emotion thick in my throat.

"They're for your companions," he says, glancing over the top of my head to where I know Elara and Ire are hiding. "Promise their safety—and yours, please."

I'm uncertain as to what will come in Tenebrae, but I nod. "I promise."

He hands over the weapons and a sheathed belt he pulled from the ground, then takes a step back, but I don't let him get far. I pull him into one more hug, whispering a soft "thank you" under my breath. I'm not sure if it's for the weapon or the freedom he is granting me.

When I return to the bedroom, I help Elara strap the weapons to her waist. While speaking, Ire has been changed into clothing far too large for her.

"Let's get my sickle back," I say.

A portal forms in my hand, swirling to life as I prepare to step toward whatever future waits on the other side.

For the Greater Good, I think to myself, welcoming the unknown and allowing the Fates to guide me into the Omnia they want me to become.

Thirty-Three

Erebus

The cold air of Tenebrae welcomes me home, glorious moonlight basking *someone* like me. I didn't expect Omnia Melania's words to sting as much as they did. I know who I am well enough—crossbred between sanguine and shadow wielder, the prince to the Tenebrae throne, and I have done more for the people of Veilia than she could even imagine—saving and protecting people because of her mother's Great Cleansing Ordinance bullshit. *Her* people are ruling this fucking land into the ground, and she has the audacity to say *someone* like me shouldn't be protecting the Omnia artifact?

The thought halts me as an image of Omnia Melania crying outside Lord Byron's house crosses my mind; the way she looked like she wanted to crawl out of her skin from the attention before dinner.

"Stop sympathizing for *someone* like her," I whisper to myself and continue forward until dense smoke permeates the air, burning wood and flesh smacking me in the face. My chest seizes, and I frantically search for the source, allowing my wings to sweep me off the ground to follow. I soar into the sky, clearing the distance so I can bear witness to the true weight of what has happened.

Nobyl is burning, and I know without a doubt, it's my fault. I've tempted Fate for far too long—my fucking penance for all the wrongs I've done. Ash blankets the landscape like fresh fallen snow. Every structure around me burns—my shack included—with everything inside. A dark gray film clings to my clothes. I lower to the ground, and the heat of the flames warm me.

Any hope my brothers and I have built over the last year burns with the fire. Dark, cold shadows trickle from my body, creating a blanket to cover the embers until only smoke remains. Breath shaking, I inhale deeply before I prepare to search the shack. Memories of building the now desolate structure float in my mind like the ash in the sky. The wooden table we had dinner at—charred. Micah's book collection—a pile of ash.

"Lelantos!" I scream, the ashen air straining my throat. "Micah!"

My only answer is the silence of a shack I knew as home; everything we stood for gone in one night. The rocking chair from Lelantos's adopted father no longer stands, and it's that final injustice that breaks me. My weight cracks the stairs, and the structure begins to crumble, taking my will to care.

Outside, someone yells for me, a female voice I've dreamed of. I stagger through the house until the night air finds me once more. My attention fixes on the stables, no longer standing, though none of the horses are inside. An ounce of hope blooms in the pit of despair that's taken root in my chest.

"Erebus," the voice sounds again.

Heavy fat tears fall from my eyes as I approach Nobyl.

Naming it makes it real, Micah said.

And real things get taken away, Lelantos added.

They knew what could happen, but I thought we were invincible. For all we've done, no one truly bothered us—until now, when I wasn't here to protect these people or my own fucking family. My limbs succumb to heaviness as I near the inflamed village. The ground is clear of bodies, and for that I'm thankful.

"Erebus," the voice whispers once more.

The woman's frame is nothing but shadows, but I can see the lines of her head bowing. Her shoulders hunch like she, too, feels sorrow as I do. Next to her, someone looks to the moonlight. Forcing my heavy limbs to move, I find a barely breathing Hamish. Bile sloshes in my stomach at the sight of a small body on the ground with her head on his thigh.

My knees hit the firm soil to reach for the girl's cold body. Deep burns cover her youthful skin, but that's not what ended her life. A dagger sized wound punctures her heart.

"Halona," I plead.

I search for a pulse as I pull her to my chest, questioning the Fates and yelling at the Mother of Death and Darkness for taking such a pure soul—someone who welcomed the shadows like they were her own. Pushing back the strands of her face, I seek life, though I know there will be none.

"I tried to save her, but she wouldn't leave until others were saved," Hamish groans through a spittle of black blood. "She wanted me to tell you she was trying to save the people like her hero." He pauses. "She was trying to be like you, King Erebus."

Like Halona, Hamish's skin is white and black from deep burns, so much damage that his magic doesn't know where to heal. Behind one hand, I can see his organs barely held in. Even if I were a healer, I couldn't fix what's happening. Not that he would let me.

"I tried to warn them, but we weren't fast enough," Hamish says, shaking his head as blood-stained tears drip from his cheeks.

"It's okay, I know, it's okay," I whisper, hoping he can hear the sincerity in my voice.

His breathing is labored, and I he won't make it much longer. I should use my dagger to end his suffering, but I need to know where my brothers are. "Who did this?"

His lips part through labored breathing. "The dark knights." He coughs up more blood, and cold air covers my skin as I realize what he said. "Accompanied by guards in white armor."

My eyes widen, fists tightening. "Was this my uncles doing?"

"He wants you."

"Where are my brothers?" I ask.

"Took them in chains." More blood surfaces through a wet rasp. I have a few more questions, and I have to be quick before the Great Mother takes him, too. "Lelantos could barely stand, let alone fight. Micah was trying to save the people." He doesn't have to add that it wasn't enough—not without me here.

"Where are the Nihils?" I ask.

Hamish's eyes close as he takes longer to answer.

"Hamish!"

They open as if he's waking from a nightmare. Panic finds me before another groan. "The dark woods," he says.

Everything darkens within me as all blood and power drains from my veins, making me an empty vessel. All the Nihils are being led to slaughter without a chance of survival.

"Tell my—" His throat works on a swallow. "M-my brother that I love him."

Hamish's hand pulls away from his stomach, and his organs fall to the ground as he takes his last breath—leaving me completely, utterly alone in the destruction of my own choices. Pulling Halona into my arms, I head for the cemetery. I'll come back for Hamish, but she deserves a final resting place more than anyone else.

My steps halt as I see the desecrated burial ground with corpses in varying stages of decomposition thrown from their graves. Stone slabs crumble to the ground, carved names beyond recognition. I've never seen anything like this before—a sacrilegious act against Esmeray, the Mother of Death and Darkness.

I lower Halona's body to the ground, preparing a place of rest for her, next to where her parents' grave had been disturbed. With a snap of my fingers, my hounds appear to guard the woods from anyone still here. When the grave is deep enough, I lift her lifeless body, her heavy weight solidifying a spot in my mind. I'll never be able to forget this.

"It should have been me," I whisper to her as I lower her into the ground. "I will avenge you, no matter what it takes." I cross her arms over her chest. "I will take that throne and make this world a better place." Tears fall, creating a bouquet of nine shadow flowers for the age she'll never see past. "A place you can be proud of," I release on a sob. I wrap her hands against the flowers that will never decay, even as her body does. "Thank you for being the hero they needed when I couldn't," My lips press to the top of her head, then I hold my forehead to hers as the tears cascade from me.

How did we get here? How did it come to murdering children so callously?

"You were always my hero and my reason for living, Halona," I mumble through a broken breath. "I will live for you." I pull myself out of the grave and reach behind me to pluck a handful of feathers—an offering to the Mothers to protect and guide her in the afterlife. "Tell my parents I love them."

The handful of feathers fall over her. It's an offering I should have given to my parents when they departed; a wrong I can begin to right with all these corpses only trying to rest.

My sobs fill the night air as I toss dirt over Halona's grave. The whole night becomes a blur, covering her body, Hamish's weight against my back as I carry him to a newly dug grave next to her—

burying them together as they had when he died. Before placing the first layer of dirt, I pull off another handful of feathers. Through the tears, I place all the corpses back into their rightful graves, each one with a feather from my wings. I'm too far gone to even care about the pain or vanity.

My hounds scope the perimeter. Butcher takes off into the woods, Ripper and Reaper following him. Damsel remains by my side with her hot, heavy breath against my hand.

"May all of you rest in the afterlife with the Mother of Death and Darkness," I say over all the graves.

I outstretch my hands as my pained wings sprawl behind me. Darkness covers the large moon, as if the Mother mourns alongside me. With a final nod to the graves and the ashes of the life I built with my brothers, I scream into the sky,

"If it's a king they want, it's a king they'll fucking get."

Thirty-Four

Melania

Tenebrae is not how I expected it to be. There are tales of the magnificent moonlight over the land, but as the three of us cross through, not a single star or speck of light illuminates the sky. Everything around us is the darkest obsidian I've ever seen. Not even Erebus's dark eyes compare—if it weren't for their distinct scent of moss and mud, I wouldn't know if Elara and Ire were next to me.

"I knew this was the land of darkness, but I didn't think it meant this," Elara says from beside me.

The center of my palms warm as a spark of fire forms—easy as breathing this time around, further cementing the revelation that Albus is my father. It's only now I realize all the clues he'd been leaving me throughout the time spent in Xannoroth.

My steps are uneasy, and the flickering flame does little to bate the unnerving energy in Tenebrae. There are things watching us—no, that's not right… they're stalking us. It's as if these creatures know we do not belong. Ire tightly clenches my hand, pulling herself closer to me.

"We may have to walk a while," I say to Elara, keeping my eyes on Ire.

Elara moves around me to lean down in front of Ire. We situate her on Elara's back and continue on, both remaining close to my side in the warm light from my flame. My hand shakes to the unsteady rhythm of my heart pounding. There's a rustling from my left, but a hissing sound from my right. I'm thankful for Elara and Ire's company, though I fear the danger I have put them in.

A sound between a hiss and a wail cuts through the air—unlike any I've heard before. I wrap my arm around Elara as our pace quickens, instinct kicking in. The ground beneath my feet shifts as the hissing wail closes in. Hot air blasts across my forearm. We try to run, but with the added weight, Elara is a step behind. Even without Ire, I doubt we'd outrun the creature gaining on us.

I glance over my shoulder to see a humanoid cat figure crawling on tiny, child-like hands, but its pawed feet are like a feline's. Its skin is an oily black with a ghastly white pointed face, four pointy ears, and the eyes are bright red, training its sight on us. Another hissing cry bellows as five more join the creature's side. Their cries splinter my ears. I've never seen anything as volatile as that monstrosity.

My power thrums inside of me.

Shoving Elara ahead, I hurl a ball of fire behind us. Three take the blast head on, but two twist aside. One launches into the air, hunting for weaker prey.

I step in its path, taking the full weight of it before it can reach Elara and Ire.

Razor-sharp teeth sink into the side of my neck.

I slam my flaming hand against its throat, but it locks its jaw, determined to tear. Another creature crashes into me from behind, biting through leather and into my thigh. I try to kick it free when a third one seizes my spare arm, wrenching it behind my back.

Its small hand grips me to the ground. Wet hair smacks against my face, slick and cold like seaweed.

The one at my neck begins to gag and hiss. White iridescent blood spills from its mouth as it claws violently at its throat.

The creature gripping my arm wails as black, sludgy blood splashes across my face and into my mouth.

A flash of black and red steel cuts through the chaos, striking the next one before it can reach me.

The one biting my leg recoils, scraping at its mouth, trying to wipe away my blood.

The power of my blood, channeling fire, burns them from the inside out.

The others—the ones struck by the fireball—either cower or lie unmoving. Elara pulls me from the ground. Ire's eyes are wide as moons, her jaw completely unhinged while Elara whispers a breathless thanks.

Even on my feet, I feel unsteady. The gashes in my flesh should be healing, but they're not. Heat overcomes my body, similar to when I was poisoned. The flickering flame in my palms dwindle, and my eyes grow heavy.

"Is someone out there?" a voice calls from the distance.

The fight within me is gone, leaving us in complete darkness.

I didn't think the Fates would lead me to this, I think before closing my eyes as Elara yells, "Over here!"

"It's been fifteen years since I've seen an Omnia," came a gravelly, feminine voice from above me.

A mane of wild, dark brown curls fills my blurred vision as I attempt to squint my eyes open. Pieces of shrubbery sprouting from her scalp catches my attention first, followed by deep burn scars over the right side of her face. Her hands are rough like bark but scarred as deeply as her face. The woman works on the bite marks on my neck and limbs, rubbing a cold balm that smells of patchouli and jasmine over them. Before I can mumble 'thank you,' she turns away from me.

Each limped step she takes is followed by a wince. Her back hunches as she hobbles to the other side of the very cramped cabin. "Fifteen years I've been waiting for this moment."

Dread tightens my chest as I wonder what's going to happen next. I try to move, but my limbs refuse to cooperate; I can't be certain if it's because of the bite from those *things* or the balm she used on me. At the thought of my capture, a deeper, more frightening fear takes root in the place beneath my sternum—Elara and Ire.

No matter how hard I fight, my limbs remain glued to the lumpy mattress beneath me as if I were bound by my mother's golden chains.

Soft shushing whispers from above, followed by clammy palms rubbing from my eyebrows to my hairline. Tears burn my eyes at the sight of Elara, unscathed from our attack, her piercing brown eyes steadying me. "You're okay. Nylisa is caring for you and the rest of us."

"The macabre have a paralytic bite," the woman—Nylisa—says. "One bite can bring down any powerful wielder, but the bite of three should be fatal."

"Except the least deserving are the ones who get to live, making the rest of us miserable. Ruining the only place we have left to survive," another feminine voice sounds.

The scent of the sea, followed by a hint of cedar, fills the room before I see who is speaking. I find her in the corner, staring at me with striking turquoise eyes and thick lashes. She has long, blonde hair, patched with red and blue near the top of her hips. Her tan skin is encrusted with dirt, and her beige tunic is stained with light blue blood.

"Funny, you say 'we' as if you understand what it means to be a Nihil," Elara scoffs.

The blonde woman jerks her shoulders back before saying, "More understanding than you, it seems."

Elara takes a step forward, stopping short of the woman as a man with black, cropped hair, cradling a small child to his chest—arms scratched and bleeding—enters the room. Round, dark brown eyes find mine, and he turns the child toward me. My chest aches, then releases at the sight of Ire, flesh unmarked as well. I don't fight the tears that fall, proud of the rain as it thumps against the roof.

"She's safe," I stutter through it all.

"All because of you," the woman says before sitting at the foot of my bed. "I knew all those years ago, you were different than your mother." She pauses as footsteps from another part of the cabin near. A few more people with different skin tones and eye colors pile into the room. The smell of moss and mud overwhelms me. Elara moves closer to my side, as if she's preparing to fight them off if she must.

Nylisa turns to the people in the cabin, gathering their attention before speaking. "Nymphs have been hunted and slaughtered for decades because of our beauty and unique way of life." She gestures to the angry, raised burn scars on her arms and legs. "We aren't like wielders who live off the land. We're like the trees, who live *because* of the land. There are few like me—crossbred between wielders and nymphs. Most can't survive the birthing process as a sapling. As a child, there was a grove of saplings protected by the elders as we learned to live within the mix of both. On the night of my tenth birthday, when I could move as a wielder without needing the root of an elder, Omnia Itzel attacked."

As I listen, flashes of my childhood come back to me—air filled with burnt wood, green blood splattered on my white dress. My pulse quickens, fingers tightening against the sheets.

"Some elders took to fighting while others tried to flee with the children." Nylisa's tone turns to sorrow as a clear, thick moisture moves from her eyes, maple wafting through the air as she weeps sap.

The tips of my fingers and toes burn and tingle through the returning circulation of blood.

"Omnia Itzel sent guards to kill us off, but they didn't make it far enough when a little girl with white hair and rainbow eyes began to crawl up the ancient hillside, playing with the Purple Providence—a sign from the Fates of hope to come." Nylisa turns to look at me, her cheeks covered in sap. "I watched as your feet created an entire hillside of those rare beauties. Did you know the gold pollen can be used as a healing component? Omnia Melania, you gave myself and the elders the strength to fight off the guards for our freedom, and if your mother didn't taint the land, more of my people would have survived."

No one breathes out of place as I rationalize what I remember against what she says. The flowers did have gold powder. People were gaining strength, but when my mother grabbed my hand that held the flower, everything changed. Agonized screams and a ghastly pale fog covered the hillside. Both nymphs and guards coughed blood as they took their last breaths.

The words my mother had told me that day rushes back: *Our power can give or take.*

I have replayed these words in my head since my youth, reciting them before every major decision in my life, but it's the first time I understand what she was saying. My mother referred to it as *our power*—the first and last time she has ever done so. Unbeknownst to me, I was the person giving, and she was the one who took all those lives without a second thought. Back then, I knew who I wanted to be before I knew what it meant—to save the lives of those who needed it.

"I am sorry," I choke out, drawing as much strength as I can in my weakened state so I can sit.

Boards shift under someone's weight as they flinch. Swooshing laps in my ears, reminding me of Irolyn. My body is heavy like molasses, and I have to fight against the urge to lie back down. Elara rushes closer to me, helping me stay upright as I take in the Nihils around me—all of them at once—for the first time.

Many wear blood-stained clothes, rags tied over what I assume to be wounds. Emotion touches their eyes, the same feelings I've learned to live with—hopelessness and desperation.

Nylisa chews on the bottom of her lip, her eyes darting in different directions around the room. Her shoulders are stiff, and she bounces a knee that shakes the entire bed. "They need your help now."

"We do not," the blonde woman bites out, stepping toward me.

Elara moves into her path, tension thickening between them. Was I really out for so long that I missed this much animosity between them?

"Get out of my way," the blonde woman says, raising a finger to Elara.

"Put your finger down less you plan to lose it," she sneers as a response.

"Enough, Addilynn," the man holding Ire shouts, startling her.

Ire raises from the crook of his arm before falling back into him with a thump. Addilynn shifts away, never letting her eyes stray from us. Her shoulders rise as she crosses her arms. I'm certain no friendship will be gained with her.

"How can I help?" I say aloud to the room.

Addilynn scoffs before mumbling under her breath. I don't have enough fight in me to care what she has to say. Aside from her heavy breathing, no one says anything, only the crackling embers from a fire in another part of the cabin offering solace from a suffocating silence.

The scent of blood turns my stomach, becoming all I can focus on. I scan the room with my senses, noticing some of the Nihils' wounds are clotting, while many others aren't. I may not be able to portal back to Xannoroth yet or create a wall of fire, but surely I can heal superficial wounds.

"Do they hurt?" I ask Nylisa, pointing to her burns on her arms and legs.

Her lower lip pulls between her teeth as she nods. My hand settles over her bark-like forearm and summons a faint, fern-colored aura glowing around my palm on her arm. The light trails up and down her body, soaking into her skin and creating a glow beneath her flesh. In the corner, someone says thank you to the First before approaching, hands shaking and face ghostly white. She has a deep gash on her shoulder. Through the bandage, blood continues to ooze.

"You're okay," I whisper.

Elara glances at her, eyes steady as her head nods only once.

"Can you remove the bandage?" I ask Elara, only for Addilynn to scoff.

"Offering to help with your powers but too snobbish to do any of the dirty work," she says.

I bite the inside of my cheek, the only way to keep my words at bay. From the way everyone looks at her, they clearly hold her in high regard. The woman in front of me keeps her eyes on the ground, defeat lingering there as if she truly believes I'm above touching her bloodied bandages.

To show them I'm not, I swallow back a gag and use all my might to lean toward her, pulling the bloody cotton between my fingers. With a wet thud, it falls to the ground, splattering blood across my clothes and the feet of those standing nearby. All I can do is breathe in through my nose and out through my mouth as the smell of blood surrounds me.

Settling my hand above the wound, I focus my powerful energy into her flesh. A collective gasp ripples through the room. Only then do I realize my eyes have been shut. When I open them, nothing remains but a faint pink hue and drying blood.

A line of people forms behind her. Elara steps forward to remove the bandages, much to Addilynn's chagrin. As I tend to the deeper wounds, I listen keenly to the whispers passing between the others.

Their village has been destroyed. The Three are nowhere to be seen.

That much I can gather beneath the murmurs. But they don't share any of it with me. It doesn't matter how many wounds I close. I know what they see when they look at me—the daughter of the enemy.

The man with Ire in his arms approaches. His cuts are minor, aside from the deep gash on his temple. Blood oozes from it, and once more, I bite my tongue to keep the stomach acid at bay. Around his narrow jawline, the red blood is smeared. Assumingly, he's been wiping it before it can drop on her.

"Thank you for protecting my sister," he says, his voice a dark timber.

"Wrath, I presume? Your sister was eager to be reacquainted." I take a step forward. "And she would be happy to have you completely healed. May I?"

"Please." His voice is soft.

Hovering my palm over his temple, I can hardly believe what I am doing. The skin fuses together as it did all those years ago when the people coated themselves in gold dust. Once Wrath is healed, Nylisa ushers the ones who have been healed to another part of the cabin, leaving me alone with Elara.

"Get some rest," she says when all of them have left.

As she parts, leaving me in the small room with a cushion settee, a mattress, and a singular window, I'm accosted by all my new realities; in one day, I found my father, found—and lost—the sickle, got attacked by macabres, saved a group of Nihils, but most importantly,

I've learned my mother's one true fear.

She can no longer control me as I take the reins on what Fate has demanded of me since I was a child.

Thirty-Five

Erebus

A sharp object digs into my stomach, rousing me from sleep. Ripper, Butcher, and Reaper pace around me while Damsel—the largest and most loyal of the four—stands guard. I rub my hand into her coarse fur, surprised by how real she feels despite being made from shadows.

"I didn't mean to fall asleep," I say to her.

Damsel nudges her wet nose into my palm to comfort me. Waves of pain course through my wings, flashing images of last night through my mind. Dried, yellow blood on my forearms reminds me of the Omnia guard I killed. He sang so beautifully as my dagger cut into his body. With each nick, he confessed his crimes. The entire raid was planned by my uncle, an attack meant to strip me of my wings and end my life before I reach full maturity. He told me where the captured Nihils were taken, and that my brothers were forced to the palace. The guard died before I could figure out how they made it across Tenebrae in such a short time. Then again, the guards wore white crested with a crown. He hadn't mentioned Omnia Itzel when

I tortured him, and Omnia Melania was with me the entire time—though that doesn't mean she's completely innocent.

Ravens croak above me as I rise from my sleep, omitting an eerie, deep sound as they fly from the branches into the cloudy, gray sky. I envy their freedom, but I can't help but wonder when I got so confident in myself that I thought I could live like one of them. My heart beats—same as theirs. My wings are the same black, tinted with hues of purple and blue. Like a conspiracy of ravens, my brothers and I flew together.

The faces of my enemies' rage through my mind. Sighing, I pull myself to my feet, working through the next steps forward. If Lelantos and Micah were here, we would rush to the dark woods, preparing to rescue all the Nihils we promised safety to. But they're not, and without them, I can't seem to think past what I truly desire.

My first steps are hesitant, as if I know I won't be able to come back from this. I promised to avenge Halona, Hamish, and the others, but who am I without the people who give me a reason to breathe?

"I could sneak into the palace, save my brothers, and wage a war against my uncle," I say aloud to Damsel, who has yet to leave my side. Her paws steady on the dried ground as her breath rasps in response to my absurd idea.

"Forget my brothers, save the Nihils, and try to save my brothers after starting a war I'm not likely to win." The words turn my stomach. If Marcus has my brothers, any act of retaliation against him could mean the end of their lives. I can handle many things, but my brothers' blood on my hands isn't one of them.

In the distance, there is the sound of another coarse caw signaling the presence of crows—an oddity for them to be near when the ravens are here. It's rumored that my bloodline stems from the ravens while the witches come from the crows—another reason Micah tells me to stay far away from those birds. We share the land, but in the eyes of the Mothers, we should never mix.

Coldness seeps deeper into my bones with each step closer to the clearing, the rhythm of my heart slowing as I make it to the opening in the woods. The trees bend like the sun itself fell into the land. My mind continues to run in circles, weighing the options, but I have to think about Micah and Lelantos. My dreams crash into my mind like a tidal wave of mangled bodies—all because I put them in danger. It's on sheer blind faith that I'm hoping Lelantos is alive. His wounds were too grave for extensive travel. I wouldn't be surprised if they left him to die—

"Don't think like that," says a gravely, masculine voice that isn't my own.

My head swings in different directions, trying to track where the voice came from. Aside from Damsel, the forest is empty, and the hound lolls its tongue, sitting unbothered as if nothing could disturb it. The other hounds stalk the forest, but none chase through the trees for prey.

"Who's there?" I shout only for my voice to echo.

Perhaps I was bitten by a hallucinogen producing snake. Sneaky little bastards. My hands pat over my body, searching for any wounds before suddenly stopping as my eyes find purchase on a woman in the woods—a woman I've only seen in my dreams.

Shadowy mist dances around her as she crouches down, her knees bent outward while her hands rest in the soil. She cocks her head to the side as long, black hair covers the lower part of her face. In place of her eyes, glowing orbs of silver, like two full moons, have taken root. I'm not scared of many things, but when she crawls forward a step, I take one back. Through the ilk-like strands of her hair, she smiles with sharp fangs, her tongue clicking against the roof of her mouth.

The woman advances at a faster speed, only to disappear before I can blink. I choke on the swallow in my throat. My fingers wrap around the hilt of my dagger. I don't know who—more importantly—what she is, but I don't want to stick around to find out.

Tendrils flicker around my fingers as a shadow portal to any-where else begins to form, only to be pulled away. Howls rip through the air, and then there's absolute silence. Not a singular caw or snap-ping of a branch. The power within dissipates, leaving an empty void in my chest.

"What do you want?" I say, rubbing at my sternum.

A bead of sweat drips from my brow, my wings rising, ready to protect me from any blind attack I can't see.

"You." The voice is cold in my ears.

A chill dances down my spine, erupting bumps over my skin. My hand holding the dagger swings out, searching for this haunting melodic voice.

"I am surprised at your idiocrasy." The woman stands before me again, but she's entirely different. Within the shadowy mist is now a woman about twelve years old. Mystical moon eyes, black hair pulled into two ponytails at the sides of her head, wearing a black gown with opaque sleeves.

"Please help me, Erebus." Her voice pleads like it did all those years ago on the night I was going to take my life. I never told Micah about the little girl in the woods who needed my aid only to vanish when he appeared. He brought me back to the light, but it was her who stayed at my darkest.

The girl is gone in a flash, followed by a small tug on my jacket behind me. Now she's about four, those same mystical eyes glaring at me with black tears streaming down her face as she repeats, "wake up, wake up, wake up," repeatedly. Flashes of the night of my parents' death strobe in my mind, showing me things I'd long forgotten. It wasn't screaming guards outside my door, nor the sounds of bodies hitting the onyx floors of the palace. It was a little girl pulling me underneath my bed, teary eyes urging me to fight—to close my eyes. Micah grabbed me from underneath.

Realization dawns on me. I wasn't trying to go back to my parents. I was trying to save the girl. My head shakes on its own, fighting the memories—knowing they're wrong. I would have remembered her.

"Lest someone made you forget," she says.

My eyes snap open, and I didn't realize they had closed. She's back in the form I first saw her in, standing at her full height at the center of my chest. Her bony fingers and elongated nails, like that of a claw, rub a bare spot in the middle of my wing.

"They will rest with my—the Mothers," she says.

Her glowing orbs are shielded by her upper brow. She smirks, dimples flaring on her cheeks. I have a feeling she doesn't do anything by accident, and her use of saying *my* instead of *the* was not a mistake.

"Will you make me forget this?" I ask.

"Yes." There's a lilt of sorrow in her tone, like it pains her to do so.

I want to argue that she can trust me, but who am I kidding? I couldn't keep my brothers safe.

"They're alive in the dungeon, trying to figure out a plan to escape," she says.

"Why are you helping me?" I ask.

She nods to herself before moving around me in a tantalizingly slow circle, her shadowy mist curling over my skin, cold like fresh snow. Before I can react, she reaches a hand behind my back and snatches the sickle, relieving the heavy weight that now leaves me vulnerable.

The sickle hisses, its aura waving uncontrollably as she touches it. Her essence moves to the blade and away from the handle as she clicks her tongue against her teeth once more. "I am helping myself, Erebus. I am tired of being idle when I want to win the fucking war."

The temperature thickens with ice. Nightmare incarnate slices the blade against my chest, digging into my shirt. Another closed lipped smile dances on her face as the missing pieces click together. She's not trying to hurt me; she has saved me from danger more times than I can even imagine, possibly stopping me before each time I would try to do something reckless, interfering with the Fates' design—

"If the Fates wanted you dead, you would be dead," she hisses once more, the blade digging further until a thin slit forms in my shirt.

"And how do you suppose we win?" I ask, more snark in my voice than there should be, considering I'm in the presence of an ancient.

She makes a tsking sound of disapproval.

"Knowing who your true enemies are should be the start." She lifts the sickle faintly and then digs it in against my chest once again. My eyes bounce over her face, searching for answers, determining whether she's telling me to trust Omnia Melania. "Always trust your instincts and the voice inside your head, whether or not it's yours." She moves another step away. Shadow vines wrap around her bare feet, climbing the base of her leg to the middle of her calf. "I can't let you remember everything, but I'm feeling generous. My name is Harlow, though I prefer nightmare incarnate, and you are the only hope to save us all."

The tendrils of my magic slam back into me, making me whole again as the heavy sickle returns to the palm of my hand. Then, I'm plummeting through the lilac sky, the name Harlow on the tip of my tongue.

"You have wings, use them!" demands the male voice from earlier.

My wings splay out behind me until I coast to the ground, adrenaline pumping in my veins as my feet land steadily in Tenebrae, far away from where I remember I'd been. A pressure forms around my temple, a hole in my memory—I can't understand if that was real or a dream.

Who are you? I think to myself—well the other voice.

My name is Malefic, and Moros hasn't worked up the courage to speak with you. We are the wraiths bound to your soul to protect you.

And you can hear my thoughts? This is fucking weird.

Not as weird as if you knew you already met us, a growly voice says. I gather Moros gained the courage to speak with me.

I never met—

My mind flashes to the night Lelantos was attacked. The two wraiths were there; they just hadn't spoken then.

You've reached full maturity, Malefic—I think—says.

My head lowers as I realize what they said. The night Nobyl was attacked was the same day I reached twenty years old— a grand birthday to me. When my head lifts from my minor pity party, opal shimmers only a few yards ahead of me. I don't know if she had any-thing to do with what happened to Nobyl, but I will make sure she pays for the crimes of her mother.

Thirty-Six

Melania

The steamy cup of herbal tea warms my hands as I cradle it between them. Ravens fly out in the distance outside, different from the harmonious sounds of fire cardinals. After healing all the people who needed it, I slept entirely too long, waking to Ire trying to braid my hair, somehow avoiding Elara, who was asleep at the foot of my bed. Many of the Nihils kept their distance, but Wrath—Ire's brother—thanked me for bringing his sister back to him. After the many revelations last night, I have one true mission left—find Erebus.

The sickle needs to be with me. In anyone else's hands, it's still a weapon, but I'm the only one who can keep it out of my mother's reach. She wouldn't spare Erebus to get it, and once she did, she'd raze the world. I'm not ready to find out what she would do with this power.

Bethany's cabin is larger on the inside than it looks on the outside. There's nothing for miles aside from land, fences and woods.

The front door opens and slams shut as Bethany limps out, her jaw clenched, and her eyes rolling, cursing under her breath. A smile blooms on my face to hear another person speak so brazenly in front of me.

"Are you alright?" I ask.

"I'm not used to this many people," she scoffs, moving down the stairs.

"Why do you live alone out here?" I ask, my curiosity getting the better of me.

"Easier than trying to live amongst others," she says, gesturing to her arms and neck. The scars aren't as noticeable as they were before; a small token, though it doesn't mean much when I know who did it.

"I am sorry for what occurred that night."

She nods, only to turn back into the cabin, leaving me to my thoughts. I always knew my mother was wicked, but to blame a child for the carnage she caused is another; to let me believe all this time that I was responsible for a massacre in the name of the Great Cleansing. Surely a way to control me. My mother doesn't run on the notion of love. She feeds off fear, and as a child, I feared death more than anything. That is, until I learned to speak with the Mothers, learning of what could wait for me on the other side one day.

The sensation of something crawling up my legs pulls me from my thoughts. Expecting to see a bug, I flinch as shadow vines move swiftly to the middle of my thighs. I try to pull them off, but I'm not fast enough as the dark scent of amber and musk reaches me. A large body shoves me against the side of the cabin, pressing a cold, long blade to my throat.

Erebus is seething, jaw clenching so tightly, he may break a fang. His eyes fill with the blackest dark of night, his veins complimenting the darkness. The hand holding the blade to my throat is steady, his pulse calm under his grasp—not an ounce of sweat on his beautiful face.

"I won't die, and I fear you do not want to make an enemy out of me."

The threat comes off my lips so easily it should frighten me, but it doesn't. Erebus' eyes scan over my neutral face. He could slice my throat, but he could never escape me. As if realizing this, the blade moves an inch away from my throat, just enough to let me breathe, but there is no illusion of safety.

"You distracted me as they slaughtered my people," he hisses, though there's an underlying, thick emotion in his voice.

"Erebus," Addilynn cries out.

He turns his direction to her, giving me the chance to push him away. He barely takes a step back, so my power surges to use necessary force.

"Step away from my Omnia," comes Elara's voice. She shoves Addilynn out of the way to get to me.

Erebus' brows lower as Elara puts herself between us, working to understand who she is to me. The moment he realizes Albus wasn't lying about my friendship with a Nihil, he lowers the dagger, but he doesn't put it back in his sheath.

Nylisa rolls her eyes as she steps outside. "In my fifteen years of living here, I've been able to avoid all royals. Now I have two in the same day."

Addilynn reaches for Erebus at the same time Elara pulls me to the side. His arms wrap around her without a beat of hesitation, revealing chunks of missing feathers in his wings, red, angry skin beneath them. Within his grasp, Addilynn sobs against his chest, and he rubs her back, whispering against her hair. "You're okay now, we're going to figure it out."

He says it over and over until it becomes tired.

Elara grips my wrist, creating a significant amount of distance, keeping her eye on the pair all the while. More Nihils filter out of the room, cheering for the savior who came for them; though none of them truly realize how their *savior* was threatening to kill me moments ago.

"You heal all their wounds, and yet you're still the villain?" Elara asks, her grip tightening on my wrist.

A laugh escapes me, self-deprecating in a way I don't mean. Wet tears tug on my eyelids at the thought that I could ever be something for the Nihils, the savior they needed. Wrath pulls Ire along by the hand toward Erebus as if to introduce them, but she keeps her eyes locked on me.

At least she recognizes all the good I have done, I think to myself.

Erebus turns in my direction; his lips curl in a scowl filled with disdain. "She can't hurt you anymore," he says loud enough for me to hear.

I scoff—loudly. Ire shakes her head, shoving away from her brother, then rushes over to my side to stand with Elara and me.

Nylisa follows. "She healed their wounds."

Erebus furrows his brow, crossing his arms as he rasps his disapproval, as if the idea is ineffable. Wrath leans toward him, whispering in his ear, then his large boots thud on the ground as he comes to our side, lifting his little sister into his arms. Erebus grinds his jaw back and forth.

Through tears, Addilynn says, "She did aid us."

He draws in a large breath, further tightening his arms across his chest, biceps bulging. Then, he cocks his head to the side and asks, "Why did you kill Lord Byron?"

Gasps fill the air, followed by low murmurs. I didn't realize many knew of Lord Byron. My brain freezes as I work through what to say through the expecting eyes watching me, but I'm not sure the truth is enough to sway them into trusting me.

"A conversation none are privy to." Elara moves a step ahead of me; there are times I believe she forgets that I'm an all-powerful bloodline, and she's not.

"Leave us," Erebus commands.

No one moves.

He yells the same commandment louder, his shoulders seizing with the slipping control he must have had earlier. Those around us flinch, then scramble all at once, like soldiers in the fray of an oncoming battle.

"Go," I say to those with me, never taking my eyes off him.

The group files into the cabin, leaving myself and Erebus alone in the open-air filled with animosity. Erebus takes a step forward, but I hold my ground, standing straighter than before. I'm not daft enough to blindly trust the man who had a dagger to my throat only moments ago, but I won't cower to him either.

"Why did you kill him?" he asks once more.

"Why did you kill the guards?" I retort.

A smirk dances on his face before he wipes it away. "You never a leave witness."

His tone is so carefree over the death of two royal guards that it leaves me speechless; baffled. I'd willingly spared their lives; they didn't deserve to die—at least not that I know of. I'm about to tell him as much, but I've been dodging his question for too long, and he knows it. Erebus moves another step, and this time, I respond with my own backward step— some twisted game of cat and mouse—and I'm not sure who's the predator and who's the prey.

"I provided Lord Byron mercy," I say finally. "My mother—"

Erebus practically growls at the mention of her.

I hold my hands up in surrender. "She punished him to stay alive in his manor after she forced him to kill his own son for being a Nihil and the other for trying to get revenge. He was living with their deaths, and only an Omnia could undo that kind of punishment. I did what was necessary."

He doesn't take a step forward this time, his boots rooted in the ground. He pulls the side of his bottom lip under his sharp fangs. "Why did you grant him mercy?"

"No one should have to live like that—with that kind of torture. Lord Byron was a good man and deserved a kind end."

King Albus had said the same words to me that day in the field. I repeat them to myself whenever memories of his and his sons' blood haunt me. For all he did for me, it was the least I could do for him.

"And your servant—"

"My dear friend, Elara," I interrupt.

Erebus sucks in a breath. "Elara; why is she keen on protecting you?"

"Because I am not the monster people believe me to be. I do not cast judgment on your kind despite all my mother has said."

"But *someone* like me shouldn't have the sickle, remember?" There's a flash of hurt in his words.

I was going to apologize for the slight before he stuck a dagger to my throat. Now I'm not too sure he deserves one. How is it that I must always apologize to others when they don't feel as if I deserve one, too?

"*No one* should have such a powerful artifact in their grasp," I say instead of choosing to apologize. "It has nothing to do with your bloodline."

"You expect me to believe you?" he snaps.

"The Fates chose me for a reason. That weapon was created for me."

"Do you know why?" He takes a step forward, but this time I don't move back.

"The Fates needed it because they were made for times of war," I say, recanting my father's words, then they hit me all at once—what they meant.

My eyes widen. I've been so focused on getting the sickle that I didn't understand what it meant for. Once I have it, the choice isn't whether I stand against my mother—it's *when*. The idea stops me dead in my tracks. Even if I continue training, it will take me years to reach my mother's level of power—power she wields as easily as breathing. And what about the people I love? If I thought her punishment for Lord Byron was tough, what could she do to me? Elara? Ire? My sisters?

"Are you sure you're ready for that?" Erebus' voice drips with condescension, like he knows me—like everyone else thinks they know me.

"I'll have to be if it's truly for the Greater Good," I say with more bravado than I thought possible.

Erebus flinches back as he did last night.

"I don't trust you," he says, more words dancing on the tip of his tongue. There's something he isn't saying. Erebus looks to anything and everything as he whispers, "But I need your help."

Erebus

I didn't expect to ask her for help, and by the looks of it, neither did Melania as her jaw drops. I wasn't lying when I said I don't trust her; a part might never, but what options do I have? To save the Nihils in the dark woods, I need a fire wielder. I refuse to leave Tenebrae until everyone I care for is brought to safety, and the crown is on my head.

Start by knowing your enemies. Harlow's words bounce back to me, and I'm still uncertain if that was a dream. Something to think about later.

"Asking for help after a holding a dagger to my throat," Melania mocks.

I didn't plan to do that. Seeing the woman who resembled the one who has caused us so much misery was my undoing. If it weren't for her threat, I might have slashed her throat, throwing my rule of hurting women out the door. Except I need to get my brothers back, and I can't risk an Omnia's wrath if I mean to keep them safe for the rest of our lives.

"I am sorry," I say through gritted teeth.

Never imagined the day I would apologize to an Omnia. She crosses her arms over her chest. I'm half expecting her to say no. It's what I would do.

"What do you need of me?" she asks.

It takes me a moment to recover. I was preparing to beg for help, even if it meant losing my pride. "The Nihils are being kept in the dark woods."

Omnia Melania lowers her brow. All Tenebrae is known for is darkness, death, and woods, something I imagine she's calculating before truly accepting.

"The dark woods are in the center of Tenebrae." I debate whether to tell her that the other side is ruled by my uncle and the other side—this side—is ruled by me, an unspoken agreement that my uncle broke last night. I choose not to as I continue. "The sun never shines there; the foliage is too thick. All monster types reside and breed there. No one would go there unless they desperately have to." Most who enter end up dying, though I don't add that last part—more for myself than for her. I would be surprised if any of the Nihils are still alive, but I have to try.

She rephrases her question. "And why do you need me?"

"Monsters are weakened by fire," I explain, and she nods like she truly understands—like maybe she encountered one already. I want to ask, but right now doesn't seem like the time. "As an Omnia, you have an abundance of fire magic to get us in and out without being torn to shreds."

Her face pales; she mentioned she doesn't like the sight of blood, and I'm guessing the idea of people being torn might be too much.

"I can help," she says with a lilt of her lips that has me second guessing once more why any of this was a good idea. "I will help you free the Nihils from the dark woods—it's the least I can do for them. But I must also ask you return my sickle to me." The ultimatum flowed from her beautiful mouth so eloquently.

She cocks her head, waiting for an answer.

I should easily be able to give it, but I can't. The sickle is all I have over the Omnias. Nightmares flash through my mind: the sickle waved in front of me, my brothers' bloody corpses. All of it because I gave up the artifact when I should have protected it.

"Not until I know which side you fight for."

Omnia Melania rolls her eyes. Her fingers thrum against her biceps. "And when will you know?"

Ravens croon over us, a cold breeze moving through the air. I wager what to say. If I don't give her the sickle, she might not help, but if I do, she could turn on all of us.

"I will know when I know." It's all I can muster.

A muscle tightens in her jaw, but her magnificent eyes remain neutral. Her only tell is the deep loosening of her breath.

"He's alive!" The silent standoff comes to an end as Addilynn crashes into me once more. "I can feel him!" she cries again, but this time it isn't from defeat—its relief; relief not just for Nobyl but for her Fated, who I finally realize is not by her side.

Others who are Fated ring out about their loved ones. I turn to Melania, and her eyes are closed, fists tight as if she, too, is feeling for something—or someone.

Thirty-Seven

Melania

A circle forms around Erebus as Nihils let tears fall from their eyes. I couldn't help closing mine, wondering if the faint blue tendril was there—one I'd never seen before being in Xannoroth. It pulsates without the vibrancy it once had.

"It's too dangerous," Erebus pleads, as if he can sense what everyone is thinking, but no one is truly listening. All their attention remains on getting back to the ones they love. I didn't realize the Three were taking in wielders. Not that there are many here. I didn't see them last night when I was healing the Nihils who needed it the most, aside from Addilynn. It's the few who are speaking about their Fated.

"I failed you all before; I cannot survive doing it again."

This time, the crowd quiets.

For a second, I think they're about to change their minds until Addilynn says, "What happened to the village isn't your fault, Erebus."

Hurt flickers in his dark eyes, followed by hatred I have yet to see in him—and I know he hates me, too.

Elara bumps her hip against mine, pulling my attention away from his domineering presence. "Do you want to tell me what you discussed?"

My head shakes, but my lips betray me, spilling everything, starting with the dagger to my throat and what happened after his question about Lord Byron.

"Are you going with them?" She nods to people gathering supplies. Erebus is a distance away, playing with a shadow in his hand, one that will surely become a portal.

I bite my nail, considering her question. I shouldn't hesitate to save the people. There's little risk for me to enter the woods. Unless my mother is hiding in there, nothing should be that dangerous. Except I'm not sure I want to aid *him* in his quest. Not when he keeps *my* sickle strapped to his back.

"He doesn't trust me. I offered my aid, but I need him to return the sickle. He refuses to do so until he knows where my loyalty lies," I say.

Elara's brows lower, holding her cheek between her teeth, biting back the words I know she wants to say—an oddity for the girl who speaks her mind even if she shouldn't.

"Out with it," I exclaim.

One of the Nihils looks at me, their nose scrunched like they're judging me. Great, another reason they can dislike me.

"I say this with the utmost respect, but do you *know* which side you fight for?"

A sigh breaks out of me before I can stop it. Having Prince Erebus ask was one thing, but it's insulting coming from her, especially after everything.

Elara lowers her brown before I can speak. "Are you prepared to stand against the woman who has beat you relentlessly? The woman who has made you feel like nothing for so long that you relate more to me as a Nihil than the most powerful wielder? Can you say, with complete certainty, that when the time comes, you can stand against your mother, her army, and your protector to defend this?" She gestures to the people who are preparing for battle.

The answer is on the tip of my tongue, but I can't get the words out. I want to save them. I want to end the Great Cleansing, but what's the Great Cleansing compared to a war between Omnias? It could mean the end of life as we know it; a complete reckoning of the kingdoms as we fight for the power to rule. Nothing my mother has done thus far can compare to the carnage that would ensue.

As for Princess La'Mia, I haven't given up on her. She may be cruel, but it's all we know. After her mother passed, neither she nor I knew what kindness meant. My mother favored her, but I wonder how much of that was for survival, to stave off the punishments I endured. When they came for me in Xannoroth, I'd never seen her look as scared as she did then. Without me there, how much does La'Mia endure? Could I risk putting her in the middle of a war between my mother and myself?

I'm not sure if I'm ready for that answer.

Elara grabs my hand. "I know the kind of person you are, and I know you will make the right decision, but can you blame him for not having the same faith in you as I do?"

I don't know when she became this wise. I gather it's from playing chess with Albus. He always has insightful things to say when you're losing the match.

Nylisa comes out of her cabin, halfway bent over from the weight of a bag on her shoulders. I quickly grab it from her as she passes by.

"Do you have your entire house in here?" I ask.

"Just about," she replies, wiping her hands together.

Wrath approaches, relieving the bag from me, carrying the weight better than I did. Elara glances over his body, a faint blush touching the apples of her cheeks.

"Are you going with?" I ask.

Nylisa nods. Clear film glosses over her eyes. "I've been so scared of what's out there that I forgot what it meant to live. Having people I can talk to and who can talk back," she chuckles. "All of this gives me a reason to continue on instead of wallowing away in the cabin. The little one was asking me about my people, and I wonder how many others forgot about my kind—or how many of my kind might be out there. My purpose was to return the favor to you, but I think it's about time I find a new one."

Tears surface again, and I'm wondering if all nymphs are as emotional as her. Elara looks at me sideways as if she is wondering the same.

Nylisa is halfway to the portal when she shouts over her shoulder, "Plus, we will be extra safe with an Omnia on our side!" Her voice is loud enough to grab the attention of everyone—including Erebus.

I can't ignore the hope in his eyes. Elara releases a breathy chuckle as Nylisa winks. She knew exactly what she was doing. Left with no choice other than to be a coward, I groan, following a step behind.

Elara doesn't leave my side, even when Erebus grips my arm and whispers close to my ear. "I'll be keeping my eye on you."

I press forward into the portal, taking a large breath as I do. On the other side, people wait in small groups for their true savior to come forth. He steps one foot onto our side as the portal begins closing behind him. I can only imagine how long he has had to use portals to become that skilled.

Around us, the grass is a darker shade, closer to black than the tan, brittle grass elsewhere. Chirping echoes from a creature I've never heard before followed by howls of beasts in the distance—not far enough away for my comfort. The air is stagnant, as if the land knows anything near or around here is better off dead. A particularly loud chirruping rings out from the gnarling woods, stretching endlessly on the horizon without a beginning, middle, or end. Darkness seeps from it as a warning and a temptation, daring those daft enough to venture in to meet their doom.

"This is as close as any of you will get," Erebus states, finality in his tone.

Another howl forces people to flinch, including the ever-fearless Addilynn. Ire tightly squeezes Wrath's hand, blue bulging from his veins. Even if I wanted to feel a sense of dread or fear, Erebus is watching me. No matter what, I have to be on his side to get the sickle back.

"We need a lot of wood," he says.

He walks in a circle, placing tendrils of shadow into the ground. Despite the fear, people search through their small items. Some ventured in pairs in the opposite direction of the trees.

"They don't have to do that, do they?" Elara asks.

"I'm not sure," I say.

Moving into a crouching position, my fingers twine with the black blades of grass. I'm not sure if Omnias have ever tried to grow anything in the land of Tenebrae—we can't access shadow magic, but it's part of Veilia.

The cool energy dances over the tips of my fingers, unlike anything I've felt before.

"What do you think you're doing?" Erebus snaps.

"She's helping." Elara steps in front of him, preparing to protect me. One day, I'm going to have to sit her down and explain what being an Omnia means and why she doesn't need to keep putting herself in harm's way for my sake.

Her hands find her hips, and Erebus takes a step to the left, but she's back in front of him. He tries again only to fail. They go back and forth until the magic blossoms around me. Ignoring their petty dance, I focus on the power as Albus told me to—feel my essence and command what is needed.

Erebus bites his lower lip, black blood dripping onto his chin.

Roots slither under the surface like snakes, creating a circle. Where Erebus marked his shadows, a thin trunk burst through with bulbous green leaves sprouting at the end. My power commands me to continue renewing the dead lands.

"That's enough," Erebus says. He pushes past Elara, his thigh in my eyesight. I call my essence back into me, stand, then look into his eyes.

Swirling mixtures of anger and astonishment overcome him as I wait for him to say something. He doesn't. Instead, he marches away, muttering under his breath.

"The training has been paying off," Elara says with a glimmer of pride.

When people return, most are empty-handed. Erebus lords over them to discuss what's to happen next, speaking loudly enough for even the monsters to hear. I sit, listening to his instructions.

"You are all going to stay here within the confines of this circle. Three of you need to stay on guard during the night. If you see or hear something, throw a burning stick in the direction," he explains. Some laugh, but his tone is completely serious.

The more he talks, the more I wonder what I've gotten myself into. Through the dense clouds, sunlight dwindles with an amethyst and lilac glow on the horizon. The color of it reminds me of the flowers I've come to see more often—the same ones that sprouted in the center of Tenebrae, the ones Nylisa called the Purple Providences.

Ire plops into my lap, making me uncomfortable in a way I've never felt before.

My eyes widen as she nestles against me, hands raising at my sides, and I'm left trying to decide what to do with them.

"Are you going to be safe?" Ire asks as she fights the gloss behind her eyes, her body shaking.

"Do you think my mother is in the woods?" I ask.

"I hope not!" she quickly replies, leaving me to chuckle.

"Then I will be safe. No one aside from my mother can truly hurt me." I don't take the time to remind her of when she stabbed me as an example. Instead, I intend to remind her to stay armed without my presence.

Erebus appears before I can.

Ire leaps from my lap when he grips under my armpit to pull me to my feet. I jerk out of his hold, surging power beneath my skin.

"Who does this bastard think he is?"

"This bastard thinks he's charming to people he likes, loyal to the ones he loves, and a bastard to the people who deserve it," he replies.

Heat blushes over my cheeks. I have to get better at thinking without speaking. Erebus strides ahead of me as Elara places the short sword Albus gifted me into my palm. Shaking my head, I return it, knowing she needs it more than I do.

"Why are we leaving now?" I ask, trying to catch up to Erebus.

"One more night in there, and all those people are as good as dead. Plus, there's no time like the present," he says with a shrug.

"If we rush it, you're as good as dead."

This time, he faces me, running his fingers through his black strands only for them to fall forward again. "If you do what you have to, we both will be fine." His large chest rises before he adds with a hint of breathy defeat, "I can't let them down again. I just can't."

I soften. "And what is it you need of me?"

"Stand at my side and keep fire around us. It's the only way we—I can survive."

He says he doesn't trust me, but in that one statement, I realize I hold not only his life, but the lives of all those people in my hands. Not to mention the ones at camp or the people of Tenebrae who thrive off his power.

Erebus turns around again, this time walking at a slower pace. I wonder how often he's had to trust another person with his life. Did his brothers protect him? And most importantly, where are they?

Erebus halts as I ask out loud, and I go crashing into his right wing. His breath shudders, followed by a broken, "Somewhere worse than there."

Erebus begins to sob, gripping harshly at himself in a hug. Without another thought, I do the unthinkable and pull him into me. His head nestles against the crook of my collarbone as my arms wrap around him to hold him closely. Erebus's weight brings us to our knees, but he doesn't let up. It's like a dam broke within him. A reckoning of who he is, and I can't help but wonder who he might become.

Erebus

The smell of lilac and spring rain engulfs me as Melania holds me against her. When I think I'm finally done, another sob releases and the crying starts all over again. I didn't expect this to happen nor as easily as it did, but the reminder of my brothers was too much, especially when all I feel is guilt.

I know they would understand why I'm coming to save the Nihils instead of them. Lelantos would applaud and thank me for doing so. It doesn't take away the ache of knowing they're left in my uncle's palace dungeon—if that's even to be believed. And if they are, I can't imagine the torture being forced upon them as they await my arrival, especially if Omnia Itzel is involved. My brothers and I have always known that she wants them in her possession, but we never knew why, aside from Lelantos being a Nihil. For all I know, she could be there, enacting her twisted punishments while I cry into her daughter's arm because I chose to save the others when all I want is to save them.

I try to pull away as another wave of heavy emotion breaks through me. Omnia Melania runs her fingers through the back of my hair, her elbow hitting against my wing. I don't have enough strength to care, even if all she wants is the sickle, something she could easily grab in my state. Except, she doesn't reach for it—hasn't tried at all. I'm beginning to wonder if the thought has even crossed her mind.

A few more moments pass, allowing the reckoning sobs to lighten. Omnia Melania pulls away slightly, dancing her ethereal, rainbow eyes over my face. Her throat bobs as if she's fighting her own bout of emotions.

"Where are they?" she asks.

"In the dungeon," I say.

She nods, her lips tight as concern etches along her brow; as if she could ever understand what it means to be in a dungeon. The only time I imagine she's seen it is when her mother is punishing another poor soul. Tears gone, the reminder of her matriarch gives me enough strength to pull away. Her eyes widen. I must be seeing things because she seems hurt.

"Once I save the Nihils, I am going to get my brothers," I say, quickly adding, "Nothing you need to concern yourself with."

Omnia Melania stands from the ground, wiping the phantom dirt from her pant legs. She skillfully brushes past me, avoiding my wings, taking the lead steadfast to the dark woods.

Addilynn had told me about the attack on Nobyl. They had separated the Nihils from the wielders, so some of the Nihils were able to slip through with them, hiding behind their bright eye colors. They stumbled through the land, trying to find anyone to offer aid until they found an empty cabin. She didn't have to tell me they planned to raid it—I know that's what anyone would do in these trying times.

Nylisa, the tree nymph, returned shortly after with a bloody Omnia and two Nihils.

Omnia Melania had healed their wounds, and for that, I am grateful, but it doesn't warrant my trust nor my kindness, especially not if it means returning the one bargaining chip I have against my uncle—my brothers' lives for the sickle.

Only a fool would deny that deal. If he does, then I will use the weapon to end my uncle and his reign. I'll need an army first before taking the throne. I'm not that much of an idiot to think Omnia guards wouldn't be there to aid in the attack.

"How long have you been in Xannoroth?" I ask Melania.

Omnia Melania scrunches her brow as she looks over at me from her shoulders. I'm as confused by my question as she is.

"Since Lord Byron's death."

Two weeks living in an entirely different kingdom, away from Princess La'Mia and Omnia Itzel. I overheard her Nihilian friend say something about training, but that doesn't make any sense. We are all born with power, but rich bloodlines demand us to wield. Strengthen our powers to protect our kingdoms. All my training occurred when I was a child—trained by my parents first, and then with Micah. She shouldn't have had to train for anything unless she was planning to come after me.

"Why are you in Tenebrae?"

"I came to get *my* sickle back." She pauses before adding, "And to apologize for how rude I was to you."

The last part is more of a mumble that I can barely hear. She brings her forefinger to her lower lip, then uses her other hand to snatch it away.

I don't ask any more questions, and neither does she. I hold a torch to stave off the whispering darkness of night vastly approaching. We should have waited until morning, but I can't trust that Fated pairs wouldn't go searching in the night. It's a risk leaving them behind while we venture into the woods, hoping they'll listen to my orders.

Nylisa enchants the burning trees to create a warm fortress to keep them distracted. Hopefully Melania and I will return safely with all their Fated and other Nihils while they sleep. The quicker we can find them all, the better.

"Wait!" Addilynn's voice rings out.

Omnia Melania and I turn as Addilynn sprints to us. Her cheeks burn bright red as a thick scent of salt drips from her sweat. She stops ahead of us with her hands on her waist, heaving to catch her breath. "You need a Fated mate to track them down." She stands upright, but her words are airy without the oxygen she needs.

Seeing Addilynn this out of breath is strange. She's in excellent shape, especially after working in Nobyl. I didn't realize we had ventured this far. In the distance, nothing remains but the smoke of the burning trees and a dim orange glow.

"It's too dangerous," I say.

Addilynn squares her shoulders, protest dancing on the tip of her tongue.

"She can guide us. There's no use sending her back now," Omnia Melania voices.

Addilynn flinches, and I'd be lying if I said I didn't do the same. I was expecting Omnia Melania to be on my side when it came to their safety. After all, she keeps a Nihilian servant she calls a friend. That alone should mean she cares for them.

Another reason she can't have the sickle.

Omnia Melania turns on her heel and leaves us behind. The chirping of the frownies grows louder. To everyone else, they are dreadblights. But those of us who live here and see them far too often call them what they are. When they contort themselves to crawl, their jagged teeth twist into a terrible frown. I can't understand why the Mother of Monsters would create such a thing. Then again, the same could be said about the macabres. I've never ventured this close to the woods before, not enough to name all the creatures that live here. Some might never leave this place, making them a complete mystery.

Cold seeps from the woods as we venture further in. Surrounded by darkness, the monsters' chirps, howls, and groans increase. Addilynn nudges closer to my side. Once we cross into the tree line, there is no going back.

We will keep you safe, my two wraiths speak.

I'm not quite sure I'll ever get used to that.

It's not me I'm worried about. It's the Nihils, but it's also venturing into such a dark place with my enemy—at least the daughter of my enemy.

"Wait," I say, stretching my arm out to block Omnia Melania from taking the step forward. I can't decide if she's hopeful I may give her the sickle or confused by my apprehension. It could be a concoction of both. "I can't enter these woods with a person I cannot trust."

Omnia Melania's chest rises as she inhales deeply.

"Tell me something no one knows."

Her head rears back. More monstrous sounds break through the thick branches of trees. When she moves to take another step, my hand snaps against her warm bicep, hot despite walking into the coldest part of Tenebrae.

"General Javon took advantage of a woman and has two daughters. No one knows about them, but they were raised in the palace with me. My mother sent them away, too afraid of the attachments I was making with them. Connections and love make a person weak." She releases a mocking laugh before continuing. "I haven't spoken to them but I've sent letters and never got a response. They reside in Quintarius, learning to hone their powers at school." She rambles on before adding, "No one knows of my sisters, and no one else shall!"

With that, Omnia Melania closes her eyes.

"By the First," Addilynn says next to me.

White flames with streaks of iridescence dance over Omnia Melania's arm, but it doesn't burn through the cotton of her clothes, fire that should be unbearable as we stand so close, but it's not. None of the flames move away from her as it sways and contorts to her body. Omnia Melania has become fire incarnate.

She doesn't glance back as she steps past me into the dark woods with a glowing aura of light amidst the darkness. Then she turns to wait for our entrance. Addilynn, wide-eyed, keeps her eyes on the light and pulls from my side to follow her, more closely than I like. Either she's found a new faith in Omnia Melania, or her survival instincts are kicking in.

They're both waiting on me now.

Shadows dance around my fingers. When I snap, Ripper, Reacher, Damsel, and Butcher snarl to life, followed by Moros and Malefic, the enormous wraiths.

"There's no going back," I say before entering the dark woods.

Thirty-Eight

Melania

The dark woods are exactly how I imagined them to be—devoid of life and light; a place where an Omnia should never venture. The animals, or maybe they're all monsters, hiss at the sudden light entering their domain. I can't help but feel for the creatures, living their life only to be disturbed by me and my companions—said companions who are practically pressed against me and my flames.

The white shimmering fire eloquently waltzes over my skin. I expected burning heat, but it's comfortable, like nestling next to a fireplace with a romance book waiting for the long-awaited kiss. I wonder if Addilynn and Erebus feel the same about my power, or if they're scared I may turn on them and burn everything around us down—them included.

My only hope is Erebus believes the truth about my sisters, and I hope it doesn't bring danger their way. It was the only secret that came to mind other than the scar on my ribs. That's a truth I'm not ready to divulge myself. I hope he realizes it was my way of relating to the love he shares for his brothers. It's not blood relation, but it's stronger. It's a connection the Fates deemed was needed, making it that much more important.

Sticks snap under the weight of our feet. I never knew such darkness existed in this world. I can't see the monsters, but I feel their eyes stalking each and every move as hissing and chirping ascends around us.

"Addilynn, follow the tendril," Erebus says.

She steps to my side, leaving Erebus behind. His wide wings curl around us. In the iridescent shimmer, more hues of purples, blues, and greens contrast against the black, mixing a beautiful, colorful mirage of light and dark.

A shadow dashes out in front of us, followed by clicking sounds. It's as if the creature is calling out to others. Goosebumps rise on my skin at the thought.

"Whatever you see, you keep going," Erebus whispers.

His hot breath fans against the side of my neck. Addilynn's eyes are closed, her hand rubbing at the spot above her chest. With limited light, my eyes finally adjust to the void. Thin trees narrow, zooming closer to us—but trees can't move. Unless the dark woods are made up of evil nymphs taunting us.

We follow Addilynn's hurried steps. At times, she slows when she closes her eyes, but not once does she stop. I'm not sure how far we've ventured when a glowing, orange orb snags my attention. Addilynn moves faster to where we're practically running. The clicking increases in volume and numbers, a chorus of monsters watching us.

Erebus groans behind me, and I glance over my shoulder. A black, catlike creature scratches into his wings. My hands clench, ready to react, only for the creature to be ripped away by—nothing?

"You're not the only one who has magic," he croons, but there's a weakness in his voice. I didn't consider monsters nipping at his back. Despite the heavy strain of using fire for this long, I push out more flames. They grow higher, basking more light around us.

With that, I turn back around, only to come face to face with a creature void of features aside from thin slits for nostrils and a crooked smile filled with rows of razor-sharp teeth. I gasp, a shriek rising from my throat, as Erebus's hand snaps over my mouth. He steers me away from the creature as quietly as he can.

"That's a dead dreadblight, but if you try to scream like that again, you will see a real one. They love the taste of fear," he says.

Go to the dark woods, Melania. It'll be fine, you're an Omnia, you can't die.

The glowing orange nears faster now. I pray to all the Gods that it's not a monster luring us. Addilynn runs forward, the creatures in our vicinity quickening with us. A shadow brushes against me, and I fight the scream that threatens to break free. I'm hoping it's one of Erebus's and not a larger version of the cat creature.

"Irwin!" Addilynn exclaims.

The orange light is a torch, but it seems to be made of an arm of some kind. The man nearly drops it to embrace Addilynn in a hug. Several more flickering lights approach, revealing battered and bleeding Nihils covered in mud and what I think is blood. Their mossy scent is thick in the void of the dark woods.

Their eyes land on me. Erebus's hand grazes my lower back, bringing me closer to them. I opt to ignore the way they all cower away from my presence despite the protecting light I project.

The white flame flickers higher without me ordering it to do so, the power threatening to consume everything in its path. Erebus remains focused on the people. He uses his finger to count the heads, making sure everyone is accounted for.

"We have to get back," I say to Erebus, hating that I have to interrupt the joyous moment, but my magic is becoming an extension of me, and there are far too many people in harm's way if it takes complete control.

When Erebus looks at me, I hope he senses the urgency in my eyes. He gives me a curt nod. "Let's make it to safety."

He guides the people as I fight for control over the flames. I grip his forearm, closing my eyes to see the glowing tendril of the sickle, its presence overwhelming. I force myself past it and focus on my magic instead.

There are seven jars made from the crystals of each kingdom inside my veins, the only one missing being Tenebrae. The ruby heart container overflows with fiery essence. I've been holding onto it for too long already—risking combustion that would destroy everything and everyone around me—but I need to keep going. The only way everyone survives this forest is by fleeing from the white flames billowing on my skin.

I can barely tamper down the essence. It won't be much longer until it drains me completely, leaving everyone in the dark with their makeshift torches.

The group moves at a much slower pace than when we came in, people far too injured without enough time to rest. Incessant chatter grates on my nerves as people talk to Erebus about the village burning and how they were able to make a break. It becomes far more difficult to draw in a steadying breath to calm my emotions, my mind anything but clear.

"Are we nearing the—"

A large click stops my words.

Someone slams into my back, but I don't care. It's as if the Mother of Monsters has dropped in front of us.

The beast towers over our group with four arms on each side of its bony torso, its skin bone white compared to the dark gray I've grown used to seeing. Trees move and contort, narrowing in, herding us like a group of cattle. Erebus comes to stand next to me, but there's nothing we can do.

"What are they?" I ask.

"Dreadblights." His voice is stern, but there's an undercurrent of fear.

A crescendo of clicking surrounds us; bones snap and contort as the tall, white, nine-foot dreadblight watches without eyes. Its long black tongue hangs from its jagged mouth. I can't be certain, but it feels as if it's challenging me—a stare down between the most powerful of the forest.

I realize then what this creature is doing and why. "Move very slowly and take the people to safety."

Erebus snaps his head to me, and the creature looks to him immediately. As if realizing he's not the prey it wants, the beast turns back to me. This isn't about satiating hunger; it's about the strongest. If the other dreadblights wanted to attack, they couldn't. I don't know why, but the white one is the matriarch of these woods—royal in her domain until I took a step in here, threatening her.

"I'm not leaving you," Erebus whispers.

Someone whimpers behind us, loosening his resolve. The decision between me and the people is easy to make. They can die—I can't. Erebus might have to sew me back together again, but my essence will always remain.

He breaks away from me. The other dreadblights click loudly as the group scatters. The matriarch brought her army, but those people aren't mine—I won't use them as such.

A sickening smile spreads across her face. Black, tar-like drool leaks down her chin. Several giant arrows jut from the center of her thin, sticklike body. One should have split her in half. It didn't. I'm not foolish enough to think I can kill her. But I will try everything to escape her in one piece.

A twisted grin pulls at my lips as the horde descends. I stop fighting for control.

Instead, I pour every ounce of anger and resentment into the surging essence.

A scream rips from my lungs as fire erupts, consuming everything around us.

The creature thought I was weak prey.

But I'm a godsdamned Omnia.

And I should be feared.

Erebus

The monsters stalking us are gone, clearing a path to safety without their presence twisting us around in a maze. People trip over each other to make it out—a feat I'm grateful for, but Omnia Melania's panicked eyes fill my head until it's all I can feel, hear, and think. I don't trust her nor particularly like her, but she kept her word… and what of me? On the other side of the woods, in the darkest part of night, white glows within the trees. I take a step forward only to stop when a visceral scream falls on my ears, one full of indescribable pain. They're probably ripping her to pieces. Feasting on the blood and skin of the finest kill they've ever had. A blast of burning lilac magic scents the air, warning us before a wave of white fire nears. Through the carnage, dark frownies run away from—

My brain catches up with my eyes, putting the pieces together.

I push into the burning energy, as hands reach my back to pull me from the fray. Pushing them away, I claw toward the forest when Melania appears through the fire of her own making. The flames lick at her skin as if they know she's their master.

Omnia Melania blazes like a star fallen from the sky. A smile blooms on my face knowing she's safe. I didn't know what to do or say; if I put Omnia Itzel's daughter and heiress in harm's way, more carnage would be at my door.

She approaches, swaying on her feet as her hands dangle loosely at her sides. Heat radiates and threatens to burn. Her head droops forward, followed by the rest of her. I catch her, the heat of her body searing my palms. I hiss, but I don't let go as I lower her to the ground.

During times like this, I wish I could heal. I scan the crowd, searching for anyone who might be able to help, only to land on Addilynn. Her blue eyes spark an idea for me.

"Conjure water," I snap.

Addilynn places a hand over her chest like I've offended her.

"Please," I plead.

Melania's skin boils. It doesn't seem to be slowing unless we counteract it. Addilynn shakes her head, then Irwin pulls her to the side, whispering something to her.

She sighs before approaching. Cupping her hands together, she drops a single tear from her eye. Awe strikes me as that one tear becomes enough to fill her palms. Addilynn drops her hands open over Omnia Melania's face, but it isn't enough.

"Is that all you can do?" Worry thickens in my voice.

"I'm not from a royal bloodline," she hisses before starting over again.

Each time, it takes longer for her hands to fill. She helps the best she can. I have to remind myself of that. The flames over Omnia Melania dwindle, but it's the fire inside her we can't get to.

Sighing—and without ideas—I reach behind me to bring forth the sickle. Gasps fill the air. The artifact seems drawn to her as spiderweb-like strings connect between her and the sickle. *I hope I don't regret this.*

Opening her palm, I place the sickle within it. The bright light intensifies through the connection. Her fingers curl around the leather wrapped handle on their own. White flames dance over the curved blade. Then, Omnia Melania stirs as the Omnia artifact breathes life back into her.

"Hot," she chokes out.

White flames smoke from her mouth; the essence is too much, even with the sickle. Addilynn tries to create another tear, but her magic isn't meant for this. Exhaling against her face, she turns closer to me, as if she means to burrow into my skin—my very cold, shadow-infused skin.

I pull her face to mine and press my mouth against hers as I push cold shadows into her. With my hand around her neck, I pulse more power. After a few rounds of breathing, I pull my shadows back.

The flames have died inside her mouth as her body cools, leaving only the white flickering flames against the trees and sickle.

"It's time for rest," I say, pulling Omnia Melania tighter into my chest.

Thirty-Nine

Erebus

It's a new day, and Omnia Melania still slumbers. Elara has been next to her makeshift cot like a sworn protector. I've seen a person step too close only to be cursed for doing so. She only allows Ire to come sit with her. An interesting story, to be sure.

"What happens next?" Addilynn asks me.

Most everyone else has left to search for food and resources. I'm not sure when the last time any of them have eaten, but I'm sure it's been one day too long.

"Now, you all make a new village while I get my brothers back from the Onyx palace," I say.

Addilynn laughs, stirring Irwin's presence. The pair, like many others, has been inseparable since reuniting—for the second time, might I add. He places a hand on her back, pulling her to reality.

"You're being serious," she says, still recovering from her fit of laughter.

Irwin glances between us, trying to make sense of a conversation he walked in on. That's why I've learned to eavesdrop well enough to know what everyone is saying at all times—it makes things less awkward.

"He wants to go the palace by himself," she says.

Irwin's brows slam over his eyes, repeating the same thing as Addilynn regarding my seriousness. It's not a mystery why these two are Fated.

"I must save my brothers, and the only way to do that is to turn myself in."

Without the sickle, I don't have the bargaining chip I need. I could try to steal it back, but I fear Omnia Melania's lapdog. Even now, it's like her eyes are watching me, as if she's waiting for my next move. I've tried to figure out any other solution to save us all, but the options are dwindling. I've even considered asking Omnia Melania for her aid, but it seems too dangerous to involve her.

"My brothers will return to help build another village," I say, running my slick palms against my torn trousers.

"And what of you?" Addilynn asks.

I bring my lower lip between my teeth. She knows the answer—we all do. My uncle won't let me go free. He made the mistake before, and I'm certain he won't make it again.

"You want to be a martyr?" Irwin bites out. My lack of an answer is answer enough. He swears under his breath, pinching his fingers between his eyes.

Tears brim Addilynn's lashes as her stricken gaze finds me. "No," she snaps. My lips part to argue. She raises her palm to my face. "You don't get to do that. Your brothers and the villagers need you, maybe more than you need them. Have you considered how they would feel if you sacrificed yourself for them? More so, I don't understand why you believe you must fight every battle alone." She pauses to catch her breath.

"You behave like you don't want to be king, but you've done everything a king would to do to protect his people. Enemies attacked our village, but it doesn't mean you get to play the martyr when we all want to fight against them. The only thing you're forgetting is that kings have armies and you're refusing to use yours." She's out of breath by the time she finishes, eyes flaring as magic circulates through her.

Irwin presses against her side. "We might not have magic, but we fought our way out of the dark woods when we could have given up. Lean on us as you would your brothers; they would want you to."

My lip bleeds, but I don't care. What they're saying makes sense. I could have an army and march to my uncle's palace to demand back the crown that should be mine. It doesn't guarantee we win, but it's a better chance than self-sacrifice.

Someone clears their throat. Elara walks over. Dark strands of brown hair frame her heart-shaped face, her deep brown eyes staring at us. Up close, I notice a fluttering of either freckles or dirt. Her lips form a tight smile. "There's someone else here who would be willing to join your cause," she says, receiving a glare that could kill from Addilynn.

"We have all the help we need," she snaps.

Irwin tries to step in front of his Fated, but she pushes past him.

"I'm not speaking to you," Elara is quick to say before facing me. "Can I speak with you in private?"

She pulls me to the side before I can give her an answer. Irwin seems to hold Addilynn back. I don't know what the story is between these two, but the tension is thicker than Omnia Melania and me.

Elara guides us closer to where Omnia Melania lies. Her eyes remain closed, but her chest rises and falls in even beats. The sickle is clenched in her fist. Somehow, I have the same sentiment for the weapon that doesn't belong to me. She seems so peaceful like this. No white flames threatening to burn everything. No crying on Lord Byron's grounds, covered in rain and blood.

"Omnia Melania is different than her mother," Elara whispers. I lean in closer as she tells me about her interactions with Omnia Melania. About her time in Xannoroth, helping Elara, treating them like people and not monsters—saving Ire despite being stabbed by her. "Her mother wanted to punish Ire for acting out against the bloodline, and Omnia Melania spared her. She isn't perfect by any means, but she's kind. One of the best people to have at your side when things get hard. I don't know all that she's endured, but there takes a special strength to march into the dark woods and burn it all down to protect people who care so little for her, don't you agree?"

Elara makes sense, but I can't find it in me to have the same faith in her as she does. Not when it comes to the safety of the Nihils or my crown. Yet, I ask, "Would she even help?"

"You could ask me," Omnia Melania says, voice groggy.

She lies on her back, eyes bouncing between us as her words hang in the air. Addilynn's comment about me fighting alone didn't mean asking Omnia Melania to help. I mull over my options. "Would you sign the Great Cleansing Ordinance?"

"No," she replies without an ounce of hesitation.

"Will you help me find my brothers?" I ask.

Omnia Melania's rainbow irises dart around Elara, Addilynn, Irwin, and me. She picks at the side of her thumb, and I realize it's her nervous tick. Before the white frownie descended, she was doing the same thing.

"I have to be home for Princess La'Mia's coronation at the end of the week," Omnia Melania says.

She's neither saying yes nor no. It's my turn to mull over her words, waiting for the pieces to connect in my mind. It's the twenty-eighth of the month, two days since my birthday and the attack against Nobyl. Two days ago, my brothers were left in a dungeon. In two more days, Princess La'Mia will have her coronation. There isn't much time before things could escalate. Elara is right; I do need

Melania. It would make our chances of winning significantly better, and we could divide and conquer. For the first time, this plan makes absolute sense compared to turning myself in or leading the Nihils into slaughter.

"When everyone returns, we rally and leave for Onyx City." There's a renewed confidence in my voice.

Part of me is eager to venture into the city where I learned to walk; people praising my parents for their boundless blessings. Hearing the songs of shadow wielders and sanguines praising the Mother's blood moon. The first and last time I drank from my mother was on my ninth birthday during the blood rite—the same night my uncle killed his own sister and brother-in-law. The praises to the mother haven't been sung nor has a blood moon appeared since then.

"I will aid you," Omnia Melania says, drawing me away from the mixed emotions of joy and immense sorrow. "And when the crown is on your head, I shall depart for Omnius."

I try to ignore the sadness in her voice or the way her eyes flit to Elara, as if they're communicating something. "Thank you," I whisper before departing.

I won't try to understand the relationship between the two of them, but there's something special. As they speak, I strategize the best places to attack. From its position on the hill, there are too many spots that would leave us vulnerable. Guards are always posted at the wrought-iron gates that line the grounds. Portaling inside the palace could work, but it leaves the Nihils vulnerable to walk in without me. As for Omnia Melania, she's going to have the most important job.

To save and heal my brothers.

All the Nihils have since returned as the sun sets, some covered in blood and others empty-handed. Omnia Melania turns away from the sight. I'm reminded of our dinner together at King Albus's palace two days ago when she nearly squirmed at the sight of the bloody broth; a dinner that feels like months ago.

Irwin tends to the fire as Wrath cooks the meat, his sister, Ire, cuddling beside Elara. Seeing the child was almost too much. I considered giving her a shadow flower, but I fear I'll never be able to craft another one without thinking of Halona. The memory of her has me standing from the ground, startling those closest to me. Out of the forty people, only half of them will be fit to travel, and that's including Nylisa and the children.

Omnia Melania clenches the handle of the sickle, sitting away from the group. I've become accustomed to the distance she creates between people. I think to gather the crowd, but the words never come. Omnia Melania holds the blade in front of her. With a lunge, she strikes at the air, only to go back to her center. Over and over, she keeps doing this, but her form is wrong as she strikes without a leading foot, body too tense to land a solid strike.

She pays me little attention as she practices a slash with the back of the blade. The one portion of the sickle that shouldn't be sharp, but it is. The end was once dull, only to sharpen with each passing. A double-edged blade is completely lethal.

"Would you like help?" I ask.

Omnia Melania jumps. Her empty hand lands on the center of her chest. Sweat lines her hairline and above her lips. Faint pink touches her cheeks, whether from exertion or embarrassment. "Is it that obvious?"

"To me it is, but I've been using weapons for more than half my life and was trained under the toughest warrior I know."

Omnia Melania glances from my head to my toes. She nods her permission.

"The weapon is an extension of you. Feel the blade and the energy it has. Let it feed off you."

"That's how I ended up with an Omnia artifact as a sickle," she quips.

"It wouldn't have been my first choice either," I say.

A small smile blossoms on her face. One of my own answers back to it. I begrudgingly don't hate her. I wouldn't seek her out in a crowd, though—

Liar, Moros says.

Shut up, I snap back. Malefic is now my favorite for his silence. Moros could learn a thing or two about that. Before Moros can retort, my attention shifts solely to Omnia Melania.

"Do you mind?" I ask, moving closer to stand at her back.

She shakes her head, but I'll need more than that before pressing her against me. "Use your words," I say. Not something I'd ever thought I would say to someone other than Lelantos.

"It's okay," she responds, her voice quieter.

My hand wraps around hers, gripping the blade, trying hard to focus on the sickle and teaching her how to wield it while keeping her ass from my groin. With my empty hand, I shift her into a fighting stance using my foot to part her legs, ensuring the weight is on her dominant foot.

"Relax," I whisper.

Wispy pieces of her hair shift. Her shoulders rise as she draws a deep breath. Her lilac scent is grounding. Omnia Melania follows my movements, shifting from a neutral stance to one for fighting. With the hand wrapped over hers, I move the blade in a slashing motion. If an opponent were in front of us, it would slice from their shoulder to hip. I show her both ways for her to learn if it comes to that, then help her thrust against the soft part of the opponent's metaphorical stomach.

"If you're dealing with armor, it's best to use magic against them," I say, backing away from her.

"Thank you," she says.

There are many things I didn't expect to hear in my short twenty years of life, and an Omnia thanking me was one of them. Her eyes bore into me, and for the strangest reason, my attention flits to the bare skin under her collarbone. Disappointment finds root in my chest. Pale pink tone flushing her skin. It's my turn to be embarrassed when realizing where I was staring.

"And if it comes to slicing their throat, well you know how to do that." The words tumble out of my mouth as I attempt to stave off the awkwardness. I couldn't take them back even if I wanted to.

Omnia Melania's head snaps back as she mumbles, "Thank you," then returns to Elara.

Any growth between us is gone with my poor choice of words in an awkward moment. Something that rarely happens to me. If she succeeds in saving my brothers, perhaps there are more chances for me to redeem myself later.

But first, we have to get there.

Forty

Melania

Erebus returns to the fire, barely able to keep my eyeline. I should say something about the comment he made. From the red in his cheeks, I knew he didn't mean it, but the delivery surprised me. Like having my worst moment thrown back in my face, as if I won't regret that day for decades after—especially if any more people die for wanting to give mercy.

"The time has come when hiding is no longer an option," Erebus' raspy voice rings out.

Everyone drops what they're doing. Elara perks up. He hasn't told the people what comes next, but everything is about to change. It's the same feeling I had when I ended Lord Byron's life. The same certainty that settled over me when I swore I would end the Great Cleansing.

The Fates are setting their plan in motion. No matter how many times we think we can outrun our destiny, we can't. Everything comes to fruition one way or another. This time, it's Prince Erebus standing at the center of it instead of me. But even saying that feels wrong. Our fates are no longer separate, bound by the damned sickle strapped to my chest.

"As you all know, Micah and Lelantos have been captured. The wrongful king wants my life for theirs, but we're not going to let that happen. My parents were King Ezra and Queen Elanora Ravenheart. Neither of them raised me to give up when things became too hard. I am only sorry it's taken me this long to remember.

They lost their lives over the crown. It's time my uncle loses his, so I can gain back what is rightfully mine. I need the help of all those able to fight alongside myself and Omnia Melania." He finds me in the crowd, and all eyes turn with him. This attention is different from my mother's palace; here, there's hope, a chance to see change for the Greater Good—and it's because of me and Erebus. Gone is my mother's puppet, the docile and demure daughter following orders with a fake smile.

"Going into this battle, I will carry the courage of Lelantos Reviers, the man who has earned the reputation of being more beast than man—the Nihilian king. His courage to change his Fate from captive to guiding me to fight for what is mine."

A chorus of cheers rings out, but I've never heard of Lelantos the Nihilian king. The most lucrative of the Three. A fierce hunter with little to few words.

People are still cheering when Erebus exclaims, "I will carry Micah Fenwick's bravery within me; the man who pulled me from the palace the night we were overthrown. He could have left me behind, but he knew there was more destined for me." Erebus pauses, his throat working on a swallow. His orbs of darkness settle on me as he finishes his message. "I will seize the throne for all of you. A new way of life for all beings of Veilia. A cause my parents died for, and one I fight for.

It will be my courage to guide those through the darkness. My bravery to stand against tyrants. My power and strength to protect us from those who wish us harm. It is my people to whom I pledge my fealty to. To all of you, I promise the Great Cleansing will end with the start of my reign."

The crowd roars, pounding their fists over their chests and against the ground. They chant *King Erebus Ravenheart*. I hadn't understood why the Fates brought us together, but after his speech, it's become very clear. *We* are the beginning of a new way of life, starting with crowning the rightful king of Tenebrae, Erebus Ravenheart.

After quick goodbyes where I had to swear to Ire nothing would harm Wrath and Elara, we left with the minimal crowd of twelve, a poor-looking army compared to the one we're about face. Then again, I alone could fend them all off, fail, and come back to life. An exhausting battle, to be sure.

As we near the City of Onyx, disappointment settles over me. The dead grass and gnarled branches are gone, replaced by a city somehow even more depressing. I saw more life in the dark woods than here.

Elara bumps my shoulder and points toward the palace on the hill. My jaw drops at the sight of the gothic structure, built entirely from onyx. It perches above the city as if lording over everything below, a stark contrast against the lavender sky. The stone gleams so dark and smooth, I'm certain anyone inside could see their reflection in its walls.

My attention shifts to Prince Erebus, searching for any reaction, but there is none. His dark eyes match the color of the palace, cold and empty. His feathers ruffle.

Erebus guides us to the entrance of the city. My disappointment quickly turns to shock. I expected to see something more like Umber. A booming town with merchants lining the streets. The scent of food and ale drifting through the air. Instead, the streets reek of body odor, feces, and rotting flesh. The stench is nearly unbearable. I breathe through my mouth to tolerate it.

Slate stones mark the path beneath our feet. On either side runs a narrow canal filled with stagnant brown water. A woman leans over the edge and splashes the murky liquid onto her face. Then, cupping her frail hands, she drinks from it.

"I think I'm going to be sick," someone says.

I have the same notion as the woman drinks from her hands without gagging. A necessity for survival, I suppose. Prince Erebus stands still as a statue, his eyes darting from the eroding slate, onyx, and ebony wood buildings back to the people lying in the streets. Barely clothed and mostly skin and bones. I can't read their emotions, but it's written over their faces and bodies—complete and utter hopelessness. They're suffering.

I lean down so my hand hovers above the water, focusing on anything but the smell of excrements. My eyes close as I imagine the turquoise blue bottle of water magic. The hardest one yet for me to wield, understandably so, since my father is the king of fire. I push anyway, removing the cork stopper of the vial, then focus on the sound of the crashing waves of Brilore. Salty breeze against my face. Sand squishing between my toes as I run into the high tide.

Movement sounds around me, but I ignore it as I focus my energy on cleaning the water. I can't make them food, but I can give them this. When I feel as if I have done enough, my eyes open to the shining canals. Addilynn kneels on the other side of the path as she makes silent peace with me.

Erebus assists me with standing even though I don't need it. His raven wing brushes against my side.

"Thank you." His voice cracks.

The people pay us little attention as we move deeper into the city. Lines form near the river as they wait for their turn to drink and fill buckets. Once Prince Erebus sits upon the throne, I wonder what decisions he will make. Providing the Nihils a safe place is important to him, but it's not just them anymore. All these shadow wielders who have been forgotten will need help rebuilding their city, starting with food. I consider sending aid from Omnius to transport goods to the people. I can't enact it until the crown is upon my head, though, and my coronation is three months away; the first day of spring when Quintarius blooms fully with plants and animals.

"What're you thinking?" Elara asks.

Two guards in white armor entering the other side of the city catches my eye before I can answer. Erebus turns quickly, ushering us into a building that threatens to break under our weight.

Long, wooden pews made from dark oak face a small dais in the front of the room. A portrait of a young woman with long blonde hair smiles at us with sharp fangs, revealing a deep dimple on the right side of her mouth. She has maroon eyes under thick eyelashes.

On the other side of the dais is a portrait of—

My mouth dries at the sight of a young man with raven wings. A metallic crown circles his head, its onyx points rising like the steeples of the palace. Raven feathers are engraved into the dark slate, weaving through the band between embedded stones. His hair falls to his shoulders, and his eyes are darker than the night sky. Aside from the smile, Erebus is the very image of his father, starting with those domineering, abyssal eyes.

On the back wall, beneath a hanging floral arrangement of dead flowers, is an oil portrait of the late king and queen holding a baby with small wings. A miniature crown rests on his head, matching his parents'. His chubby hand squeezes his mother's thin finger. The royal family, captured in paint, marking a new dawn with the princeling in their arms. I can't help but glance at Prince Erebus, wondering what kind of man he might have become if they had never died. He stands on his toes, leaning against the frail wall. As if sensing my stare, he nods for me to flank his right side. He peers through a thin slit in the stone, too high for me to reach. I choose a lower one in the wall instead.

If we weren't in a desecrated church, hemmed in by memorial portraits of the murdered king and queen of Tenebrae, it might almost be funny to see us like this—two royals pressed against a filthy wall, spying on the approaching guards. Their bodies are coiled tightly as they make their way toward the city, shoulders drawn high beneath helmets crested with rainbow feathers that mark their allegiance. Longswords hang at their iron belts, metal-clad hands gripping the hilts, ready to draw.

One glances at the clear water flowing through the streets. His head tilts toward the other. My heart beats in my chest. I didn't mean to put anyone at risk.

"We are here by decree of the king," the taller guard says. "It's been brought to his attention that people are conspiring with Nihils in Tenebrae; an unlawful lack in accordance with the Great Cleansing Ordinance. We will search your homes. If anyone is harboring a Nihil, they will be sent to Omnius to receive judgement by Omnia Itzel."

Prince Erebus tenses, his breath breaking into uneven pants. The sweat-slick bodies of the Nihils press in on all sides, setting my skin on edge. I don't fight the urge to bite my nail—it's the only thing keeping me grounded through this sensory nightmare and the rising dread of a guard search.

"Everyone, stay very still," Prince Erebus whispers.

Realization dawns on me; they don't know what's about to happen. Wisps of shadows emerge like a fog over a lake around Prince Erebus's clenched fists, spiraling over his forearms and biceps. A cold tendril runs past me, inciting a chill over my neck. Elara's wide gaze finds me as they cocoon us together.

I immediately spring into action, watching between the shadows as he focuses solely on weaving shadow around us. It's the only way quiet the shame gnawing in my chest. I was brought here to help, but what good am I if all I can do is hide? Elara's hand drifts along my back, as if she senses my unease… or perhaps it's her own.

The guards move swiftly through the cracked homes, the fractures making checks easier. They're only one house away when the shadows conceal us wholly. Part of me wonders if they'll avoid the sacred church we've found ourselves in.

As if they could read my thoughts, one of the guards says, "How about this place?"

"That place is desolate like the rest of the town," the other guard responds. I exhale sharply as they move in another direction.

Shadows lighten slightly, Erebus's shoulders relaxing with them. I struggle to understand any of this. My mother warned me to avoid Tenebrae—to fear all shadow wielders as if their power were contagious. And yet, her own royal guard patrols these streets, her own influence catching like wildfire.

My thoughts lead me to wonder what truly happened to Prince Erebus's parents. I only saw them once as a child, and then never again after that. My brain wracks to remember what the meeting was for. It's rare for all royals to be in one place unless they're enacting a law throughout the kingdoms.

The missing piece clinks into place. The enactment of the Great Cleansing Ordinance. I didn't know what they were arguing about, but the discussion was heated. A week later, people mourned the king and queen of Tenebrae. Then Queen Gaia died, and The Great Cleansing Ordinance was enacted the same day.

Heat moves over my skin, knowing the cost for my mother to enact her own agenda. I've always known her to be wicked, but to kill another king and queen for the sake of it is beyond me.

"Omnia Melania, calm down," Prince Erebus whispers, worry

evident in his tone.

I open my eyes, not realizing I'd closed them—and understand their panic. White flames gutter, thinning the shadows that keep us hidden.

Deep breaths, Melania. In for four, out for four, I think, reminding myself of what Albus told me to do when it all suddenly felt like everything and nothing in the same breath.

The flames dim, but the damage has been done. The shadowy cocoon barely covers our legs. Erebus's eyes flare wide. My heart drums in my ears, leaving me to worry if everyone else can hear it. Through the thin slit, the guards are still outside searching. We are safe as long as no one makes a—

Irwin sneezes, then recovers with panicked eyes. Prince Erebus struggles to summon more shadows to encompass us once more, a fruitless endeavor as my skin glows.

The door begins to budge, shaking loose dust from the walls. Before it's able to open, someone yells out, "Why would Nihils even come to this desolate place?"

Through the slit, a burly, bald man with biceps larger than my head approaches, drawing the guards' attention. Prince Erebus glances out, his breathing quickening. When he looks back at me, it's like he's seen a ghost.

"Leave us to do our duty," a guards responds, coming into view. The other one must be at the door, deciding whether or not to open it.

"Judging by your armor, your duties are far from here," the burly man argues.

I can't decide whether I'm grateful for the distraction or scared for his safety as the guards close in on him. His deep-set, dark eyes leer down at them, sharp and unbothered. A smug smile tugs at his mouth until his gaze shifts to the chapel—right where I'm looking.

The strike happens so fast I nearly miss it—one guard's helmet is sent flying from his head, and I recognize him instantly as a guard who used to patrol the east wing door in Omnius. He was playing cards with another guard the night I killed Lord Byron.

The burly man shoves the guard away. He stumbles, and the other surges in, arms and fists flying. Both guards, disposable foot soldiers for my mother, have lost their helmets now. They pant, faltering with cheeks flushed, sweat slicking their foreheads. A crowd gathers, watching as the man makes light work of those meant to protect Omnius—in a way, it's pathetic.

One reaches for their sword. The bald man is too distracted by the other to see the blade thrust into the center of his stomach. His large hands cover the wound as the foot soldier pulls it out, and black blood oozes from the blade onto the ground. Prince Erebus sighs, mumbling something under his breath about the Mothers and his soul. A guard shackles the man's wrists as his wound bleeds heavily. Bile stops in my throat as the guards force him to walk with them, tugging him along to the Onyx Palace, though I know it's unlikely he will make it that far. The man looks over his shoulder at us, a smile on his face—he knows exactly what is going to happen next.

"That was close," Prince Erebus says.

"We have to save him," I whisper.

Eyes settle on me as if I grew another head and four arms, Prince Erebus being one of them as he stares at me through his thick lashes.

"We rest tonight and venture to the palace tomorrow."

The man won't make it that long, even if he has superior healing. What was it Erebus said when he rushed us into the dark woods? "There's no better time than the present." I echo it back with a faint, smug shrug.

Erebus drags his lower lip between his teeth. His gaze shifts past me, scanning the crowd. Elara stands at my side, wearing a matching, devious smirk. There's a hunger in the people. They want battle. Vengeance for the burning of their village, yes, but it runs deeper than that. To rise against a king…

It's the beginning of change for generations to come.

"Let's go to battle," Erebus says.

Forty-One

Erebus

Harold used to be a general for my father, one of the best fighters back then, and it seems he still is. My chest cracks knowing he's Hamish's identical twin. When he was stabbed, I hoped he would have died right then and there, so he could be reunited in the afterlife with his brother. Then Omnia Melania had to suggest saving him—a notion I felt deep down but was too scared to voice.

Fear has warped its way into me in a way it never has before. These people look to me to lead them in battle, and all I can think about are my brothers. I know what I said in my speech, except when I said it, the words felt different than they do now with the prospect of adding action.

Omnia Melania flits around the chapel, healing everyone to their finest. I shouldn't worry about her, but I wonder about the strain she's putting on her body by doing so. She has to remain strong if we have any chance of succeeding. Then again, we have no choice but to succeed, lest we all die or face the wrath of Omnia Itzel.

"We are ready to go." Omnia Melania's voice is more chipper than it was before, practically vibrating at the idea of beginning a battle I was certain she wouldn't want to partake in. During the last few days, I've learned to see her as Omnia Melania and not the spawn of my enemy.

Nodding, I try to reconcile my past and present, wondering how I got to this moment. Standing in a long-forgotten place of worship with memorial paintings of my parents that used to hang in their bedroom, preparing to conjure a portal to the woods on the outskirts of the garden. I'm not sure how I'll react seeing the palace grounds so closely. Would it trigger the scent of my mother's sugary hot tea or the booming voice of my father pretending to be a giant I had to defeat with a wooden dagger? I'm not quite sure I can handle it. Not after seeing what the Onyx City has become.

How could I abandon my people like this? To see them drinking water from canals that contained things I don't want to think about, frail as skeletons with barely any flesh on their bones. I thought my uncle was ruling the people as he wanted to, but I realize he's more wicked than I thought. My fists tighten at the notion of Omnius guards prancing around the city, searching for Nihils when I've built Tenebrae to be a haven.

"Are you alright?" Omnia Melania asks, clutching my arm and leading us away from the people before I can respond and into an abandoned dining area.

A broken table and chairs scatter across the room. Stained glass windows reflect broken light on the other wall. Omnia Melania waits for me to answer. I could lie and tell her everything is just fine, or divulge the truth.

"I don't think I can do this."

Her rainbow eyes catch the light from the window as she nods slowly. Light within the darkness. Without thinking, I pull her against me, seeking comfort in her tense body, but she doesn't pull away, and

I cling to her like she's another lifeline in the absence of my brothers.

"What if I fail?" I ask against the top of her head.

Her response is immediate. "What if you succeed?"

I pull away, my eyes dropping to her pink lips, noticing the rounder curve of her bottom, leaving a permanent pout. Lost in the clash of right and wrong, fear and bravado, failure and success, I lower my lips to hers. They're just as soft as they were when I breathed shadows into her after the dark woods.

Her hands land against my chest, leaving me eager for a deeper kiss. She pushes me away instead, leaving me staring at blown pupils in place of her rainbow.

"I don't know what overcame me," I say.

"It's quite alright." Her voice is meek, and I can't decipher if she wants it to happen again or not.

Before I can ask, Addilynn enters the room. "Someone's here to see you," she says, looking right at me.

Dread fills me as I leave them behind, not feeling an ounce better than when I entered. The Nihils gather, staring at a man in the doorway with long black waves down to his navel. He has a slender build, like many of the other city folk. His clothes are torn, and on his waist is a sheathed short sword. I tense, broadening my shoulders as I prepare to fight if needed, as long as it means protecting my people.

"I'm Alexander, the blacksmith to the king."

My hand wraps around the handle of my dagger. "What do you want?"

"We want to help," he responds, lowering to a bow.

"We?" I question.

Alexander moves to the side to reveal a group outside with swords and shields in hand. They're stocked to the brink with weapons on their waists.

"We served your father, and we want to serve you!" a woman outside exclaims.

Tears I've been holding back threaten to fall. The fear of failing refuses to fade, even with this newfound motivation. More numbers mean a greater chance to win, even if we are being hasty.

"Thank you," I respond.

Leaving the chapel, our new followers pass out swords and shields, reprieving us from our lack of preparation and stock.

Then, we review the plan, starting with me and Omnia Melania separating. She will go to the palace to save my brothers while my group prepares to battle outside and take out the rest of the guards. And then there's the notion of finding my uncle, ending his life, and placing the crown upon my head. I keep that to myself.

"All Hail King Erebus," the crowd chants when I finish divulging the information.

Omnia Melania chants with them. The ushering of a new dawn starts today—one that will be written into history. All I can hope for is that the Mothers and Fates are on our side. In my palm, a portal forms. Omnia Melania moves to create one of her own to lead closer to the palace.

"Wait," I exclaim. I don't want her walking the streets of Onyx unprotected. I don't want her unprotected at all. But once she has my brothers, I know she'll be safe.

She glides back to me, her long, white gown hissing against the floor, a woman fitted for royalty—not battle. I don't know when she was able to change, but she did. I search her, realizing the sheath for the sickle is no longer strapped to her chest. Panic flares.

"It's safe with me," she says.

Part of me wants to ask her where it's at, but I fear I've already crossed too many personal lines by kissing her. I'll reflect on my actions after the battle, not before.

"When you reach my brothers, find the tall one. Micah is more understanding than Lelantos. He'll be able to keep Lelantos from attacking you," I explain, and her eyes widen. Lelantos didn't gain the reputation of being more beast than man for his charming personality, so I continue, fear and all. "Whatever you do, under no circumstances, do *not* touch him."

I hope she can hear the urgency in my tone. She graces me with a closed lip smile before saying, "Don't touch Lelantos. Got it."

I really hope she doesn't. I can't afford for Lelantos to go feral nor her powers retaliating against him. She turns away from me, and I watch her step through the portal as I place my own on the ground.

I hope I don't regret this, I think to myself before ushering the wave of people through.

Only time will tell, Moros and Malefic answer in unison.

Forty-Two

My steps are heavy as I walk up the giant hill to the Onyx Palace. The gothic building grows more breathtaking the closer I get. A tall iron fence, tipped with sharp points, surrounds it—keeping intruders out. Two guards in black armor stand at the gates, lifeless as statues, yet I can feel their eyes on me, tracking every step. By the time I reach them, I'm winded and regretting the gown over my leathers. Then again, the plan is contingent on it—on me donning the mask of Omnia Itzel's obedient daughter. A wolf in sheep's clothing, one far too many people underestimate.

"I am here to speak with King Marcus." My voice is steady despite the lack of air.

"We weren't expecting you," the larger guard says, his words muffled behind the black helmet crowned with protruding raven wings. I can't see his eyes, but his stance is meant to intimidate—one hand resting on the hilt of his blade, ready to draw. If I were anyone else, I might be afraid, but I've been around guards my whole life.

Their tactics are child's play compared to General Javon's.

I scoff. "What are your names?"

"Lucian," the same one says before pointing to the other one. "This is Enzo."

"Well, Lucian and Enzo, I don't expect low-life guards to be privy to the inner workings of the royal proceedings."

They glance between each before deciding to open the squeaky gates, the sound grating against my eardrums. When King Erebus takes the throne, he'll need to fortify the palace with more than a rusty gate and fence. The guards step aside to let me pass, though the gap is barely wide enough.

"What does Omnia Itzel want?" Guard Lucian says.

"Nothing you need to know about," I snap.

Neither of the guards speak further. My teeth graze against the inside of my cheek, a new habit I've learned does help against the nerves. My heart pounds regardless as sweat blossoms above my upper lip. I would have been happier leading the Nihils and retired soldiers into battle than tasked with saving Prince Erebus's brothers. If I fail—or if they're already dead—I don't think I can fix him ever again. I couldn't imagine if I tasked him to save my sisters and then learned he didn't succeed. There's a chance I would do something I regret in my wave of despair and anger.

The towering palace is unsettling with lifeless brown grass overgrown like a dead meadow. Onyx barely peeks through as long shadows cast over me the closer I get to the domineering structure. Ravens circle above, loosening raspy caws into the night. They soar above spires with shards jutting out.

Crisscross patterns stretch across the high, arched windows. Columns of chiseled onyx rise on either side, carved into the likeness of shadow figures, each with a raven perched along its outstretched arm. They support a massive slab of onyx above the entrance. Everything about the gothic palace is hauntingly beautiful.

There's a door, but it blends seamlessly into the structure, nearly invisible. Only the twin knockers, shaped like raven heads, betray its presence. In the polished onyx, I catch my reflection: rainbow eyes glimmering with the power in my veins, long iridescent white hair falling to my navel, shoulders pulled back with confidence I've never known. Like I've finally stepped into the place I was always meant to stand, away from the shackles of my mother.

I can't help but smile, realizing I found the freedom I've longed for in the shape of a rebellion.

One of the guards begins to push the slab open. It groans as it yields. A smile touches my face as I take my first step into the palace. The heavy stone slams shut behind me, leaving me alone within the onyx walls—my reflection surrounding me on all sides.

Above, dark candelabras sway in a phantom breeze, their maroon candles flickering just enough to guide my path. Twin staircases rise ahead, leading to the next level of the palace. Guards in black armor stand so still along the walls that I hadn't noticed them at all.

"Omnia Melania."

I flinch hearing my name.

Glancing around, the guards still have not moved. My name echoes again. With heavy, hesitant steps, I move toward the sound, though I can't be certain where it came from. The palace feels like a grand maze, leading me nowhere.

I come upon two massive obsidian slab doors, an arched crest above them bearing the symbol of a crown.

"Omnia Melania." The whispers form into my voice, clear now.

As I push the heavy door open, my eyes widen at the black-and-white checkered floor, laid out like a chessboard. Arched alcoves line the walls where I assume portraits once hung.

Against the back wall sits a raised platform, with two narrow staircases leading up to it. A grand throne towers at its center, one that puts my mother's to shame. Its back is carved from uncut onyx, jagged and severe, sharp angles jutting like shards. An open window behind it reveals the courtyard, the lowering sun casting a lavender hue across the stone, turning the edges into something like stars in the night sky. At the throne's highest point, two daggers cross in an X, a raven perched on a skull between them—an emblem of Tenebrae. Yet, none of the guards wear it.

Seated upon the throne is the false king. His graying skin sinks against his bones, hollow and brittle. Long, stringy hair—void of color and life—hangs to the center of his chest. The crown of Tenebrae barely clings to his head. His royal garments hang loosely, ill-fitted to his withered frame. A vial of white, iridescent liquid rests around his neck. My power comes alive seeing it, a sloshing sensation taking root in my stomach.

"Your visit is unexpected." His voice is weak. Flecks of dust fall from his mouth when he speaks.

"One long overdue, it seems." My terse tone is too similar to my mother's. I should hate it, but I can't. Not when I know I'm speaking to the false king who killed his own blood to get to the throne. Like the portrait of Queen Elanora, his eyes are dark maroon, perusing my body like he owns it. He fixes his gaze on the main artery in my neck, thrumming with blood and power. His magic doesn't come from Veilia like the others, drawing strength from the elements or from the light and shadows of Princess La'Mia and Prince Erebus. His comes from taking—from drinking power from others, using their blood to wield them like puppets. I've often wondered why my mother never attacked Sanguines. Seeing Marcus and the vial around his neck gives me my answer.

"It's custom to bow when an Omnia is in your presence." My voice drips with disdain as my resolve weakens, untapped power in me threatening to rage against him and the hypocritical, tyrannical reign of my mother.

Marcus' bones crack as he peels himself away from the chair, leaving a worn spot in the velvet cushion from his body. He presses most of his weight onto a cane in his right hand, then bows his head before returning to normal. Another slight of his lack of respect for me.

"Lower," I say with cool command.

A hiss slips past his sharp fangs, the crown tilting forward on his head. He snatches at it, nearly toppling over with the sudden movement. The scent of lavender and dust drifts toward me. A drop of his shimmering maroon blood hits the floor. I force my gaze back to him, away from the abhorrent liquid.

"Rise," I demand.

A deep, twisted part of me wonders if my mother would be proud of the wickedness in my voice. Could she look upon me now and feel pride for the woman she birthed?

"Why are you in my kingdom?" King Marcus asks as his wound fuses back together.

"My mother sent me to retrieve the outlaws."

Marcus' eyes flare. His tongue darts out to lick the blood on his hand. I choke on a swallow, fighting the bile to keep it down.

"Your mother, Omnia Itzel, sent *you* to retrieve them?"

Sweat forms on my palms. He cocks his head to the side, eyebrows raised, waiting for my response.

"Don't play coy. You know who my mother is, and you should be aware she doesn't take kindly to people who displease her," I snap.

"Of course she doesn't. The guards will escort you to the dungeon." His voice is cunning like a snake circling its prey before biting.

Two guards from the city enter the throne room, their helmets gone, revealing red marks where their skin healed from the fight with the man who saved us near the cathedral.

They flank my side with nervous energy surrounding them, never once touching me, as if they're scared to be this close to me.

King Marcus smirks. "Oh, Omnia Melania, I'm sure General

Javon would like to pay you a visit after dealing with my nephew."

I swallow the panic rising in me, thinking of General Javon. He never goes anywhere without my mother—but I would know if she were here. Her presence is unmistakable, like a vile force draining life from my soul. I strain to listen for anything beyond these walls, but the palace is too thick.

Somehow, Marcus knew I was coming. He knew I was with Prince Erebus. I rub the back of my neck, gritting my teeth as the mark I was born with rises beneath my skin. Someone else is here; the only other person my mother would want General Javon protecting.

And this time, she won't have to answer to my mother. It'll be me.

Before the doors close behind me, I whisper in the ancient tongue taught to descendants of ancient bloodlines, "I hope you choke on your dried-up power and blood as the rightful king crushes your impenitent body to get his throne."

The guards lead me through the darkened palace. As we enter the study choked with cobwebs and dust, I wonder where they're taking me. The one who always watches me on the palace grounds steps forward and pulls a book from the shelf. A mechanism clicks, unlocking something hidden as a door slides open. Beyond it, a winding staircase descends into the damp depths below.

"It's for the Greater Good," he says.

Then he leads me down the slick spiral staircase, one guard ahead with his head bowed, watching his steps. I sigh, knowing what's about to happen, and it's going to hurt like hell. I throw myself back, dragging both the guards with me. Limbs tangle and crack against the narrow walls and unforgiving steps as we tumble down.

Umph.

My body lands on the ground, taking the air from my lungs. I knew what was going to happen the minute the guard said, *it's for the Greater Good.* They just didn't realize I'm playing for my own Greater Good now. I push to my feet, my arm hanging at an awkward angle. I don't even flinch as I snap it back into place. Nothing compared to when I was learning calligraphy, each miswritten letter earning a broken wrist.

The guards groan, but I don't give them a chance to recover. Thick ivy vines erupt from the ground, entwining over their bodies to keep them rooted in place. No matter how hard they try to break free, it won't work. Reaching down, I pull the keys from their waist as the vines cover everything but their nose.

"Are you alright?" It's the voice of the man from the village.

"Fan-fucking-tastic," I retort.

And for the first time, I can hear the battle raging above us—swords clashing; people screaming. Time to get Prince Erebus his best fighting chance—the AWOL soldier, the Nihilian king, the gigantic general, and an Omnia who is taking control of her own life, ready to burn down the world for the true Greater Good.

Starting with the seizing Tenebrae from the inside out—exactly how we planned it.

Forty-Three

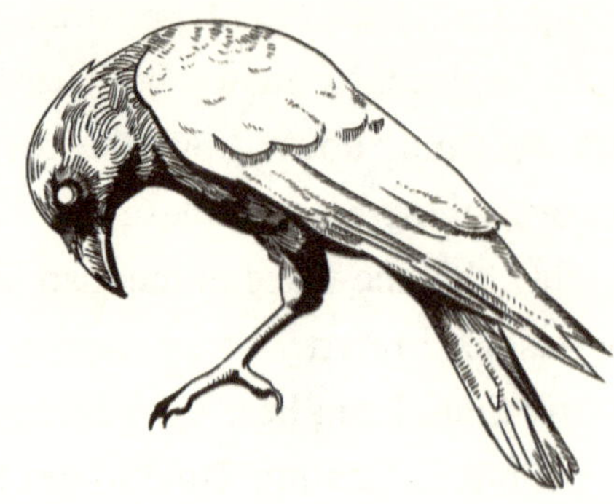

Addilynn and Irwin flank my sides, but it doesn't feel right without my brothers. Through the gnarly branches and thorns, heavy trepidation fills the surrounding air. The land is a melancholic dark violet as dusk begins to settle over the land. No animals or birds flitter about. My body and wings tense with the sensation of being watched, but I can't decipher if it's from paranoia.

Addilynn moves her head on a swivel, and Irwin tightens his fists against his sword. The Nihils and a few shadow wielders prepare to rage against the king as they break through the foliage, revealing the glorious palace, tarnished by the memories inside those reflective black walls. Doubt blossoms in the center of my chest. How can I face the man who took everything from me?

Air whooshes past my ear, followed by a pained groan next to me. Irwin roars unlike anything I've ever heard before as Addilynn falls backward with an arrow protruding from the center of her chest, aqua covered blood pooling against the cotton of her shirt and into the firm soil.

More arrows rain down upon us. I splay my wings wide to protect Irwin and Addilynn. Everyone else holds their shields high, but an arrow still strikes Elara's left arm, even with Wrath's shield protecting them both. Those who aren't fast enough fall to the ground.

Rage consumes me. Howling snarls break away from my arms as the shadows I've been holding at bay release. Betrayal. Someone had to tell these soldiers where we were.

Metal clangs against the ground, rushing us.

A sword flies toward my wings. The blade barely hits sensitive tissue before it snaps. I thrust a dagger into the soldier's neck, right through the tiniest sliver of an opening.

Irwin drags Addilynn's pale body from the fight.

Three guards charge toward me, two in white armor and one in black. Moros tears into their flesh without prompting. One soldier in white slices his blade through him, and into the other soldier.

The one in black swings wide toward Irwin.

Elara steps in, thrusting her fiery short sword into his throat with her one good arm, maroon blood spewing from his mouth.

Irwin nods a thank you, then continues staunching his hands around Addilynn's wound, blue blood staining his skin. Her life force is draining faster than I want to admit.

"Erebus, watch out," someone shouts.

The guard without a helmet, blond hair slicked back with dark eyes, swings wide at me, the tip of his sword slicing into my wing.

"I can't kill you, but I can make you suffer," he hisses through a twisted smile, his blade already raised again to strike.

I try to summon the darkness, but it doesn't answer my call.

The woods are lighter than they should be.

My attention is pulled back to reality as he plunges his sword into my wing again, releasing a guttural growl from me as the pain of my muscles and feathers severing flares down my spine.

My hands find my dagger, and I prepare to strike him.

His footwork is as good as Micah's. He flits away from my attack, a smile gracing his face as if this is all just a game to him.

Another bout of rage consumes me as I lurch forward, throwing any teachings from Micah out the window as bodies fall around me, warning me about knowing the enemy and keeping emotions in check.

Butcher's howl cuts through the chaos, drawing my attention just as a ball of light slams into his misted form. He's gone in an instant. The loss settles heavy in my chest.

The soldier seizes the moment, driving the hilt of his sword against my head. The blow drops me to the ground. A heavy boot slams into me, flipping me onto my stomach. Pressure crashes down on my wings beneath his heel.

I wince but force my eyes open to see the fallen bodies clearly. Elara and Wrath protect Addilynn and Irwin, but there are too many assailants. Moros and Malefic are weakened by whatever is happening in the woods. More Nihils cake the ground as some attempt to stand, only to fall against the ground bloodier than they were before.

"This was always a losing battle, you fucking murk," the man says above me. His boot twists against my wings.

I let out a pain-filled wail from deep within my chest.

Desperation plucks me, and my eyes bounce around the land, searching for anything to help me when my focus settles upon a shadow woman hanging upside down from a branch in the woods. Completely odd and at ease as if we aren't losing this battle.

"You wanted this! Now fucking help!" I cry out.

Glowing white eyes snap open, and I can sense her smile. A crow's call shifts the air, followed by a sharp, clicking sound that turns my blood to ice. Women clad in black appear in the blink of an eye, tattoos curling over skin of every shade. At their sides, small frownies and macabres linger like obedient pets. One woman, her hair and eyes as dark as a crow's wing, slips a thorn bracelet from her wrist. It cracks through the air toward a soldier pinning Elara beneath him, his sword grinding against hers, blood blooming bright at her jugular. Wrath fights to reach her, fending off two guards. One seizes him by the neck, tearing off his helmet to reveal elongated sanguine fangs. He doesn't get the chance to bite as the whip snaps against his throat.

Rigid thorns bite into his neck, sawing deep between muscle and bone. A frownie's jaw unhinges, tearing the soldier's head clean from his body—the one who had Elara pinned. Two macabre descend on the other soldier near Wrath, dragging him down in a blur of limbs and teeth. Another soldier stands over a Nihil, clutching at his throat. His deep maroon eyes blow wide as murky black-green water pours from his gaping mouth.

The weight on me vanishes.

I glance to the side—he's already running for the palace.

A fucking coward.

Don't worry about him. There's someone else who will give him the judgement he deserves, Harlow says in my mind.

I search for her only to come face to face with a woman wearing a heavy black veil. Her hands sink into the soil as she speaks the ancient tongue under her breath. Green spirits emerge from the depths. Feathers—my feathers—attached to their clothing. I move to my knees at the sight of a real necromancer conjuring before me, blurring the lines between life and death as the spirits battle the living. I don't make it far when a small hand appears, halting me. My breath catches as the dark green spirit of Halona forms with a bouquet of black shadow flowers in her other hand, with mist emitting from them.

"I always knew you could do it," she says, then skips away with her flowers.

Soldiers collapse to the ground, gripping at their throats, as she passes by. Hamish's ghost swings a great axe, a smile plastered on his face. My feathers coat the spirts as they did the witches, vengeance strong in their souls.

My energy slowly returns as I face the palace. I take a step, then falter. A spirit hovers over Addilynn. Witches move through the chaos, some fighting, others bent over the fallen. Their healing is nothing like what I've seen before. Dark green and black light pours into the wounds, forcing them closed.

"Addilynn," I break.

The little witch in the black veil appears before me as if made of air, like the spirits. "You have to win the battle." Her ancient voice doesn't belong in this world. "Find your uncle and avenge my people." She forces me to my knees without even touching me, clutching my dagger and slicing into her wrist. Black blood rises to the surface. Then, she forces my mouth against her wrist.

I drink greedily through the decadent temptation, taking in the taste of moss and fresh spring water. It's how I imagine the swamp water near their coven tastes. My fangs dig into the flesh to keep it near, thrumming the darkness in my chest to life. The world darkens in a way it's never been before.

The witch pulls my head away, bringing me to my full height, even though I want more.

"Finish this," she hisses before kneeling beside Addilynn, clutching the spirit close to her body.

I blink and then I'm suddenly under my childhood bed. My black bat stuffy lies beside me. I clutch him close, just as I did the night my parents were murdered. My legs stick out from beneath the frame, my cheek pressed to the floor, trapped in the narrow space. I know why Esmeray, the Mother of Death and Darkness, brought me here—back to the night it happened. Back then, I was too small. Too afraid to do anything.

But I'm not anymore.

I push myself from beneath the bed, rising to take back what belongs to me.

Forty-Four

The dungeon smells of mildew and rotting meat as water rises to the bottom of my heavy dress. In the first cell is a skeleton chained to the wall. The man who started the fight with the guards to save us sits in the second cell with a deep gash in his stomach healing slowly.

There are so many keys, it takes me a moment to find the right one, pressing them into the lock as quickly as I can. When it finally clicks open, I rush inside, unbinding him from the chains pinning him to the wall. Relief flickers through me—at least this time, someone doesn't need to die.

"Why did you come?" he asks.

"To partake in a rebellion," I shrug, realizing Erebus's smug personality is rubbing off on me more than I like to admit.

With the chains off, the man groans as he stands, the motion forcing blood from his wound. I instinctively press my hand against it, emitting my glowing sage aura. The skin fuses together beneath my palm.

I wipe blood against the skirt of my dress, trying my hardest to ignore it.

"Thank you," he says, lowering into a bow.

I nod and flick my head for him to go, then leave him behind as I search in the other cells to find Erebus's brothers, but they're not down here.

"Follow me," the man says.

He brushes past me until we come to a dead end of cobblestone. The man presses a sequence of stones, and the door opens slowly to reveal a deep cavern reeking of death. My heart pounds as I pray to any of the Gods that it's not Lelantos and Micah rotting.

"How did you know?" I ask.

"I was the right hand to King Ezra. There were times we had to use this chamber for Marcus when his hunger for blood was too much," he says, moving into the room.

My eyes water from the smell, but he keeps pushing forward, so I do as well.

"Why did you help us?" I ask, needing anything to keep my mind distracted. A giant rat runs past me, and I scream so loudly, I hurt my own ears.

"I have been waiting sixteen years for Erebus to take the throne." He takes a side path I didn't see. "My brother and I swore an oath to many kings before to protect the Ravenheart bloodline, and I took my oath seriously."

A smile blossoms on my face at that kind of loyalty, born in love and harbored through friendship.

"Why are *you* helping?" he asks.

"I want to see the rightful crown on the throne."

He leads us into a back room. Three cells line the circular chamber, dark vines creeping over the cobblestone walls. Flickering torchlight spills through the space—a welcome relief after the tunnels. Two cells are occupied.

Erebus's brothers.

The one with turquoise eyes—Micah I presume—straightens as best he can, his neck bent at an awkward angle. He scoffs, his large fingers gripping the small bars. "A sick twist of Fate if an Omnia is here to save me."

Angry red patches spread across his skin. Shirtless, his torso is all lean lines of muscle, broken only by pale blue gills over his obliques, rimmed with the same irritated rash. He clears his throat, and heat rushes to my cheeks.

I find the key much quicker this time. Micah steps out before the door fully opens and nearly tackles me to the ground. My neck cranes all the way back to see him at his full height. I thought Harold was tall, but Micah is a few inches taller than him. He rotates his neck from side to side, stretching his large arms to reach the top of the cavern.

Before I have a chance to open the other cell, Micah shoves me against the back wall. Harold tries to pull him back, but he's stubborn in his intentions as he presses his forearm against my throat. "What did you do to Erebus?" He flashes his sharp canines, eight-pointed edges barred right in front of my face.

My power rages beneath the surface, ready to lash out against his onslaught.

"Erebus is fighting with the Nihils to make their way to the castle," Harold snaps.

Micah pulls away from me, his eyes darting between mine, fighting whether or not he can believe it.

"I am here to put the rightful king back on the throne," I say.

His eyes widen, and his shoulders visibly relax as he exhales. Heavy eyes shift to the other occupied cell to where a muscular body lay naked and curled into a fetal position, left for dead—certainly not the man they call the beast. His shoulders rise and fall in slow succession. Dried blood cakes the splits in his back, remnants of a whip.

"They would make me watch as they lashed him over and over," Micah chokes out, tears bridging his eyes.

A twinge flares in my chest, as if the pain is somehow mine to bear.

"He hasn't woken up since the lashing last night."

As I open the cell door, Erebus's voice cuts in—warning me not to touch Lelantos.

I move anyway.

A strand of red hair falls across his face. I brush it aside and freeze. It's him. The man who shot an arrow through my ribcage. My hands shake. My eyes fall shut. The fading blue tendril between us pulls taut.

Lelantos isn't just the king of the Nihils.

He isn't just Prince Erebus's brother.

He's my Fated.

My hand trembles as I cradle his jaw, thumb brushing his cheek. A soft, instinctive touch. Sage-green light blooms across my palm, spilling into him. A tear slips free as the power takes hold—and only then do I realize what I've done. It's too late to stop. Muscle knits beneath my touch, fusing with a sickening pull. A low growl rumbles from his chest. His head nuzzles into my hand like a cat, almost a purr. Until his eyes snap open.

And he sees me.

Lelantos moves too fast for me to prepare or track the movement. His hands wrap around my neck more firmly than Micah's. My power surges from the threat, taking everything in me not to fight against the hold. His sapphire eyes with blown wide pupils stop me as he wars within himself. There's a fresh, faint sage mark on his skin that I know will never go away, even in the afterlife.

Harold and Micah pull at his body to get him off me. He releases a deep, primal growl. My head and lungs feel like they're going to burst from the lack of air.

"Lelantos," Micah pleads.

Like a band snapping, he jerks free and collapses against Micah. I struggle to catch my breath, forcing my gaze anywhere but the sprawl of bare flesh on the filthy ground. Micah recovers first, pushing himself upright. I'm already moving out of the room before his hand lands on my shoulder. He turns me back, fingers brushing my neck, searching for something… Then it hits me.

"There are no marks," he whispers, his slender fingers gentle over my pulse. "He may not say thank you, but I will."

With that, Micah scouts ahead, Harold slipping out after him. None of us speak about what happened in that room—though I wouldn't know how to begin. Lelantos follows, naked as the day he was born, my slender handprint still marked along his jaw, brushing the line of his lips.

His eyes flit to my neck, a low rumble building in his chest.

He brushes past me as if I didn't save his life. I stumble after them, tripping against the cobblestone. I claw at the leather, begging for reprieve from the suffocating fabric.

"This godsdamned gown," I bite, only able to rip the sleeves.

"For fucks sake," Lelantos mutters.

He turns me around, tearing at the tied corset in the back, ripping it in two. I mutter a thank you under my breath and run ahead in my white leather, the sickle strapped against my chest. Micah glances at it before looking over my head at Lelantos walking toward us with my gown tied around his waist like a makeshift kilt.

Harold leads us out of the second part of the dungeon. The two guards in white wait with their swords in hand.

"You didn't kill them?" Micah asks.

"I don't kill people," I say.

"That's not what we heard," Micah answers as Lelantos says, "Great. We get an Omnia to aid us, but it's the weak one."

His words sting more than his hands at my throat. Spite fuels my power as I erupt more vines from the ground. They wrap around the guards, and their blades fall. Micah reaches for them, tossing one to Harold and using the other one to decapitate the man. Harold follows suit. My stomach answers, spewing its contents against the ground, mixing with their blood.

Lelantos hisses under his breath.

They all step over their bodies as if it's another day for them. I suppose it is, being that two of them are notorious outlaws.

We make our way back to the study where more sounds echo through the palace. Metal pounds against the ground, footsteps facing toward something unseen. Through the window, more women move amongst the scattered bodies. Creatures tear into the fallen soldiers clad in black and white armor. I scan the chaos for raven wings, but he's nowhere in sight. Micah stands behind me, looming as he looks over my head.

"The godsdamned witches descended," he says.

The study door bursts open as a guard charges in. Lelantos is on him in a flash, locking his neck between his bicep and forearm. A sickening crack—bone giving way—before the body hits the floor with a heavy thud.

He snatches the fallen sword.

His eyes lift to mine.

And for the first time, I see him for the beast he is.

Forty-Five

Chaos ensues around the palace, flashes of the past and present colliding. Guards running, people screaming, all while I maneuver from my bedroom unprotected. My hard boots click against the surface of the floor. In the hallway, I can see where my parents used to sleep. All the times I used to walk from my room to theirs after a nightmare. Or the sound of their slippers after they tucked me in. A blanket extra snug against my wings.

Their portraits used to hang on the walls. I would look at them, hoping to be a great king like my father. Hoping to find a woman as beautiful as my mother. Blinking through tears, cold reality of adulthood without their guidance sets in. Each step I take carries a weight of mourning for the life I could have had, but there's no regret because the Fates' design brought me Micah and Lelantos.

Above the double-wide staircase, guards rush past, but not toward me. I move like a shadow, a ghost haunting these walls that no longer feel real. I've come to accept that part of me died the night my parents did. Every smug smile, every arrogant word—it's all been a mask, hiding the piece of me that once believed in something better. How can anyone believe in happy endings when their life has been nothing but a string of nightmares? At least that's what I believed until Micah told me about his childhood. And then we met Lelantos. His parents are alive and well… though they don't deserve the breath in their lungs.

My mother's melodic laughter hums through the wall, a song from her younger sanguine nest. She'd promised she would tell me all about the nest when I was older. Some days, my father used to have me practice from the top of the staircase to fly. I failed only to fall into his arms. I step onto the same ledge—and jump.

The necromancer witch's blood heals me faster than my own powers ever could. Patches where feathers were still growing in are completely restored now. Two guards stand outside the palace doors, clad in black armor without helmets—maroon eyes, sharp fangs. Most of the guards in black are sanguine, with little to none wielding the power of shadows.

They unsheathe their swords in unison. I don't allow them to take a step toward me. Shadows coil around their bodies, tightening until I hear their final breaths fade beneath the suffocating dark. They hit the ground with a hard thud.

My hands settle against the slab of onyx—a door I passed through countless times to reach my father's throne. I used to hide when I came here, but he always knew where to find me. He would lift me onto the throne. Even then, I feared becoming king—the lives of Tenebrae resting in my hands. Hands that have killed for coin, just to survive… hiding from who I was always meant to be.

The king of Tenebrae.

Pushing the heavy door open, I come face to face with the man who ruined the life I should have had.

"I'm home," I say.

He sits on the throne, a sharp slate and onyx crown sitting atop his wavy blond hair. His features are soft like my mother's, but there's a twisted darkness in his eyes that she never had. "I've been waiting for you."

Marcus stands and makes his way down the spiral steps, but my eyes flicker to a pile of bodies wearing white armor. I search for the blond one, but he's not there—a pity.

"I always enjoyed drinking the blood of ones who didn't wield shadows," he coos, motioning to the ones sent to a slaughter. I can only think of Omnia Itzel being callous enough to do so.

As he draws closer, I see the vial of white, iridescent blood hanging from a chain around his neck. My fists clench at the sight of it. A few yips sound behind me—my obedient hounds.

"A new party trick," he says, motioning to the shadows behind me.

"I've gotten a lot stronger than the last time you've seen me," I bite.

He nods, keeping a wide berth around me. "You know Erebus, I never wanted to kill your parents." His tone is too casual for a conversation about treason.

Baiting me isn't going to work. Not when I know I'm stronger than he will ever be. I bite my lower lip hard to stop myself from asking what I long to. He licks his mouth at the sight of my blood dripping down my chin.

"My sister turned her back on me for her Fated." He pauses for dramatic effect, like the sizable cape he's wearing. "And your daddy didn't like my insatiable thirst for blood. He wanted me to be like Elanora, turn my back against the sanguine ways, only to drink on the night of the blood moon."

He circles me. My hounds nip at him but never get close enough to bite. I should end this, but I long to know what drives a man to kill his own family.

"They chained me in the basement, only allowed me to drink from coagulated bottles. Never filling me the way I needed them to. I was about to break, follow the path of my sister, until a pretty woman in white paid me a visit. She offered me her iridescent blood in exchange for my freedom to take the throne. All I had to do was make sure the Ravenheart bloodline ceased to exist."

"But you failed," I say.

Marcus scoffs. "A sin I have been paying for, but that ends today."

He lunges at me.

I dodge.

His face twists into a smile as he comes back once more. "Do you know your mother begged for me to spare you?"

I pause and swallow at the thought.

"The only reason you're alive is because I felt like I owed my sister a kindness before draining her of our blood." King Marcus shoves me against the wall.

My right wing crunches, breaking on impact.

He rushes me.

Damsel bites into his leg to stop him.

His hand rears back, smacking against her snout. She whimpers but refused to let up.

Gaining the upper hand, I drive him to the ground. Somehow, the crown stays in place, as if it's taunting me, as if it wants me to earn it back.

A cord of shadows coils around his neck. A sickening smile curls across my lips as his face darkens to a deep shade of purple.

His right hand slips free beneath my knee. He reaches for my face, but it doesn't matter if he pushes me away. The shadows will finish the job of ending his miserable life.

He wrenches my head to the side.

My parents' bodies are pinned to the walls, heads bowed forward to the throne.

"Mom?" My voice cracks.

Her head turns to me, blood spilling from her neck. She opens her mouth, but only more blood pours out. I can't look away—can't move—until sharp fangs pierce my neck. A scream lodges in my throat.

Marcus rips away, my blood staining his lips. "I never wanted to kill you, Erebus. You were always meant to be mine—my puppet. An obedient soldier to solve all of Omnia Itzel's and my problems. Starting with your brothers and ending with her daughter."

He pierces my neck again. I try to reach for him, but my limbs won't obey. Like a puppeteer, he pulls the strings, using my blood against me.

Melania

Micah, Lelantos, and Harold make quick work of any guards who try to stand in our way. Blood coats my white leather, but I can't dwell on that. I fear if I vomit one more time, they're going to force me out of the fight. I didn't remember the walk from the throne room to the dungeon taking this long. Then again, there weren't soldiers clad in black armor and sharp fangs trying to kill us.

Each strike Micah and Lelantos throw is clean and precise, giving barely enough bodies for Harold to fight.

Through the narrow windows, the sun is nearly gone, and I find myself hoping to see the glorious moon everyone speaks about. There hasn't been one since the attack against the Nihilian village. Perhaps when the crown rests upon Prince Erebus's head, it will rise again. At the thought, blood and power thrum through my veins.

The throne room lies just ahead—the finish line, the moment

that will mark a definite change throughout Veilia. Lelantos reaches the second staircase first. Harold stays just behind me, watching for any attack from the rear. Micah finishes off a guard in black, the man gurgling on his own blood. I glance at the mane of red hair, forcing myself to think of anything else. His name is on the tip of my tongue.

A flash of silver cuts through the moment. General Javon steps from the shadows, a blade pressed to Lelantos's neck.

His blond hair is slicked back as it always is, white teeth smiling as he presses against Lelantos's wrist, forcing his sword from his hand. Micah moves to attack, but I stop him.

General Javon sneers at me, as he's done for most of my life. "I didn't believe King Marcus at first when we said you were here and fighting on the losing side."

"There are many things you don't know about me."

General Javon's eyes drag over me. Suddenly, the leather I'm wearing feels too tight. He wets his bottom lip, catching it briefly between his teeth. "Your mother would be eager to hear about this. She's been thinking of new punishments to try on you."

My stomach knots with unadulterated, feral rage. I could tear his head from his body with my bare hands, an emotion that's not like myself. My eyes fly to Lelantos, and I wonder if it's his energy coming to the surface through me.

"You know how much I love seeing her work, but there's been a few things I've wanted to try."

Lelantos snaps his head back, hitting General Javon square in the nose, forcing his sword further into his throat. Blood drips down his neck to the top of his chest. General Javon looks at me with tears in his eyes, and I relish it.

All these years I had to endure torment under him, and he still views me as the meek child begging for my mother to stop. The girl biting her tongue through each lashing while his sickening smile watched me. All the times I imagined killing him in the lonely nights in the dungeon. When he laughed as my mother choked the life out of Ben.

Deep energy brims within me, and my eyes lock onto his. A windstorm of rage prepares to destroy everything in its path. I thrust out my arm; he laughs, only for his panicked gaze to land on me. Lelantos breaks away from his hold as my hand slowly forms a fist.

"You and my mother made the mistake of underestimating me. You can choke and die on your vile words knowing that. I'm not the obedient daughter to abuse anymore. I went away and learned the true power of my strength."

The veins in his neck stand out, muscles straining as the air is ripped from his lungs. My mother's specialty is now mine to wield.

I grit my teeth. "And when I end the Great Cleansing and take down my mother for every heinous crime she's committed against me and others, it will be this moment I relish in: seeing the life leave your eyes, knowing the Mothers will give you the afterlife you deserve."

Before his eyes close for the last time, I spit in his face—for every time he did the same while I was chained in the dungeon, left to wear his contempt.

His body hits the ground with a thud, and for a moment, something like peace settles in my soul. The man who tried to break me time and time again is no more. And unlike Lord Byron, I won't lose sleep over his death—I'll savor it.

Wide eyes watch me from behind as tears coat my cheeks. Lelantos motions to say something, but it never comes as a scream erupts from the other side of the door in the throne room.

Forty-Six

Melania

Prince Erebus stands with his arms stretched wide, as if bound by invisible strings. His eyes are locked on the mirage of his parents' bodies pinned to the wall. To the untrained eye, it might seem real, but I know better. A faint light glows behind them, something that shouldn't be there. A trick I've recognized since childhood. Back when Princess La'Mia and I would play *Save the Princess,* she always cheated to win, creating a mirage of the doll we were meant to save. It took me years to look for the sparkling golden glow from her mark of power. If one were to stand closely enough, they would realize they were see through.

But I won't let her win again—not anymore.

When Micah sees the bodies, he swears under his breath. Lelantos nears Prince Erebus, trying to force eye contact. Erebus refuses to glance away.

"Erebus," Lelantos says, a subtle growl in his voice.

Prince Erebus turns away from the mirage, revealing a deep

gash on the side of his neck, his flesh torn, with a bloody black mark in its wake. A deep growl rumbles from somewhere in the room, followed by clicking shoes. Marcus appears, arms raised like Prince Erebus, black blood around the side of his mouth. A dark mass of shadow snarls at his feet.

"This is your first and only warning to leave this room without my nephew, and I'll spare your life," Marcus says to Micah and Lelantos before directing his attention to me. He flicks his maroon eyes to the pile of bodies in the middle of the floor. Exsanguinated corpses that gave him the strength he didn't have when we first spoke.

"We're not leaving here without him," Micah says.

Lelantos releases a deep growl, acknowledging his agreement.

Marcus shrugs, Prince Erebus mimicking the same motion. His sanguine power and strength control the blood within the prince.

Marcus unsheathes his weapon.

Prince Erebus lunges toward Lelantos.

His dagger is aimed to kill, but Lelantos dodges it at the last minute, and it slices into his arm.

I lurch instinctively to protect him, but a hound snaps at my feet, sharp canines bared as hot, acrid breath huffs against my leathers.

Its jaw opens to tear into my flesh. Heart pounding, I clutch my sickle and bury the light orb deep into its skin.

The hound whimpers, then disintegrates into a smoky aura of light and shadow. My eyes flicker to the banister above and land on Princess La'Mia in a golden gown, her panicked, yellow eyes on me.

Never again will she win, I think, summoning a portal at my feet. I slip through, landing right in front of her.

Metal clashes beneath us as Marcus hides behind Prince Erebus. The brothers fight against one another—protectors and guardians pitted against each other as I face my own.

La'Mia's dandelion eyes bounce between the sickle and me.

"Get his parents off the wall," I hiss through clenched teeth.

For a moment, I think she might defy me. Her eyes shut as the mirage begins to fall away, raining golden glitter. I watch it, and Princess La'Mia tries to move around me, her weight shifting away from the sickle at her throat. I throw myself forward, pinning her against the banister. She groans as her angelic, dove-like wings smoosh behind her.

"No more running," I snap.

"You don't want to do this," she breathes, her voice pleading through a hint of spite, as if it pains her to be nice to me—but she knows she's at my mercy, in a position she'd never thought she'd be in. That thought alone has me standing taller to sneer at her.

"And why don't I want to do this?" I hiss through clenched teeth.

"I have knowledge about you that could affect all of the kingdoms." She swallows. "You were born on the fall equinox, but your mother has been telling you it's the spring equinox. You're twenty years old Melania, the rightful age to ascend the throne."

I search her face for the lie, but she remains neutral, despite her eyes wide with panic.

"And why should I believe you when you've always supported my mother over me? When you were always the one who stepped on my back to make me seem smaller? What grounds do you believe you have to say any of that to me and for me to believe you?"

The words spill out as fast as the tears falling down my cheeks, and I hate myself for it. A steady beat of rain echoes against the palace walls. The sickle in my hand shakes—whether from the truth being revealed or the anger I've kept locked away.

"You're the one with a sickle pressed to my throat, Omnia Melania."

Metal clashes below us. Someone bellows out in pain. I have to help them fight Marcus. End the blood spell he currently has Erebus under.

"If what you say is the truth, then there's a bigger choice for you to make. My side or my mother's. I will not be a pawn in either of your games any longer."

"If she finds out I told you that you're the rightful Omnia, she'll skin me alive only to bring me back to life. You can't imagine what she did when she—" Princess La'Mia stops speaking.

I press the sickle closer to her throat, leaning into her. "I can imagine what she will do, which is why neither of us will tell her of what has happened here."

La'Mia's mouth parts, but I press harder. A single dot of golden blood blooms to the surface. Nauseous alludes me, and that should scare me because the smile that forms on my face is cold. Far too similar to my mother.

She steadies herself. "Have you spent too much time away that you've forgotten the true nature of your mother? She will find out what happened here and rage a war against Tenebrae. Would you hold a sickle to your own mother's throat for the people who are only using you for their own gain?"

Elara asked me a similar question. Could I handle fighting a war against my mother and my protector? But it's different this time because La'Mia is trying to manipulate me. There is no worry for me; it's for her fear infested self, scared of what it would mean to stand against my mother and me, forced into a position between us.

"Seizing this throne was my idea. Defending them from her and *you* was my idea. Every decision I made after the Imposition has been of my own choosing, because I'm not afraid of either of you anymore. I want to be remembered as a hero who isn't afraid to stand for what they believe in."

I step closer to her, and more blood wells to the surface. She's trapped as the fighting continues, followed by the smell of moss and bark. A guttural growl roars from below.

Daring a glance, I see Lelantos underneath King Marcus, his fangs centimeters from his throat. Micah tries to fight off Prince

Erebus. They're all bleeding as they throw blows against one another.

"Make a fucking choice," I seethe, my voice firm despite the feral energy coursing through my veins.

"You," she snaps.

With the sickle at her throat, I use my other hand to conjure a portal to Xannoroth, revealing King Albus working at his desk in the office. The sight of him sends a pang through my stomach, wondering if he knew of my actual birth date, or if this is another ploy from Princess La'Mia. Regardless, I will find out the truth after we finish this.

I snatch La'Mia's arm, pulling her from the railing, the sickle pressed to her wings. "You will stay in Xannoroth until I come for you. If you even think of leaving that palace, I will cut your wings from your body and mount them to my bedroom wall."

Without another word, I shove her forward.

Erebus

Lelantos yells as Marcus's teeth clamp onto his jaw. Through the haze clouding my mind, I know this is wrong. Fighting them—forcing it until only one of us survives—is wrong. But I can't stop. My mind and body are no longer my own. No matter how many times I try to resist, I can't. Trying feels like swallowing shards of glass—each one tearing through me as it moves.

Not nearly as painful as seeing Micah bleed, knowing I'm the one causing it. A deep gash splits across his gills, blue blood spilling from the wound. When his face twisted in agony, the pain echoes through me, but it didn't stop me from striking again.

I should be on my ass, coughing up blood against Micah. His

strikes are steady, meant to wound, not kill. He pulls his punches, avoiding my wings when he knows they're my biggest weakness.

Lelantos thrashes against the ground, trying to tear Marcus off, but Marcus's jaw is locked at his neck, feeding. He finally pulls away, and Lelantos sputters for air.

Marcus wipes the blood from his mouth with the back of his arm and rises, drawing my attention. His maroon eyes are lost to bloodlust. He uncorks the small vial around his neck, drinking greedily. A blood-curdling growl rips from him, the heady concoction of my blood and an Omnia's coursing through his veins.

He hurls Micah against the wall without even lifting a hand.

I drag my feet to my brother, fighting against everything in my body to do so. Marcus demands Micah's blood.

Lelantos rolls to his side, one hand pressed to his neck. Blood pools beneath him, drawing Marcus's gaze.

"There's nothing as potent as Omnia blood," he says before his foot collides against Lelantos's face, preying on the weakest man just because he can. Now it makes sense why Omnia Itzel chose him. His soul is as dark and twisted as hers.

A flash of white drives King Marcus to his knees. His wide eyes snap to mine, trying to command me to fight against her.

Micah wraps around my legs, dragging me to the ground. My face slams into the obsidian floor, chipping my right fang.

No matter how I fight, I can't break free. He's too strong.

Omnia Melania towers over King Marcus. "Do you know what's more potent than an Omnia's blood?"

She glides her sickle across his throat, blood spraying in a crimson arc.

"An Omnia herself."

Omnia Melania slices until his head hits the ground. His shimmering maroon blood soaks her white leathers. And just like that, the fog cloaking my mind clears with my uncle's final breath.

Silence follows, broken only by our ragged breathing and the hollow roll of the crown as it spins across the floor. It slows, wobbling to a stop at my feet like a coin coming to rest after spinning on a table. The sound echoes against the walls, matching the pounding in my chest.

Omnia Melania steps forward. The woman who once refused meat at the sight of it drags her fingers through Marcus's still-warm blood, then smears it across the crown. Rainbow light surges in her eyes, fearless and unrelenting.

She sheathes her sickle.

"I'm quite familiar with slicing someone's throat."

Micah rises from my back, keeping his distance from her, a strange look of either fear or awe clinging to his aqua eyes.

He rushes to Lelantos—bloody and barely conscious—his attention still focused on her.

She lifts the crown in both hands. "Kneel."

The command shakes the candelabra above us.

I pray we all remain in her good graces when her reign begins.

If not, I pray she kills me swiftly.

Forty-Seven

Melania

Prince Erebus kneels before me, raven wings sprawled wide behind him, his eyes wholly dark as the night sky. Without a moon, there's only the flickering flame of the candle and my aura casting light upon us all.

"Do you solemnly swear to protect and serve the people of Tenebrae?" I ask, using the ancient tongue.

His brows lower. I clear my throat, realizing he would have been too young to learn when his parents died. Too young for them to teach him.

I repeat the question in the modern language.

"I swear to protect and serve the people of Tenebrae," he says, his voice wavering thick with emotion.

"Do you vow to use your power for the Greater Good of Tenebrae?"

"I vow to use my power for the Greater Good of Tenebrae."

I prepare to place the crown on his head and call him the king, but there's something more pressing in my mind. The conversation with Princess La'Mia. There will be a war, one I am not equipped to fight alone.

"Do you swear to aid me in the upcoming war against my mother?"

Erebus nods without hesitation. "I swear to aid you, and any future Omnia, for what you did for me today."

My face remains neutral despite the kindness of his words. I take a step forward, placing the bloodied crown on his head. "All hail the blood king." Blood drips against his face. "The Rightful King Erebus Ravenheart of Tenebrae."

Fists pound against the ground as Lelantos, Micah, and Harold kneel. Erebus takes one step between us, then pulls me into a hug.

"Whatever war we may face, you have the strength of Tenebrae," he whispers in my ear before breaking away from me, his steps slow as he makes his way to the throne. His boots trail blood behind him.

Lelantos sneers in my direction, but I'm grateful to see the bleeding has stopped in his neck. Micah nods in appreciation before finding his spot below the throne next to Lelantos.

They lower at the waist as King Erebus runs his hands over the shards of onyx. I wish I could see his thoughts, if only to understand what this moment means to him. All these years hiding from his duty of being king leading to this moment.

He waves his hand, and two wraiths come to life, flanking the sides of the throne, followed by raspy barks of shadow hounds guarding the main doors. I bring myself into a bow to acknowledge the rightful king of Tenebrae as he settles into his throne.

The moon rises through the windows in the back, covering the entire horizon and stealing my breath. The throne room bathes in a red light as the blood moon marks the Mother's happiness. To see it is another thing entirely.

King Erebus settles his black eyes on me.

We won.

The Great Cleansing is no more, marked by his reign.

Except this is far from over—especially if Princess La'Mia was telling me the truth.

Forty-Eight

Erebus

My brothers climb the stairs, each taking turns hugging me. Lelantos remains tentative, but I'm grateful for his willingness to try. His brows lower and nostrils flare, as if he can't believe he embraced me either. Probably has something to do with the sage handprint against his face.

Micah brings me to his chest, fat tears soaking me as he whispers, "Your parents would be proud."

I can't help but look at where their bodies were. I don't know what caused them to be there, but when I find out, someone will pay. The heavy door clicks open, and Omnia Melania departs with her head lowered.

"Her? Really?" Lelantos growls.

I glance at the mark before smacking it twice. "I think she'll be around a lot more often."

Lelantos nips at my hand before he glances at the door she exited from. I pull my arms over their shoulders, allowing myself to feel the emotions of being king. I won't have the freedom to do as I want anymore, leaving a pressure of ruling an entire kingdom in my chest. But for the first time in fourteen years, my brother and all Nihils are safe. The people of Nobyl can begin again in Tenebrae completely free from Omnia Itzel.

Addilynn and—

I dart out of the throne room before I can stop myself. The little witch was holding Addilynn's spirit safely, but I don't know if that's enough. "Omnia Melania!"

She whips around, a smile blossoming on her face.

"I need your help," I say.

"Again? It's going to cost you." She laughs at her own joke, holding me mesmerized by the sound.

Following her lead, I say, "I'll give you my first born as a token."

She laughs harder before returning to her serious self, the gleam in her glowing eyes remaining. I envy Lelantos, wishing my magic had marked her skin instead of him.

A portal forms in front of us, and we emerge in the woods. The blood moon hangs in the sky as people dance and sing, but I can't rejoice with them. Not as I see the only witch here with her hands hovering over Addilynn. I guide Omnia Melania there, but people keep pulling me away, praising me for taking back the throne. Harold lowers into a bow in front of Omnia Melania, reaching for her hand and kissing the back of it. Lelantos appears from the portal behind us, striding forward to shoulder check him.

Elara sprints toward us, nearly knocking Omnia Melania to the ground, squeezing her tightly before pulling back to see the blood covering her clothing.

"Are you okay?" she asks with panicked eyes.

"When will you learn I'm an Omnia? Very little can harm me," Omnia Melania responds.

Elara nods but never leaves her side again. Lelantos studies her as if he can't believe Omnia Melania befriended a Nihil—or perhaps a Nihil befriended her.

When we reach the top of the hill, her steps slow. The little witch glances over her shoulder. None of us can see her face through the thick veil. I stretch forward, hoping to catch a glimpse as Addilynn's dark green spirit hovers above her body.

"You involved the witches?" Micah hisses.

"The Mothers asked us to," she says, her eyes falling to Omnia Melania. "We can't ignore the call of the Mothers."

Part of me still fears Omnia Melania might turn and leave Addilynn for dead, but she doesn't. She pushes past our small group, brushing her hand against Irwin as she kneels across from the witchling. His eyes are swollen red. He rests his against Addilynn's forehead.

"What's your name?" I ask.

The witch breaks her gaze from Omnia Melania. "Salvinia."

Her name sparks within my chest, and I fear I'll never forget it. I was destined to meet her. My lips part, but Harlow appears in the woods, her ethereal form staring at Omnia Melania and Salvinia. She nods her head, drawing the ancient tongue from the witchling.

Omnia Melania responds with, "My life, your death."

Melania

There are things I shouldn't do, but today is determined to damn me to them all. Salvinia keeps one hand over Addilynn's waning spirit, holding her there with a piece of her veil. I know little about the witches, but I know they're one of the few things to scare my mother.

I pull the other side of her veil up and over my head. Beneath the veil, I catch my breath. The witch is beautiful. Pale skin like moonlight. A thin black line runs from her lower lip to her chin. Dark paint smears beneath her eyes, as if she's been crying. They're as dark as King Erebus's, but flecked with silver, like stars caught in shadow. The moment I saw her, I understood what she was doing—holding Addilynn's soul from slipping into the Mother of Death and Darkness's domain. Now she needs me to heal the wounds, to give Addilynn a vessel to return to.

Salvinia guides my hand over Addilynn's pulseless heart, placing hers over mine. The blackened tips of her fingers brush my skin—she's a necromancer. With steady pressure, she forces my hand deeper. A twinge of Addilynn's power remains inside her, calling for help.

Ancient power coils around us.

The connection locks into place.

There's no going back.

"We're testing the Fates," I say, more to myself than to her.

"She doesn't deserve to die because we were late," she says. "Let the Fates be damned just this once."

Cold air dances on my cheeks.

Come to think of it, she feels entirely too cold for a steady heart-beat.

"Living between life and death," the witchling says, reading my mind. Moving closer to my face, she whispers, "There's no going back."

She presses her lips against mine. My light recoils from her darkness.

I push past it, forcing my power to the surface. It becomes a struggle, a push and pull against ancient magic far darker than anything King Erebus commands.

Salvinia's hand threads through mine, binding us further. Beneath my hand, pressed to Addilynn's chest, a flicker sparks.

The first beat of her heart.

Her dark green spirit floats back into her warming body.

Salvinia pulls her lips from mine as Addilynn's chest rises. I meet the witchling's gaze and catch my reflection in her dark eyes. Something changed.

Where my hair should be white, it's black, streaked with iridescence. The color in my eyes shifts, something moving beneath the surface.

I lean closer, but Salvinia snaps back.

Irwin shoves me aside as Addilynn gasps, breath tearing into her lungs. My body goes hollow. Like I crossed into something I wasn't meant to see.

Elara touches my shoulder. My heart booms from my chest as I face her. Her eyes search me with so many questions. But this time I don't know if I can tell her if I'm okay or not because I don't know what I am.

Salvinia glances over her shoulder. Heaviness settles in my chest—she saw it, too. I decide right then and there.

We shall never speak of what happened when we brought Addilynn back to life—no matter the cost.

Forty-Nine

Melania

Three large pyres burn under the blood moon. I'm not sure of anything anymore. In one day, I marked my Fated, killed two men, threatened my guardian, found out I'm already at the age to reign, placed the crown upon King Erebus's head, and kissed a witch to bring someone from the brink of death.

When will this dream end? When will I wake up and find myself in the clutches of my mother's dungeon—the true nightmare?

Leaving the palace feels like a lifetime ago. Back then, I was searching for sanctuary after killing Lord Byron. I didn't expect it to lead to all of this—especially not in Tenebrae.

Elara makes her way up the hill to where I sit with my knees pulled tightly against my chest with my cheek resting against them. She drops next to me, a bottle hanging in her hand.

She raises it, shaking it back and forth before I finally decide to take it. The wine is bittersweet, nothing like the bubbly wine in Omnius or the burning cherry whiskey in Xannoroth.

"Where did you get this?" I ask, taking another deep gulp. It warms my empty stomach.

"A few of us raided the palace's wine cellar when the Three went through the portal," Elara sighs, her voice softer as she shrugs, as if stealing from the palace isn't a crime.

King Erebus and his brothers—whom I've learned aren't blood related—left to bring the helpless here to the palace, King Erebus leaving me in charge.

"Elara," I say, staring off into the distance. Her eyes flash to mine and my stomach sinks. "I have to return to Omnius."

"Can we stay for the night and leave in the morning?"

I swallow one more large swig of wine, accepting the liquid courage. Elara has protected me more than I could ever ask for, but it's time I protect her. Instability threatens the kingdoms as the Great Cleansing Ordinance unravels with King Erebus's reign. Once my mother figures out I had a major part in it, she'll take all her anger out on the people I love the most—starting with Elara.

"Stay here in Tenebrae where you can be safe."

Her head jerks toward me, lips twisting in a scowl. I place the bottle between us and unclasp the sheathed sickle from my chest. Elara shakes her head as I buckle it against her.

"I have to keep you and this sickle out of reach from my mother. She will not be happy with me, and I can handle her anger, but I cannot bear the thought of her using you to get to me. I *need* you to remain here with the sickle at all times, and I *swear* by the First, the Mothers, and my life that I will come back," I plea, hoping she understands the seriousness in my tone.

Elara rubs her hand against the brown leather. Heavy tears threaten to spill over her dark lashes. She doesn't speak, instead pulling me into a breathtaking hug, washing her scent of moss over me, a welcoming comfort despite the unease of leaving them both behind.

"Who's going to braid your hair?" she laughs.

A soft, sorrow-filled laugh escapes me, echoing hers. I can only imagine what the Nihilians and shadow wielders think—an Omnia and a Nihil clinging to each other, laughing and crying all at once.

We stay like that for a long while before cheers pull us apart.

A swirling dark void tears open. Nylisa steps through the portal, Ire's hand in hers. Wrath runs to greet them, blood streaking his face, but she doesn't hesitate as she throws herself into his arms. His broad forearms cradle around her, pulling her tightly against his chest.

Elara presses her hand to her heart as she watches them reunite. Wrath glances our way, a bright, unguarded smile splitting his face, the small gap between his front teeth showing. Elara leans forward—just an inch—before settling back beside me.

"Enjoy the night. This is a new start for all Nihils," I whisper, nudging her shoulder with mine.

She lowers her brows, questioning my decision. I give one more encouraging nod, and she sprints toward the pair. Then, I take another swig of wine as more Nihils enter through the portal to reconnect with their loved ones. Many search for Irwin and Addilynn as they cozy near the fire.

Micah steps through the portal next, as if waiting for someone. Lelantos follows, his deep-set, piercing gaze locking onto mine. A scowl twists his face, like I'm less than a bug. The sage-green mark along his jaw brightens, whether from my presence or the flames, I can't tell. For a moment, it looks like he might step toward me. Micah's large hand presses to his chest, shaking his head.

Lelantos shoves him off, turning to storm in the opposite direction, Micah quick at his heels. Erebus finally steps through the portal, and a fresh wave of cheers rises around us.

The blood moon casts a red hue over his pale skin. The flickering flames reflect off the onyx gemstones and black banded crown as his wings sprawl wide behind him. Covered in blood—a king returning from war.

He glances at me, taking one step toward my direction only to be stopped by the swarm of people approaching him. A spike of envy curdles my blood. For all that I've done for them, I'll only ever be Omnia Itzel's daughter—the enemy.

My mind wrestles with the idea that I didn't do enough. For years, the Three have put themselves in danger to protect the people from the Great Cleansing Ordinance, whereas my efforts started by killing Lord Byron only to end in killing King Marcus. Sure, I risk the wrath of my mother, but there's nothing she could do to me that would scar me the way she has these people.

Then, there's Princess La'Mia to consider; I spared her life with a threat, but I can't trust her to keep this from my mother. What danger could I bring upon these people for believing in someone who has never believed in me?

Bitter wine sloshes in my empty stomach. The answer is so painfully clear it scares me to even think of it. These people don't need a king sitting on the throne when my mother has proven she can overthrow it without an ounce of hesitation. My mother has the other six kingdoms to wield as she sees fit.

What the Nihils need in order to live a life without fear is an Omnia who stands to fight for them. One who doesn't cower or hide at the prospect of fighting for the Greater Good.   The   people need me to be her: cruel and calculated, showing no mercy to those who affect our agenda. I've been so scared by the idea of becoming my mother's daughter that I didn't realize it was the answer all along.

A tantalizing plan begins to take shape in my mind, threading together like a spider's web. I've heard my mother say it countless times—know your enemy—whenever she addresses her generals. But she never took the time to learn my weaknesses or desires. She never saw me as the enemy, and how could she? I'm Omnia Melania. The girl who weeps at injustice. The one who flinches at the sight of blood.

All this time, my mother has been waging war against the Nihils, blind to what stood beneath her own roof. A wolf in sheep's clothing.

Like all the others, I was overlooked because my strengths were perceived as weaknesses. A life I once accepted until I learned what I truly am.

I wasn't born to be silent.

I was born to be an Omnia.

"I know the face of scheming when I see it." Erebus's cool voice pulls me from my planning. I realize my nails are bleeding and chewed to shit.

King Erebus plops down next to me, his raven wings coiling around me like my own personal blanket. For some odd reason, my eyes flash to Lelantos. His lips press into a hard line, his jaw set tight. I'm not sure if he's aware, but this is the closest he's been to me all night.

"What are you planning?" Erebus asks, jarring me back to him.

"If I told you, I might have to kill you," I tease.

He places his hand over his chest, feigning offense as a playful smile reveals his sharp fangs, a dimple digging into his right lip. "You wound me, Melania." His eyes flare. He quickly clears his throat. "Omnia Melania, I mean, but I thought we could drop the formalities with our newfound friendship seeped in murder."

"Thank the First for that. It's been entirely too annoying to refer to you as Prince and King in my internal monologues."

An unrestrained laugh bursts from him, followed by a deep snort. I jerk only to follow with my own hysterics. Our laughter flits through the air, and for a moment, I question if the Fates are wrong—or perhaps it's the wine getting to me.

When our laughing fades, Erebus asks, "So, what were you scheming about?" He nudges his knee against mine. "Since we're friends now."

The man beside me is nothing like the one who once held a dagger to my throat. It's easy to see why people flock to him—there's a brightness to him, even wrapped in darkness. I almost laugh at the irony. I've known light wielders who climb over others for power, yet Erebus… he feels different. He didn't rise without loyalty. I just hope some of it belongs to me. So, I tell him everything—what Princess La'Mia revealed, and the reckless plan that's taken shape because of it.

When I finish, he starts to clap. Slow at first, then faster, his palms striking together in rapid beats. At last, the sound dies. He turns to me, abyssal eyes flickering between mine, as if he's seeing me for the first time.

"I swore an oath not only to the land of Tenebrae, but to you, too. Neither of them I take lightly." He pushes the strands of hair that have fallen forward, then stops. "When do you plan for all of this to come to fruition?"

"In my mother's style, it has to be memorable." I pause for dramatic effect. "Princess La'Mia nearly ruined your coronation. What do you say we ruin hers?"

Erebus's eyes spark like the portal to Tenebrae—dark, swirling with shadow and the promise of death.

A slow smile spreads across his face.

"I say we collect your fucking crown."

Fifty

The palace bustles with servants and guards, welcoming guests and ushering them toward the main throne room. Princess La'Mia glides from one person to the next, thanking them for attending—as if it weren't mandatory. The beading on her golden gown hisses against the marble floor, loud despite the lack of fabric. High slits climb both sides of the skirt, leaving little to the imagination. The open back reveals her gold-dipped dove wings, while the bodice—two sleek panels of gold—expose much of her stomach and sides.

Gold dust shimmers across her dark skin. Her brown hair is pulled into dozens of fine braids, threaded with flecks of gold. She looks like the embodiment of light, only missing her crown.

My mother descends the stairs overlooking the sea of people. Her iridescent hair is more lackluster than normal, hued with more gray than shimmering white. Like La'Mia's, her white, silky dress displays more leg than fabric with a high slit cut up the side. Her bodice frames the middle of her navel. She adorns her neck with gold draped between her breasts, gemstones cut in the metal of every kingdom—all but Tenebrae. My jaw tightens as my attention flicks to the crown of Omnius upon her head, knowing it belongs to me. The few patrons in the room bow to her—then to me. Her eyes settle on me, overlooking the guests. For this plan to work, I have to play the role of an obedient daughter, but I refuse to bow to that woman any longer.

She continues toward me, stopping to pull a guard to her. "Where is General Javon?"

"He hasn't returned," the guard says.

She pushes him away, dismissing him.

Princess La'Mia must not have told her everything that happened in Tenebrae. Despite this, I know her. She can lie beautifully; hide information from those she claims loyalty to. I can't fully trust her.

My mother slithers next to me, curving her blood-red lips. "I haven't forgotten what you did to Lord Byron."

"Of course not, mother," I say with more bite.

She sneers at me. I take solace in the red staining her front teeth, and I don't dare tell her about it. Princess La'Mia joins us, flanking my side instead of my mother's.

"You both look beautiful," she coos, glancing down at my white tulle ballgown. The corset is encrusted with diamonds that scrape against the insides of my arms. The dress was left hanging outside my bedroom door this morning, with no servant waiting to help me into it. I'm grateful for that. I can't stand the idea of someone other than Elara doing my hair.

"Princess La'Mia, you are perfection," my mother says, cutting her eyes to me.

"Your wings look exquisite," I say, rubbing a finger against the strong boning.

Princess La'Mia gives me a tight-lipped smile, and I hope she can taste my threat on her tongue.

The orchestra marks the start of the coronation.

"You better behave," my mother says, reaching for my forearm with her sharp fingers. I jerk away from the touch, no longer afraid of the woman who gave me life.

I do not fear the weak.

Her jaw snaps shut as she walks to the high marble doors. Two guards swing them open, revealing the beauty of the grand throne room.

The chandeliers are covered in dust, with sheets covering the thrones, windows, and long marble benches for people to sit on.

A hint of envy brews in the pit of my stomach, knowing my rightful day for coronation has passed. This beauty should have been revealed to me on my twentieth birthday.

Our shoes fall softly against the white carpet, trimmed in gold. Golden petals are scattered across it, placed imperfectly enough to feel intentional. Three grand chandeliers catch the glorious sunlight, cascading brilliant reflections, as if it knows someone of The King's bloodline will sit on the throne once more.

We make our way deeper into the room, and the guests lower. My mother tilts her chin, soaking in attention, taking strength from it. The large dais chiseled above the rest of the foundation creates a circle where all the thrones for the eight kingdoms await.

The orchestra strikes up Omnius's anthem, its heavy beat closer to a war march than a coronation.

I try to ignore it, but my attention drifts to King Albus, Queen Pria, and Princess Priscia. Like the other royals, they stand at the base of the dais, bowed as they wait for my mother to take her seat before claiming their own.

As if he can feel me looking at him, magma orbs lock with mine. I had made good on my promise to return to Xannoroth to retrieve La'Mia. She woke before Albus and I could delve into the important matters at hand—why he allowed my mother to lie about my age. I can forgive him for keeping his patronage a secret, even understanding his potential desire to keep me safe, but I won't be fully satisfied until I know all the secrets he harbors for the sake of my vile mother.

I break eye contact with him and focus on the order of the thrones and the stained-glass windows. At the center of the circle is the throne of Omnius, domineering with a high back, streaked with gold at the sides, crafted from the same material as the rest of the palace. A white velvet cushion holds its shape in the center despite the many Omnias who have sat upon it. A high window with different panes of glass representing the rainbow arches behind the throne. The structural lines are painted gold and made in the shape of a crown in the center. Its magnificent light basks my mother, myself, and the throne in rainbow.

The throne to the right of the window sits before a smaller, arched pane of glass. Set within panels of pale blue and white, two wavy lines cast radiant light over the seat, white diamonds forming the throne of Irolyn—the kingdom of air. Beside it stands a matching throne in shape and scale, but forged from silver, its surface dusted with blue and white quartz like frost settling over the land. A perfect reflection of Jeadrenia—the kingdom of ice—echoed in the window behind it, where pale glass frames a single snowflake.

Brilore's throne seems to be made of sandstone and pearls, arched by a window of cobalt blue and indigo. Waves cast light, ebbing and flowing with a mirage of water. The colors of the rainbow are out of order. I nearly roll my eyes at yet another feat I'll change when the throne is mine.

The throne of Quintarius is carved from bark, ivy-green vines winding over its surface. The light that filters through the window is like standing in a meadow at the height of summer.

Xannoroth's throne is much smaller than the one in their throne room, made from lava stone with red glass on the window flaming volatile light, as if it may erupt the moment King Albus sits on it.

Tenebrae's is made of Onyx, missing two pieces on the sides to support wings. A raven sits on a skull at the top. Indigo and violet cover the window, a color that reminds me of Erebus's wings in the sunlight.

The final throne is left open; a crown rests on a feathery white pillow. Like Tenebrae's, sections of the throne are cut away to mirror the window behind it. At the crest of Laelithra's throne, a golden sun rises, a small dove perched at its center. It's pale, yellow rays feel almost gentle beside the richer colors surrounding it; if only the same could be said for its future queen.

I trip on the edge of my skirt as I reach the bottom of the stairs. My mother's eyes cut to me, I'm sure restraining herself from backhanding me for my mistake. She glides to the middle of the dais instead, but the rainbow light rejects her as it selects me to bask in its glory.

My mother ascends the stairs, and I follow; it's an act of rebellion. Only the rulers of kingdoms get to stand or sit on the dais. She grinds her teeth.

Good. Her resolve is breaking her down—exactly as I planned.

She settles onto her throne, reaching for my forearm to force me into a kneel at her side. I remain an arms-length away, hoping she and everyone else notices I'm one step ahead of it, too.

My mother clears her throat before announcing to the crowd, "You may rise."

The sea of guests moves as a unit, a few rubbing their backs, preparing to have to bow again once Princess La'Mia walks through. Attention settles on me.

My skin crawls, but I can't buckle. Not to the royals with confused expressions, and especially not to my mother's glare.

The orchestra begins to play Laelithra's lyrical anthem, adding in the high pitches of a flute. The wide doors open once more, and

Princess La'Mia makes her way down the carpeted aisle. She stutters a step when she notices where I stand. This time, I don't hide my smile.

The bowing crowd misses her misstep, but the other royals do not. She quickens her steps, reaching the top without ascending onto the dais. Only when the crown sits upon her head will she take the step to her throne, marking her reign as the Queen of Laelithra.

Princess La'Mia turns to the crowd. "You may rise."

People lower into their own packed seats. Princess La'Mia bends to her knees against the plush carpet, her throat working on a swallow. My mother stands from her throne and pulls the golden crown from the plush pillow; the metal gleams in the soft light.

Around the golden band are varying high points, like the rays of the sun. Feathers are engraved in the banding to represent the wings she and all her ancestors were born with. Like that of Tenebrae. Tiny diamonds encrust the spacings of the bands. Even with all that, Princess La'Mia is likely to take that crown to a royal jeweler and have them add more flair to it.

My mother stands in front of Princess La'Mia, casting a shadow over her. The music comes to an end as everyone waits for the short crowning to begin. "Princess La'Mia Lumens of Laelithra, today you commit yourself to the people and kingdom."

I swear she's choking back tears. I don't bother hiding my eye roll. The Fates were wrong—Gaia should have been my mother and La'Mia a daughter to mine. If it weren't for their guidance on this journey, I would say they were wrong about far more—especially with my Fated.

My mother lifts the crown higher, letting it catch the light, its brilliance untouched since Queen Gaia last wore it.

"Princess La'Mia, do you solemnly swear to protect and serve the people of Laelithra?" she asks in the ancient tongue.

"I swear to protect and serve the people of Laelithra," she responds quickly, breathlessly.

"Do you solemnly swear to use your power for the Greater Good for Laelithra?"

"I swear to use my power for the Greater Good for Laelithra." Princess La'Mia's eyes flicker up to the crown, her teeth chewing on her lower lip as her hands vibrate.

"All hail Queen La'Mia Lumens of Laelithra," my mother says, placing the crown upon her head. A single tear falls from my mother's eyes, yet no rain beats against the palace.

She reaches down to help Queen La'Mia to her feet, taking her first step together with the rest of the royals—and me. She sits on the throne, and everyone claps and cheers. The orchestra of Laelithra rings out through the room as everyone readies for the ball.

Now the *real* show begins.

Fifty-One

The crowd makes its way toward the formal ballroom set up to drink and feast in celebration. My mother's glare cuts to me, but she isn't given the chance to speak before Albus approaches. His large hand settles against my lower back, guiding me away to the grand entrance. Guests gawk at the royals, while the others rush to find their spots in the ballroom.

"You left Xannoroth before we could really speak." His voice is quiet.

I know he wants to know about what happened in Tenebrae, but I can't form the words to speak about it when all I wonder is why he lied to me, harboring another secret for the sake of my mother.

"When was I born?" I ask, barely loud enough for him to hear.

His head snaps back, magma eyes searching my face. My jaw tightens, waiting to see if he will lie or not.

"During the fall equinox," he resigns.

My head bobs. Hearing him admit it solidifies why I'm doing

what I have to do today. I want to tell him as such, but my mother starts down the aisle straight toward us. "We can discuss this later."

Her rainbow eyes narrow, her jaw clenched. I pray someone steps in to intervene, anyone, but no one is foolish enough to stand in the way of Omnia Itzel.

No one but me.

"You're planning something." He bites the inside of his cheek, closing his eyes and looking to the sky, as if he's praying to the Gods.

My mother nears, and my heart pounds against my chest. I guess being courageous doesn't mean being fearless.

King Albus turns to stand between my mother and me. "Omnia Itzel."

He holds out his hand, and she places hers within his. Then he lowers into a bow, pressing his lips against her knuckles. When he comes to his full height, he smiles. "Omnia Melania was just telling me how she needs to freshen up."

He settles his hand against my mother's lower waist, thumb swiping over her ribcage as lovers would. I expect my mother to fight against the hold, but she doesn't. Her eyes fill with longing. I use that advantage to flee toward my bedroom, ready for the next part of the plan. But first, I can do very little while wearing this much tulle.

As I retreat, Queen Pria and Princess Priscia hold each other's arms as Priscia says something to her mother. Unlike my mother, Pria's slackened jaw and eyes hold a knowing defeat, like she can never compete where she doesn't compare. If only she knew King Albus did it for me, but either way, he chose an Omnia over them.

I force myself to move away from the tragic scene of unreciprocated love and toward the east wing. The long hallway covered in portraits of Omnias before me looms over me. They wore the crown of Omnius on their heads, the pressure of eight kingdoms resting upon them. A responsibility I am rushing toward so I can stop the tyrannical reign of my mother—at least that's what I keep telling myself. I'm doing this for the people, but if I'm completely honest, it's mostly for me. A chance to show everyone that I'm not the weak Omnia they thought I was born to be, but a reminder to myself and all the others who feared my mother that they can revolt against her.

After tonight, there will be a portrait of my face in this hallway. I hope the future generations of Omnias look to my portrait to see the strong woman I've become. Before entering my bedroom, my fingers trace over Omnia Matilda, who wielded the Omnia artifact to fight for the people. I pray it's her fierceness I carry with me for the battle ahead. I find Omnia Arabell with the bow strapped over her chest; I pray it's her bravery I keep to stand against the monster in my life—Omnia Itzel.

Inside my room, I don't allow myself another chance to second guess about what's going to happen. I deserve to reign, and this is the only way.

The portal to the Onyx Palace forms. I helped Erebus get his crown; he's going to help me get mine.

Erebus

The mystical tendril of the portal forms where King Marcus died. For a woman sickened by the sight of blood, she sure has a sick sense of humor. I step away from the throne, the heavy weight of the crown weighing on me now more than ever.

Micah and Lelantos enter the throne room. Like me, they wear black breeches and court doublets over a maroon tunic, the only pop of color in all black and silver regalia. Over their chest is an embroidered silver skull with a raven on it.

Micah carries General Javon's helmet in his left hand.

Lelantos keeps his bow over his chest, the quiver buckled to his thigh. He let his red beard grow thicker in an attempt to hide the sage handprint. Once Omnia Melania left, he didn't rage like I expected him to, but I'm willing to wager he knew before seeing it. He fidgets with the collar around his neck.

I whistle. "Neither of you look ready for a ball."

"Are we certain this is a good idea?" Micah asks.

Omnia Melania's spiral portal grows larger, revealing her pacing the floor in a white ball gown, hiding her delicious curves underneath. Lelantos grumbles, sensing where my thoughts have gone.

"It's not a good idea." I pause for effect. "It's a great one."

I step into Omnia Melania's bedroom, the temperature spiking ten degrees. She nods as Micah makes his way through. He leans down to maneuver through it as if it might hurt if he hits his head, then he flanks my left side.

All eyes settle on Lelantos. His chest heaves, and he bares his teeth, preparing to step through some imaginary burst of flames. After what feels like an eternity, he makes a step forward, only to stop. His lips move, but I can't hear who he is speaking to.

Elara comes forward with folded clothes in her arms. She shoves them against him before nodding and waving to Omnia Melania. A whole wave of Nihils enter the throne room with a hand over their chests. I tense, stepping forward to yell at them. Micah pulls me away.

Our friends from Nobyl, the shadow wielders, everyone there during the battle lowers to a bow. Not for me—their king—but for the next Omnia, destined to save them from damnation. Well, everyone except Lelantos, who forces his way through the portal, shoving the clothes into Omnia Melania's arms. She stares at the group behind him, lips parted, touching the rosy hue in her cheeks as tears brim her eyes.

She glances to the clothes, revealing her Omnia artifact on top of white leather. Her wide eyes find Elara, who smiles widely at her. If it weren't a sweet notion, I would be hurt that she didn't think we could defend her, but she was right to do it. We can't defeat an Omnia. Only Melania can.

The people of Tenebrae stand. Melania inhales sharply and begins to close the portal. A knock sounds at the door.

My blood pulses in my ears. Micah and Lelantos search the area for an escape.

Melania looks to me for answers. She throws the clothes against the bed, and the heavy sickle lands against the ground with a thud. I wince as I watch such a special weapon tossed around like nothing.

"Melania, are you in there?" calls a muffled, familiar voice.

Melania's shoulders slouch forward as her shaking hand settles on the doorknob. Lelantos and Micah hide, and I'm left in the center of the room. She gestures for me to move, and I make quick to stand behind the vintage room divider near her closet.

A flood of white offends my sight. I don't think she owns anything other than these gaudy gowns—certainly not the style of the woman who beheaded a man.

"Albus," she answers, her voice shaky. "What are you doing up here?"

"It's later. I came to speak with you about what happened in Tenebrae. And to find out what it is you're planning now that you know the truth about your birth date."

My heart pounds. I didn't realize she'd told him.

I've learned to trust King Albus, but this isn't exactly something to speak about inside the walls of the Omnius Palace.

"I'm not—"

Lelantos sneezes loudly.

"Who is in your room?" His tone is stern.

She doesn't have a chance to formulate a lie as a chorus of more sneezes ring out, this time from Micah. After this, I am going to have a stern talk to my brothers about what it means to hide and the high stakes we are facing.

The heavy door swings open as King Albus forces himself in. I try to move closer to the closet, but he's already looking behind the divider. I've never seen the male look so betrayed; then again, I am alone in his daughter's bedroom.

"Albus," Omnia Melania snaps. Her tiny foot stomps against the marble floor, slamming the heavy door behind her. "I am planning something, but I will not risk your safety by getting you involved. If you want to help, you keep my mother occupied until I make my arrival."

"What about him?" he asks, pointing at me.

Omnia Melania shakes her head no.

King Albus pinches the bridge of his nose, releasing a deep sigh before making his way toward his daughter. "Whatever you're about to do, please know I am on your side," he whispers before sneaking out to the hall once more.

Melania's shoulders slump forward. She reaches for the clothes and sickle near the bed and disappears. Lelantos and Micah stand from their hiding spot as Lelantos rubs under his nose. He sneezes as if he's allergic to royalty.

"That was close," Micah says.

An understatement of the year.

Lelantos remains quiet, more silent than normal. He moves around the room, as if he's searching for information about Melania without ever having to ask her.

Melania comes out of the closet in an outfit that absolutely takes my breath away. Lelantos moves in front of me, blocking my view and improving his. I shove him to the side to see Melania in white leather pants with a matching long-sleeved top. The hem of the shirt is elongated like the skirt of a gown covering the sides of her legs beside the front. The inside of the train is painted like a rainbow. Her white boots are embellished with gold. The sleeves end with lace around her wrist. The buttons on the front of her chest are made from the different gemstones of the eight kingdoms. Around her thigh is the Omnia artifact. The only thing missing is the crown on her head.

"There's no going back." Her rainbow eyes churn with the power that's been kept at bay for too long. Her lips are painted red and I can't understand why Lelantos would feel disdain being her Fated.

"All hail Omnia Melania," I say with a flourishing bow.

The heavy reality hits me; this moment will be embedded in history forevermore.

Fifty-Two

My feet are heavy, like they've been encrusted in stone. Melania leads us through the palace, and I can't help feeling like we're cattle being led to slaughter. Erebus has always been too trusting with people, but I expected him to have more sense than to trust Omnia Melania so blindly. All of this could be her mother's plan to capture The Big Three.

The only ounce of safety I have is the mark on my chin. I've tried to scrub it away time and time again, but alas, it remains. A sick fucking joke from the Fates to demand I bond and mate with an Omnia. If she even tries anything, I'll tell her to shove it where the sun doesn't shine—though being Itzel's daughter, she might like that.

The palace walls are suffocating. Gaudy chandeliers are made from diamonds, gold, and marble, like people aren't starving while they bathe in wealth. There are portraits on the walls, staring at us, almost like the Omnias of the past know we shouldn't be here and will intervene from beyond the grave if necessary. But I'm not quite sure Omnias even die. They could all be held below ground, leaching the life from others to stave off death.

Two guards approach Melania, but she's steadfast until she comes to stand at their chests.

"They are not on the—"

Thick vines cord around their bodies, covering every part of them aside from their nostrils. She tried to tell me she doesn't kill once, but she killed three men already—two of which I witnessed. Melania might have my brothers believing in her ideas of a better future, but I know better than to fall to her feet and worship the ground she walks on just because she's an Omnia.

Her little legs take wider strides until we reach high arching doors made entirely out of marble. I try hard not to roll my eyes at the tackiness of it.

Melania stops behind the doors, pressing her small palms against it. A nervous energy I've never felt before radiates through my veins, releasing a small groan of unease from my chest. Her doe eyes settle on me. I bite the tip of my tongue to stop from reacting to the plea within them.

Erebus places his hand on her shoulder before nodding. I don't care if he's touching her or if he finds her attractive. What pisses me off is how he can't control his desires. One day it's going to get Micah and me killed because he has a weakness for a pretty face and tight ass.

With his hand still on her shoulder, she pushes open the marble doors. Her steps are confident, but I can taste the apprehension like it's my own. Everyone turns in our direction. That doesn't last long. Melania whistles softly, papers descending from the ceiling at her call. Everyone reaches out to see what it says.

Some gasp while others turn back to us. One of the papers comes to rest at my feet. Words are written in loopy penmanship that I don't understand.

Micah leans over. "It says: all rise for the new king of Tenebrae, The Blood King, Erebus Ravenheart."

I'm certain no one else heard that. I'm not able to speak over the hysterics in the ballroom. Itzel approaches our small group, clenching a piece in her fist. I move beside Erebus, who stands to the right of Melania. Micah comes right next to her, only a foot ahead—a born protector.

"What is the meaning of this?" Omnia Itzel snaps.

She stops at the sound of metal rolling against the ground as Micah tosses the helmet of the general to her feet, face smug.

"Next time, send a larger army," Erebus says.

He smiles wide to show off his long white fangs, though the right one is slightly shorter. Itzel doesn't look at Erebus, but at her daughter, releasing a cunning cackle.

I didn't think that monsters were able to do that—well, that's kind of insulting to monsters.

"Unless an Omnia places the crown upon your head, then you cannot be king." She gestures to the crowd. "And I certainly would never crown shadow scum."

"No, mother, you'd only give a sanguine your blood for him to slaughter nearly the entire Ravenheart bloodline," Melania says before taking another step forward. "But he couldn't kill his nephew and never planned to. His thirst for blood was stronger than the loyalty he felt for you." She continues until they're face to face, her words shaking the chandeliers above us. "You didn't place the crown upon his head, but I, the rightful Omnia of Veilia, did."

Omnia Itzel takes a step back. I search the crowd to see if they saw her move away like I did, or if I were imagining it.

The queens of the air and ice kingdoms, Elowen and Arya, glance at each other, communicating with only their eyes, admiring Melania. Xerxes, the King of Quintarius, has long forgotten the men and women surrounding him. I don't like the way his eyes are roaming over Melania's body, like she's a prize to be won. I nearly growl at my interest in her. I shift my attention back to the ground. Albus has never looked as proud as he does now, but there's the hint of fear in his tense body. Who does he choose to stand with—his Fated or his daughter?

Caspian, the King of Brilore, speaks under his breath to his crossbred daughter, Brianna, her hooded eyes focused too intently on Micah. I scan around me to find La'Mia, but either she's blended in with the light, or she's not present for the showdown of the ages.

"You are not the rightful Omnia until the spring solstice." Itzel's mask slips from anger to pure rage. Her fists ball tightly at her side.

"Must we keep telling lies, mother?"

Itzel searched the crowd. The party has ceased with the familial drama unfolding. I thought I had family issues, but nothing compares to this, and I killed my brother.

"Are we suddenly speechless, or should we ask the only other person in the room who was present for the consumption and birth to enlighten all the royals about my pedigree and the day I was born," Melania snaps.

One of the chandeliers crashes to the ground, causing people to jump back.

"I didn't crown you Omnia because you don't understand the weight of the crown and eight kingdoms as I do!" Itzel roars.

"But you do? Slaughtering an entire species and claiming it is for the Greater Good is not the way an Omnia should rule." Melania takes another step forward, holding her sickle in the air between them, while Itzel moves back.

"Anyone who is impure should be slaughtered!" Itzel screams, though her eyes flash to the weapon, blown wide with fear.

I prepare for the ground to crack or for another chandelier to fall to pieces, but nothing happens. And that's the glaring truth: Melania is the strongest and rightful Omnia.

The crowd murmurs, seeing the same lack of power. Others whisper about her wanting to kill those who are impure, including crossbreeds like Caspian, who favors his daughter over all nine of his pure-blooded, Veilian sons.

"You seize a throne, and suddenly you believe your power." Itzel's voice is a calm before a storm raging against the land. "Did it take having a shadow wielder fuck you to give you a backbone? Perhaps you let his Nihilian—"

Omnia Melania smacks her across the face with the hilt of her sickle, drawing blood to her cheek. "I grew a fucking backbone through every beating you forced me to endure. That is what made me strong, mother. To withstand being chained and starved in a dungeon or being whipped in your study for General Javon's and your sick twisted pleasure. I grew a fucking backbone when I granted mercy to a man who didn't deserve for his sons to be murdered. I grew a fucking backbone when I took the life from General Javon, but mostly it happened when I realized you only beat me because you fear me." Melania's screams echo off walls. Cracks of thunder shake the foundation.

"And I was beat my entire life until I killed my own parents," Itzel seethes, touching her face to wipe at the blood. Her confession is stunning. No one truly knew what happened to her parents—at least everyone except Albus. He lowers his head. "If you want to rule the kingdoms and burn it all to the ground, then here!"

She pulls the crown from her head and places it right on top of Melania's.

My jaw drops, though my shoulders tense. Could it really be this easy?

Omnia Itzel step forward, as if realizing what she's done, and claws for the crown of Omnius. The smell of singed flesh invades my nostrils. She pulls her hand away, revealing a burn deep to the bone.

"All hail Omnia Melania, the reigning Omnia of Veilia," Albus says, lowering himself into a bow.

Melania lifts her chin, preparing to speak. As she parts her mouth, La'Mia reaches through a portal behind Omnia Itzel, tugging her.

"This isn't the end," Itzel says before La'Mia pulls her through, leaving behind the Omnia she was born to protect.

Melania looks ahead with a twisted smile, the crown of Omnius on her head and the threat of war on the horizon.

End of Book 1

Acknowledgements

First and foremost, it's an honor to be writing this for all of the amazing people who have helped me on this journey with their love, patience, and kindness. I want to thank my partner for being my best friend and confidant. If anyone else loves the school scene, he was the one who gave me the idea for it. Without his love and support, knowing when I need to work hard or take a break for video games, I don't think I ever would have finished.

Thank you to my amazing parents. For my mother who has been my sound board from the very beginning. Thank you for buying me those colorful pens and all the notebooks I could want to make this story a reality. Without your support of listening to the same songs over and over again, along with your love, none of this could have been a reality. Thank you to my father who has pushed me to pursue my dreams from a young age, whether it was becoming a pro golfer or author. Your hard work has inspired me more than you will ever know. I love you both endlessly for all the love and support you have given me.

To my eight siblings whose personalities inspired not only these characters, but many more. All of you were my first friends before my characters were ever born, and for that I'm grateful. I wish I could name you all, but there's limited spacing! Please know you all are my biggest role models and I am proud and eternally grateful you all are my siblings.

A special shout out to my talented brother Inkstrider for the cover design and artwork in the book. Cheers to all the late nights when we imagined where our dreams and talents could take us. I hope you enjoy the ride as much as I am.

As for my nieces and nephews, you all are too little to read this book, but if it weren't for you guys I wouldn't have been able to write this. Like Erebus, there were many times I wanted to give up, but when I held each of you in my arms, I knew I needed to stick around to be your aunt. Thank you for saving my life when I needed it the most.

A special shout out to my crowbar sisters; your endless guidance has brought me to this moment. I appreciate you all for taking in the 24-year-old author and helping me grow into the writer I am today. I love you all so much!

To Samantha Vargas who has been my editor and mentor through this journey. Your endless guidance has helped make this book a reality. Thank you for all your criticism that not only made me a better author, but to help me love the story I created. You are my Elara to my Omnia who will support me, but not afraid to tell me when I need to step up. Thank you for everything, especially for all the commas you had to add and delete. I love you!

To my readers who decided to read my debut novel. When I was six years old, I dreamt of this world. As I grew older these characters became my closest friends through every trial and tribulation. I can only hope these characters can comfort you in your times of need as they have for me.

Finally, and the strangest acknowledgment, I want to thank my one-in-a-million benign tumor for reminding me life is short. It's especially too short not to chase my dreams. If it weren't the tumor I never would have decided to take a chance on myself to write this book.

About the Author

Jay Montana has been dreaming of stories since she was six years old. Outside of writing, Jay pursued her dream of becoming a collegiate golfer. Through the many hours spent on the golf course, she continued to draw inspiration from nature. Jay went to college, earning her bachelors in psychology with a double minor in addictions counseling and leadership. She wasn't ready to give up on the dream of becoming a writer. Wanting to combine psychology and writing, she pursued her masters in Creative Writing.

Jay has been a fan of fantasy her entire life, but has a soft spot for romantic comedies and reading as much romance as she can. She is a true nerd at heart, playing Baldurs' Gate with her partner and creating backstories for the characters. Jay's hard work is fueled by Diet Coke and The Human Bean. If she isn't writing she spends all of her time with her nieces and nephews, napping, or watching television with her parents.

Follow me for more!

And as always, if you enjoyed this book, please leave a review!